Finding Forever

Boulder Bodyguards Book 2

Nika Rhone

Book Cover Design by 100 Covers

Published by Park Nine Publishing

First edition published 2017. Second edition published 2023.

Printed in the United States of America

She believed she could, so she did.

Chapter 1

The party was a raging success.

Everyone who was anyone from Connecticut and Washington was there, nibbling on imported caviar and drinking overpriced champagne. Smiles and air kisses were exchanged. Handshakes dispensed. Photo opportunities given—discreetly, of course—to the lucky few reporters granted entrée to the first of the gatherings leading up to what was expected to be the society wedding of the year, if not the decade.

Too bad the only one not impressed by it all was the bride.

Sipping the too-dry champagne she'd been nursing, Amelia Westlake contemplated how much of her not-inconsiderable trust fund she'd give to be just about anywhere but at the center of the juggernaut propelling her toward her fate as Mrs. Charles Wilson Henry Davenport.

A fate that, up until tonight, she'd been perfectly happy with.

Or at least she'd convinced herself she was.

Because if she was absolutely honest with herself—something she tried not to do very often these days, lest the thin veil of complacency be shredded—she'd been approaching her marriage with all the enthusiasm of a prisoner heading for the gallows.

Or maybe the Coliseum was more apt.

Her wedding was all about spectacle, after all. Lots of flash, very little substance.

"Kind of like Charles," she murmured into her glass as she swallowed the last sip.

"What was that, dear?"

Whoops.

Amelia gave an insipid smile to the jewel-encrusted woman standing next to her. "I said I should go find Charles. If you'll excuse me, please?"

She slipped away without waiting for a reply. A big nasty etiquette faux pas, but she honestly didn't care anymore. She knew she should, but she just...didn't.

After swapping her empty champagne glass for a full one from a roving waiter's tray, she slipped through the crowd, trying to look as though she was moving with purpose, when all the purpose she had was to simply keep moving. If she didn't, she'd be cornered by whichever of the Davenports' guests was closest when she stopped.

Normally not a problem for her, having been drilled in social etiquette from birth. She could fake polite interest with the best of them.

But tonight...

Tonight, her tolerance for meaningless chitchat and name-dropping one-upmanship was at an all-time low. In fact, her tolerance for everything seemed to be low, quickly thinning toward nonexistent.

Especially for her fiancé. Whom she hadn't seen more than a quick glimpse of since they started welcoming guests to his parents' mausoleum of a mansion.

A bright splash of color in the middle of the crowd caught her eye. Her heart lightened for the first time all evening.

Thank God.

She didn't see anyone she brushed past to get to that vibrant beacon of hope. Much as she wanted to barrel straight into her two best friends for a group hug, her mother's voice screeching in her head about decorum reined her in at the last second. She stopped short in front of them, swaying slightly on her dainty high heels.

"You're really here."

She sounded pathetically needy, but it didn't matter. Not with them. She'd grown up with Thea Fordham and Lillian Beaumont. They'd all seen each other at their best and worst, and they all loved each other no matter what.

They loved *her* no matter what.

"Like we wouldn't be here for you." A petite cloud of citron and charcoal silk, Lillian pulled her into a tight hug.

After an evening of air kisses and cool, limp finger-touching, she sagged into the embrace with a sense of wild relief, barely noticing when someone plucked the glass from her grasp. A person could only survive so long without real human contact before going a little bit crazy.

And right now, she felt about half a step from insane.

With great reluctance she withdrew from the embrace, keeping a tight hold of her friend's hands as she stepped back to take in the colorful creation she wore. "You look amazing." The swirl of vivid yellows and subdued grays should have overwhelmed Lillian's diminutive five-foot-two frame, but the expert cut of the dress and the intense energy that emanated from the woman herself made it work for her. "Is it one of Des's?"

"A certified D.F. original."

With a dramatic twirl, Lillian showed off what was sure to be another instant hit in their friend's newest entrepreneurial endeavor. It was amazing how much raw talent the man had, and in how many different directions he could fling it.

"It looks truly incredible on you. Des is a genius."

Which was exactly what she'd thought when she'd tried on the gown he designed for her to wear tonight. The one with the brilliantly tailored cut that had complemented her delicate bone structure, and whose soft lavender silk brightened her pale complexion to a healthy peaches-and-cream.

The one still hanging upstairs, vetoed by her mother for its lack of designer-name cachet.

Of all the things she hadn't put her foot down about for this party, and there were too many to count, she regretted that one the most.

Lillian grinned. "As he'd say if he were here, 'Thank you, kitten, but did you really expect anything less from the brilliance that is *moi*?'" She ended with an arm sweep *a lá* Desmond.

Despite her dejected thoughts, Amelia laughed. She could totally picture Des saying it just that way. She turned to her other best friend, Thea, who was also wearing one of Des's masterpieces.

She looked amazing.

The sheer panels of black lace at the sides offset the slightly baroque style, keeping the bronze sequins from overpowering either the gown or the woman wearing it. Her thick chestnut hair had been upswept into an elegant style, with a few tendrils teasing at her high cheekbones and along her neck. The look was both chic and sexy.

The total opposite of her own long, blonde locks, which were constrained in a lacquered, formal style more suited to someone her mother's age. She was only twenty-three. She didn't want to look like her mother. She wanted to look young, and sophisticated, and yes, damn it, a little bit sexy.

Great. Now she not only had dress envy, but hair envy as well.

As she gave herself up to another exuberant embrace, she tried to bury both. It was far too late for regrets now.

Even if her dress did make her collarbones stand out like chicken wings.

And the silver lamé washed her out until she was practically invisible.

And the boat neckline made her breasts look almost nonexistent.

God, I hate this dress.

I hate this night.

I hate my life.

Blinking in surprise at the traitorously honest thought that sneaked in, Amelia stepped back from the hug, only then realizing she'd missed whatever Thea said.

"I'm sorry, what was that?"

"I asked if you were all right."

"I'm fine." No, she was a big, fat liar. "Des really outdid himself, T. You look fabulous."

It wasn't just a compliment to deflect Thea's attention, which was a bit too keen. It was also the truth. Less than a year ago, Thea had been a mess of insecurities and self-doubt. Now, she looked cool, confident, and crazy in love with the tuxedoed man standing at her side holding the champagne glass Amelia only now realized she was missing.

Retrieving the glass and accepting a kiss on the cheek in greeting from Thea's fiancé, Amelia realized it wasn't the dress that gave her friend such an air of self-possession and poise. It was him. Once he'd gotten over his hang-ups, Brennan Doyle had dedicated himself to showing Thea how madly, deeply in love with her he was.

Nauseatingly so.

Tipping back her glass, Amelia drowned out the spiteful little voice of jealousy with the last of her champagne. She was happy her friend had found that kind of love. Really, she was.

Happy, happy, happy.

She just wished she saw a fraction of that adoring devotion from the man she was set to marry in—God help her—ten days.

"Mellie, have you had anything to eat tonight?"

Blinking a bit owlishly at Lillian, who studied her with an expression of concern, Amelia nodded. "We had an early family supper. Duck a l'orange with shallots and parsnips. They have it every Wednesday. It's one of the chef's specialties."

"Sweetie, you hate duck."

"But Charles and his father love it." She saw a lot of unhappy duck dinners in her future.

She saw a lot of unhappy in her future, period.

Amelia raised her glass to her lips, only to be disappointed by its emptiness. "Oh. I need more champagne."

"Maybe you should wait on that." Thea plucked the glass from her hand and passed it off to Doyle, who deposited it on a passing tray.

He did not, Amelia noted with great disappointment, exchange it for a full one.

As she watched the waiter disappear with her liquid courage, Amelia's gaze ran into another familiar form standing unobtrusively off to the side of their little group, like a sheepdog guarding his flock. Which was exactly what he was doing.

Although, dressed in dark formalwear tailored to his broad shoulders and lean frame, Daryl Raintree looked more big, bad wolf than dog. Thea's bodyguard literally stood head-and-shoulders above the rest of the guests, his dark gaze intimidating enough to scare off anyone stupid enough to approach without invitation.

As always, Amelia was a little awed by the raw masculinity and understated power Daryl seemed to exude. She gave him a tentative smile and extended her hand.

"It's good to see you, Daryl." When he hesitated, she realized she'd just made another faux pas, her second—third?—of the night. You didn't shake hands with security. They were usually treated like inanimate objects, important for their purpose but otherwise ignored.

Well, screw that. Daryl had helped save her best friend's life not so long ago. That made him more than just hired muscle. Anyone who didn't like it could go suck lemons.

Taking her hand carefully in his much larger one, Daryl said in his soft, deep voice, "Thank you, Miss Westlake, it's good to see you, too. You're looking very well this evening."

No, she wasn't. Interesting to find he could lie with such a straight face.

Lillian let out a small eep sound. Thea stared like she'd just grown a third nostril.

Whoops.

Had she said that last bit out loud? Daring a peek up at Daryl and seeing the combination of amusement and concern in his eyes, she guessed she had. Well, at least he didn't look angry about being called a liar.

"Mellie, sweetie," Thea said.

Pasting on her party smile, Amelia interrupted before she could say anything more.

"Come on, let me show you around. Lil, I think you'll love the gallery leading to the library. There's a wonderful little landscape there they think might be an unknown Monet. There's a huge debate over how to go about proving the provenance, but even if it's not one of his, it's still one of the most beautiful canvases I've ever seen."

She chattered on, hardly aware of what she was saying as she led them through the crowded ballroom, down the wide hallway that connected the more public rooms to the private family area at the back. As she'd hoped, no one else was there.

No longer under the cynosure of the glittering throng her parents and future in-laws considered two hundred of their closest friends and potential campaign donors, her whole body sagged with relief.

Which, of course, her friends noticed.

Thea put a hand on her arm. "I know you said you were fine, but sweetie, you really don't look all that fine right now." She chewed her bottom lip, a sure sign she was anxious about something. "Is it...do you want me to go?"

"What?" A shot of pure panic raced through her, straightening her spine faster than one of her mother's disapproving glares. "No! You can't go! Why would you want to go?" Heart racing, her gaze darted between her two friends. "Please, please, don't go."

Tears prickled her eyes. Horrified, she used every bit of willpower she had left to battle the emotions bubbling up. What happened to the ironclad cap she normally kept them locked down under?

It had to be the champagne.

And the stress.

And the duck she'd forced down that had forced its way back up an hour later.

It couldn't possibly be the realization of what a colossal mess she'd made of her life.

"Why..." She sucked in a breath and smoothed the hitch out of her voice. "Why would you ever think I'd want you to leave? I want you all here. I *need* you here."

Knowing her friends were coming for the entire week of events leading up to the wedding was the only thing that had kept her from dissolving into a full-blown panic attack. Kind of like the one that was threatening now.

Relief softened Thea's pensive expression.

"It's just, I know the dragons were giving you a hard time about me being involved in any of the wedding events. And after I found out about the cancellation, I thought maybe you'd decided to keep the peace and, you know, distance yourself a little. Which would be perfectly okay if you did," she said in a rush when Amelia just stared at her in confusion. "The last thing I want to do is add any more problems to your plate."

"No." Amelia shook her head, although she wasn't certain if she was disagreeing or simply clearing her thoughts, which were suddenly spinning in cloudy champagne-tinged spirals in her head. "I mean, yes, Mother and Mrs. Davenport were a bit...apprehensive about the press making some sort of reference to last year's incident when they saw you, and stirring the whole thing back up again instead of focusing on the wedding. But, no, I didn't change my mind about having you here."

Though she had changed it about having Thea as one of her bridesmaids. Or, rather, had it changed for her.

Oh, Thea had stepped back on her own before Amelia was put in the awkward position of having to ask, but they'd both known she would have. Despite limited success in finding her backbone when it came to dealing with her mother, Amelia had yet to withstand the combined might of both her mother *and* future mother-in-law.

Duck wasn't the only thing that made her stomach miserable.

By habit, she reached for one of the rolls of antacids she always kept handy. Only her tiny evening bag with its precious cargo was still on her dressing table, vetoed in much the same way Des's beautiful dress had been.

Even as Amelia considered an escape upstairs to go pop a few tablets like a drug addict scoring a hit, Lillian held out her hand. "Here you go, sweetie."

"Oh, God, I love you." Ripping open the roll, Amelia practically inhaled two of the discs. The fruit flavor didn't mix well with champagne, but she didn't care if it tasted like garden dirt. All she wanted was to soothe the gurgling that erupted in her belly the moment Thea mentioned leaving.

The familiar motion of chewing had a calming effect, and after a moment her tight muscles loosened. This was good. Her stomach was settling down. Her friends weren't abandoning her. All was right with her world.

Well, not all, but enough that she had a shot at making it through the rest of the party without losing control again.

It was only as she was slipping a third insurance tablet into her mouth that the rest of what Thea said cycled back around and repeated itself. She cocked her head at her friend in confusion.

"What cancellation?"

⚬

There were few things Daryl Raintree considered a worse way to spend an evening than being on a security detail at a society party.

One of the reasons he'd enjoyed working for the Fordham family the past six years was that most of the parties they hosted or attended were oriented toward family or Frank Fordham's business. "Society" held little appeal to them despite their wealth.

Unfortunately, there were still times when it became necessary to venture into that glittering world, and when they did, so did their security.

He adjusted his stance against the wall just outside the hallway with more paintings than a wing at the Met, ignoring the sidelong looks from passing guests.

At six-four, with his father's Lakota heritage stamped plainly on his bronzed features, and the slight crookedness of his nose that said he hadn't spent his life sitting behind a desk and playing tennis at the country club on weekends, he didn't exactly blend into this type of crowd the way Doyle could.

Not that his boss was usually in the field these days.

Doyle was too busy running his fledgling security company to be the Fordham chief of security anymore. But since Daryl and the others from the staff had signed on with him, life continued on at the Fordham estate with barely a hitch, with Frank Fordham as Praetorian Security's first client.

Doyle being Doyle had balked at the nepotism at first. Frank being Frank had bluntly asked if he was willing to entrust the safety of his fiancée and future mother-in-law to anyone else. Since Doyle adored Evie Fordham and loved Thea more than life itself, it had been a no-brainer. Praetorian got the job, Red Fields took over as on-site security chief, and everyone was happy.

Except for Daryl, who was currently hating his life choices right about now.

And I have no one to blame but myself.

He could have requested to be on the senior Fordhams' detail. They weren't arriving until next week. It was only Thea who'd flown in to do the pre-wedding party train. Ten days of Society hell, and he'd volunteered for it.

Dumbass.

But after what happened nine months ago, he wasn't taking any chances. He didn't much care for the senior Westlakes—the mother was an ice-cold bitch and the father a pompous blowhard—but it was the Davenports he didn't trust. His instincts itched whenever he was around them, and that wasn't just his aversion to Society chaffing at him.

Something bad was definitely going to happen.

"Amelia, sweetie, wait!"

Daryl straightened from his relaxed pose to alert readiness as a tiny bundle of blonde and silver stalked out of the hallway where Doyle had accompanied the Royal Court. He ignored Amelia until the other two women hurried after her, followed by Doyle, who looked annoyed but not concerned.

Looking his way, Doyle gave the all-clear signal. Whatever drama was going on wasn't a danger to Thea. Not yet, anyway.

Being half a head taller than most people in the room made it easy for Daryl to follow the women's progress through the crowd. Amelia led the way, looking like an ice-breaker forging its way through the North Sea, with Thea and Lillian two colorful anchors being dragged in her wake.

It was an odd sight.

In all the years he'd known them, he couldn't remember a single other time when Amelia had taken the lead on anything the three friends had done. She was the follower, the Princess, the one the other two fussed over and protected. It was her security code name that had been picked first back when the girls were in school.

The other two quickly followed. Thea was the Lady, the group's moderator and voice of reason. And Lillian was the lead troublemaker, their Queen of chaos. If there was a plot or plan in evidence, she was the one most likely to have thought it up and convinced the other two to join in.

Hence, the Royal Court had been born.

And while Lillian and Thea had been known to surprise their

security details and act out of character once in a while, Amelia was the one least likely to go off-script. Her entire life was run by her mother with an efficiency Patton would have envied.

Which was why her sudden change in behavior now was so disturbing.

"Do we have a problem?" Daryl asked as he and Doyle followed the women.

"Oh, I'd say there's definitely a problem. I'm just not sure whose it is yet."

But it involved Thea in some way. Daryl could tell by the slight growl that edged his boss's voice. If Daryl was hyper-vigilant of Thea's safety, Doyle was fanatical. Unfortunately for them both, Thea wasn't the type of person to sit back and let others take care of her problems for her.

Which was why they were following the three women instead of charging ahead to slay whatever dragons stood in their path.

When they caught up to where the women stopped, Daryl realized he'd been closer to the truth than he realized. In front of them were Meredith Westlake and Constance Davenport. Both of these particular dragons were elegantly gowned and coiffed, and wore identical expressions of disapproval. Presumably in response to the belligerent expression on Amelia's normally neutral face.

Yet another odd sight.

The break from the norm was unsettling, but it also raised his alert level from yellow to red. Any problem that could force someone who'd spent twenty-three years allowing herself to be molded into the perfect little princess to break form—in public, no less—had to be one hell of a doozy.

Sometimes I really hated being right.

Chapter 2

I can't believe she did this.

After listening to what Thea told her, even the acid sloshing around in Amelia's stomach became an afterthought. All she could think was, *she's not getting away with this.*

Actually, she might have even said it out loud. She wasn't sure.

The only thing she knew with any certainty was that she needed to deal with this. Now.

And while acting rashly in the heat of anger might not be the smartest move—Thea's worried words as Amelia stalked away—she knew if she let her temper cool even a little, she'd lose any chance at winning this fight.

Forward momentum fueled by rage was all she had going for her.

The cause of that rage was holding court on the side of the ballroom with the seventeenth-century tapestry of Saint George slaying the dragon hanging under glass.

The irony didn't escape her.

Reaching deep, she dredged up the politest tone she could manage. "Mother, may I have a word with you, please?"

"Amelia." Her mother's voice held the familiar whip of reprimand. "You remember Mrs. Pendergrass and Mrs. Cates. They were just telling us how lovely the spring has been down in Washington."

Which really meant, *these are very important people, so kiss their* wrinkled asses.

Normally, her Pavlovian response would have been to do just that.

Now, she barely glanced at them as she said, "Very nice to see you both. If you'll excuse us, though, I need to have a private word with my mother."

"Amelia, I don't think you under—"

"What did you do to my furniture order?" If her mother wasn't willing to do this in private, Amelia would accommodate her. She locked gazes with the woman who'd raised her to be nothing more than a pretty accessory and refused to let herself be backed down by the censure radiating back at her.

This was her Rubicon. She wouldn't let herself lose one more battle.

She couldn't.

Unexpectedly, it was the second dragon who stepped into the breach. Waving a hand that held more gems than Amelia's entire jewelry case, Constance Davenport gave a soft chuckle.

"Oh, dear. It would seem we have some last-minute jitters over wedding details that need to be soothed. You know how these young brides can be. So very needy." She said it with a sense of camaraderie and bonhomie, as though including the two women in a private family moment even as she gently shooed them on their way with promises to catch up later.

There wasn't a drop of that good nature left in evidence when she wheeled back toward Amelia. "That was unconscionably rude and unacceptable behavior from you, missy! What on earth were you thinking?"

Amelia ignored her and repeated her question. "What did you do to my furniture order, Mother?"

"Obviously, you already know the answer to that, so don't play coy, Amelia Ann. You aren't any good at it."

"How dare you?" She was almost vibrating with the rage that threatened to spill out. "Do you have any idea how many weeks Thea and I spent picking everything out? Making sure it was absolutely *perfect*?"

Her mother's gaze flicked past Amelia's shoulder, mouth twisting in disdain.

It shouldn't surprise her that her friends had followed. She'd just been too forward-focused to notice. But knowing they were there gave her confidence an added boost.

"No." She pulled her mother's attention back to her. "This isn't about Thea. This is about me. Charles left the decorating of the townhouse up to me, and you had no right to interfere."

She'd wanted to reward that unexpected show of faith by making the end result a true blending of their two very different tastes. With Thea's expert eye and a lot of hard work and compromise, Amelia felt they'd achieved the perfect result.

And now it was all undone.

"The expectation was that you would be using a *professional* to decorate his home," her mother replied. "With his position, there are certain standards that are expected to be maintained."

"Thea *is* a professional decorator, Mother, as you well know." Her mother had never liked either of her friends, but her animosity toward Thea had increased exponentially over the last nine months. "And it's going to be my home, too, not just Charles's. Even if I decided to decorate it with purple flamingos and lime green shag carpet, it still wouldn't give you the right to interfere!"

Her mother's surgically thinned nostrils flattened as she sucked in an indignant breath. Amelia braced for the next verbal volley, but to her surprise when her mother spoke, it wasn't to her.

"You were right, Constance. It would have been a terrible mistake."

Mrs. Davenport inclined her head. "As I told you."

Amelia's head whipped toward her fiancé's mother. "You played a part in this?"

Stupid question.

There hadn't been an area yet in Amelia and Charles's relationship she hadn't somehow inserted herself into. Sometimes Amelia wondered—only half-jokingly—if she planned to come along on the honeymoon as well.

Then again, with the amount of interest Charles had shown in her lately, it probably wouldn't make all that much difference if she did.

Focus. One dragon problem at a time.

"It doesn't matter."

"Of course, it doesn't matter," her mother said with a sniff. "I don't know why you worked yourself up into such an unpleasant—"

"It doesn't matter," Amelia said a little louder, "because I'll get it all back. Every stick of furniture, every piece of artwork, every yard of drapery." She wasn't certain if that was possible, but she'd damn well do her best. "So, I don't care what furnishings you ordered in their place, you can cancel them first thing in the morning because I won't be needing them."

There was a long, tense moment of silence where even the soft roar of hundreds of voices faded into the background.

Mrs. Davenport's brisk tone broke the spell. "Obviously, you don't have all of your facts, missy. A dangerous mistake for someone about to become the wife of a political candidate."

The solid ground of conviction began to crumble around her feet.

"And what facts am I missing, exactly?"

"That the furnishings you're so vociferously defending weren't cancelled because they were found lacking. Although your behavior of a few moments ago has certainly brought your judgment about what is *acceptable* into grave question."

Normally, such a verbal rebuke would have twisted her stomach into knots any sailor would be proud of. This time, there was barely a ripple. She was too focused on the subtext of what *hadn't* been said.

"Then why?"

"Because you won't be needing it, of course. Any of it."

"*Why?*"

"Because you'll be moving in here."

Like a fist hammering for escape, Amelia's heart thudded against her breastbone. The crumbling ground broke away to form a yawning chasm before her. All it would take was one good nudge to push her in.

She shook her head. "What? No. We're moving into the townhouse."

"The townhouse has been let go."

"No. We...you can't..." Suspended over the long drop to hard reality, she floundered for a reason, an explanation, *anything* to refute what she was being told. "I don't believe you. Charles would never allow it."

"Charles is fully aware of the change in plans," his mother said. "In fact, he approved wholeheartedly."

And with that final blow, Amelia soared off into space, all sense of connection to what was going on around her lost in the terrifying sensation of free-fall. Her heart pounded, wild and painful, as she fought the sense of vertigo Mrs. Davenport's bombshell had triggered.

It can't be true. It can't be.

She and Charles had spent weeks house-hunting, looking for the perfect place to start their new life together. Alone. Without his family or hers constantly watching over their shoulders, although she'd agreed his bid for office later this year meant staying in Connecticut. It was where he could cash in on his senator father's reputation and name recognition with voters.

She'd wanted a house, Charles a condo. They compromised on a townhouse, and she'd been in love with it since the moment they signed the lease. Finally, *finally*, she'd have a home of her own, where the only two people in the world she had to worry about pleasing were Charles and herself.

What a ridiculously naïve notion.

How had she, for one single minute, believed her life would

somehow magically become her own? Especially when the family she was marrying into was even more politically driven and power hungry than her own?

Had she been willfully blind, or just that pathetically desperate?

Voices buzzed around her as she stumbled through her internal fog. Her mother was saying something. She didn't know what. She didn't care. Thea's voice joined in the fray, and Lillian's, but it was all simply noise. It existed outside of her. Distant. She was too filled with this strange drumbeat in her ears, in her throat, in her chest, for anything else to get in.

Charles was aware. He had approved.

Those two thoughts swirled above the other chaos in her brain. He'd let his mother do this to them? Without talking to her? Without asking what *she* wanted to do?

She'd thought they were growing closer again these past few months. Back to the way it was when he first led her on a whirlwind courtship full of romantic dinners and nights at the symphony.

And flowers. No one had ever bought her flowers before him.

He'd given her a dozen perfect red roses the night he proposed. She hadn't expected it; it had been too soon. But she'd accepted, anyway. Their union felt like the right choice. She'd thought he was "the one."

Back when she truly believed she loved him, and that he might just love her back.

Stupid, stupid, stupid woman.

With no conscious input from her brain, her feet took her away from the voices that were sounding more strident by the second. Away from the overpowering sense of doom those few simple words created. She didn't see the people she passed. Didn't hear them. She simply walked.

It wasn't until she was standing back in the empty painting-lined hallway that she came back to herself enough to realize someone else was there with her.

"Miss Westlake?"

The soft, Midwest-flavored voice identified her shadow. Thankfully, she was still too disconnected to feel humiliated about Daryl Raintree seeing her in this state. She was too disconnected to feel much of anything at all.

"Miss Westlake? Amelia?"

The use of her given name was unusual enough to make her realize she hadn't responded or even acknowledged him, but it didn't make her care enough to want to do either. Maybe she could just stay disconnected for the rest of her life.

"Is there anything I can do for you? Anyone I can get?"

Get. Yes. *Yes.*

"Yes." This time she made sure to say it out loud. "Charles. I need to speak with Charles." Because Charles could fix this. He'd approved the change in their living arrangements. He could change it back. Then everything would be fine again. She wouldn't be stuck in this mausoleum of a house, watched and judged and corrected every second of every day.

She wouldn't be trapped, once more, by a dragon.

"All right. Do you know where he is?"

"No." The last she'd seen him, he was ensconced in a corner with his campaign manager, his father, and another man who, judging from the avaricious way they were monopolizing him, was someone with a healthy disposable income.

She was only marginally aware of Daryl's voice as he spoke in low tones to someone via the mic discretely clipped to his sleeve. A few moments later, she started when his hand touched her arm, and realized she'd once again failed to respond when he said her name.

"Charles was last seen heading to the second floor about twenty minutes ago."

Which was off-limits to guests. Perfect. She could talk to him in private, without having to pry him away from any potential campaign donors.

"Thank you, Daryl." Her mind already structuring the best way to approach Charles about the housing debacle, Amelia headed for the small service staircase at the end of the gallery hall, past the library that also served as Senator Davenport's office when he was in residence. She'd catch hell for using it if anyone saw, but she'd choose that over another possible confrontation with either her mother or Mrs. Davenport any day.

The stairs let out through a door in the upper hallway not far from Charles's suite. Her own was across the hall. They were the only two suites occupied at this end of the family wing. She'd wondered at the room choice when they arrived at the beginning of the month, but hadn't questioned it. Now she wished she had.

Had the decision been made all the way back then that she'd be denied her own household?

The possibility was so real she had to tuck it away and ignore it. Just for now. She'd take out that nugget of betrayal and examine it again later. Right now, she had to focus on getting Charles to change his mind.

Somehow.

Because if he didn't, she wasn't sure she could live with the consequences.

※

Standing in the barely open doorway at the top of the stairs, Daryl watched Amelia hesitate in front of the door to what he presumed was Charles Davenport's room. Whatever impetus drove her upstairs had clearly deserted her. She looked like a porcelain doll about to crack into a million pieces.

Not my problem.

He shouldn't have even followed her upstairs. She wasn't his charge, wasn't his responsibility. And even if she had been, this was clearly a matter that fell well outside the bodyguard purview. Unless someone threatened her physically, there was shit-all he could do for her.

Still, leaving wasn't an option now.

He'd been too far away to overhear what went down in the ballroom, but it must have been something staggering. When Amelia had turned and walked away, she'd seemed in such a daze she reminded him of someone who'd just taken a blow to the head.

Thea had looked at Doyle in that silent communication the two sometimes shared, and Doyle signaled for Daryl to follow her while Thea stepped between Mrs. Westlake and her retreating daughter, just like she always did.

So now here he was, babysitting the Princess until Thea and Lillian came to claim her.

Taking a huge breath, Amelia stepped forward and opened the door, slipping inside and closing it softly behind her.

Daryl shook his head. Whatever she hoped to accomplish, there wasn't much chance of her succeeding. She didn't have enough fire in her gut. Oh, flashes of something showed through now and then, tiny hints she wasn't one-hundred percent doormat.

But how long would it be before even those faint sparks were extinguished under the smothering effects of her soon-to-be in-laws?

He gave it a year, tops.

Less than a minute later, the door opened again. As silently as she'd gone in, Amelia slipped out, closing it with the careful motions of someone either very drunk or trying very hard not to lose their shit.

He'd seen that same door-closing precision from his stepmother after learning her brother had died in a car accident. She'd hung up the phone, carefully closed the door to her bedroom, and proceeded to smash everything she could lay her hands on.

Amelia might not be the smashing things type, but she was very clearly at her breaking point as she stood staring at the closed door, one hand still on the antique glass knob. Whatever had happened between her and her fiancé, it wasn't good.

Daryl grimaced. He sucked at the emotional crap. That was Thea's thing.

Where the hell is she, anyway?

Before he could request an ETA from Doyle, Amelia swung away from the door and walked a few steps to the center of the wide hallway and stopped, looking as though she had no idea where she was.

Shit.

Abandoning the stairwell, he approached with care. "Miss Westlake?"

She turned too quickly. Daryl's hands came up to steady her when she teetered on her high heels.

"Are you all right?"

Her face was flushed, a vast change from the paleness of just moments ago. From this close, her cheekbones were a little too sharp, her face a little too thin, her deep green eyes a little too shiny. Oh, hell. If she started to cry, he was seriously screwed.

He dropped his hands from her arms as though burned. Where the *hell* was Thea?

"I'm..." She gave a short, confused sounding laugh. "I don't know what I am right now. I have to..." She turned in a half-circle as though orienting herself, then walked to the door opposite Charles's and went in.

Daryl stared after her, debating his next move. He earned a very nice paycheck, but there wasn't enough money in the world to make him willingly deal with a crying woman if there was another option. No sane man would.

Still, the instinct to check on her was compelling. He'd been taught from a young age that the strong always looked out for the weak, and Amelia was one of the most fragile people he knew. To leave her all alone while she was in pain was an act of unadulterated cowardice, plain and simple.

Just then, familiar voices drifted from the servants' stairs.

Thank God.

Okay, yes, he admitted it. When it came to tears, he was a coward.

After giving a brief recap of what had happened since Amelia left the ballroom, Daryl indicated the still open door she'd disappeared through. Thea and Lillian rushed in after her.

"Can I ask what in the hell is going on?" Daryl asked Doyle as soon as the door shut.

"The quick version: Amelia found out she isn't getting the house of her dreams, that she's moving into the castle with her wicked monster-in-law instead, and good old Charles okayed it all without talking to her first."

"Well, fuck."

Had he said a year? Hell, he'd be surprised if Amelia made it to the end of the summer before she was bulldozed entirely flat.

"Yeah, that pretty much sums it up." Doyle glanced toward the door the women had disappeared behind with a scowl. Neither of them was happy Thea was out of sight, but neither was brave enough to go in after her, either.

What was it about crying women that made even the most fearless man's blood run cold?

"Did the girls do their usual song and dance for the dragons?"

"They tried, but Constance Davenport is a lot harder to divert than Meredith Westlake." Doyle grimaced. "It got a little ugly there at the end. I practically had to drag Thea away before she clawed the bitch's eyes out."

Well, that didn't bode well for Amelia.

Usually, whenever her mother's tongue got too sharp and drew blood, Thea or Lillian did or said something to redirect her anger onto them. Her words couldn't hurt them because they truly didn't give a damn what the woman thought. Their only concern was to protect their friend, who, after all this time, still hadn't figured out the simple task of how to protect herself.

After only a few minutes, the door opened and Thea and Lillian came out. Daryl expected Amelia to follow, but Thea closed the door, giving it a pensive look as she did, as though she could still see her friend through it. And was worried.

"How is she?" Doyle moved closer so he could run his hand down Thea's arm. She smiled up at him and stepped into his embrace.

Daryl repressed a snort. The two of them had been disgustingly touchy-feely ever since Doyle got that ring on her finger. Watching their hard-ass former Marine boss go all soft and squishy over his fiancée was a favorite pastime for his staff.

"She's okay. I think."

"A lot more okay than I expected her to be." Lillian sounded a little confused.

Daryl could understand that, because the Amelia he watched stumble through that door like a sleepwalker had been nowhere near okay. She'd been on a dangerous edge. The kind that sometimes led people to do very rash, stupid things.

"Did she say what happened with Charles?" Doyle asked.

Thea shook her head. "No. She just said she had some things to think about, but she'd wait until after the party, when she could concentrate better."

"Then she kicked us out." Lillian sent a baffled look at the closed mahogany door. "Can you believe it?"

"She didn't kick us out, Miss Drama Queen. She just said we should go back to the party, and she'd be down in a few minutes."

"For Mellie, that's practically the same thing."

"She just wanted to be alone."

Daryl sympathized with the slight thread of confused hurt underlying Thea's words. But for fuck's sake, Amelia was a grown-ass woman. She needed to start handling her own problems, sooner rather than later.

"Okay, fine, let's go back to the party, then. That should be loads of fun." Lillian rolled her eyes. "Especially when Mrs. Davenport has us escorted off the property and blackballed from the rest of the week's festivities."

"We wouldn't get that lucky," Doyle muttered under his breath, grunting when Thea's elbow connected with his ribs.

Not wanting to call attention to where Amelia was by using the main staircase, which would deposit them right into the middle of the party, they retreated down the way they'd come. As they mingled back into the crowd, the two men ranged behind the women like the guard dogs they were.

Lillian's joke about being escorted out wasn't beyond the realm of possibility. No one was getting to Thea or Lillian without dealing with them first.

"Ho-ly hell!"

Lillian's awed whisper made Daryl tense. Scanning for potential trouble, his eyes snagged instead on Amelia, who was descending the grand staircase.

"Oh my God." Thea let out a disbelieving giggle. "Her mother's going to shit flying monkeys!"

"Thea..." Doyle's admonishment fell on deaf ears as she leaned over to whisper something to Lillian that elicited an evil chuckle.

Amelia walked with a gliding gait that made it appear as though she were floating along on her own personal cloud. Damned if she didn't look like a real princess coming down from her tower.

"Why did she change her dress?" Because he remembered her in some silvery thing that made her look like an underfed twelve-year-old. What she had on now...

Well, she definitely wasn't twelve.

"She's making a statement," Thea replied.

"Yeah." Lillian grinned like a shark watching chum hit the water. "She's giving her mother a great big 'screw you' without having to say a word. It's brilliant."

If that was the case, then Daryl had to agree. Sometimes knowing your own weaknesses and playing to them was the only way to win a battle. Since Amelia couldn't stand up to her mother directly, finding an indirect route to declare war was her best alternative.

Of course, being able to win that war was another matter entirely.

He watched Amelia walk through the crowd, intrigued by the subtle changes in her. Even to his "guy-eye" the light purple gown was a much better choice for her than the one she'd been wearing. The soft fabric wrapped around her body like a lover's touch.

She'd pulled her hair down from its tight confinement as well, leaving the blonde curls loose around her shoulders. The slightly tousled look was surprisingly sexy, a description he never would have applied to Amelia Westlake before.

But it wasn't just her appearance that was altered. It was the way she walked, the way she stood as she stopped to talk to people. There was a confidence in her posture that had been lacking before. A very definite poise and calmness.

Or maybe it was just the "screw you" he was seeing.

Either way, he found himself adjusting his earlier assessment. If she managed to survive the rest of the night, maybe she had a shot at winning the war after all.

Chapter 3

Amelia stared at the dark-paneled hotel room door. Her composure was hanging on by its very fingernails. Much like her.

I can do this.

Sheer stubborn willpower had gotten her this far. But everything she'd been suppressing for the past fourteen hours was bubbling up, a seething mass of emotions threatening to blow out the tight seal she had on them at any second.

And she needed to be on the other side of that door when it did.

With a deep breath that almost seized in her throat, she knocked. First too soft, then again too hard. Flustered, she snatched her hand back and wrapped it around the strap of her purse to keep from knocking again.

Despite the thinning threads of her composure, she managed a weak smile for Doyle when the door opened. "Is Thea here? I need to talk to her."

His gaze ran first over her, then the black tote bag at her feet before flicking down both directions of the empty hallway.

"Sure. Come on in. Here, I'll get that." He picked up the bag before she could. "The girls are out on the balcony plotting either a shopping spree or world domination. Daryl and I are steering clear until they decide which."

The subtext being they wouldn't come onto the balcony unless summoned. Amelia gave a jerky nod but couldn't manage even a weak smile this time. "Thanks, Doyle."

The room was a suite with bedrooms on either side, and a living room with elegant yet understated furniture anchoring its center. A table with the remnants of breakfast sat near the floor-to-ceiling windows. The door Doyle disappeared through likely led to the adjoining room Daryl was using.

Leaving her alone to talk to her friends.

Her stomach did another of the slow rolls it had been performing all morning. She dug into her purse and chewed through an antacid tablet with grim determination.

I can do this.

Squaring her shoulders, she clutched the purse strap even tighter and walked through the French doors to the balcony.

"Mellie!"

She withstood the barrage of greetings and tight hugs, blinking fast several times when her emotional seal began to falter. By the time they had her seated on one of the comfortable rattan chairs with a cup of tea beside her, she had her composure pretty well back under control.

For most people, anyway.

Thea and Lillian weren't most people.

"Not that we're not happy to see you, sweetie," Thea said, "but we weren't exactly expecting you this morning. Is everything all right?"

"Of course." The assurance rolled off her tongue before she realized she'd spoken it out of habit.

Thea looked doubtful. "Really?"

"Because you don't look like everything's okay." Lillian added a little "Ow!" when Thea kicked her in the ankle. "Well, she doesn't, and I'm not going to lie about it."

Amelia knew exactly what she looked like. Her bathroom mirror had been brutally honest. She'd done her best, but makeup wouldn't fully cover the mauve hollows beneath her eyes unless she slathered it on with a trowel.

"No, she's right." Her stomach twitched again. She reached for the tea and took a few small sips, hoping to settle it, and also buying herself a few more seconds. When she put the china cup down, it rattled against the saucer, betraying her unsteady hand.

I can't believe I'm really doing this.

"I gave Charles back his ring."

There was a small amount of satisfaction to be had in the dumbfounded expressions on her friends' faces. It wasn't often that she got to surprise them, much less shock them into total silence.

Which only lasted for a second before Lillian leaned forward in her seat. "Okay, I must have heard that wrong. You did what, now?"

"I gave Charles back his ring." Amelia rubbed her left hand, still not used to the bareness of it. "I talked to him this morning, and I told him I wasn't going to marry him."

"Oh." Still looking stunned, Thea reached out and grasped Amelia's hand. "Oh, Mellie. Sweetie. Are you sure? I mean, are you *really* sure that's what you want?"

"Of course she is!" Lillian all but launched herself off the chair, pulling Amelia to her feet and into a hug that nearly knocked the breath out of her. "It's the best thing she could have possibly done! Maybe not the best timing, but..."

Her burst of enthusiasm faltered. Pulling back, she gave Amelia an uneasy smile. "You *are* sure, right? This is what you want? Because if not, I'll just sit down and shut my big mouth, right after I pull both my feet out of it."

"It's what I want." Amelia looked at Thea, who still had a doubtful look on her face. "Really. It's the best decision I've made in my...entire...life." The last words were more sobbed than spoken. The tears that followed were the ones she'd refused to shed before. If she had, she might have lost the resolve to get her through what needed to be done.

Arms came around her from both directions. The show of unconditional love from the only two people who had ever given it to her made her cry even harder, until she was all but being held up entirely by their embrace.

They didn't tell her it would be all right, or try to calm her down and get her to stop crying. They just held on until she didn't have the strength left to cry anymore.

Then she went into the bathroom and threw up.

There was a fresh cup of tea waiting for her when she came back, along with a small package of crackers. It was comforting her friends knew her that well, but it was also embarrassing. Neither of them ever cried so hard they'd vomited.

What did it say about her that she did it often enough for them to find it so unremarkable?

"So?" Lillian prompted after a few silent moments of Amelia sipping fragrant Darjeeling and slowly chewing the dry crackers.

Amelia put down her cup. At least this time it didn't rattle.

"You both must think I'm the biggest idiot walking the face of the planet." She shushed their automatic protests. "I know you never liked Charles very much. But despite everything that's happened, I truly believed I could make things work between us."

Could, or had to?

She still wasn't sure.

Her hands started pleating the linen napkin in her lap. "But then after last night..." She shook her head. "I knew that was never going to happen."

"Because of the townhouse?" Thea asked. "Did you talk to him about it?"

A bitter laugh escaped her. "Oh, I went to talk to him, all right."

"And?"

"And I found him with his pants around his knees and his..." She broke off, unable to verbalize the picture forever burned into her brain. Not even bleach and a sharp stick could dislodge it. "Let's just say he was too busy *polling* one of his constituents to talk with me."

"He...he..." Thea stuttered, clearly at a loss for words.

Lillian had no such impediment.

"That slimy bastard!" She slapped the arms of her chair with both hands. "That two-faced, lying son of a bitch!"

"Lil..." Thea tried to break in.

"How dare he do that to you! At a party being given for your *wedding?* A freaking *week* before you're supposed to *marry* him?"

"Lillian..."

"He needs to be castrated! No, that's too good for him. You need to hit him where it'll really hurt. You need to find a way to make him suffer. Slap him with a lawsuit for infidelity or breach of promise or...or just being a major douchebag or something. Oh! Maybe we can get him drunk and tie him to a lamppost in front of City Hall wearing nothing but a sign that says 'lame duck' tied around his—"

"Lillian!"

"What?"

Thea glared at her. "Shut. Up."

With a growl, Lillian slapped the chair's arms again. "He needs to die."

"I know, but this isn't about him right now."

Lillian swiveled in her seat and sent Amelia an apologetic look that didn't cancel out the fury still burning in her dark eyes. "I'm sorry, sweetie. I got a little carried away. What can we do?"

"Nothing. Although I did kind of like the sound of that last idea you had." Amelia surprised herself by almost grinning. And being only half joking. She'd never thought of herself as a spiteful person before.

Then again, after what she'd seen and heard, she was entitled to enjoy just the tiniest bit of spite, wasn't she?

"What did he say when you told him you were calling off the wedding?" Thea asked.

That memory hurt almost as much as the first one.

"That I was overreacting. Being childish. Unreasonable." Realizing she was no longer pleating the napkin but strangling it, she smoothed it out on her lap and picked up her tea. "I don't think he believed I would do it."

"Overreacting? *Childish?*"

Lillian's shrill tone meant she was about to wind up again, so Amelia was quick to say, "I didn't tell him I saw him last night. I only brought up him letting the townhouse go without talking to me first." Which was only the latest in about a dozen other things he'd done without her knowledge or input. Things that affected not just him, but *them*.

Sometimes she wondered if he remembered there *was* a them.

"Why the hell wouldn't you slap him right upside the head with it?" Lillian asked.

"I wanted to hold it in reserve to use if I needed it." Plus, she'd been a little too afraid to hear the reasoning behind his infidelity. Somehow, some way, he'd turn it around and make it *her* fault that he'd cheated.

Thea frowned. "He had to believe you when you gave him back the ring,"

Amelia thought back to the exact expression on Charles's face when she'd placed the platinum set two-carat ring on the desk blotter in front of him. Not surprise. Not concern. Not even hurt.

No. What she'd gotten when she gave him back the symbol of his supposed commitment to her, to their future life together, was impatience.

"He put it in the desk drawer and said he'd hold on to it until I realized how ridiculous I was being."

"Ridi—*ow!*" Lillian shot Thea a scowl and scooted her chair out of kicking range. To Amelia she said, "I'm all-in for castration. Just say the word."

Amelia tried to smile, but she was too tired.

Tired of the stress, the tension, the stomach-churning anxiety of the last few weeks. Of always being the one to bend and give and accept less than, or other than, what she wanted. Tired of being everyone's chess piece to move around willy-nilly as they needed her.

"What about your mother?" Thea broached the subject with all the caution of someone approaching a bomb.

Amelia's fingers tightened on the cup. "She was on her way out to brunch at the Westlake's country club when I told her. She said we'd discuss it when she got back."

"She didn't think you wanting to call off your wedding was important enough to cancel her plans?"

"She was joining the First Lady and the governor's wife. Trust me, nothing short of the zombie apocalypse would make her cancel *those* plans." Not when she expected her pathetic, weak-willed daughter to be dutifully waiting on her return as instructed.

Not this time, Mother.

Just thinking it filled her with a strange combination of giddy elation and stark terror.

"Are you going to go back and talk to her later, then?" Thea asked.

"No." She'd made her decision. There was no going back. Just like last night, she was relying on forward momentum to carry her through.

I am doing this.

"So...what can we do?"

Amelia took a deep breath and ignored the slight heave in her stomach when she said, "I need a ride to the airport."

• • •

"I'm sorry you had to come with me."

It was probably the fifth, no, the sixth, time Amelia Westlake had issued the apology since they left the hotel suite, and they weren't even over Kentucky yet. Only the pity he felt for her and her circumstances kept Daryl's annoyance at bay.

"It's not a big deal." And it wasn't. It was a job.

Just not the job he'd gone to Connecticut to do. *That* job was still sitting in her hotel room with Lillian Beaumont, planning to stay clear of the shit-storm that would fly once Amelia's departure became common knowledge.

But as Doyle had pointed out, with the wedding called off, there wouldn't be any parties for Thea to attend. Nor would she be staying the extra week to oversee the decorating of the already-moot-anyway townhouse during Amelia's honeymoon as planned—her wedding present to her friend.

That meant the extra security Daryl had come along to provide for those events was no longer needed. Which left him free to accompany the erstwhile bride back to Colorado.

Lucky me.

At first, Thea wanted to fly back with Amelia herself. So had Lillian. If they had, though, Doyle suggested—rightly so—that it could be misinterpreted as them applying undue influence on Amelia and her decision to cancel the wedding and run off. *Willfully* misinterpreted, if past experience was any yardstick.

The Davenports and Westlakes loved nothing so much as a scapegoat.

Thea hadn't cared. Her friend needed her, and she wanted to be there for her, damn the consequences. As usual, Lillian stood at her side, backing up her decision, the two of them ready to take on the world for the sake of their darling Princess.

It was Amelia who'd told them no.

Not a word they were used to hearing from her, judging by their stunned expressions. It had been entertaining to watch Thea lose an argument to Amelia. Right up until she'd given in under the condition Amelia not make the trip alone.

Daryl turned his head to look at his charge. She was half in profile, staring out the plane window, her posture so rigid and straight it had to hurt.

A pinch of guilt nipped at him. His response had been a little too flippant. Just because he'd been relegated to babysitter didn't mean he had to act like an ass.

"I don't mind escorting you home." That didn't seem like enough, so he added, "I'm just sorry things turned out the way they did for you." It was pretty inadequate as apologies went, but he couldn't say what he was really thinking. Which was more along the lines of "why did you wait so damn long to stand up for yourself?"

Amelia lifted a shoulder, acknowledging his words but not replying.

He'd tried. He should let it go and enjoy the rest of the trip in silence, tense as it might be. But his damned conscience kept poking at him.

"If my opinion matters, I think you're doing the right thing."

That earned a soft, cynical laugh. "Running away, you mean?" She continued to stare out at the passing clouds. "Doesn't that make me a coward?"

See, this was why he should have kept his mouth shut. That was one of those questions that just didn't have a right answer, like "do you think my sister's pretty?" Even tense silence would have been a better choice.

"No."

"Liar."

The word was so soft he almost missed it under the steady roar of the engines. If he hadn't been looking right at her and seen her mouth move, he would have.

Anger welled at the accusation, the second one in as many days, only to ebb away when he realized that, on some level, she was right. A part of him *did* think she was taking the coward's way out by jumping on a plane and running home to hide, rather than sticking around to deal with the fallout of her decision.

Then again, knowing her parents, if she stayed there was a better than even chance they'd get her to change her mind. They'd had a lifetime of obedience from Amelia. It was doubtful they'd allow that to stop now. So, was it really cowardice to avoid a confrontation you knew you couldn't win?

As he'd thought last night, sometimes you had to play to your weaknesses.

"Leaving doesn't make you a coward. It makes you smart enough to accept when a strategic retreat is called for."

There wasn't an immediate response to that. But after a few long seconds, Amelia shifted in her seat to look at him, her posture easing just a little. "I don't feel very smart at the moment, but...thank you."

He gave a curt nod of acknowledgement before turning his attention to the screen embedded in the seatback in front of him that showed their flight route on a map of the country. Just over three hours left.

Fucking wonderful.

His mind jumped ahead to what he needed to do once they landed in Denver. The only luggage between them was Amelia's small carry-on tote, so they could head straight for the car Doyle had arranged to pick them up. After that, it was a forty-five-minute drive to Boulder. Once he dropped Amelia at the Westlake estate, he'd been given the next few days off.

That was Doyle's plan, anyway.

His plan was to head back to the airport and catch the first return flight to Connecticut. Because his gut was telling him there was no way the political powerhouses of Davenport and Westlake were going to accept the disruption of their carefully laid plans without a fight. And he intended to be there to help protect Thea if they tried to bring it to her doorstep.

Chapter 4

That worry still preyed on Daryl's mind as their car swung into the wide, garden-lined cobblestone driveway of the Westlake estate almost two hours later. An accident on Route 36 had slowed traffic to a near standstill, delaying them and screwing up the timetable he'd worked out in his head for catching the five o'clock flight back east.

If they could offload their charge with a minimum of fuss, he jettisoned the idea of eating, and Sam broke a few speed limits getting him back to Denver, he still might have a chance at making the last flight of the day.

But it would be close.

He was already opening his door as the car glided to a stop at the base of the ornate granite steps. Even though he was eager to get this over with so he could get back to his actual job, habit had him scanning his surroundings. As he did, he gave a nod of acknowledgement to the two men flanking the bottom of the steps.

He stepped to the rear of the Town Car, reached for the handle.

And paused.

Something was off.

Giving the area another sweeping look, Daryl searched for what was pinging his radar. It made no sense for there to be any kind of danger here. Senator Westlake employed more security than Frank Fordham did, even if most of it was currently back in Connecticut with him and his wife.

Well, shit.

Turning his body away from the car, Daryl looked again at the two men by the stairs. *They* were what was wrong. Like extras out of an old Kevin Costner movie, they were doing the classic bodyguard pose, one hand grasping the opposite wrist. There was no reason for it. Just like there was no reason for them to be there in the first place.

Unless there was trouble.

"Phillip. Mitch." He didn't know them well enough to read, but they seemed much too tense, way too on alert. He didn't like it.

"Daryl." It wasn't either of the two men who spoke, but rather the older man striding down the steps toward him.

"Leon." Daryl echoed the careful tone the Westlake security's second-in-command had used. He let his hands drop casually to his sides. Not aggressive, but ready.

He just didn't know for what.

Leon stopped a few paces away. "We expected you over an hour ago."

Daryl stilled. "I wasn't aware you were expecting us at all."

"Paul contacted me from the jet with your flight info."

One short sentence, but it conveyed multiple levels of information and innuendo.

Paul Kent was the head of the senator's security, Leon's boss. If he was on the senator's private jet, that meant he was on his way back to Colorado. And since he rarely left his boss's side, that meant the senator was on his way back as well.

"Interesting how he got that information so quickly," Daryl said.

"Could be he made a lucky guess."

"Or could be the senator asked someone in Homeland for a favor."

Leon's wide shoulders rose in a faint shrug. "Senator Westlake knows a lot of important people." Nothing in his expression gave anything away, but Daryl couldn't help feel that it was some kind of warning.

Damn, he really hated mind games. "Look, Leon..."

Before he could continue, the car's tinted rear window slid down and Amelia looked out at him, a small frown pinching her already pale face. "Is there a problem?"

"That's what I'm trying to figure out."

She looked past him and smiled. "Hello, Leon. Is everything all right?"

A responding smile spread over the older man's face, gentling features that spoke clearly of more than a few years in a boxing ring. "Miss Amelia," he said with a respectful dip of his dark, bald head. "I'm sorry things don't seem to have worked out the way they should have for you."

"Thank you." Her lips twisted into a wry smile. "So am I."

"If you could just give us another minute, please?"

For some reason, Daryl felt a small tug of satisfaction when Amelia looked to him before answering. He gave a small nod. Something was definitely going on, and he wanted to know what it was.

With a tiny huff and a roll of her eyes, the window went back up.

Daryl turned his full attention to Leon. He knew peripherally that Sam had stepped from the car, leaving the driver's door open and the engine running. Sam wouldn't know *what* was going on, but the small bit of conversation he would have just heard would be enough to let him know *something* was.

"So?" Daryl asked. "Do we have a problem?"

Rocking back on his heels, Leon slid his hands into the front pockets of his well-cut suit trousers and studied the sky. "As you can guess, the senator and his wife aren't exactly thrilled at the most recent turn of events. They're both on their way home to...discuss the matter with their daughter."

Daryl would have expected them to stay in Connecticut for at least a few days to work damage control alongside the Davenports, but what did he know? Maybe the Westlakes decided distance would lessen the amount of insanity the press rained down on them.

"When Paul called to let us know Miss Amelia was on her way

home, he relayed specific instructions from her father." There was an emphasis on the word *specific* that sharpened Daryl's attention. Leon was still staring up at the sky, jingling some change in his pocket.

"What instructions?"

"Now, see, I really can't tell you that, of course—"

"Leon..."

"—but if I could, I'd probably say I was told that once Miss Amelia stepped foot on the estate, we were to make sure she stayed put until the senator and his wife got here." He tipped his head and looked at Daryl with a grim smile. "But since I can't tell you that, it means you didn't hear it from me."

Daryl realized two things at once. One, that Leon had a quiet respect and affection for Amelia Westlake, which surprised him. Although maybe it shouldn't have. Amelia might be quiet as a church mouse most of the time, but she was unfailingly polite and kind to those around her.

Like the other two members of the Royal Court, she was a genuinely nice person.

The second thing was that his simple escort and delivery job had just turned into something a whole lot more serious. Leon was talking about holding Amelia at the estate, against her will if necessary.

That wasn't acceptable. Not by a long shot.

He did his best to keep Mitch and Phillip in view without diverting too much attention from Leon. His heart started to pump a little faster as "fight or flight" kicked in, although he didn't alter his posture or expression by so much as a twitch.

"That could prove to be a problem, since we're already here and all."

"Well..." Change jingled again, marking Leon's agitation. "See, here's the thing. The senator is always talking about how things are never black and white, but more a bunch of nuances in between, to be interpreted depending on the circumstances. I was specifically instructed to detain Miss Amelia once she stepped foot on the estate. Now, the way I see it, she hasn't actually *stepped foot* anywhere yet. So as long as she doesn't get out of the car..." He shrugged.

Daryl couldn't keep the incredulous half-laugh from escaping. "So, the car is what? Like sovereign territory?"

"Hey, if foreign countries can declare their diplomats untouchable while they're in their embassy cars, I figure as long as Miss Amelia is inside one of the Fordham cars, she's technically still on Fordham property."

"Nuance, huh?"

"Works for me."

For him as well. But Daryl didn't think the senator would be quite as charitable with that loose interpretation of his orders.

"Of course," Leon added, rocking back on his heels again, "this all becomes moot if Miss Amelia decides she *wants* to stay."

True. Daryl didn't know what her reaction would be to her father's order, or the news her parents were on their way home. She probably wouldn't be happy. But unhappy enough to defy them and leave? He wasn't sure.

But she'd damned well have the choice.

"I guess I'll ask her, then."

"You may want to take a ride while you're doing that," Leon said, interrupting Daryl as he reached for the rear door handle. He tapped a finger to the Bluetooth earpiece he wore. "Private jets land a lot closer than Denver."

Understanding the warning that the senator might already be on the ground at the local municipal airport, Daryl swore and motioned to Sam with a quick jerk of his head. He ducked back into the driver's seat and slammed the door.

"We may be back." Daryl yanked his door open. "Or we might not. Whichever it is, you can be sure it'll be her choice."

"Can't ask for more than that."

As he slid into the front seat of the Town Car, Daryl shot a quick look at Mitch and Phillip. Both continued to stand in their statue poses, making no move to stop them, although Mitch inclined his head in a nod of either acknowledgment or agreement. Evidently, they, too, were willing to risk the senator's wrath to help Amelia make her escape.

"Daryl, what's going on?" Amelia slid forward on the seat as she asked, only to give a soft *oof!* as Sam put the car into drive and his sudden acceleration dumped her back against the dark leather.

"There's been a slight complication." He didn't want to have this conversation over his shoulder in a moving vehicle, but he didn't want to leave her completely in the dark, either. "We need to find someplace to park so I can talk to you about it. Okay?"

"A slight complication?" There was a long silence. "Okay, sure. Whatever you think is best."

What he thought best was to have never gotten on that plane with her in the first place. But Doyle had tasked him with seeing her home safely, and one way or another, he was going to do just that. Hopefully without making things worse than they already were.

Although honestly, he didn't see a single way this could go that wouldn't end in a complete and utter clusterfuck.

As the Town Car slid out through the high wrought-iron gates they'd entered only minutes before, a dozen questions swirled around in Amelia's brain like leaves in a windstorm.

Why had Leon, Mitch, and Phillip been waiting outside the house when they arrived? Why hadn't Daryl wanted her to get out of the car? Why were they leaving, where were they going, and how the hell had her life gotten so absurdly out of control?

Pressed back into the buttery soft leather seat, she struggled to maintain her composure.

She'd been counting on being able to retreat to the quiet safety of her room to vent the anger and frustration threatening to choke her. Had literally counted the minutes during the long, silent ride from the airport.

Having to keep up the calm façade even longer when the end had been in sight was almost physically painful.

The car pulled into a strip mall parking lot at the outside edge of downtown. Daryl and Sam both got out. Amelia waited, expecting one of them to open the door for her to get out as well.

It was a surprise when it opened and Daryl slid into the backseat with her instead.

The vehicle was large and roomy, but with Daryl sharing the seat, it suddenly seemed cramped. Not that he was huge. While taller than anyone on her father's security detail at four or five inches over six feet, he wasn't as bulky as Leon. Rather than being built like a bodybuilder, he had more of a lean-hipped, broad-shouldered build, like a runner or a swimmer.

Or a cowboy. She vaguely remembered Thea mentioning once Daryl had done some rodeo riding in his youth.

No, it wasn't his size that seemed to take up all that room. It was his presence. Daryl Raintree might be a quiet, intense, watchful man, but no matter where he was, he always seemed to own the space around him.

A trick Amelia envied him for, since she'd never managed to learn it herself.

Turning sideways on the seat to face him, she braced for whatever bad news he was about to deliver. Because what else could it be?

"Okay, what's happened?"

He hesitated, and she wondered if he was going to lie to her. Again.

"Your parents are on their way back to Boulder." His voice was soft, as though he were trying to lessen the blow.

It didn't work. But as she had so many other times, she absorbed it without a flinch. "I see." She gave a grim smile. "They didn't waste any time, did they?"

"It wouldn't seem so." His fingers tapped out an angry staccato against the seat.

Judging from his agitation and obvious reluctance to tell her, there was still worse to come. "You might as well just spit it out. It won't get any better with age."

"You're right." He struggled a moment longer with his words before letting out a frustrated breath. "I'm just trying to find a way to say this without causing trouble for anyone."

It only took a moment to decipher his dilemma. "You don't need to worry about anything getting back to my father. This wouldn't be the first time that Leon *didn't* tell me something I needed to know."

Did he really think she'd tattle to her father? Well, that was a little insulting. She liked Leon. He was kind of what she imagined a gruff old uncle would be like.

Or a cuddly grizzly bear.

"Leon's orders were to keep you at the estate until your parents got there."

Amelia waited for more, but that was it. She frowned, replaying his words, trying to find what had upset both men to the point of whisking her away.

"That makes sense. I mean, if they're flying all the way back, I would expect them to want to talk to..." Her words trailed off as a horrible possibility arose. "Wait, you don't mean *keep* me there, do you? Like, *keep* me, keep me? As in, not let me leave?" She waited for Daryl to correct her, but he remained grimly silent.

"No, that has to be wrong." It had to be. "Leon must have misunderstood what my father said. He might be furious with me right now, but he wouldn't have me forcibly detained. He *wouldn't,*" she said again, but it was herself she was trying to convince.

"Maybe I shouldn't have interfered." Daryl's deep voice was troubled. "You most likely wouldn't have left before they got there anyway, and you would never have known. But," he said, laying emphasis on the word, "I thought you had the right to make an informed choice."

Choice? Did she have one, really? That was her home. She'd burned her bridges in Connecticut. Where else could she go?

But the thought of what her father instructed his security people to do smoldered like an angry ember in her chest. *Keep* her there? To what, wait on his convenience?

He could have just asked her to stay put until they got there. But no. The senator didn't ask. He told. And if he'd told her to stay there, she probably would have. He was a hard man to disobey.

Instead, he'd chosen to humiliate her with what amounted to house arrest.

Past evidence notwithstanding, there were certain hard limits to what she was willing to endure for the sake of familial harmony. Last night she'd found one of them.

It looked like she'd just found another.

"I can have Sam bring us back if you want."

Daryl's stiff words broke into her silent outrage. She shook her head. "No. No, don't. I'm not ready to face them yet."

She pressed a hand to her stomach, where the anger burning in her chest seemed to have dropped a few white-hot sparks. One-handed, she opened her purse and popped an antacid into her mouth, leaning her head back to study the roof as she chewed. It was rude, but at that moment, she couldn't find it in her to care.

Once she had a grasp back on her composure, she rolled her head to the side on the seatback to look at Daryl. He was still watching her, his dark brown eyes maybe seeing a little too much for comfort.

"Thank you. I appreciate that you—both you and Leon—thought to give me the chance to make my own decision." It was sort of a novel experience. "You're right. If I hadn't known about my father's orders, I would have been there when he arrived, simply because I hadn't planned to go anywhere else today."

She took a breath. "That being said, there's an enormous

difference between being there, and being *kept* there. And knowing he ordered the latter leaves a very bad taste in my mouth."

Not to mention the arrow it sent straight through her heart.

If ever she'd needed an indicator of the place she held in her father's affections, this would do it. The only thing the man truly loved was power.

Amelia pinched the bridge of her nose, forcing back the burn of tears. God, she was exhausted. Both physically and mentally. Not to mention being about an inch away from emotionally crashing in a big, ugly, embarrassing way.

"I'm sure either the Fordhams or Beaumonts would be happy to have you stay with them until you decide what you want to do."

Oh, yes.

Evie Fordham and Patricia Beaumont were like surrogate mothers to her, showing her the love and easy affection never present in her own family. They were just what she needed right now.

But she shook her head.

"That's the first place my parents would look for me. I wouldn't put it past them not to show up at their front doors and cause a scene." If her father was angry enough to chase her all the way back to Colorado to yell at her, he wouldn't have any qualms about venting his frustration on anyone who got in his way.

"So, a hotel, then?"

It was the logical choice under the circumstances.

But she was feeling too raw to be alone right now. Too needy. She needed someone who would understand and sympathize with her. Someone she could let down her barriers in front of and not be humiliated by whatever came pouring out unfiltered. Who would keep her from shattering into a million little pieces.

Normally, that would be Thea or Lillian. But they were a thousand miles away.

That left only one other person in Boulder she could think of to turn to.

"No, I have someplace better to go. Sam knows the way."

Chapter 5

"Drink your juice, kitten. You still look about five shades beyond pale."

With a wan smile, Amelia accepted the heavy glass tumbler from Des and took a sip. The freshly squeezed orange-mango mix tasted delightfully sweet and tart on her tongue, waking taste buds that had long ago gone dormant for lack of interest. She took a larger swallow, draining half the glass before setting it next to her plate.

"Delicious," she told him, and was rewarded with a grin.

"Of course it is," he said without modesty. "Now finish your eggs. It would be a sin to waste a bite."

She rolled her eyes at him, but picked up her fork and dug in. He was right. Anything that came out of the kitchen when his roommate was cooking was bound to be good. Better than good. Sheila might be a master pastry chef, but her skill wasn't limited to desserts. The egg white omelet was delicately seasoned, as well as fluffy and light enough to not lie like a rock in her stomach.

Heaven.

Across the table, Daryl was working his way through what had to be the largest Denver omelet she'd ever seen. It had all but hung over both sides of the plate when Sheila brought it out, anchored in place by slices of golden toast and accompanied by several small jars of homemade preserves.

Clearly, it had been meant to impress.

Daryl, however, was too busy inhaling his breakfast to notice that, or the very thorough and appreciative perusal he got from the meal's creator. Or maybe he had noticed and chosen to ignore it. After all, Sheila was just as big a flirt as Des. And if Amelia wasn't mistaken, she'd dated Daryl's coworker Sam for a while the previous year.

Daryl struck Amelia as the kind of guy who'd consider Sheila off-limits for that reason alone.

Not that Amelia could really fault Sheila for flirting. He was a good-looking man. Even with a dark morning scruff and wearing the previous day's wrinkled clothes—with their height difference he couldn't borrow anything of Des's the way she had Sheila's—he looked, to use one of Lillian's favorite descriptions of him, hunkalicious.

Des filled the mealtime with his usual funny/snarky chatter, alternately gushing about the moderate success his new clothing line was receiving and lambasting the critics who were stingy with their praise. Especially the one who had called him out for "simply cashing in on his gay cachet."

"I mean, really, *gay cachet*?" He looked caught between horrified and amused. "What does that even mean? It sounds like a bad name for a men's cologne."

"Sounds to me like he couldn't find anything with your work to bitch about and decided to go with a personal attack instead." The hint of an Irish brogue flavored Sheila's blunt assessment. She chased the last of her eggs around the plate with a wedge of wheat toast, then used it to point at Des. "I think he's still pissed at you for turning him down on New Year's Eve."

"Hmm." Fiddling with his coffee cup, Des gave a half-hearted shrug. "I suppose he might still be holding a grudge. Patrick always was a bit of a bitch."

"A bitch?" Sheila snorted. "If he was out, he'd be a full-blown diva."

"And his not being out publicly is why I turned him down, despite his very delicious Johnny Depp good looks." Des offered a disappointed moue before he grabbed up the glass carafe from the center of the table and refreshed everyone's coffee as he spoke.

"He's free to make the choices that are best for him, of course. But I've reached a place in my life where I'm very comfortable with who I am. Dating someone who isn't out means a lot of sneaking around and lying to people I care about, and I'm not about to be chased back into the shadows because someone else is still hiding in them."

"It sounds like you've done that before," Amelia said softly.

"Once." Des sighed. Not one of his usual over-dramatic ones meant to entertain, but a sigh that spoke of true regret and more than a little unhappiness. "I thought...well, I was wrong. In any case, nothing good can ever come of trying to be something you're not, or trying to be what everyone else expects you to be. The only way to really be happy is to be you."

Words of wisdom? Or warning?

She swallowed and looked down at her plate, then back to the wealth of understanding warming his dark, Mediterranean eyes. "What if you don't know who that is?"

"Oh, kitten." He placed his hand over hers on the table. "I think you know exactly who you are. You just have to be brave enough to step out of your shadows and embrace it." He gave her hand a pat and retrieved his coffee cup. "So, are you still planning to beard the lions in their den today? Because you might want to reconsider. Moving to neutral territory may make things easier. Even the playing field, so to speak."

Daryl tipped his head between bites. "He's not wrong."

"If you want it, *mi casa* and all that. Sheila and I can make ourselves scarce for a few hours."

Sheila nodded. "Just say the word, and we're the wind."

"Thanks, but I really think I need to go to them." Amelia couldn't imagine the response if she suggested her parents expend the effort to meet her someplace other than at home for the coming talk.

Although *talk* might be too optimistic a term.

Everyone thought her mother was the worst of the two when it came to being unpleasant, but it was her father who had the truly ugly temper. She didn't see it often, but then, she'd shaped her entire life to be as accommodating as possible so she wouldn't have to.

It had been hard enough putting off the coming confrontation until today. Her mother had called her cell not long after she and Daryl arrived at Des's duplex yesterday afternoon, demanding she return to the house at once.

She'd almost relented as the harangue went on and on about ungrateful children and selfish actions creating disastrous consequences for others. But Des's warm hand on her shoulder had grounded her enough to remember she had the right to say no. Even to her parents.

So she did.

It hadn't been pretty.

She'd been on the verge of tears when Daryl plucked the phone from her fingers and told her mother that Amelia would call her back after everyone had a chance to calm down. And then he'd hung up.

On. Her. Mother.

When he handed her back the phone, she'd had the incredible urge to kiss him for that simple act alone. There weren't many people who dared defy Meredith Westlake. Even Des had looked a little awed.

After a dinner she only went through the motions of eating, Amelia had reluctantly made the promised call. And found there was something even worse than her father's anger: his condescension. She'd forgotten just how cruelly and effectively he could wield it.

It was then she'd decided she wasn't in any shape to go home and face them yet.

If five minutes on the phone could leave her feeling like her skin had just been flayed off her body, there was no way she'd survive the full-on lecture that awaited without quietly bleeding to death.

She'd told her father she'd present herself at the house by lunchtime today. Then, while she'd marshalled her courage to end the call if he protested, he'd beaten her to the punch. With a curt "see that you do," he'd hung up first.

Her mother might be the queen of the dramatic exit, but her father was the master of the last word.

Daryl's phone rang. After a few quick words, he excused himself and left the kitchen. A moment later, the front door opened. There were quiet voices before the door closed, followed by another door somewhere else in the apartment.

After helping to clear the table despite Sheila's protests, Amelia aimlessly wandered the bright and airy living room, propelled by nervous energy. The room was a combination of Thea's expert eye and Des's eclectic taste, with pieces of Sheila's Irish heritage to make it all feel like one cohesive space. A true, comfortable home.

Just how I thought my house would be.

Except there was no house of her own now. She was right back where she started, trapped in her parents' home. Only now it was going to be ten times worse. Somehow, someway, they were going to make her pay for humiliating them like this.

The delicious omelet that had gone down so easily was suddenly caught in the whirlpool of stomach acid her nerves started pumping out by the gallon. She thought longingly of the antacids in her purse, but she couldn't bring herself to get them in front of Sheila. It would be an insult to her delicious cooking.

Instead, she paced and worried, and let the acid flow unchecked.

The worst part was, whatever recriminations her parents were going to throw at her, they'd be right. She *had* backed out of the wedding a mere ten days from the event. She *hadn't* given any hints in the past few months that she'd been having doubts or second thoughts. Her actions *would* create problems for both families. Not just socially, but political ones as well.

And while Senator Davenport would probably ride out the scandal with only a few bumps and bruises, it was Charles's budding career that would suffer the most. Might, in fact, implode.

Because of her.

"You're thinking much too hard about something." Des took her by the shoulders and led her toward the sofa. As they sat, he pressed two familiar discs into her hand.

She could have cried in gratitude.

"I was just wondering if I could have handled things different. Better."

With a wince of apology to Sheila, who shook her head and rolled her eyes in response, Amelia popped the antacids and chewed with a desperation that betrayed just how close to becoming ill she'd allowed herself to get.

"Probably," Des replied in his usual pragmatic way. "But should-haves and could-haves are a useless waste of energy and a wonderful way to make yourself sick." He gave her an admonishing look before patting her knee. "Concentrate on the here and now. You made a decision about what was best for you. It doesn't matter what anyone else thinks."

"But that decision didn't just affect me." And that was the crux of the problem. Her parents weren't angry about her ruining *her* life. They were angry about how her decision impacted *them*. No amount of justification in the world could fix that.

"Maybe not," Sheila said, "but you have to stop owning all the blame. I'm sure there's plenty to go around."

There was. More than enough.

But Amelia wasn't about to admit the scene she'd walked in on the night of the party. Telling Thea and Lillian had been hard enough. Though she supposed she'd have to tell her parents, if only to explain why she'd ended things seemingly with no reason.

It was a *big* effing reason.

Although even Charles's infidelity might not be a good enough one to satisfy her father. Not when it meant the end of his dream of a son-in-law who was being groomed to one day make a run for the White House.

A short time later, she accepted hugs from both Des and Sheila as she left, working hard to summon a smile in response to their words of encouragement. The tote bag she'd dragged with her all the way from Connecticut she left in Des's care. The only thing it contained was the gorgeous dress she now associated with her first step toward taking back control of her own life. She hadn't left it behind for fear something might 'accidentally' happen to it. Her mother could be spiteful that way.

Her father's dreams of breathing rarified Washington air one day weren't the only ones Amelia had upended.

She followed the red brick walkway from the front steps to the sidewalk behind Daryl, who was now clean-shaven and wearing a fresh pair of dark slacks and a crisp white dress shirt. Courtesy of whomever had been at the front door earlier, judging by the black knapsack slung over one broad shoulder.

Guilt nipped at her conscience at how much he'd been forced to put up with in the past twenty-four hours because of her. Not the least of which was a night sleeping on Des and Sheila's sofa. As cushy as it was, it probably wasn't all that comfortable as a bed. Especially for a man of his size.

She hadn't expected him to spend the night. As far as she was concerned, he'd already done his job. More than, actually. But it seemed Daryl took his orders a little more literally. He'd been charged with seeing her home safely, so until he delivered her to her front door, he was in full bodyguard mode. That meant staying wherever she stayed.

It also meant refusing her offer to switch places and let him have the queen-sized bed in the guest room. Which was just silly, in her opinion. It wasn't like he needed to place himself between her and the front door. She wasn't in any physical danger the way Thea had been last year.

No, the threat she faced wasn't one any bodyguard could shield her from.

Even so, despite it all feeling like overkill, she was still glad he was there. Something about his strong, silent presence lent her some strength of her own. And God knew she'd need every bit she could get.

Not to mention it was just nice not to be alone. For a little while longer, at least.

Amelia hesitated at the sidewalk, not seeing the expected Town Car waiting. Instead, Daryl pulled a set of keys from his pocket and thumbed the fob. The lights flashed on a big, black four-door truck parked at the curb that looked about a mile off the ground. He opened the front passenger door and waited.

"Yours?" She rolled her eyes at herself. Of course, it was his. She cast a wary eye at the open door. At five-eight, she wasn't short, but it still wouldn't be an easy ascent.

"I thought it might be better if we showed up in a personal vehicle, rather than one of the Fordhams' cars. Here, put your foot on the running board and grab the handle." He tapped a handgrip molded into the inside of the doorframe.

"Hmm." It still looked tricky, but Amelia did as instructed. She should have borrowed a pair of Sheila's jeans rather than the skirt and kitten heels. The long, flowy skirt had helped hide the few inches too short it actually was, but it also tangled itself around her legs as she maneuvered into the high seat.

"No, the other foot. There you go. Now just turn...wait, not...just...here, this way." Daryl put his hands on her waist and hip and guided her into the seat. He closed the door, went around the front of the truck, tossed his knapsack in the backseat, and got in, cursing under his breath as he whacked his knee on the steering column. "I told Sam not to let Kirsten drive it over," he muttered.

Amelia was still sitting frozen by the strange zing of heat that had accompanied Daryl's touch. It hadn't been inappropriate. In fact, Daryl had touched her much more as he guided her through both airports the day before, using his size and personality to create a jostle-free zone for her.

But for some reason, *this* touch, fleeting as it was, sent a shiver deep inside where she'd never shivered before.

It was disconcerting, to say the least.

Lucky for her, Daryl was too busy readjusting the seat, mirrors, and radio, all the while softly cursing Kirsten—another of the Fordham security team—to notice her flustered state. After buckling her seatbelt, Amelia sat watching him, trying to understand her strange reaction.

Nerves. It had to be nerves.

Plus, thanks to Lillian, she was more aware of Daryl physically than she was anyone else on either her or her friends' security teams. Lil was forever commenting on his broad shoulders and long, muscular legs, and how her fingers itched to sketch him. Preferably shirtless. Though as far as Amelia knew, she'd never gotten around to asking him to pose.

But oh, what a picture that would be if she ever did.

Finally finished reclaiming his space, Darryl turned to her, jarring her from that errant thought.

"Are you okay with showing up in this? Like I said, I thought that since you wanted to keep the Fordhams out of things, it might be better than using one of their cars. But if you'd rather, we can stop by their estate and switch it out for the Town Car or limo. Sam said they offered the use of either one if you wanted it."

She shook her head.

"This is fine. Besides," she added with a wry grin, "I really don't think my parents will be waiting outside for me, do you? I could show up on a Segway and they wouldn't know the difference. Or care." No, the only thing that would matter to her parents was that she presented herself as demanded.

"A Segway, huh?" Daryl's lips twitched.

Amelia lifted a shoulder in a half-shrug. "They're fun."

"I've never tried one. They look a little dangerous."

Says the man with the Godzilla truck.

"Not after you get the hang of it. The three of us used them when we went down to Denver last summer. It was kind of cool. Until Lil started goofing around and nearly got us kicked off the tour we were on." She smiled a little at the memory.

"Why don't I find that hard to believe?" He checked traffic and pulled away from the curb. "What did she do, chase pigeons?"

"Pedestrians."

She regaled Daryl with the story of how she and Thea had fought a losing battle to rein in their impulsive friend when she'd gotten bored of the historical sites and started cruising the crowds for artistic subjects instead. There had been one man in particular she'd been keen to get permission from to take some photos so she could do a sketch later on.

His wife had *not* appreciated Lillian asking.

She'd appreciated it even less when her husband said yes.

Lillian had snapped her shots, and they'd hightailed it back to the tour before things got too ugly between the couple. Amelia had picked up a few new words of Italian that day. Complete with hand gestures.

"I hope she learned her lesson."

Amelia snorted. "What do you think?"

It wasn't until her phone rang and interrupted that she realized they were almost at her parents' estate. Reminiscing about the Segway fiasco managed to both distract her and help settle her nerves, both of which she would have thought impossible under the circumstances.

Yet another thing to thank Daryl for.

Recognizing Thea's ringtone, Amelia slipped her phone out of her purse, a faint smile still on her lips. "Hi, T."

"Mellie, sweetie. Where are you?" Thea sounded tense, which was enough to make Amelia tense up herself.

So much for settled nerves.

"We're a couple of minutes from my parents' house." She'd spoken with Thea the night before, bringing her up to speed on everything that had happened and what the plan was for today. "Why? What's wrong?"

There was a long hum of silence on the line, long enough that Amelia started to think she'd lost the call. But then Thea spoke.

"Sweetie, we got a call just a few minutes ago from Louisa about the luncheon scheduled for today."

Louisa. The wedding planner's snooty assistant.

She wasn't going to miss dealing with those two.

"To cancel," Amelia murmured. The tightness of extreme anxiety pinched her chest at the thought of all the people getting the news this morning about the wedding being called off.

"No. To reschedule."

Amelia froze. "What?"

"She said that they were pushing the luncheon off until tomorrow, and that tomorrow night's dinner reception would start two hours later than planned to accommodate the guests who were invited to both events."

Unease and confusion fluttered in Amelia's chest like trapped birds.

"Wait, why would they do that? It makes no sense to have the parties when the wedding is cancelled." Unless they were trying to drum up sympathy for Charles by parading him in front of their guests as the jilted groom putting on a brave face?

Thea's next words disabused her of that possibility.

"That's what I'm trying to tell you, sweetie. It hasn't been cancelled. *Nothing* has been cancelled. The wedding is still on."

Chapter 6

"**B**reathe."

Daryl dragged his hand up and down Amelia's back, trying to coax her into taking in enough air to keep from passing out. Which she looked in imminent danger of doing at the moment. Either that, or throwing up.

Neither was a desirable outcome.

He had no idea what brought on the extreme reaction. One minute she'd been talking to Thea on the phone, the next she'd been wheezing for breath like a ninety-year-old asthmatic. He'd nearly taken out two cars in his haste to pull the truck to the side of the road.

Hampered by the wide center console between them, he got out and went around to the passenger side. He yanked the door open and unclipped Amelia's seatbelt to remove any possible restriction to her breathing.

It didn't help.

Thea's voice came from the phone clutched in her hand, faint but demanding. He ended the call and dropped the phone to the floorboard next to Amelia's feet, realizing only after he did it he probably should have said something first.

Sure enough, the phone rang again almost immediately. He ignored it. Amelia was his priority at the moment. He rubbed her back, his voice quiet and firm as he urged her to relax and just *breathe*.

After a few moments, the phone on the floor fell silent, but the one in his pocket vibrated almost at the same time.

This one he couldn't ignore.

He thumbed it on, said "Call you back in five" and hung up. Both phones stayed silent after that, although he was sure Doyle was having a hard time on his end convincing Thea to lay off the speed dial.

Slowly, Amelia's body unclenched and her lungs accepted precious air more readily. As her breathing deepened, Daryl changed from a brisk up-and-down rub to slow circles. He was pretty sure the crisis had passed, but wouldn't stop until he was certain.

It was only then he noticed he could feel all of her delicate bones through the soft cotton top she wore. Shoulder blades, vertebrae, ribs. Damn, the girl had absolutely no meat on her. She wasn't exactly tiny, but she'd never reminded him more of a porcelain doll, pretty and delicate, and easily smashed with one careless gesture.

Judging by the almost translucent paleness of her face, whatever news Thea imparted had been of the smashing kind. He'd find out what when he called Doyle back. Right now, he was worried about the young woman in front of him. She was too pale, too quiet.

Too broken.

Fuck.

Give him a car chase or shootout any day. *That* he could handle. Crazed stalker with a gun? No problem. But this? This was emotional shit, and he didn't know dick about how to protect against that.

So, he just kept rubbing her back in what he hoped was a comforting way, and prayed there wouldn't be any tears. Tears were usually his signal to head for the door. That wasn't an option here, though.

Please God, don't let her cry.

Finally, Amelia took a huge breath and let it out with a shaky sigh.

"Better?" He didn't ask if she was okay. A single look in her eyes told him she was miles from that. But if she was at least past the anxiety attack, or whatever the hell that had been, he could risk stepping away for a minute to get a sit-rep from Doyle.

Not meeting his eyes, Amelia gave a tiny nod.

Daryl waited a minute, but she remained silent. Realizing his hand was still on her back even though he'd stopped rubbing, he snatched it away. "I'm going to call Doyle. I'll be right at the rear of the truck if you need me, okay?"

She nodded again. Still no eye contact.

He hesitated. He'd feel better if she actually said something, but it didn't seem like she was back together enough to manage it yet. Instincts torn, he walked to the rear of the truck, far enough to be out of earshot if he spoke low, but close enough to hear if she had trouble breathing again.

Doyle answered on the first ring. "Is she all right?"

"She had a panic attack or something and couldn't catch her breath, but she seems to be past the worst of it now. What the hell did Thea say to her?"

There was a moment of muffled talking while Doyle conveyed his words to Thea before he answered. "So far, nobody here has said anything about the wedding being cancelled. The lunch Amelia was supposed to host today was pushed off until tomorrow, but nothing else has been changed or called off."

"Son of a..." Swallowing the curse, Daryl glanced toward the open passenger door and lowered his voice. "What the hell do they expect to accomplish? The bride called the wedding off. Period. Hosting parties isn't going to change that."

"No, but it buys them time." Doyle's tone was grim.

"For what? To figure out how to word the press release?"

"Or to change the bride's mind."

Daryl froze. They wouldn't dare.

The fuck they wouldn't.

Neither the bride's nor groom's parents were the kind to take *no* for an answer if *yes* suited them better. So far, only a small group of people knew about Amelia's decision. If she changed her mind, they could have her back in Connecticut and saying "I do" before anyone else was the wiser.

There was only one problem with that plan.

"Amelia's not going to change her mind."

"Maybe. But she doesn't exactly have the best track record when it comes to standing up to her parents. Isn't that why she left in the first place? Add the Davenports to the dog pile on her back, and how long do you think it will be before she crumbles?"

Considering the way she'd been second- and third-guessing herself already this morning because of the guilt? Not long at all.

Shit.

Daryl clamped down on his temper. "What can we do?"

"Not taking her to her parents' place would be a good start."

No shit.

"Problem is, even if I don't drop her on their doorstep like a present, they're not going to just give up. They'll keep calling her and try to browbeat her into going home. And she can't stay with her friend Des again. There are zero options for security there."

Not to mention another night on that sofa would turn him into a pretzel.

"She can hole up with the Fordhams. Thea already talked to her parents. They're beyond livid about the whole thing, and Evie told her to have you bring Amelia to the house asap."

"I don't think she'll go. She doesn't want to cause trouble for them, or the Beaumonts. And you and I both know the Westlakes wouldn't hesitate to apply whatever pressure it took to pry Amelia loose from their protection once they knew she was there."

William Westlake might be retired from politics, but he still had a long reach in the state.

Doyle sighed. "I think you're probably right. Much as Evie would love to take a swipe at Meredith Westlake for how she's treated Thea, and Amelia, it would just create more problems than it would solve. Amelia needs to be out of Boulder altogether. Proximity is a major part of the problem here."

"Being predictable is the other," Daryl said. "We need to get her someplace they wouldn't expect her to be. Someplace she's never been before."

"As soon as she buys an airline ticket or books a hotel room, it'll no doubt send up a red flag somewhere. Same for anyone connected to her or to either family."

Doyle sounded as annoyed as Daryl felt about the probability one or both of the senators had called in a favor from one of the alphabet agencies. It was the only explanation for how fast they'd known about Amelia coming back to Boulder, right down to the flight she'd been on.

Besides being borderline illegal, it made keeping Amelia invisible for the next few days a hell of a lot harder.

"Are you willing to stick this out for the duration? No matter how long it takes for them to back off and finally cancel the damn wedding?"

A spark of annoyance flared at Doyle's question.

"Boss, if anyone but you asked that question, they'd be picking up pieces of their ass with a pair of tweezers."

"I just need to check." Doyle didn't sound the least bit apologetic. "Once you leave Boulder, it'll just be the two of you. So, if we're going to switch things up, it's got to be now."

He was right, damn it.

Daryl put aside his outraged sense of honor and considered the situation.

Could he handle being with Amelia for the next three, four, maybe more days? Being not only her sole source of protection, but in her constant company, day and night, no matter how much they might get on each other's nerves?

Though she was a Society princess, she'd never been a prima

donna, at least not that he'd ever known. She wasn't a chatterbox like Lillian, so she wasn't likely to talk his ear off. And while quiet and a little introverted, she at least had a brain in her head. They could probably manage a few days together without driving each other too crazy.

"Unless she'd prefer Kirsten or Francine, I'm in." She might feel more comfortable being stuck in close quarters with one of the female bodyguards.

"Good." Doyle sounded pleased by his answer.

Maybe a little *too* pleased.

"I have an idea how you can stay off the grid," Doyle said, confirming Daryl's suspicions.

"What is it?"

"You need someplace that's less than a day's drive, so there are no hotels or airlines to book."

"Right."

"Someplace you know well enough to feel safe at, but not someplace many people know about."

Feeling like he was being led down the primrose path, Daryl said cautiously, "Yeah."

"Someplace isolated but not totally cut off from civilization, where she wouldn't be recognized if someone saw her."

Warning bells started to ring. "Doyle..."

"Someplace you could just drop in anytime, unannounced, and know there's always a bed, or two in this case, waiting for you if you need it."

Oh, *fuck* no.

"Forget it." The words were a growl. "No way in hell."

"It's the perfect solution."

"No."

"You can be there by what? Midnight?"

"If I was lucky. That doesn't mean—"

"I suppose you could always stop and find a discreet hotel for the night if you had to," Doyle continued, rolling right over him. "But there's less of a chance for the senator's *friends* to get a bead on you if you drive straight through. Besides, the later you arrive, the fewer people that are likely to see you."

"There are reasons I don't go there very often." Daryl gripped the phone so hard he was surprised it didn't crack.

"Are they more important than Amelia's safety?"

No, damn it.

But still. "This is not a good idea."

"Give me a better one."

He wanted to. But he couldn't. "Fuck."

"You'll need to get on the road as soon as you can. Thea said Amelia's welcome to raid her closet, but you'll probably still have to stop at a store somewhere along the way for her to pick up toiletries and whatever else she needs."

"She might not agree to go." He latched onto the possibility with desperate hope.

There was a terse silence from the phone. "Convince her. Amelia means a lot to Thea. If she ends up marrying that asshole, I may have to kill him just to keep Thea from doing it."

If it came to that, Daryl would probably end up sharing a cell with him. Anyone who could leave the bruised look in a woman's eyes like Amelia's had held the night of the party deserved to die.

"This is a bad idea."

"It's all we've got. Make it work."

Daryl slid the phone back into his pocket with a heartfelt "Fuck me" as he struggled to come to grips with this latest turn of events. Doyle was right. They needed a place to stash Amelia that was safe, out of the way, and not connected to her in any way. This fit the bill.

But damn it all, he really, *really* wished it didn't.

Walking to the front of the truck, he was relieved to see Amelia was no longer paler than the bleached sheets his stepmother used to hang on the clothesline every Sunday. Her eyes were closed, head tilted back against the headrest on the bucket seat, hands clasped in her lap, but she in no way looked peaceful.

She looked exhausted.

"We need to talk about some things." Daryl stopped when she lifted her phone from her lap for him to see.

"Thea filled me in while you were talking to Doyle." She opened her eyes and rolled her head to look at him. "I guess it's a good thing you didn't leave me there yesterday, or I'd probably be on a plane back to Connecticut right now, memorizing my apology to Charles and his parents for inconveniencing them with my silly little attack of nerves."

There was a bitter bite to her sarcastic words, but she wasn't wrong.

"They can't force you to go or to change your mind."

She shot him a *get real* look. "Like everybody doesn't know I'd fold like wet tissue paper once they started working on me. So much for my 'strategic retreat,' huh?" She took a deep breath. "Thank you for not just leaving me to my fate."

He shrugged. "Thank Leon."

"God, Leon." Worry darkened her mossy green eyes. "Is there any way to check on him? If he lost his job because he helped me..."

If he did, Doyle would most likely hire him on the spot.

"I'll look into it. But right now, we need to talk about what we're going to do."

Amelia gave a brittle laugh. "Do? If I don't want to end up Mrs. Charles Wilson Henry Davenport by this time next Saturday, I need to get out of Boulder for a while."

It was good she realized that. One less hurdle to overcome.

"Out of the state would be better."

"Okay. I can go visit my Aunt Josie in Texas."

Daryl had a vague recollection of the woman from the engagement party the year before. She was Meredith Westlake's aunt, making her Amelia's great-aunt, and while she was as rich as Croesus, she was also about as old as dirt.

He shook his head. "It would be one of the first places your mother would think to look once they realize you're not in town."

That deflated her a little, but she nodded. "You're right." She thought for a second. "You can take me to the airport. I'll buy a ticket on the next flight to any random city, and just check into a hotel there and...what?" she asked as he shook his head again.

Where to start?

"Okay, first off, buying a plane ticket would mean having your name in the airline's database, which we've already seen your father capable of somehow tapping into for information. So, if you get on a plane to anywhere, he's going to know it. Same goes for checking into a hotel."

She looked chagrined. "Okay, then I could drive somewhere, and use cash to get a hotel room under a fake name."

"The only place you could check into without giving them ID is a no-tell motel, and you sure as hell won't be staying in one of those." The thought of classy, elegant Amelia Westlake staying in a by-the-hour dive like that was almost sacrilegious.

"Oh."

He hated knocking her ideas to the ground like so many bad apples, but she needed to realize none of what she was thinking would work. That would leave what he was about to propose as the only possible way forward. No matter how outlandish it sounded.

But for that to happen, he needed to clear up one last misconception first.

"And to be clear, *you* won't be going anywhere. *We* will. So whatever plan we come up with, it'll involve the two of us, together."

"We?" She practically squeaked the word. "Together?"

"Yes, we, together." He wasn't sure if he should be amused or insulted by her reaction.

"But, why?"

"Because you have some very powerful people angry with you

right now, and I don't trust them to play fair when it comes to getting their way." He paused. That might have been a little too honest for his pay grade. "Look, I know they're your parents, and I'm sorry if that sounds insulting, but…"

"No, it's not, because you're exactly right. They *are* angry. And they really, really want this marriage to happen, no matter what. But why should *you* have to come along and babysit me again?"

"Would you be more comfortable with Kirsten or Francine? Because it's no problem if you do. We just need to take care of the switch right now." Not to mention they'd need a whole new plan.

Funny how the idea of passing her over to someone else suddenly rankled, when just a minute ago he'd been cursing both Doyle and his idiotic idea.

The dismay on Amelia's face was genuine and immediate.

"No, that's not what I meant." She placed a hand on his arm. "I'm perfectly comfortable with you, Daryl. It's just…I hate that you're disrupting your life for me like this. I'm sure babysitting me for the next few days isn't your idea of a fun time."

Realizing her objection hadn't been *about* him but rather *for* him eased whatever had tensed inside his gut.

"I don't think it'll be yours, either." He said it in a wry manner, trying to lighten the mood, but that didn't make it any less true. "But if you're willing to suck it up, so am I."

She gave a small laugh. "Okay. Deal."

"Deal."

He accepted the delicate hand she offered just like she had the night of the party, taking great care not to squeeze too hard. It felt cool, and he was tempted to cover it with both his hands to warm it. Thankfully, she withdrew from the clasp before he could embarrass himself by giving in to the odd impulse.

"So." Some of her normal poker-back posture returned as she straightened in the seat. "Where are we going?"

He worked hard to control a grimace, because he needed her to love the idea even though he hated it. "How would you feel about meeting my parents?"

Chapter 7

Everything moved fast after that.

So fast, in fact, that Amelia was sitting in the passenger seat of the black monster truck heading north without being a hundred percent certain she'd ever actually agreed to the plan. Because as if she wasn't humiliated enough about the mess she'd gotten herself into, now she'd have to involve total strangers?

And not just any strangers. Oh no. That would be bad enough. No, she'd be throwing herself on the mercy and hospitality of Daryl Raintree's *parents*.

What was he thinking?

And what was she thinking to go along with it?

Oh, right. That she was willing to do just about anything to avoid the wedding that was evidently moving full speed ahead back east, missing bride notwithstanding. She still couldn't quite wrap her head around that.

Yes, she might have waited until almost the last minute, but she'd been very clear when she spoke to Charles. I don't love you. You don't love me. This marriage would be a mistake. I'm sorry, but I can't marry you.

She'd given him back *the ring*. It couldn't get any plainer than that, could it?

The. Wedding. Was. Off.

Except...it seemed it wasn't.

And Daryl might say no one could force her to say "I do," but he didn't know what her parents were capable of making her do. For twenty-three years, she'd knuckled under and gone along with whatever they wanted. She learned at an early age it was pointless to try to argue, object, or worst of all, rebel.

Her mother may have never raised a hand to her, but she had honed the art of drawing blood with her words to an art form. That, in Amelia's opinion, was a much more effective weapon to use against a child than any fist or belt.

When the one person who's supposed to love and cherish you the most tells you that you're a disappointment in everything you do, it isn't long before you start to believe it's true.

And are willing to do whatever it takes to try to make her proud.

No matter what she'd done, though, Amelia never seemed to measure up. She'd never been quite pretty enough, accomplished enough, or graceful enough to garner the prize of her mother's approval. It wasn't until Amelia had gotten engaged to Charles she'd finally seen a glimmer of pride in her mother's gaze.

Too bad it turned out that pride had all been for Charles.

Charles was smart. *Charles* was ambitious. *Charles* was going high places in politics, maybe even as far as the White House. He was the answer to all her parents' dreams, while Amelia was merely the means to obtain it. Once they were married, her parents would finally have the son they'd never been able to conceive themselves.

She might have been willing to live with that—*had* been willing to live with it—if only she could have gotten the one thing she craved the most from Charles. Not love, although she wanted that, too.

No, what she wanted was much harder to come by, at least in her experience.

Respect.

If she had a husband who respected her, maybe she could block out her mother's negative voice in her head every time she tried to think for herself. Maybe she could mend the gaping wounds to her self-confidence that sometimes managed to scab over but never really heal. Maybe she could get through a day without scarfing down two rolls of antacids just to keep her stomach from going full-blown Chernobyl.

If she had a husband who respected her, then maybe she could finally respect herself.

Because when she looked in the mirror, she didn't like who she saw. Hell, lately she barely even *recognized* who she saw. And that was what scared her the most. Every day, the real Amelia faded just a little more. How much longer would it be before one day she was gone entirely, leaving behind only the pretty, useless shell her parents helped construct?

God, she was a psychiatrist's wet dream. Her mommy issues alone could put his kids through grad school.

From her surprisingly comfy seat, Amelia glanced out the truck's window, but the view was the same as it had been for the past several hours. I-25 was crowded with cars and eighteen-wheelers and getting more crowded by the minute as rush hour crept ever nearer.

About forty minutes later, Daryl eased the truck through the now bumper-to-bumper traffic to the exit ramp and zipped off the interstate. When the little gold Subaru darted in front of them at the last second, Amelia flinched, certain they were going to hit it.

But Daryl's driving skills were up to the task. There was a chirp of brakes and a small jerk from the seatbelt, but the smaller car skimmed in front of the truck unscathed, with no more than a sneeze's clearance between their bumpers.

She scowled at the car, which nearly rear-ended the SUV in front of him before braking hard. "Freaking dumbass."

Daryl made a noise, and she looked over. The amusement on his face made her realize she'd said that out loud. The telltale heat of a blush started to toast her cheeks. "Sorry, that just slipped out."

"Don't be," Daryl replied with a lazy grin. "That's actually tame compared to what I was thinking."

Even so, she needed to be more careful. Saying whatever came into her mind was a dangerous habit to get into. One she'd been indulging in too much around him lately.

"Where are we going, anyway?"

"I figured we could make a quick trip to a store for whatever you need, then get some food and gas before hitting the road again. The worst of the traffic should be over by then."

"Okay. Shopping won't take long. I don't need much." She'd raided Thea's closet while Daryl had gone to his apartment to pack a bag for himself. But she still had to pick up a few things.

It didn't matter how tight you were, you just didn't borrow your bestie's underwear.

As for getting something to eat, it surprised her to find she was actually hungry. Never one to take the appetite unicorn for granted when it made one of its rare appearances, she almost suggested they start with the meal and then go shopping.

But Daryl clearly had a plan in mind of what they needed to do. He was already doing so much for her. The last thing she wanted was to start being difficult and demanding. So, they'd shop first, and find a restaurant afterward.

She just hoped her appetite lasted until then.

It wasn't long before Daryl located a strip mall anchored by a super-sized Walmart, where she made the mistake of trying to get out of the truck on her own. She'd forgotten about the huge step down.

Stupid Godzilla truck.

While she sat with one foot on the running board, she tried to figure out the proper way to turn her body to step down and hold on without her skirt tripping her again. Before she could work it out, two large hands steadied her around the waist and practically lifted her to the ground.

She swallowed a yip and managed a small smile instead.

"Thank you."

Good. She sounded normal. Not like she was rattled by that same odd zing of warmth from his touch. Her whole body felt like she'd stuck her tongue on a 9-volt battery.

What on earth was wrong with her?

The only things she had to get were toiletries, shoes, and underwear. Once inside the store, Amelia zipped through the first two without issue, although it did take longer than expected to pick from the unfamiliar brands lining the shelves. Why did there need to be forty different types of body wash?

It wasn't until she got to the last item on her list that she balked.

There was no way she was shopping for underwear with Daryl hanging over her shoulder. The mere thought made her insides squirm. But unless she wanted to rinse out her panties and bra in the bathroom sink every night, she needed to buy more, and that meant getting Daryl to step away for a few minutes.

"Could you wait over there, please? I'll be quick." She pointed to a display of socks about ten feet away from the lingerie department.

"No."

His unequivocal answer left her nonplussed.

"But...I just need five minutes."

"Not even for one."

"Daryl..." The heat burning her face meant she was probably turning one of her unpleasant shades of red. The curse of the fair-skinned. "I can't shop for"—her voice dropped to a strangled whisper—"*underwear* with you watching me."

"Just pretend I'm not here."

Right. Pretend the six-four man with the shoulders of a god wasn't watching her choose between bikini briefs and boy shorts.

She considered her imagination pretty good—hell, she'd managed to convince herself she was in love with Charles for the past year, hadn't she?—but somehow she didn't think she'd be able to pull that one off.

Amelia considered trying another tact to sway him, but the resolute expression on Daryl's face said he wouldn't budge.

Okay. Fine. She could do this. She was nothing if not skilled at the art of doing things that made her uncomfortable. Taking a steadying breath, she squared her shoulders and turned toward the lingerie department.

"All right, then. Let's get this over with."

Because really, in the grand scheme of embarrassing things that were happening in her life, how bad could this one possibly be?

⚬

Daryl tried to give Amelia as much space as he could, so she at least had the illusion of privacy. But the tall racks of packaged underwear meant he had to shift aisles every time she did to keep her in sight.

Overkill? Maybe. But though he was ninety-nine percent sure they hadn't been followed, they were still too close to Boulder for him to feel comfortable letting her out of his sight just yet.

Even if lurking in the lingerie section felt a little bit creepy.

As he watched her compare the plastic-wrapped panties, a small frown puckered her forehead. Had she ever bought prepackaged underwear before? She came from money, and money shopped in boutiques, not big-box stores.

Well, unfortunately for her, they'd be sticking with the anonymity of places like this from now on. He wasn't about to leave an easy trail for anyone to pick up. Going to a smaller, more exclusive store might be more in Amelia's comfort zone, but salespeople in those places tended to remember their customers.

Especially ones who looked like Amelia.

She might not be his type, but he could still appreciate that she was attractive. It didn't matter if her personality was so subdued as to be almost nonexistent. She still had the kind of looks that caught a man's eye. All that curly blonde hair, those wide green eyes, and that almost translucent skin that showed every emotion she was feeling better than a mood ring.

He'd never known anyone who could blush so many different shades of red.

Amelia changed aisles. He followed suit, frowning when he got a good look at her profile under the harsh store fluorescents.

She was much too thin for her height. Her face was all sharp edges and shadows, and he could swear his hands had touched when he'd put them around her waist earlier.

The girl was in definite need of a cheeseburger.

Not that she was purposely starving herself like some women did. He hadn't missed the extra-large bottle of antacids she'd buried at the bottom of the shopping cart. It was obvious she had a delicate constitution. Hence her tendency to revert to timid mouse status whenever faced with any type of conflict.

Well, most of the time.

She'd definitely shown a hint of backbone these past few days. It was a good look on her.

He just hoped it would be enough to get her through what was to come.

Daryl glanced at his watch and pushed down his rising agitation. Not that they were taking too much time to get where they were going. It was the opposite, in fact. His unease was increasing in direct proportion to how close they were getting to their destination. He didn't relish the thought of spending the next week sequestered on his family's ranch with a runaway bride.

Hell, he didn't relish the thought of spending a week on his family's ranch, period.

There were reasons he hadn't been home in almost two years. But none of them were enough to trump Amelia's immediate safety.

Damn it.

Doing another visual sweep of the area as they changed aisles again, he nearly swallowed his tongue when he saw Amelia had moved on from the packaged panties to the racks of bras. She fingered one that was dark blue with black lace around the edges.

Holy hell.

For one intense, insane moment, his mind flashed him a picture of her wearing it, the deep cobalt contrasting her pale skin like a jewel against satin. Then rational thought snapped back into place and wiped the too-vivid image away.

Mostly.

What the hell was *wrong* with him?

Not only had it been the most inappropriate thing to think about someone who was under his care and protection, but to think it about someone like Amelia Westlake? Someone so far removed from the type of woman that attracted him she was all but in another time zone?

Ridiculous.

Wrong.

A mistake.

And yet, he couldn't deny it had happened. But it couldn't happen again.

It *wouldn't* happen again.

When Amelia approached a few minutes later and dumped her choices into the cart, he breathed a sigh of relief there was nothing blue and black in the mix. If she didn't buy it, then he didn't have to worry about wondering whether she was wearing it.

After a quick detour to add bottled water, some snacks, and a cheap burner phone to their haul—he'd shut down both his and Amelia's phones before they left Boulder—they found the shortest checkout line. As Amelia transferred her purchases to the belt, Daryl surreptitiously added a few rolls of the antacid tablets her friends always kept on hand.

It wasn't until Amelia opened her purse to pay that the trouble started.

"No, I've got it." Daryl took out his wallet. The way her back snapped straight warned him he was going to have a fight on his hands. That, he couldn't allow. Anything that would make them memorable to the cashier was something to be avoided.

"That's not necessary."

If he were prone to frostbite, her tone would have had him counting his fingers and toes.

"Actually, it is." Handing cash to the teen, who was thankfully more engrossed in texting on her phone than in her bickering customers, he raised a meaningful brow at the credit card in Amelia's hand.

She grimaced and pushed it back into her wallet.

There would be no plastic used on this trip for either of them. They'd be living off the grid. Which was why Doyle had known the Raintrees' South Dakota ranch would be the perfect hiding spot, since it wasn't just off the grid, it was still in the Stone Age.

Okay, that wasn't entirely fair. Or true.

But his father's adherence to the motto "if it ain't broke, don't fix it" was just one of the many things they'd butted heads over for most of Daryl's life.

Gathering up the bags, he led a somewhat subdued Amelia out of the store. After stowing everything in the backseat, Daryl helped boost her into the front and got them on their way. Try as he might, though, he couldn't stop thinking about just how delicate her tiny waist had felt in his hands. How fragile she seemed.

He'd almost been afraid of breaking her.

This was why he didn't date women with smaller body types. He always felt a little like the character Sloth in the eighties movie *The Goonies* when he was around them. An oversized freak, awkward and clumsy in his own skin.

Granted, six-four wasn't exactly giant height. But when you were around women a good eight to ten inches shorter than you, it could certainly feel that way. So, he avoided them whenever possible.

Only avoiding Amelia wasn't an option. Like it or not, he was as stuck with her as she was with him. But what he *could* avoid was touching her any more than necessary. Once they got to the ranch, that would be a lot easier. Until then, he just had to suck it up and make sure he didn't hurt her.

Although after the past twenty-four hours, he was beginning to think that it would take a lot more than his clumsy hands to make this little mouse break.

Chapter 8

"**I** don't think I've ever actually thanked you for helping me."

Daryl glanced at his passenger, who had been quiet ever since they'd gotten back on the interstate. She was curled sideways in the bucket seat so she was looking at him, her hand playing along the strap of the seatbelt where it crossed her chest. Her voice was soft and a little sleepy, as though she'd started talking to keep herself awake.

"You don't have to thank me."

"Yes, I do."

"Okay, then you're welcome."

She huffed out a small laugh. "I'm serious. I know you think you're just doing your job, but I'm pretty sure this wasn't what you had in mind when you first agreed to do it. Taking me away from Boulder, bringing me to your parents' home? That's totally above and beyond, and I wanted you to know I really do appreciate it. Thank you."

There was a level of sincerity in her voice that told him she wasn't just mouthing the expected platitudes. In that, Amelia was very like Thea. He'd never seen either of the women treat their parents' staff with anything other than genuine warmth and friendliness.

Unlike Amelia's parents, who were some of the biggest snobs he'd ever met. As someone else's hired help, he'd been so far below their notice as to be all but invisible.

Which would only aid their current strategy.

"I'm happy to help. But I would have done it even if it wasn't my job."

And he would have. Even if Doyle hadn't sanctioned this little game of hide-the-bride, he would have taken some of the time off he had coming and done it on his own. Of course, he wouldn't have chosen to go to his parents' place, but in that, Doyle had been right on the money.

Damn him.

"Really?"

He wasn't sure if the surprise or the hint of doubt in her voice bothered him more. It was hard not to take either personally. But then, when your own parents tried to screw you over, how could you really trust anyone to be looking out for your best interests?

"Really." He glanced over at her again and was pleased to see a small smile teasing at her lips even as she struggled to keep her eyes open.

"You're a very nice man, Daryl Raintree." She raised a hand to cover a yawn. "Sorry. I don't know why I'm so tired all of a sudden."

It might have something to do with the chicken sandwich, fries, and shake she'd all but inhaled at the diner they stopped at. He wasn't surprised her body had put itself into a food coma. If she were an anaconda, she'd hibernate for a week.

She'd popped one of the antacids from her jumbo bottle once they got back to the truck, but it had seemed more of a precautionary act than anything. Regardless of everything else that had turned to crap in her life, putting distance between Amelia and her parents seemed to be good for her stomach.

"Go ahead and get some rest. It'll be a few hours yet before we get to the ranch."

"Your parents live on a ranch?"

Shit.

"Yeah, sorry. I didn't think to mention it before." She'd probably been expecting to stay in a nice house with central air conditioning and reliable hot water. Unless things had changed a whole lot at the Circle R since his last visit, she wasn't getting either.

"I'm afraid it's not anything fancy, like a dude ranch, if that's what you're thinking. If I had someplace else to take you—"

"Don't."

He threw her a quick look, not used to hearing that sharp tone from her. "Don't what?"

"Think I need or expect special treatment. Just because they call me Princess doesn't mean I act like one." She shifted in her seat so she was facing forward again, her head turned away toward the door so he couldn't see her face.

Even so, he got the feeling he'd somehow hurt her feelings.

He should just let it drop. But the longer the silence stretched, the more it bothered him. Finally, he said in a tone more grudging than conciliatory, "I didn't think you'd turn your nose up at the place. I was just...embarrassed."

The admission stung because it was true. His words had been about *his* discomfort with the state of the ranch, not hers.

There was a long silence. Just when he decided she must have fallen asleep, she asked, "What kind of ranch is it?"

"Horses, mostly. And some chickens and cows." And the last time he'd been back, a couple of piglets, which had most likely been turned into bacon by now. His stepmother might love animals as much as her husband and children, but she was also a practical woman. Every animal on the ranch had a purpose, and for some, that purpose was being breakfast.

Just one more reason he didn't miss living there.

"Horse training or breeding?"

"Both, although Dad's more interested in the bloodline aspect of the operation." Training had been Daryl's forte. But that was a bone of contention best left alone. "Do you know how to ride?"

Amelia shifted in her seat. A quick glance from the corner of his eye showed her curled back around to face him again. Evidently, his apology had been accepted. Why that gave him a warm, satisfied sensation in his chest he didn't understand, but it did.

"I took lessons when I was younger. English-style riding, and later on dressage." Her enthusiasm gave away how much she'd enjoyed it. "I trained for about five years before I had to give it up."

Daryl had a hard time wrapping his brain around the thought of a miniature-sized Amelia perched on top of a thousand pounds of prancing horseflesh. "Why did you stop?"

"I took a bad fall during a training session and broke my arm." The joy that had bubbled in her voice just a second ago went flat.

He'd been thrown more times than he could count. Broken more than a few bones, too. But the image in his brain of Amelia being the one tossed to the ground like a rag doll was enough to steal the spit from his mouth.

"Well, it's normal to be nervous about getting back on a horse after a nasty fall. Maybe while we're at the ranch, we can help get you past your fear and back on a horse again."

"Thank you, that's sweet of you to offer. But I'm not afraid of horses."

"Then why did you quit?"

There was a small pause. "Because my parents got the instructor fired after the accident, even though it wasn't his fault. But they wanted a pound of flesh, and because they were rich and powerful, they got it. I didn't want that to happen to anyone else, so I never went back."

"Didn't your parents ask why you gave up something you loved so much?"

Amelia's laugh was soft and derisive.

"They didn't care if I loved it or not. It wouldn't have mattered if I'd hated it. They wanted me to train because it would have looked impressive if I'd gotten onto the Olympic equestrian team, which had been their plan from the day they signed me up for my first lesson. When I refused to go back, they were upset with my decision for *their* sake, not mine."

Just when he thought he couldn't dislike them any more than he already did.

Some people shouldn't be allowed to be parents.

"Well, the offer stands. I'm sure Dad would be happy to put you on the back of any horse you like."

"Thank you, Daryl."

They drove in silence for a while. Only when he was certain she was asleep did he relax. It wasn't that Amelia was difficult to talk to. He just didn't know what he was supposed to talk to her about.

Well, fuck.

That could be a problem. He'd been so focused on where to take her, he hadn't given any thought to what he was supposed to do with her once they got there.

At least the ranch had a tv and the internet. Would that be enough to keep her entertained? What the hell did a Society princess do to occupy her time, anyway?

Whatever it was, he was pretty sure they wouldn't have it at the Circle R. He could only hope the Davenports and Westlakes conceded defeat and announced the wedding was off before Amelia discovered just how substandard her temporary accommodations truly were.

Consciousness came to Amelia in slow sips.

First, she became aware of the sun shining on her face. Next, she realized she was lying down, which meant she wasn't in the truck anymore. The third—and most disturbing—thing was that she had absolutely no idea where she was or how she'd gotten there.

That last was enough to make her sit up with a jolt.

Heart pounding, she looked around the small room for

something, anything, familiar. Almost immediately, she spotted the small suitcase she'd borrowed from Mrs. Fordham on the floor near the door. Next to it was the bag from Walmart. Her purse sat on top of the dark wooden dresser nearby.

Okay. Her things were here.

Those touchstones gave her rabbiting brain something to latch onto.

Initial panic waning, she continued her inspection of the room. It was small, so it didn't take long. There was the dresser with a simple round mirror above, a nightstand, and the bed. The beautiful rug covering most of the worn wood-plank flooring looked hand woven and expensive, which was at odds with the simple wooden furniture.

On the wall above the bed hung a thin branch bent in a circle, laced with white threads to resemble a spider web, with several feathers dangling from the bottom. A dream catcher. That, along with the design on the rug, finally made the where click into place.

They'd arrived at the Raintree ranch.

What she couldn't retrieve from her memory, however, was how she'd come to be in this bedroom. Or this bed. The last thing she remembered was talking with Daryl about horses. After that, total blank.

Oh my God, did Daryl carry me inside and put me to bed?

Shoving down the covers, she groaned when she saw she was still wearing yesterday's clothes. It seemed the answer was yes.

Mortification didn't come close to what she felt, along with a pinch of unease.

She hated when this happened. *Hated* it. Normally, she was a very light sleeper. But when her body was on the last dregs of its reserves, it would shut down like she'd been given a sleeping pill. One moment awake, then next so deep asleep not even a bomb could wake her up.

Or, it seemed, being toted around in the middle of the night by her bodyguard.

She covered her face and groaned again.

So much for insisting I didn't need to be treated like a princess.

Her stomach gave a massive growl, startling her out of her humiliation. There was no clock in the room, but the sun shining through the large window said she'd slept through most of the morning. And likely breakfast.

First things first, though. She had a pressing need to find a bathroom.

There were three doors. The smallest was probably the closet. She flipped a mental coin and tried one of the other two.

Yes!

An en suite bathroom. At least she could get cleaned up without having to leave the sanctuary of her room. Running into her hosts with wrinkled clothing and morning breath wasn't the first impression she wanted to make.

Or would it be the second?

Trying not to think about the probability at least one of them had witnessed her undignified arrival the night before, she gathered her newly purchased toiletries. As she set them on the sink, doubt began to niggle at her. Was it all right for her to just use the shower without asking? Was that being too presumptuous?

She shook the thought away. Of course, they'd expect her to use the shower. She needed to stop worrying so much about doing and saying the right thing all the time. That was what had gotten her into this mess in the first place.

Just like that, the entire weight of her problems came rushing back, pressing down on her chest, making it hard to breathe. She dropped onto the edge of the tub as she fought for air. Oh, dear lord. What had she done?

Had she really broken her engagement and run away like a spoiled child, leaving everyone else to pick up the pieces of her mess? What had she been thinking?

Simple. That she needed to escape while she could. That she needed to be as far away from Charles as she could get. That she needed a place to hide and lick her wounds until the worst had blown over.

Had she overreacted?

Possibly.

But would anything good have come of her sticking around to deal with her decision in person?

Absolutely not. Her parents' presence in Boulder proved that.

Slowly, the tightness in her chest eased and her breaths smoothed out from the choppy gasps of her mini panic attack. She needed to focus on something mundane, something routine, to stop her brain from spiraling back out of control.

Resolutely, she lined her bath products up on the edge of the tub and turned the water on. As she waited for it to warm, she stripped, folding each garment with precise care. It didn't matter they were going into the laundry. The act of control was soothing.

Twenty minutes later, she was squeaky clean and dressed in one of Thea's soft cotton tees and a pair of her jeans. They hung so loosely off her hips she wished she'd thought to pack a belt as well. Hitching them up, she went back into the bathroom, only to realize there wasn't a hair dryer in evidence.

Swallowing her discomfort about snooping, she checked the cabinets under the sink. All she found was a stack of worn but clean towels and some cleaning supplies. Damn. If she'd known they wouldn't have a hair dryer for their guests, she would have bought one.

"It's not anything fancy, like a dude ranch, if that's what you're thinking."

Daryl's words popped into her head, and she was instantly ashamed.

His parents were offering her shelter, and she was getting pissy about frizzy hair.

She ran her fingers through the tangled curls, trying to find some semblance of order, then gave up. It would dry however it dried.

She'd deal with it later.

Her mother's voice screeched in her head that a lady never allowed herself to appear at less than her best. Amelia took in her damp, messy hair, ill-fitting clothes, and makeup-free face in the mirror.

And grinned.

"Screw you, mom."

Hitching up the jeans again, she went back into the bedroom and opened the third door. The short hallway outside led to a fairly spacious living room with a high, timbered ceiling. Like the bedroom, the furniture was simple, with lots of dark wood and slightly worn fabrics, and there was another of those amazing geometric design rugs on the floor in front of the sectional sofa. Anchoring the room was a massive stacked-stone fireplace that soared to the ceiling.

The scent of food cooking drew her through the empty room to the kitchen, where she hesitated in the doorway. There was only one person inside, and it wasn't Daryl.

Amelia waffled. It would be better if she waited for Daryl to show up and introduce her. Then again, she didn't know where he was or when he might be back. And whatever was sizzling on top of the huge six-burner stove was making her mouth water.

The decision was taken out of her hands when the woman at the stove turned. A welcoming smile creased her bronzed face. "Good morning! Come, have a seat." She indicated the chair in front of the one spot at the table that was set.

Which meant everyone else had already eaten and gone, leaving her to be catered to.

Damn.

"I'm sorry that I slept so late," she said, only to be silenced by the woman's waving hand.

"We have to listen to what our bodies tell us. Yours was saying that you were in need of a good, deep sleep."

You have no idea how deep.

Falling back on the manners that had gotten her through other uncomfortable moments in the past, Amelia smiled and stepped forward, hand extended. "I'm sure Daryl already told you, but I'm Amelia. I want to thank you for opening your home like this with no warning. I'm sure it must be a huge inconvenience for you."

The woman seemed to hesitate before reaching out to take Amelia's hand. There was strength in the slightly calloused grip. Unlike her own perfectly soft, perfectly manicured hands, which hadn't seen a single day of hard work in her pampered, privileged life.

"I'm Kimama. And this is my son's home, too, even if he chooses not to visit it as often as he should. You're his friend, so of course you're welcome to visit as well."

She wasn't sure *friend* was the right term. But since she didn't know what Daryl had told his parents about them being there, she just hummed in noncommittal agreement.

"Please, sit." Kimama waited until Amelia complied before turning back to the stove. "I hope you're hungry."

"Thank you. I am." Surprisingly, it was true. "May I help with anything?"

"No need. Everything is ready."

Amelia straightened the silverware on the woven placemat with restless hands. She would have preferred not to be waited on by Daryl's mother, but what could she do? She picked up the steaming mug that was placed beside her and took a cautious sniff of what looked like tea. It had an interesting undertone to it she couldn't place. She sipped, enjoying the pleasant but still elusive flavor.

Kimama deposited a brightly colored plate piled high with food in front of Amelia before taking her seat across the table. "Eat."

Eat? All that?

She stared at the breakfast in dismay. There was no way she'd get through even a fraction of that much food. But Mrs. Raintree had gone to the trouble of making it for her, so manners dictated she try.

Picking a starting point, she dug in. "Is Daryl around?" She popped a tiny bite of crispy maple cured ham into her mouth. Her tastebuds just about had an orgasm.

Mmm. Delicious.

"I was afraid he was going to wake you, sticking his head into your room every ten minutes to see if you were awake. So I sent him down to the barn with his father to work out his fidgets with the horses."

The ham nearly choked her on the way down.

Daryl had been watching her sleep?

Granted, she'd been fully clothed. And he'd obviously seen her asleep in the truck. But sleeping in a bed just seemed so much more...*intimate* somehow.

"He should be back soon." His mother didn't seem to have noticed her reaction. "If he's not by the time you finish eating, I can take you to him if you like."

"That would be great. Thank you." Although it might be tomorrow by the time she finished the mountain of ham and eggs on her plate. "This is delicious, by the way." A lot more than her usual unbuttered toast and fruit breakfast, or the occasional egg-white omelet when she was feeling particularly hungry.

Which lately was never.

Kimama gave a small nod of thanks. She sipped from her mug, studying Amelia with a contemplative expression as she slowly made progress through the scrambled eggs. Which were not only tasty, but somehow weren't causing her stomach to rebel despite the quantity she was shoveling into it.

In between bites, Amelia studied Daryl's mother in return. Her dark skin and hair, tied back in a messy knot at her neck, clearly spoke to her Native American heritage. Her light hazel eyes, however, hinted at something else in the genetic mix. The combination was striking.

Though Kimama looked to be in her late thirties or early forties, Amelia knew that couldn't be right, since Daryl himself was at least thirty. Some women just aged really well.

Unlike her mother, who prayed at the altar of her plastic surgeon on a regular basis.

The only sound in the room as she ate was the click of knife and fork against the plate. Normally, manners would force her to make small talk to fill the silence. But for some reason, this silence was peaceful rather than uncomfortable. She was happy to let it go unbroken.

She was able to finish almost half the food she'd been served before she placed her utensils across the plate in defeat. "That was delicious, Mrs. Raintree. But I'm afraid I can't eat another bite."

The woman studied her for a long second before giving a shrug that could have meant anything. "Come. I'll take you to my son."

Amelia stood, only to have to grab at her jeans as they started sliding toward the floor. Mortified, she stammered an apology and retreated to the bedroom, where she stripped off the jeans and replaced them with a pair of sweatpants. Those, at least, had a drawstring to help keep them up.

Barely.

What the hell?

She and Thea had shared clothes almost as long as they'd known each other. Her friend always had a bit more oomph in her butt and bust, true, but her clothes had never just fallen off before.

Yes, she'd lost some weight the past few months. Even the seamstress had commented on it after she'd had to take her wedding dress in.

For the third time.

Lifting the bottom of her t-shirt, she ran a hand over her concave stomach to her too-prominent hipbones and finally had to admit the truth. She'd done more than just lose a little weight. She looked like a poster child for the warning signs of anorexia.

How had she let this happen to herself?

How had she *done* this to herself?

Suddenly, the delicious breakfast was a hard rock in the pit of her stomach. She grabbed the bottle of antacids from the Walmart bag and grimly ate her way through three of them. Penance for her earlier enjoyment of the meal.

It was a struggle, but she refused to give in to the nausea that gurgled and pinwheeled through her gut. Her nerves had sometimes gotten bad enough to cause her to vomit in the past. How many more times had that happened in the last few months?

Much more than she'd been willing to admit, it seemed.

The combined assault of her mother's micromanaging and her future mother-in-law's constant biting belittlement had worn her down until she'd practically wasted away to nothing. Why had she given them that power? Why hadn't she fought back before now?

Slipping one more fruit-flavored tablet into her mouth, Amelia squared her shoulders and made a vow. No matter what else came of this disaster, she was never, *ever* going to allow herself to be treated as though she didn't matter again. As though her wants and needs fell below everyone else's.

She *would* stand up for herself, damn it.

She just had to learn how.

Chapter 9

Daryl leaned against the split-rail fencing of the main training corral, watching one of his father's hired hands put a sweet bay-colored mare through her paces. The horse circled the man on a lunge-line, small ears pricked forward as she listened to the soft clicks of his tongue that signaled her to change her gait from a walk to an easy trot.

Muscles flexed under her sleek reddish coat as she picked it up a notch, tail swishing to show her enjoyment of the faster pace, the small kick in her step hinting she was eager to go even faster despite the human's insistence to temper her speed.

Daryl chuckled, knowing Chaska would have seen the mare's impatience and keep her to a trot for longer than he might have, just to make sure she knew who was boss. When animals outweighed the humans by eight hundred or more pounds, it was important to establish the proper amount of respect or people—and animals—could get hurt.

Shifting his weight to prop one booted foot on the lower rail, a momentary sense of contentment descended over him. With the scent of horse and leather in his lungs, the sun beating down on his shoulders, the only sounds the clomping of hooves on hard-packed dirt and the bridle's jingle, the universe centered and righted itself for the first time in...years.

Damn, but I missed this. Why the hell did I ever leave?

A boot scraped against the rail next to his. "That should be you out there."

Right. *That* was why.

"She's a beauty." Daryl ignored the comment and focused on the one thing he and his father had ever been able to agree on. Horses.

"That she is," his father said after a long hesitation, apparently accepting they still weren't going to talk about it. "It's more than just looks, though. She's got heart."

"And a bit of attitude." Daryl grinned when the mare gave a little buck to express her displeasure at not being brought up to full speed when she so clearly wanted to run.

"All the best ones do."

True enough. His old rodeo horse, Jasper, had had the heart of a champion, but he'd still dump Daryl right over his head whenever he felt slighted. It had kept each of them from getting too complacent with the other.

The old twinge of regret he felt over having to sell that wily old bastard still needled his heart. He'd been one damn fine horse.

He turned his attention back to the mare.

"Is she one of yours or a boarder?" The ranch had gained enough of a reputation for the techniques they used with the horses they bred that people had started bringing their own horses to his father to be trained.

People thought Hank Raintree was some kind of horse whisperer. Daryl wondered what they'd think if they knew his success had more to do with the pure bull-headedness he'd gained in the Marine Corps than from his ranching acumen.

"One of ours, out of Black Ember."

He didn't recognize the name of the mare's dam. But then, he hadn't been around much over the past six years. Or really, even in the years before that, not when he could help it. He'd been too busy riding the rodeo circuit all over the southwest back then, trying to figure out what it was, exactly, he was supposed to do with his life. Where he belonged.

Because it sure as hell hadn't been on the ranch. *That* much he'd known for a lot longer than he'd been looking.

"So. This girl you brought with you. What's really going on?"

His father had accepted the bare minimum of explanation when Daryl had appeared at the door late last night. Early this morning, really. It had been closer to one by the time he'd pulled his truck into the building where they stored the tractor and other large equipment—one more precaution he hoped was unnecessary.

It was a sign of supreme restraint on his father's part that he'd waited this long to be fully read into the situation.

As succinctly as he could, Daryl explained the events of the past few days. It was clear from the tightening around his father's mouth he saw the same implications in her parents' actions that Daryl had.

"Has she spoken to them since you didn't show up for the planned meeting?"

"Spoken, no. But she sent them a text saying she was taking some time for herself to let everyone's tempers cool off."

"Talking would have been better."

"I know." Daryl grimaced, remembering the look of absolute devastation on Amelia's face when she'd realized the truth. "But I don't think she would have been able to handle it. Not yet." Not while her parents' betrayal was still so fresh and painful.

"So, you're hoping to just hole up here and wait them out until they no longer have the option of coercing her back to the altar?"

"That's the idea. The best one we could come up with on the fly, anyway. If you have any other thoughts, I'd be happy to hear them." His dad might not have any experience with unscrupulous politicians, but after eighteen years in the military, he understood strategy.

"Hmm. I'll think on it some."

They watched Chaska work the horse for a few more minutes. Finally satisfied with the mare's cooperation, he allowed her to pick up her pace. Her gait was smooth and effortless as he paid out the line, giving her a larger circle to gallop until she was running within a few feet of the fence line.

"How important is she to you?"

The question surprised Daryl into twisting to look at his father. His dad kept his eyes on the mare, but Daryl knew most of his father's attention was on him. "She's just someone who needs a little help."

"That's all?"

"That's all."

The soft grunt his father used when he was neither agreeing or disagreeing had Daryl shaking his head. He turned back to the action in the corral. There wasn't anything more to his helping Amelia than that. She seemed to bring out the bone-deep protective streak he had for the weak and helpless.

Not to mention frail. Hell, he'd been afraid of snapping one of her delicate bones with his big Sloth-like hands when he'd carried her into the house. She'd weighed no more than a baby bird in his arms. How could he *not* feel protective?

"It would be safer if no one knows who she is or why she's here. Especially Winnie." Chances were low anyone from the Westlake camp would track her to the ranch, but small communities sometimes bred the biggest mouths. And his little sister owned the biggest of the big.

If she knew who Amelia was, it wouldn't be long before *everybody* knew.

"Your sister has her own secrets these days. She won't have time to be worrying about yours."

Warning bells clanged.

"Aw, hell, what's she gone and done now?"

"You should speak with her while you're here."

Daryl waited, but it seemed that was the only answer he'd get. Great. As if he didn't have enough to worry about.

The mare reversed direction and went through several other

maneuvers, her black tail high as she nailed every action requested of her as if she knew she'd been a model student.

"Do you really think the parents would try to force their daughter into a marriage she doesn't want?"

Daryl thought over the times he'd come into contact with the senior Westlakes throughout the years. They were cold, shallow, manipulative people. He couldn't remember a single time either had shown a speck of human warmth toward their only child. Maybe they were different when they were in private, but he doubted it.

"Yeah, I do. But there wouldn't be much force involved. They're so damned skilled at manipulation she'd go back thinking it was her idea in the first place."

"Sounds as though this young lady is weak-willed at best."

Annoyance stirred in his gut.

"Not at all. If she was weak, she never would have found the courage to break the engagement in the first place."

"But she chose to run rather than stand her ground. Twice. That makes her weak."

He heard the echoes of Amelia saying the same thing to him on the plane. He gave his father the same answer he'd given her.

"No, it makes her smart. She knows what her weaknesses are, but that doesn't mean *she's* weak. She was molded her whole life to think a certain way, do as she was expected. That's not something that can just be changed overnight."

"True, habits of a lifetime are the hardest to break."

"Exactly." But there was something in his father's tone that had Daryl wondering if there wasn't a double meaning to his words. As Chaska brought the mare down into a cool-off walk, Daryl glanced at his watch.

"She'll be fine without you hovering at her bedroom door."

Somehow, his father always seemed to know his thoughts. One of many reasons living on the ranch had become so uncomfortable as a teen.

"I should still check on her. She'll be waking up in a strange place."

She'd been so deeply asleep when he carried her into the house, he doubted she'd even registered the move. Going to sleep in one place and waking in another, especially an unfamiliar one, could be disconcerting at the best of times. And these weren't.

"Looks like she managed just fine." His dad tipped his head in the direction of the house.

He turned and let out a silent sigh of relief at the sight of the two women walking toward them. Amelia might have been in need of a good night's sleep after the day she had, but he'd started to get concerned when the hours kept passing and she still didn't wake up.

The last thing he needed while they were in hiding was for her to get sick.

She didn't look sick, he decided as she got closer. She didn't look the perfect image of health, either. Her cheeks were drawn and her skin seemed dangerously pale in the bright sunlight. But the bluish tint that skimmed in half-moons under her eyes had lessened, and she'd lost some of the overall about-to-shatter quality of the day before.

At least it was a step in the right direction.

Something else was different about her as well, though he couldn't put his finger on it. Maybe it was the sweats and t-shirt she wore. Had he ever seen her dressed that casually before?

Whenever she'd hung out with Thea, she'd always dressed in what he privately thought of as young Grace Kelly chic. Slacks, blouse, heels, hair and makeup done, the whole nine yards. Even the day before, wearing borrowed clothes, she'd been almost as put together as usual.

He didn't think he'd seen her looking like a normal, everyday person before.

It was a little disconcerting.

"Good morning," he said as they arrived at the corral. "I'm sorry I wasn't inside when you woke up. Did you sleep okay?"

"Perfectly, thank you."

Was that a hint of a blush on her cheeks? He had no idea why there would be, but it sure looked like it to him. The color looked good on her, eating away the paleness.

"You've obviously met Kim. This is my father, Hanska Raintree. Dad, this is Amelia Westlake."

"It's a pleasure to meet you, Mr. Raintree." Amelia offered her hand. "I want to thank you for allowing me to impose on your hospitality. Your wife already said it wasn't necessary, but I still wanted to apologize for just showing up in the middle of the night like we did."

He shook her hand. "Nice to meet you too, and Hank will do just fine. And Kim's right. No apology needed. Daryl knows the door is always open whenever he chooses to stop by, no matter the time or the reason."

Amelia wouldn't hear the small chastisement in the words, but Daryl got the point loud and clear. He shot his father a disgruntled look, but he was still looking at Amelia. Studying her, actually.

Damn.

He knew that look. It was time to nip the inquisition in the bud.

"Have you eaten yet?" he asked.

"Yes, your mother made me a delicious late breakfast, although she shouldn't have gone to all the trouble." She aimed a grateful smile at Kim, who gave a gracious nod.

"Good."

He'd have to ask Kim later how much of that delicious breakfast Amelia actually ate.

"Oh." Amelia's soft exclamation of admiration diverted him from his next question. He followed her line of sight to the mare in the corral behind him.

"That's Giselle. She's a beauty, isn't she?" Daryl invited her with a gesture to join him at the fence for a closer look.

"Oh, she is." Amelia stepped next to him and peered over the top rail. "She truly is."

Daryl didn't see it, but his father must have signaled to Chaska to bring the horse closer. After first greeting Hank with a blowy snuffle that nearly knocked his hat off his head, Giselle turned her curious gaze to the two strangers.

Amelia made another of those little "oh" sounds as she craned her neck back to look up at the horse, who stood nearly sixteen hands tall.

"Here." Daryl grasped her by the waist and swung her up so she could stand on the bottom fence rail. He'd done the same thing a hundred times for his sister, so the action was automatic. It wasn't until afterward he realized he probably should have asked before manhandling her like that.

Not that Amelia seemed to care.

After her initial squeak of surprise, she was all about cooing to the horse, who had brushed right past Daryl and was eating up her attention, dipping her head so Amelia could scratch behind her ears.

His father grinned as they watched her baby-talk the thousand-pound beast. "Careful. She can get a little lippy when she's in a mood."

Nodding, Amelia continued to run her hands along the mare's head and down her neck while the horse snorted and pranced in place.

"That's a favorite spot of hers right there, miss," Chaska said, the horse uttering what could only be called a groan of pure pleasure. "Just watch that she doesn't—"

Only reflexes honed from years of working around horses allowed Daryl to step behind Amelia and brace her with his body against the unintentional push the horse gave with her head, trying to get Amelia's hand right where she wanted it. Amelia gasped, then laughed as Daryl steadied her.

"—do that," Chaska finished wryly, shaking his head. "Sorry about that. She's still a bit like a big puppy. She doesn't understand her own strength."

"No harm done," Amelia said with a grin, "but I'll definitely pay more attention next time." She stuck out one hand, continuing to stroke the horse's neck with the other. "I'm Amelia, by the way."

Looking a little bemused at the delicate hand being offered, Chaska finally took it. "Chaska Everheart," he said, giving her hand an almost reverent shake. "But you can call me Chaz."

Amelia smiled. "Well, Chaz, it's a pleasure to meet you. I hope I didn't interrupt your training session."

Chaz seemed a little dazzled by the wattage of the smile aimed at him.

"No, we were just finishing up. I, ah, do need to take this little lady to get rubbed down and turned out, though." He shot an odd look at Daryl and ducked his head, but not before Daryl saw the grin that quirked his lips.

It was only then Daryl realized he was still standing behind Amelia, his hands gripping the top rail on either side of her, the front of his body snug against the back of hers, like a stallion covering a mare.

He let go of the fence and stepped back as though singed.

"Daryl and Miss Amelia will be visiting for a spell," his dad said.

"Well, then, I'm sure we'll see each other again sometime soon. Miss. Ma'am." With a dip of his head to both Amelia and Kim, he gave a quick click of his tongue and led the mare towards the barn.

Chaska hadn't meant his comment in any way other than being factual, but Daryl found himself irritated anyway. And he blamed Amelia. She needed to be a lot more careful where she aimed that smile of hers. Didn't she understand its potency on unsuspecting men? He might have understood she was merely being her usual polite self, but some men might get the wrong idea from a smile like that.

Some men like Chaz.

Suddenly, he wasn't all that sorry for the impression he'd given earlier by his possessive stance, unintentional as it had been. Since he couldn't explain who Amelia was or why she was there, it would be helpful if it was assumed she was already spoken for. That meant there would be less people he needed to pound into the ground when they started hitting on her.

And judging by the look on Chaska's face, they *would* be hitting on her.

"Daryl, why don't you show Amelia around so she has an idea of where things are?" his father suggested.

Daryl looked at Amelia as she stepped down from the rail. Drag the princess through the muck and manure? "I don't know if—"

"I'd like that."

"Are you sure? It can get pretty dirty."

"I've been around barns and horses before, remember?" Smiling at his parents, she said, "Thank you again for your hospitality."

The tour helped Daryl reacquaint himself with the ranch. There had been several changes since he'd last been around, the most notable being the second barn. Although on closer inspection, it turned out to be an indoor training arena. A suggestion he'd made more than once in the past, to allow training to continue during the sometimes brutal South Dakota winters.

A suggestion his father had shot down every time he brought it up. Until now, it seemed.

Not sure what to make of this apparent change of heart, a change his father had never mentioned during their admittedly sporadic phone conversations, Daryl tucked it away for later consideration.

He concentrated instead on the woman who was chatting away with another of his father's hands. They'd interrupted him as he mucked out the stall of the very pregnant mare cross-tied in the aisle, her swollen sides making her look like a tick about to pop.

Daryl stroked the mare's neck as he half-listened to them talk. The hand, who couldn't have been more than seventeen and thin as a rail, was hanging on Amelia's every word like it was manna from heaven.

He really did need to tell her to tone down the smile she flashed at the kid before leaving him to his work. There was a look of pure adoration on his face as he watched her go.

Right up until he saw Daryl watching him watch her.

The look in the kid's eyes changed to panic, and he turned back to his chores so fast he nearly tripped over his rake. Only youthful flexibility and sheer dumb luck kept him from going headfirst into the steaming pile of hay and manure.

Amelia, lucky for the kid, noticed none of it.

By the time they reached the house, the tip of Amelia's nose was turning pink. Daryl realized he should have found her a hat to wear before dragging her around in the bright sun. With her fair skin, she'd burn up like a crisp in no time.

Boots, too, if she was going to be tromping around the horses instead of staying safe and clean inside the house. She'd need something with a bit more protection than her new white sneakers, which already looked a little worse for wear. Maybe he could borrow a pair from Winnie.

That thought reminded him of his father's earlier cryptic remark about secrets. What kind of mess had his pesky little sister gotten herself into now? At least asking her about the boots and hat for Amelia was a good excuse for him to go find out.

It turned out, he didn't need an excuse to go to her. She was already there.

As soon as they entered the house, Winnie's exuberant greeting nearly knocked him on his ass. She jumped on him, hugging him so hard that he couldn't help but feel what his suddenly numb brain was telling him.

He tried to deny it, but the firmly rounded belly she was sporting under her loose blouse didn't lie. His baby sister—his twenty-one-year-old *single* baby sister—was most definitely pregnant.

Chapter 10

"**I**'ll kill him."

After freezing for a brief second at his growled words, Winona unwrapped her arms from his neck and took a step away from him, her back straight and proud. "It's good to see you, too, Mato."

Unwilling to be diverted by either her stick-up-the-butt attitude or her use of his middle name, the one she only used when she wanted to annoy him, Daryl asked in the same lethal tone, "Who is he?"

"Do you think I'd tell you after you just threatened something like that?"

"Do you think I can't find out even if you don't?"

This was an old dance between the two of them. Their love for each other was fierce and loyal, but they rarely, if ever, could get along for longer than two minutes in each other's company. Just another of the myriad reasons he stayed away.

Not to mention, the ranch was more her home than it had ever been his.

Or, at least, it had been.

She'd moved out almost a year ago according to his father, when he'd said to use her room for the sleeping Amelia. She was sharing a rental house with her best friend, Kaitlin Blackhawk, who taught at the same elementary school she did. Why no one had bothered to inform him of the change was something he'd look into another time.

Right now, he needed to find out who'd knocked up his little sister and make him suffer.

"Who is it, Winnie?" He was having a hard time keeping his gaze from dropping to her belly. His little sister was *pregnant*. How the hell was that possible? "Give me his name, and you'll have his ring on your finger by the end of the day."

He couldn't guarantee what shape the groom would be in by then, though.

Winona poked his chest. "And *that* is exactly why I won't tell you."

"What?" He took a half step back and rubbed the spot she'd jabbed. The girl still had bony fingers. "He got you pregnant. He can damn well pay the price."

"Well, isn't that just romantic as hell?" Winona's lips curled into a disgusted sneer. "To pay the price. What a lovely reason to get married. Just what every girl dreams of."

"You gave up your right to romance when you started being responsible for that little person growing inside of you." He tried not to feel like a total shit as hurt flashed across her face. "You have to think about what's best for the baby."

"Maybe what's best *isn't* having parents who got married because they had to instead of because they wanted to."

Daryl winced as the barb about their father's marriage to his mother hit its mark. "Why don't you want to marry him, Winnie? You obviously liked him well enough to sleep with him." An ugly thought entered his head. "Did some bastard force you? Is that why?" It made sense. Why else would she be fighting a marriage so hard?

Someone was definitely going to die.

Confusion, then shock, then something close to outrage showed in his sister's expression.

"No! Nobody forced anyone. It wasn't like that. It..." She blew out a frustrated breath. "I just *knew* you were going to react like this."

How the hell else was he *supposed* to react?

"Then why, Winnie? Why don't you want to marry him?"

"I do want to marry him," came the sulky reply. "He just hasn't asked me yet."

"Give me his name, and he'll ask."

Winona shot him a glare that would have seared his eyebrows off if he wasn't immune.

"He'll ask," she said, stubborn as ever. "You'll see. Just as soon as he gets back, he'll—" Her mouth snapped shut.

"When is he coming back? And from where?"

"Butt out, Mato." Winona crossed her arms over her chest. A mistake, since that only emphasized the small protrusion of her belly under the brightly colored blouse.

"Winnie..."

"No." She slashed a hand through the air. "I'm done talking about this with you. This is my business, not yours. Stay out of it." She stalked out of the living room.

Not his business? The hell it wasn't. He might not have been around as much as he should have the past five or six years. Or maybe even a few more years before that, when he'd been following the rodeo circuit all over creation. But Winona was still his baby sister.

And if there was one thing no one messed with, it was his family.

⊷○⊶

Amelia jumped when the bedroom door swung open and nearly crashed into the wall.

To her surprise, it wasn't Daryl who stormed in. It was the young woman she assumed was his sister, based on their similar looks and what little she'd heard of their conversation before she slipped away to give them privacy.

Muttering under her breath, she slammed the door. The only

words Amelia could make out were "stupid men." It wasn't until the woman—Winnie, had Daryl called her?—turned that she caught sight of Amelia. Her body tensed and her eyes narrowed.

"Who are you?" Recognition lit her expression. "Oh, right. You're the one my parents told me about. The woman my brother brought with him on his first visit home in almost two years."

Frozen in the act of hanging one of her borrowed tops in the small closet, Amelia offered a tentative smile. "Yes, hello. I'm Amelia."

"I didn't know they'd put you in my room." Winnie propped her fists on her hips. "Not that there was anyplace else to put you, I suppose. But it would have been nice if someone had bothered to mention it."

The room held no personal possessions, and the closet and dresser were empty. It might well be the other woman's room, but she clearly wasn't living in it at the moment. Still, Amelia didn't want to cause problems.

"I'm sorry," she said, feeling a little confused and a lot uncomfortable. "This was the room I was put in. Should I ask to be moved?"

That got a harsh laugh.

"Ask to be moved? You do know this isn't a hotel, right? The Circle R is a working ranch. People *work* here. No one is going to have time to wait on you and make sure you're not bored or stub a toe or whatever."

"I..." Taken aback by the verbal attack, Amelia stammered out, "I never expected anyone to."

"Oh, really?" Winnie tipped her head to the open suitcase at Amelia's feet. "Louis Vuitton, right? And I bet that top you're holding is Donna Karan or Vera Wang or some other expensive designer, isn't it?" She snorted. "It probably cost more than one of my car payments."

"I'm not—"

"He won't marry you, you know."

"I...what?" Amelia's brain hurt from all the left-turns the conversation kept taking.

"It doesn't matter how pretty you are. He won't marry you." Winnie sniffed. "Rich girls with nothing but time and money to waste might be a step up from the buckle bunnies that used to chase him all the time, but he'll still just keep you around until he's tired of screwing you and then move on. It's kind of what he does."

There were so many things wrong with Winnie's bizarre assumptions she wasn't sure where to start.

"I don't know what a...a buckle bunny is, but I can assure you that I'm not sleeping with your brother. And I certainly don't want to marry him."

"Why not?" Winnie's chin tilted at a belligerent angle. "What? He's not good enough for you?"

"No! I mean, no, that's not the reason." For the first time in a long time, Amelia's usually glib tongue failed her. "I'm sure Daryl is a very nice man. I mean, I know he is." What other kind would put his life on hold for someone else the way he had? "But we have a...a *professional* relationship. There's nothing personal between us. At all. Really," she said when Winnie continued to look skeptical.

"Professional, huh?" Winnie's gaze darted to the designer luggage again. "So, you're one of those rich people he works for down in Colorado?"

"Technically, he works for my friend's family, but yes."

"But you're rich, too, right?"

"My parents are. Me? Not so much."

And that was the sad truth. She had no money of her own. No credit rating. No anything. Even her car was in her father's name. Aside from the cash she had in her wallet, she was dead broke.

"Oh." The belligerence slid away. Winnie dropped onto the bed and asked in a much more reasonable tone, "Then why would he bring you here instead of some posh resort?"

Amelia sighed. "Because I'm hiding out," she said, opting for the truth. She had a feeling Daryl's sister wouldn't settle for anything less.

"Really?" Winnie's dark eyes widened. "From the IRS?"

Yet again, the other woman's train of thought surprised her. "Um, no. My family."

"Oh."

Amelia was starting to feel a little silly standing in front of the closet, clutching the blouse like a frightened ninny. "So, is it okay for me to stay here?"

Winnie waved a hand at the closet. "Go ahead, finish unpacking. I was just feeling extra bitchy when I came in here is all, and I took it out on you." She scowled. "My brother makes me so mad sometimes I could just scream. You know how they can be."

"I don't have any brothers, so no." She often wondered how different her life might have been if she did. If there had been someone else for her parents to mold and shape in their image instead of her. Then, maybe, they would have left her alone.

It was a horrible, selfish thought, but sometimes she couldn't help thinking it.

Amelia forced her thoughts from that dangerously deep well of self-pity.

"I guess I can sort of understand what you mean, though. My friend Lillian has three brothers, and she's always complaining about how high-handed and annoying they can be. Especially her twin. He drives her absolutely bonkers."

"There's nothing worse than a big brother who thinks he knows everything." Winnie darted a dismayed glance at Amelia. "You, ah, didn't happen to hear…"

She must have given the answer away somehow, because Winnie collapsed onto her back with a groan.

"I only heard the very beginning," Amelia rushed to assure her. "Just the part that you're, um…"

"Knocked up."

"Um, yes. That."

Winnie smoothed both hands over her belly and sat back up. "I'm not sorry about it. I love this baby. Just like I love K—his father. And he loves me. We're going to get married and be a family. It's just...complicated."

"Trust me." Her lips tilted wryly. "I know all about complicated."

Winnie was instantly diverted. "Guy troubles, huh?"

Amelia hummed her agreement as she hung the last top, not wanting to get into the mess she'd made of her life. But Winnie wasn't that easy to dissuade.

"Did you get dumped?"

"No, actually, I was the one who ended things." She closed the empty suitcase and put it inside the closet before shutting the door.

"Ooh, I bet he didn't like that." Winnie snapped her fingers. "That's why you're here. You kicked him to the curb and now you're waiting to see if he wants you bad enough to come after you. That's so romantic!"

"No, it's not."

Winnie looked confused by Amelia's vehemence. "You don't want him to?"

"God, no." The thought of Charles coming after her turned her stomach into a seething swamp of acid. "My situation isn't anything like yours. I don't love Charles, and he doesn't love me. And the reasons we were getting married...well, suffice it to say, they were the wrong ones all around. No marriage should be built on business ties and bloodlines."

"Oh, my God! You were in one of those, what do you call them? Arranged marriages."

"No, it was nothing like that." But...in a way, wasn't it *exactly* like that? She dropped onto the bed beside Winnie. "People should only marry for love."

"That's what I told Daryl. I want Kyle to ask me to marry him before he finds out about the baby. I want him to want to marry me because of *me*."

Winnie probably didn't even realize she used the name she'd been trying so hard to keep a secret. But that wasn't the part that made Amelia do a mental double take.

"He doesn't know about the baby?"

A mulish expression eerily similar to the one Daryl had given her when she asked him to give her five minutes alone in the lingerie department crept across Winnie's features.

"Not exactly."

"Not exactly? How can he not know when you're..." She waved a hand at the obvious baby bump.

"He's been away." Winnie fluffed her blouse so it hid the evidence better. "Like I said, it's complicated."

More like a disaster in the making.

But then, who was she to judge?

"Well, I hope everything works out the way you want it to."

"It will." Winnie's voice was a lot more certain than her expression.

Awkward silence descended. Taught from the cradle to fill such things, Amelia asked the only question she could think of.

"So, what's a buckle bunny?"

⚬

"What a shame your pretty fiancée is still feeling too unwell to attend her own luncheon. I do hope it's nothing serious."

Holding onto the smile he'd been wearing for the past two wretched hours of similarly insincere platitudes and leading questions, Charles Davenport replied with practiced ease.

"Just a touch of a stomach bug, Mrs. Johnson. Inconvenient, but not serious. The doctor recommended she take a few days to rest, so she's back to one hundred percent by next Saturday."

"I see." She raised the nose her husband's millions had recently paid to have reshaped into a dainty button. Which, in Charles's opinion, was akin to paying to build a beautiful gazebo in the middle of a swamp. "I had hoped to meet the girl before the ceremony."

Her and about a hundred other of his father's biggest political contributors. Soon to become *his* contributors, if all went according to plan.

Which, thanks to his little bitch of a fiancée, they weren't. She'd thrown the past two days into utter chaos with her ill-timed temper tantrum. A fact for which she was going to pay very dearly when she returned.

"I'll make certain that Amelia and I speak with you and Ralph as soon as she's feeling up to resuming her bridal duties."

Leaving the barely pacified old cow behind, Charles broke away from the crowd of people littering the back patio of his parents' estate. He slipped through the French doors that led to the library and sighed as the peace and quiet wrapped around him.

His first stop was the wet bar, where he poured himself a tall shot of the expensive Tennessee whiskey his father favored. Without hesitating, he tossed it back and poured another.

"You do know you're supposed to sip that stuff, right?"

Charles tensed at the unexpected voice.

Sneaky, light-footed bastard.

"Desperate times and all that." Saluting his father's fixer with the glass, he threw it back like the first and let the burn clear away the last of the unpleasant aftertaste of dealing with his guests. "You have good news for me, I hope?"

"Afraid not."

The glass hit the polished mahogany bar top with a sharp crack. "That's not what I wanted to hear."

Vaughn shrugged. "I can't give you what I don't have."

"My father pays you to handle messes like this. Right now, I'd say you're not exactly earning your exorbitant paycheck."

"It's not my fault your little pigeon bolted before you could seal the deal."

Charles seethed at the hint of amusement in his tone.

There was a lot of leeway given to Vaughn, considering the delicate nature of his employment for the Davenport family. But there were still boundaries that needed to be respected. It would seem he needed to be reminded of that little fact.

"But it is your fault her ass isn't back here hosting this damn party like she should."

"If she'd gone to her parents' estate like she was supposed to, she would be."

And that pissed Charles off even more. One of Amelia's greatest attributes was her clockwork predictability. She did what she was told, the way she was told, every single time.

Except, it seemed, when he really needed her to.

What had possessed her to think she could call off their wedding in the first place? Hell, if anyone was going to call it off, it would have been him after the fiasco of their engagement party.

If the polls hadn't come back saying he'd take an even bigger hit in voter popularity, he would have happily washed his hands of the mousy bitch back then.

But to think *she* could leave *him*? Waltz into his study and calmly announce she'd changed her mind, so sorry, here's your ring, there's the door? Did she honestly think he would just accept her decision? It seemed he'd been remiss in clarifying her position in their little arrangement.

An oversight he couldn't remedy until she was returned.

"What about that aunt of hers, the one in Texas?" The one with all the money she'd taken great glee in telling him his campaign wouldn't get one thin dime of.

Tight-fisted old bitch.

"I have someone watching her estate, but so far it doesn't look like she went there."

"Then she's got to be hiding out with one of her nosy little friends. She doesn't have anywhere else to go." God, he hated those two. He didn't know which one was worse, the loud-mouthed little troublemaker or the one who always looked at him like she smelled something rank.

Without invitation, Vaughn walked to the wet bar and poured himself a small tot of whiskey. Charles bristled at the impudence.

"I already checked on that. There's no way to be a hundred percent certain without getting inside, of course, but it doesn't appear as though she's at either the Fordham or Beaumont properties. It's strange, though." He took a sip and made a sound of appreciation.

It irked Charles to have to ask. "What's strange?"

"Those friends of hers that you don't like? They're still here. Not *here*," he said when Charles's gaze flicked to the French doors. "Not that I've seen, anyway. But they haven't checked out of their hotel yet."

That news gave Charles pause. Since it had to be those two troublemakers who were behind Amelia's uncharacteristic act of rebellion, it didn't make sense they hadn't returned to Colorado with her. Unless...

"Are we certain she was actually on that plane?"

Vaughn nodded. "Airport security footage confirmed it."

"Then where the hell *is* she?"

"I'm working on a few possibilities."

"Work faster, damn it. I need her back here. Now."

Vaughn downed the last of his whiskey and dipped his head in a gesture more mocking than deferential before leaving.

Asshole.

Furious, knowing Vaughn would never dream of disrespecting his father that way, Charles poured himself another drink, but put it down untouched. He needed all of his faculties intact to deal with the guests outside who wanted their pound of flesh in exchange for their financial support.

Begging for bucks was the part of the political business he least liked. And why he'd specifically chosen Amelia to be the woman who graced his arm. She might be a washed-out little mouse, but she knew how to charm the crowds into pulling out their checkbooks.

She should be here taking care of their guests and making his life easier, instead of forcing him to make excuses for her absence. It was unacceptable behavior from his future wife and hostess. A fact he'd be sure to impress on her after the ceremony. Oh, he'd have to act the simpering bridegroom to keep her happy and smiling for the cameras on the day.

But once she was legally bound to him...she would regret every second of embarrassment she ever caused him.

Chapter 11

Dinner at the ranch was an experience like none Amelia had ever encountered.

While the hands had their lunch out in the small building near the bunkhouse that served as their mess hall, breakfast and dinner were eaten in the main house with the family. Since most of the time that meant just Kim and Hank Raintree, it made good sense.

In theory.

In actuality, it made for a loud, somewhat claustrophobic group of very large men and two medium-sized women squeezed in around the massive kitchen table. With Daryl and Amelia there was barely enough room for everybody to fit, but no one seemed to mind.

As long as there was enough food, they were happy.

Amelia ended up sitting between Daryl and Chaz. Since she'd already met Chaz, she was pleased with the arrangement. Daryl seemed less so. In fact, he seemed downright surly while Chaz entertained her throughout the meal with stories about the various rodeos he'd ridden in when he was younger.

Which had to have been *very* young, considering he couldn't be much over forty. He'd evidently taken a lot of championships before coming to work on the Raintree ranch, and he wasn't shy in bragging about them. Several of the other hands made occasional rude comments in return, although they kept it clean in deference to her and Kim.

Seated across the table, Manuelo, the young man who'd nearly fallen into the horse manure earlier—something she'd never admit to witnessing—was hanging on Chaz's every word.

When he stopped talking long enough to fork some of the delicious pot roast into his mouth, Manuelo said to her, "Chaz took the All-Around *six times*." The awe in his voice was palpable.

The term was foreign to her, but it sounded like something worthy of extra boasting. "That's very impressive."

Chaz grinned at her. "You have no idea what that means, do you?"

"I'm sorry, no," she replied with a small laugh. "I'm not familiar with rodeo. But I assume that's a lot to win?"

"It was a record." The twist of his lips said he wasn't thrilled about the past tense of that statement. "Until some young buck came along and bested me out of the title."

She didn't need to ask who that young buck was. Not the way Chaz's gaze shifted past her to the man sitting on her right, who hadn't opened his mouth at all during the meal other than to put food into it.

Although to be fair, Chaz hadn't given anybody else much of a chance to speak.

Manuelo's jaw was all but on the table, avid eyes darting between the two men. "Awesome."

Amelia took a sip of water to hide her smile. Like it or not, the teen's hero worship had just found another target. She turned to look at Daryl, who was focused solely on his plate. "Do you still hold the record?"

"No idea."

She blinked at the abrupt reply.

Oo-kay then.

Clearly, Daryl wasn't interested in bragging about his accomplishments. How strange. In her experience, when men had something they considered brag-worthy, they wrung every last drop out of it.

Falling back on her training, Amelia shifted the conversation to less prickly ground with a comment about the pregnant mare. That led to a discussion about the breeding program the ranch ran, which in turn led to a litany of bloodlines that were on the wish list for future pairings.

Rather than diffuse things, however, the horse talk only seemed to wind Daryl even tighter.

They were seated close enough that she could feel the coiled tension in his long, lean body. He was like a rubber-band propeller on a model airplane that was being stretched turn after turn, until it either had to be let loose, or snapped.

Daryl, thankfully, chose the first option.

Laying his knife and fork across his empty plate, his chair screeched as he pushed it back from the table. With a brusque thank-you to his mother for the meal, he exited through the kitchen door, not slowing as he grabbed his hat from one of the pegs driven into the wall there for that purpose.

Conversation stumbled to an uncomfortable halt as the door banged shut behind him.

Amelia's tummy did a tiny pinwheel. Clearly, she'd misstepped somehow. She just didn't know in what way.

She summoned her most encouraging smile. "So, which horse do you think would be a good fit if I get up the courage to try my hand at riding tomorrow?"

Everyone had an opinion, and the rest of the meal passed with no more mention of rodeos or Daryl's abrupt departure.

Once pie and coffee had been inhaled, the men made their way out to do whatever evening chores they had. Each one thanked Kim for the meal and made a point to nod or tip an imaginary hat to Amelia and wish her a good night. Hank gave his wife a quick kiss on the cheek before following them out.

Finally, it was only Kim and Amelia left in the kitchen, surrounded by a mountain of dirty dishes. As she brought her plate to the garbage can to scrape off, Amelia shook her head.

"I don't know how you managed to make such a huge meal and end up with zero leftovers. I thought for sure you'd made enough to last for the whole week."

Kim shrugged, gathering empty plates from the table. "Ranching is hard work. The boys won't get much done if I don't fill the hole in their bellies."

Turning from the garbage, Amelia noticed for the first time hers was the only plate that needed to be scraped of uneaten food. Every other plate was the next thing from licked clean. Even Daryl, with his early departure, had managed to finish his meal first.

Embarrassed, she added her plate to the stack Kim set next to the sink. She'd left a good portion of her food uneaten the last time Kim had fed her, too. Although, to be fair, both times the food had been served to her, so she wasn't responsible for the portion sizes.

"I'm afraid I'm not used to such big meals," she said, even though Kim had given no sign she was upset about the wasted food.

"You don't eat like you're on one of those starvation diets." Kim put the last of the dishes on the counter before grabbing a sponge and dampening it in the sink. "Even though you look like you are."

Amelia winced, the disturbing reality of her too-flat stomach still painfully fresh.

"I'm not."

She was on the my-nerves-are-shot-to-hell-and-I-keep-puking diet.

"And I don't want you to think it has anything to do with your food, which has been delicious. My stomach has always been a little touchy, and lately it's been a lot worse. It's going to take me a little time to build my appetite back up to where it should be."

Kim gave her a considering look. "If I had to guess, I'd say your stomach problems have something to do with the reason you're staying with us for the next little while. No." She held up a hand when Amelia started to speak. "I don't need to know what brought you here. Daryl said not to ask, so I won't. But don't you worry. We'll get you fed up while you're here." A finger to her lips, she hummed in thought. "Smaller meals, I think, and more of them. And more of my tea. It will help your nerves as well as your digestion."

A pang of sadness showered over Amelia like a melancholy rain. Kim had known her for less than a day, and already she'd shown more awareness and consideration of Amelia's eating issues than her own mother had in the past six months.

But then, there had been an important wedding for her mother to plan. There hadn't been time left to spare for her daughter, even if she was the bride.

Which she wasn't anymore.

Thank God.

Watching Kim wipe down the table, Amelia felt like a useless lump. She considered excusing herself to retreat to her room, but Winnie's voice rang in her head.

"This isn't a hotel. People work here."

Well, that meant she was going to work, too.

Since asking would put Kim in an awkward position, she took a page from Lillian's book of 'easier to ask forgiveness than permission' and started rinsing the stacked plates and loading them into the dishwasher. When Kim didn't comment, she took that as tacit acceptance, and they worked in companionable silence setting the kitchen back in order.

Squeezing the last plate into the dishwasher, Amelia felt an unfamiliar sense of accomplishment. "What's next?"

Bringing the first of the pots to the sink, Kim replied, "I can finish these up."

"Really, I can help."

"These just need to soak until the dishwasher is free. I can manage. But thank you for your help with the rest."

Oddly deflated, Amelia managed a smile. "Of course. My pleasure."

Kim gave her another of those contemplative stares.

"Mike's wife, Ella, usually helps out with the meals. But with her visiting her sister until her newest nephew is born, an extra set of hands would be a big help. If you've a mind, that is."

Relief was immediate. "I'd love to."

"Just be certain. Crack of dawn isn't just a saying around here."

When the alternative was sleeping in, knowing everyone else on the ranch was already up and hard at work, it was a no-brainer.

"I'll be here." She hesitated. "In the spirit of full disclosure, I'm not a very good cook, just so you know."

Kim raised a shoulder in a negligent shrug. "You'll get better."

That simple, easy vote of confidence warmed Amelia like a burst of sudden sunshine after a long, cold winter. She smiled.

"Yes, I will."

⫘⬦⫘

"You'd rather spend your evening out here with Lolly than inside with that pretty little gal of yours?" Chaz leaned his shoulder into the open stall door, a sardonic smile on his lips. "Boy, you must be tetched in the head."

Daryl didn't bother looking up from the brush he was running over the left flank of the horse he was grooming. "She seemed to be enjoying herself just fine when I left."

Damnation.

He hadn't meant it to come out sounding like he was jealous. He was *glad* Amelia hadn't felt uncomfortable. She was used to dining with millionaires and heads of state, not a bunch of rough-mannered cowboys, but she'd handled the situation just fine.

He'd been the one itchy and out of sorts.

Daryl kept working with the brush, stopping every so often to knock off the loose hair and dirt the curry comb had already loosened up. It was repetitive, mind-numbing work. After all the talk around the table, he needed to not think for a little while. Brushing down the horses had always been one of his go-tos for that.

Undaunted, Chaz said, "I don't know why you get all bent out of shape when people bring up your rodeo days. I'm the one whose record you broke. If anyone should be pissed, it should be me."

"Since you're the one who brought it up in the first place, you have no one to be pissed at but yourself." Although, to be fair, it wasn't the rodeo talk that had really gotten his temper worked up. It was the ranch talk. Which was stupid because it had been *his* decision to walk away from it in search of...something.

And left an opening for Chaska to step right into.

He now held the right-hand-man spot his father had expected him to settle into. Only Daryl had never been one to settle. He'd joined the rodeo circuit young and worked it hard, all with one goal in mind: to earn enough prize money to buy a place of his own.

Only his plans had blown up in his face.

One too many injuries had cost him his dreams, but it was a misplaced sense of pride that had cost him his home. Coming back to the ranch had just seemed too much like tucking tail and admitting defeat. So instead, he stayed away, eventually taking the security job down in Colorado.

His choice. All of it.

So why did he still resent Chaska his place here, then?

This was why he stayed the hell away. It was a lot easier to ignore the regrets his decisions stirred up inside him with a few hundred miles of distance between him and what he could never have.

"So, how long have the two of you been together?"

"Not long." The lie rolled off his tongue with no input from his brain. Chaska might have been a good twenty years older than Amelia, but the man had never let a little thing like age stand in the way of a good time. Young, old, pretty, plain, rich, poor. He bedded them all.

His only redeeming quality when it came to women was that he didn't poach.

Finished with the left side, Daryl switched to the right. As he stroked the short-bristled brush over the white mark on the gelding's chest, he grinned, remembering how outraged he'd been on the horse's behalf when Winnie had chosen the ridiculous name of Lollipop because of its shape. No amount of coaxing, begging, or threatening could persuade her to pick a different one.

She might have only been six, but once his sister had her mind set on something, there was no changing it. Winnie had definitely gotten the Raintree stubborn gene.

But she hadn't gotten the horse-crazy gene. Despite her desire to name the horses on the Circle R—something she was thankfully never allowed to do again—she showed little interest in riding them.

She could, of course. Their father would have accepted nothing less than total equine competence. But as she'd gotten older, she'd been less drawn to the horses and more to the men working them.

Not that a single one would dare look at her with anything but complete respect.

His father might be getting up in years and be more laid-back now than he'd been during his years as a Marine, but he could still be one scary bastard if you got on his wrong side. Anyone laying a finger on his baby girl would be annihilated. Which was probably why she was keeping the name of who had gotten her pregnant such a big—

His hands froze mid-stroke.

No. Even Chaz wouldn't be that stupid.

Would he?

His gaze snapped to the man who was still slumped in a lazy pose against the stall door, a stalk of hay tucked in the corner of his mouth, hat cocked back on his head. The very picture of a bored cowboy.

It was a look that had gotten him into the panties of more buckle bunnies than any other rider on the circuit, whether he'd won his events that day or not. Even when Daryl had been riding years later, they still talked about the legendary Chaz Everheart, man of steel.

And they *hadn't* been referring to his stamina on a horse.

Slowly, Chaz's lazy posture changed in response to Daryl's glare. Eyes narrowing, he straightened, his loose limbs going stiff. "I have no intention of chasing your woman. You should know me better than that."

"It's not Amelia I was wondering about."

Did Chaz look a little nervous? Maybe even a little guilty?

Or maybe just confused, because that was how he sounded when he asked, "Then what the hell's with the death stare? Who...son of a bitch!" He tossed the piece of hay to the ground, confusion giving way to anger. "Tell me you don't think I had anything to do with getting your sister pregnant. Tell me you don't think I'm that much of a twisted prick."

He didn't give Daryl a chance to reply. Stalking away then retracing his steps, he threw his arms up in the air.

"Christ on a crutch, boy, that girl is like family to me. Taking her to bed would be like sleeping with my niece. And you can *damn* well believe that if I'd gotten *any* woman in the family way, I'd own up to my responsibilities. Damn. *Damn!*"

He stalked away again, muttering under his breath.

The tension in the air had Lolly stamping his foot in agitation. Daryl reached out automatically to soothe him.

Damnation.

He'd screwed that to fuck and back. If he'd taken more than two seconds to consider, he'd have known there was no way Chaska would have taken advantage of his sister. The man had been on the ranch for over ten years. He was right. He *was* like family.

And Daryl felt like a complete and utter ass.

He found Chaz ten minutes later, sitting on the ground with his back up against the rear of the bunkhouse. With one knee up, he was contemplating the horizon, another piece of hay crammed in the corner of his mouth.

Wordlessly, Daryl sat down beside him and handed him one of

the cold long-neck bottles he'd taken from the mess hall fridge. Chaz tipped it up and took a swallow.

"I was a jackass." Daryl took a long swallow of his own beer. He didn't drink it often, but the sharp bite was welcome.

"You were."

"I'm sorry."

"You should be."

They drank in silence for a few minutes. He could feel the angry tension seeping out of Chaz now that the smear to his honor had been cleared away. Daryl watched as the setting sun turned the sky a brilliant flag of reds and pinks streaked with purple before darkening to twilight.

He'd missed that. Seeing Mother Nature's nightly light display. And the one that came again every morning with sunrise. And the crisp fresh air hung with an edge of horse and leather. Hell, he'd missed a lot of things.

Just not enough to come back.

"You want to know the other reason there's no way I would have ever messed with little Miss Winona?" Chaz asked after the sun had completed its fall. "It's because she's a forever kind of girl. And guys like me don't mess with girls like that. Ever."

"Well, someone sure as hell did."

"Have a little faith." Chaz poked Daryl's ribs with an elbow. "She's a Raintree. She might not have the scary stare you inherited from your old man, but she's sure got his brains. When that girl sets her sights on a goal, she doesn't stop until she gets it. Just wait. Things'll come out right in the end."

Daryl wasn't as certain of that, and waiting wasn't an option. Not when Winnie wouldn't be able to hide her condition under baggy clothing much longer.

"You know who else is a forever girl?" Chaz asked. "Little Miss Amy."

Daryl finished the last of his beer, ignoring the small nip of jealousy at Chaz's easy use of the nickname he'd heard no one ever use before. Damned if it didn't suit her, though.

"Maybe. But she's definitely not *my* forever." The mere thought was laughable.

"I don't know." Chaz stared at his bottle as though it held the secrets of the universe inside before upending it and drinking down the last swallow. "If you ask me, forever with her is exactly what you need."

Chapter 12

Breakfast hadn't turned out as bad as she'd feared.

Stacking the last of the dishes in the dishwasher, Amelia felt a sense of giddy pride that her first attempt at pancakes hadn't totally sucked. Aside from the very first batch, of course, which had been burned on the outside and runny inside.

Lucky for her, Kim was a patient woman. After scraping that first failure into the garbage, she'd coached Amelia through the process until she was pouring and flipping like a pro.

Maybe I can get a job as a short order cook.

She snorted softly, but it wasn't really funny. God knew her parents wouldn't welcome her back with open arms after what she'd done. She was going to have to figure out what came next for her.

But not today.

Today, she was going to the barn to pet the horses, and maybe, if Daryl remembered his promise, ride one of them. The thought of getting back on a horse after so many years sent a rush of anticipation through her.

She hadn't lied about loving to ride when she was younger. There had been an incredible sense of freedom while on the back of her horse. Of control. Away from her parents and all their suffocating expectations, that ring had become her own little bubble of autonomy.

Then, like everything good that came her way, they'd taken it from her.

It didn't matter that the horse had just taken a bad stumble. Or that she'd landed wrong. Someone had to be held accountable. If only she believed their outraged reaction had been over her wellbeing, and not how any visible flaw she might have ended up with would diminish her worth as part of the perfect family portrait they portrayed.

But Amelia had never believed in fairytales, and she'd always known she wasn't destined to get her Disney princess happy ending. She'd been willing to settle for it simply being better than *un*happy.

Which was why she'd been willing to settle for Charles.

Wiping her hands on the dishtowel hanging by the sink, she shook her head, disappointed with herself. Why had she decided she couldn't have anything better? That she didn't *deserve* better?

Because there was simply not getting your prince, and there was getting a warty, two-faced ogre instead.

Not projecting much there or anything.

Even with just a few days' perspective, she was seeing things so much more clearly. It was like being woken from the fog she'd been trapped in for the last year, able to finally see what her friends had been trying to oh-so-gently tell her.

She really had escaped by the skin of her teeth.

Speaking of teeth, she needed to go brush hers. They felt a little sticky after the syrup-covered stack of pancakes she'd just put away. True to her word, Kim had given her a much more manageable portion of pancakes, bacon, and eggs on her plate this morning, and for the first time in recent memory, she'd finished a meal with nothing left on her plate.

Stupid to feel a sense of accomplishment over that, but she did.

Once her mouth was minty fresh, she went in search of Daryl. Last she'd seen him, Manuelo had been chewing his ear off as they walked out the door. The boy still hadn't run out of questions about Daryl's rodeo days.

Amelia didn't blame him. She was more than a little curious herself.

She'd only seen clips on tv, but it seemed to her that riding bulls and roping calves and whatever else they did called for not only skill, but a certain amount of bravado and devil-may-care attitude. Those two traits were ones she'd more likely use to describe someone like Chaz. She had no problem picturing the flirty cowboy strutting around the rodeo grounds, oozing sex appeal and trailing a cluster of buckle bunnies eager to catch his attention.

She grinned as she stepped around a pile of fresh manure.

Who knew there was an entire subculture of groupies just for rodeo riders?

Thanks to Winnie, she'd had her eyes opened to that little bit of information. As well as to the fact Daryl had once been a much sought-after prize himself. But even if he'd won as many contests as last night's dinner conversation alluded to, she had a harder time thinking about Daryl as a chick magnet than she did Chaz.

Daryl was attractive, yes, but he was so big. And stoic. And intimidating. While she'd always felt totally safe whenever he was on Thea's security detail, she also couldn't help feeling just a little overwhelmed by his presence.

Except...she'd just spent the past forty-eight hours in his company, and she couldn't remember even once feeling overwhelmed *or* intimidated. Not even when they'd been stuck in his truck together for hours on end.

Funny how a little thing like having your entire life go nuclear could change your perspective on people.

She had a fairly accurate layout of the ranch stored in her head, thanks to yesterday's tour. Her freakishly good memory was what had made her so indispensable at her father's fundraisers. She could memorize the entire guest list and feed him names before he greeted people, making every potential donor feel like they were a close, treasured friend of the good senator from Colorado.

Ha! If they only knew.

Coming around the corner of the bunkhouse, the training ring she had visited the previous day with Kim came into view. Today, as then, two tall men stood with their boots propped up on the bottom of the split rail fence, watching the action going on inside.

From the back, father and son were so much alike it would have been hard to tell them apart if it hadn't been for their hair. While Hank's slightly graying black locks were cut military short beneath his Stetson, Daryl's hung over the collar of his shirt in an inky wave. Other than that, they were the same. Same height. Same frame. Even their body language mirrored one another.

She slowed as she approached, trying to see Daryl the way a buckle bunny might.

His broad shoulders did wonderful things to his shirt, stretching the blue-and-white checked material taut as he leaned forward on the top rail. That wide expanse tapered down to a lean torso that ran into trim hips and long, muscular legs that were encased in denim jeans that looked like they'd seen a lot of use. Not the already distressed ones from the store, but ones that had seen more than their share of hard work and numerous washings.

She tried not to stare at the way he filled out the back of those jeans, but Lillian was right. The man had one very fine butt.

So, okay, yes. He was physically appealing. And good looking. But she still didn't get why he would have attracted so many women like bees to clover. It was obvious she was missing something important.

A shout sounded from the training ring.

As if they'd choreographed it, Daryl and his father swung themselves over the fence in response to whatever had happened. Panic fluttering in her chest, Amelia broke into a run. She skidded to a stop, hands gripping the top rail, trying to make sense of what was going on.

Hank knelt next to Zeke, who was curled up on his side on the ground, holding his left leg and cursing up a storm. And Daryl...

She sucked in a terrified breath, heart pounding.

Daryl had put himself between the injured man and the big black horse that was snorting and prancing like a crazed demon all around the ring. He moved along with it using slow, measured steps, always keeping himself between it and the two men on the ground, arms raised out to the side.

The horse shied away from him. After a few canters around the ring, it slowed, until it came to a fidgety stop on the far side, blowing hard in agitation and fear.

Movement dragged Amelia's attention back to the other two men. Zeke was now on his feet—or rather, foot—with his arm slung around Hank's shoulders for support. She wasn't the only one who noticed. The horse snorted and pawed, dancing a few steps to the side as though it was going to break into movement again.

Daryl countered, stepping closer to draw the horse's attention to himself, talking in a low voice to it. Heartbeat tripling, Amelia couldn't hear what he was saying, but the horse could, its dainty ears twitching toward the sound.

Torn between helping and watching Daryl perform his horse whisperer trick, she forced herself to walk slowly to the gate further down the fence line. She opened it for Hank and Zeke, then quickly closed it behind them. Zeke's pant leg was torn and bloody, but at least the rest of him appeared intact, if a little dusty.

"Are you okay?"

"Nasty bastard kicks like a mule," Zeke said through gritted teeth. "Don't think he broke it, though. Shoulda known he was gonna try something, he had that look in his eyes."

"Let's go get you checked out," Hank said, turning them toward the house.

"Can I do anything to help?" Even as she asked, she could hear other ranch hands approaching at a run.

Hank jerked his head back towards the ring. "You can stay and make sure my fool son doesn't get his head kicked in by that brat."

From the gruff tone of his voice, it was clear he wasn't happy Daryl had taken on the more dangerous job of wrangling the unruly horse for himself.

It was clear Hank's agitation wasn't because Daryl couldn't handle the job.

As Amelia watched, heart in throat, Daryl slowly built a rapport with the black beast. It was like watching a snake charmer, except instead of music he used his voice to mesmerize, speaking in a soft, crooning tone. He managed to get a few steps closer before the horse realized it and retreated a step itself.

On and on it went, Daryl gaining two or three steps and then losing one or two back. Every once in a while, the horse would paw at the ground rather than retreat, sending Amelia's pulse racing as she waited for it to bolt or strike out with its deadly hooves.

But it never did. Daryl would stop moving and change the pitch of his voice, waiting for the animal to settle down before starting the dance again.

Unable to take any more, Amelia turned to Ned, who was watching the scene unfold from next to her. "Shouldn't you go in and help him?"

"More people would just spook him again."

Maybe, but that didn't stop her from being terrified by thoughts of the thousand and one things that could go wrong with what Daryl was attempting.

"Then why doesn't he just get out of the ring and leave the horse to calm down on its own?"

"Can't," Mike said from her other side. "See those reins trailing in the dirt? Horse gets his feet tangled up in those..." He shook his head. "The black's too valuable to risk getting a broken leg, or worse."

And Daryl isn't?

She swallowed the angry words and went back to watching Daryl slowly work the huge beast toward the side of the ring. It felt like hours before the horse's rump finally touched the fence.

Then everything happened all at once.

The horse let out a startled squeal. It tried to rear up, but with the fence behind it could only get its front half a few feet in the air. Daryl stood his ground, avoiding the flailing hooves. As soon as the horse went to all fours again, he darted in and grabbed hold of the dangling reins.

That brought on another attempt to rear, but this time Daryl had the means to yank the horse's head down lower than its shoulders, preventing it.

Blowing and prancing in place, the horse fought a little longer before signaling its surrender with a long, heartfelt sigh. The tension left its body, and its neck relaxed, allowing Daryl to loosen up his hold on the reins.

Only then did Mike and Ned climb over the fence and make a slow approach.

Daryl didn't relinquish his hold on the horse to them right away. Instead, he spent a few minutes stroking its long neck, still talking in that low voice, transferring the reins to Ned's hands as he did so the horse didn't even realize someone new was holding them. After a quick word with Ned, Daryl gave the horse one last pat and turned.

Her heart still pounding from the thrill of fear she'd felt for his safety, Amelia watched Daryl walk across the ring, bending to scoop up the hat he'd lost somewhere along the way. He dragged a sleeve over his face, which glistened with sweat, before shaking his hair back and securing the Stetson on his head while he strode toward the gate.

There was something...different about the way he moved.

His long-legged gait was more fluid, almost a strut. The satisfied look on his face one of a triumphant warrior leaving the field of battle.

Oooh.

Amelia struggled to moisten her suddenly dry mouth, unable to tear her gaze from this Spartan warrior version of Daryl. Her body thrummed in response to the glitter in his dark eyes.

Okay. *Now* she got it.

"Boy's still got the mojo," Chaz said from where he suddenly appeared at her side, startling her from her sudden epiphany.

Or maybe he'd been there for a few minutes. She'd been too focused on Daryl to notice.

Why did she feel like she needed to fan herself?

"He's, um, always been this good with horses?"

"Better. And for someone not doing this from the cradle, that's saying something. It's in his blood, no matter how hard he tries to pretend otherwise." He grinned when Daryl broke direction from the gate and instead hopped over the fence right beside them. "Bring back some memories?" he asked in an almost mocking tone.

"Yeah," Daryl replied. "That horse wrangling's damn hard work."

"And catching bullets for a living isn't?"

Daryl's gaze flicked from Chaz to Amelia for a quick second. "It has its moments." He shifted, and somehow, she wasn't certain how, he was between her and Chaz. "Where's Zeke?"

"Bunkhouse."

With a nod, Daryl collected Amelia with an arm around her shoulders.

She went along without complaint. There was still that air of the warrior fresh from battle about him. It was slowly fading, or he was clamping down harder to contain it, but she still felt it vibrating off of him like a live wire shooting off sparks.

Her body practically sizzled every place it touched his.

But as they walked toward the bunkhouse, one question kept demanding an answer. If he was so amazing with horses, if the ranch was in his blood, then why wasn't he here doing what he'd so obviously been born to do?

Chapter 13

When did I lose control of the situation?

Two hours later, Daryl thrummed his fingers on the truck's steering wheel, trying to figure that out. He scowled at the small procession of vehicles ahead of them, kicking up dust as they drove down the long road from the Circle R to the main road.

"You know this isn't smart, right? The whole idea of you being here is to stay out of sight."

"It's only church." Amelia ran a hand over her skirt as though to iron out some imaginary wrinkle. "We're going to go in, sit down, listen to the service, and leave. No one's even going to notice me in the crowd."

If she honestly believed that, she was delusional.

She might think wearing a simple white top and another of those long, flowy skirts made her blend in. But with those golden curls and that smile she couldn't keep from stunning every male she let it loose on, she would most definitely be noticed.

Add to that the fact it would be the first time in close to six years since any of the good people of Hayden had seen *him* crossing the threshold of the town's tiny brick church, and they were going to be a goddamned spectacle.

"Besides, your mother asked us to go. It would have been rude to say no."

"Step."

"I'm sorry?"

"Kim is my *step*mother. My mother died when I was seven." As soon as he said the words, he wanted them back. He never talked about his mother. To anyone. Ever.

"Oh, I'm so sorry."

"It was a long time ago." He tried to sound as repressive as possible, hoping she'd take the hint.

She didn't.

Instead, she reached over and laid a gentle hand on his arm. "That doesn't mean you can't still miss her."

Deciding not replying was his best course of action, Daryl concentrated on the road even though he could have driven the route into town blindfolded. There was only one road that ran through the area. Well, one paved road, anyway.

There were others—some gravel, some dirt—that branched off of it, but no signs to tell you where they led. As far as the locals felt, if you didn't know what was at the end of a road, you had no business being on it in the first place.

Not big on outsiders were the people of Hayden.

Which was why he wasn't surprised when just about every head turned as they walked through the heavy wooden doors at the rear of the church. Like a breeze moving across a field of wheat, it started at the back with the first people who noticed them. That was followed by whispers and more turning heads until, pew by pew, the effect rippled forward.

Oh, sure. In and out. No one will notice us at all.

He gave a mental head shake as they slipped into the back pew after the rest of the contingent from the ranch, taking the aisle seat. He glanced at Amelia, sandwiched between him and his father. She wore her calm and composed face as she looked around, as though unaware of the men sitting in front of them nearly twisting their necks off to get a better look at her.

Then her back went rigid and she made a small, unhappy sound.

Daryl tensed. Snapping into bodyguard mode, he scanned the crowded church for any sign of trouble. Damn it, had someone actually managed to track them down this fast?

But no. All he saw were the ranchers and townspeople in their Sunday best, making small talk and trying not to be too obvious as they stared. Nothing and no one seemed out of place.

Before he could ask what she'd reacted to, Amelia tapped his leg urgently and whispered, "Get up."

He did, allowing her to shoo him out of the pew and into the center aisle. But instead of beelining for the rear door and outside as he expected, she marched—*marched!*—up the aisle until she came to a pew about halfway to the altar. Only then did he see what she had.

A wave of anger crashed over him.

Despite the fact that every other pew was at least partway filled, this one contained only one person, sitting so rigid and alone she looked ready to shatter.

Amelia slid into the pew beside Winona and pulled her into a hug. "Thank you for saving us all seats. Sorry we're late. A little accident out at the ranch earlier made the whole morning kind of crazy." She urged Winnie further into the pew so that Daryl could sit as well.

Looking confused but grateful, Winnie latched onto the conversational gambit like a lifeline. "What kind of accident? Is everyone okay?"

As Winona—and everyone around them, no doubt—listened to Amelia tell the story of Zeke's run-in with the stallion in hushed tones, Kim and his father slid into the pew from the other direction. The rest of the men followed them, filling the pew to capacity.

Daryl gave each of them a nod of gratitude.

By the time the priest started the service, it was clear to everyone inside the little church that the Circle R family stood as a united front alongside Winona. It wouldn't keep all the narrow-minded bigots in town from ostracizing her, but it would give a lot of people pause.

Hayden wasn't large enough that it could afford to lose the ranch's business to one of the neighboring towns.

Daryl didn't hear a single word the priest spoke over the next hour.

He spent it quietly seething, staring down anyone who dared turn and peek at the women sitting at his side. The minutes ticked by so slowly he felt like he might suffocate on the heavy scent of incense if he didn't get out into the fresh air soon.

Or maybe it was just his anger he was choking on.

When the time finally came for them to leave, he stood and stepped into the aisle, blocking the flow of people like a dam, allowing Amelia and Winona to exit the pew unimpeded. He fell in behind them as they walked to the back of the church, Amelia chattering away to his sister as though they'd been best friends for years.

Winnie held her head high and ignored everyone around them, but Daryl saw the death grip she had on the arm Amelia had linked with hers.

Skin prickling, it took everything he had not to unleash on them all for doing that to her. This was her town, damn it. Her home. How dare they make her feel unwelcome in it. *Especially* here, in a place of God.

Once they made it outside, the press of bodies thinned. Kim moved up to walk on Winnie's other side, while the rest of their group ranged around the women like herding dogs protecting their flock from predators.

And there were several.

Daryl spotted them lying in wait as they passed through the opening of the low stone wall surrounding the church grounds. Nasty old biddies whose sense of morality was offended by his sister's apparently not-so-secret condition, and felt the need to let her know it in meant-to-be-heard stage whispers.

"Some nerve, stepping foot inside a church in her condition."

"The girl has no shame."

"Dirty Jezebel."

Daryl's temper notched higher with every inch his sister's shoulders hunched under the impact of the insults. But when that last one flew, he saw red.

Not today, bitches.

He wheeled around, but before he could say anything, Amelia peeled herself away from Winona's side and walked with stiff determination toward the cluster of old crones. Like Macbeth's witches, they huddled together under the large dogwood tree that had dominated the front of the church since before Daryl and his father had arrived in Hayden.

"'Judge not, that ye be not judged,'" she said in a firm, loud voice. "'For with the judgment you pronounce you will be judged, and with the measure you use it will be measured to you.'"

The three women were so taken aback, they didn't respond right away.

"You don't like that one? Then how about this? 'And he said unto them, he that is without sin among you, let him first cast a stone at her.'"

Mouths gaping, the women stared at Amelia like she was some strange new life form. Daryl knew exactly how they felt.

Who *was* this Amazon?

"No? Then here's a simple one you should recognize. 'You shall love your neighbor as yourself.' *Love*," she repeated, stabbing a finger at them that made all three flinch. "Not judge. Not ridicule. Not shun and turn away from in their time of need. And shame on all of you for choosing to use God's house and His day to serve your own sanctimonious agenda."

She glanced around at the people standing nearby, silently including them in her reprimand. A few ducked their heads and turned away.

"Perhaps your time would be better spent contemplating

your own shortcomings rather than attacking those you so self-righteously perceive in others. 'Why beholdest thou the mote that is in thy brother's eye, but considerest not the beam that is in thine own?'"

Much as he was enjoying the captivating sight of Amelia in avenging angel mode, now seemed a good time to make a strategic exit. Before the crones found their tongues and lashed back.

He could guarantee his words then wouldn't be nearly as civil as Amelia's.

Seeing Kim and the others had already hustled Winnie away, Daryl took Amelia's arm and they turned their backs on the still sputtering women. As they walked toward the parking lot through the small crowd that had gathered to watch, there were more than a few people trying to hide grins. One or two looked like they wanted to break into applause.

He knew he did.

Two of the ranch trucks had already left. Winona stood beside the one remaining, shaking her head at whatever her mother was saying. As soon as she saw Amelia, Winnie threw herself at her, hugging her tight.

"Thank you." She pulled back and swiped at the tear that stole down from one eye. "You were amazing." She looked at Daryl, eyes still glistening. "Wasn't she amazing?"

"Very." Though he was still trying to wrap his head around that out-of-character performance. Who'd have thought the little mouse could roar like that?

"Tell your sister she should come back to the ranch with us," Kim said, interrupting his study of Amelia's pinkening face.

"Mama, I told you, I can't." Winona untangled herself from Amelia with seeming reluctance. "I have work in the morning, and lesson plans to get ready today."

"You shouldn't be alone."

After what he'd just witnessed, Daryl agreed, but he recognized the stubborn look on his sister's face. It was the same one Kim wore. In sheer will, mother and daughter were evenly matched.

"I don't like the idea of you being all alone, either," he said.

"I won't be. Kaitlin is there."

"And where was she when you needed her here?" Kim asked with a hint of temper.

"She didn't feel well this morning, so she stayed home. Plus, neither of us knew *this* was going to happen." When her mother's worried expression didn't ease, Winona sighed.

"Mama, really, I appreciate your concern, and I'm more grateful than I can say about the way everyone came to my defense inside. But I'm not going to run away and hide at the ranch whenever someone hurts my feelings. I got myself into this situation, and I'll handle the consequences." She smoothed her hand over her belly.

The very adult reasoning along with the protective gesture made Daryl's gut clench at the reminder his baby sister had gone and grown up while he wasn't around to notice.

And he had no one to blame for missing it but himself.

As Winnie was hugging her mother goodbye, Daryl met his father's gaze over their heads and gave a small nod to the unspoken request he saw there.

After Winnie had given Amelia another bone-crushing hug, she went into Daryl's embrace and whispered against his ear, "Don't let this one go, Mato. She's a keeper."

The words, so eerily similar to the ones spoken by Chaz the night before, left him more than a little rattled. So much so that he all but tossed Amelia up into the high seat of his truck in his haste to minimize the contact. Even so, his fingers tingled long after they pulled out of the parking lot.

This wasn't good.

Maybe he should just tell everyone the truth of why he'd brought Amelia to the ranch, rather than have them keep jumping to all the wrong conclusions. Then he could go back to thinking of her as just a client.

He ignored the sardonic chuckle from his inner bullshit meter.

"Are we following Winnie home?" Amelia asked after they'd made the second turn that kept them trailing behind his sister's dusty little Honda.

"Yes."

"Good."

The hint of avenging angel still in her tone made his lips twitch.

A few minutes later, Daryl pulled to the curb in front of a ranch-style house in a slightly shabby neighborhood. He ran an assessing gaze over the nearby houses. They all had the same neat but worn appearance Winnie's rental did of owners who just didn't have much money to spend on curb appeal.

His sister parked under the carport next to a dented white Jeep Cherokee, then walked to the front door. She was too far away to see, but he was pretty sure she rolled her eyes at him when she waved before disappearing inside.

He didn't pull out right away.

Instead, he stared at the house, wondering if he'd done the right thing in not trying to convince her to come out to the ranch. For all she was practically a force of nature, his sister still had the tender heart of a child.

How long had people been treating her the way they had today? What other slights and recriminations had she been subjected to that no one knew about because she was too damn proud to say anything?

He turned off the ignition.

The hell with it. She was coming back with him, whether she liked it or not.

Which she wouldn't.

Which meant they'd probably fight, and she'd get upset all over again, and that couldn't be good for her or the baby.

Damn it to hell.

He restarted the truck and pulled away from the curb before he changed his mind again.

They drove in silence for a few minutes before Amelia spoke.

"I didn't expect that kind of animosity. Pregnancy outside of marriage has become almost commonplace these days."

"Not in a small town like Hayden. People here aren't the open-minded sort."

"Surely you can't paint the whole town with the same brush like that?"

The hell he couldn't.

But he reined back his own issues with the good folks of Hayden and gave her as honest an answer as he could.

"I suppose not, but all it takes is a few sharp tongues to cause a wound that bleeds." He glanced over at her. "Speaking of words, the ones you used to knock those women down off their high horses were perfect. What do you do, sit around memorizing Bible quotes for fun?"

"For fun?" Amelia uttered a harsh noise that wasn't quite a laugh. "No. For my father. He liked to pepper his speeches with the appropriate religious flourishes when he was speaking to certain groups of constituents." She sighed. "I probably shouldn't have gone after them like that, though. That was very un-Christian of me."

"Are you kidding? Those three witches were long overdue for a taste of their own sanctimonious medicine."

"Why do I get the feeling there's a story there?"

Probably because there was.

Those three bitches figured prominently in the earliest memories he had of living in Hayden. Twenty-two years later, they'd only gotten older and nastier. And had shifted their bitterness and intolerance onto a different Raintree offspring.

Only this time, they wouldn't be able to drive their chosen victim away so easily. He hated to admit it, but his little sister was made of sterner stuff than he'd been at her age.

Rather than answer, he said, "I just realized this time it's me who hasn't said thank you. For what you did for Winnie. Twice."

"You don't have to. I like your sister. Besides, anyone would have done the same."

Damn. The woman didn't take gratitude any better than she did a compliment.

"But anyone didn't. *You* did. So, thank you."

"But—"

"You're welcome, Daryl." He singsonged it over her protest.

Amelia sputtered for a second before laughing. "You're welcome, Daryl," she parroted back. "But really, if you think about it, you're helping me and I helped your sister. I'd say we're even."

Even? Not by a long shot. What she'd done for Winona had been personal. And undoubtedly uncomfortable. She'd jumped into the fray unasked, when he knew for a fact she despised confrontation.

His decision to help her was less altruistic. It had been his job, plain and simple. He'd gotten involved because Doyle had asked it of him, then continued to help her out of a sense of honor-bound duty.

And maybe a little pity.

But all that changed the second she'd taken on the Hayden Harridans for a girl she'd known less than a day. Like it or not, Amelia Westlake had just earned herself a champion, and come hell or high water, Daryl was going to slay her dragons for her.

The only question was just how singed he was going to get in the process.

Chapter 14

She'd forgotten how much she loved riding a horse.

Tilting her head back and taking a deep breath of the warm, grass-scented air, Amelia closed her eyes and let the sun beat down on her face, trusting the sure-footed animal beneath her to find her way. Cleo hadn't seemed to need much direction during their lazy ramble over one of the huge grazing fields. She was too enamored with Daryl's mount to do anything but follow where he led.

As if to prove it, Daryl drew Pepper to a halt and Cleo took the opportunity to come up beside him and reach over to lip at his neck and mane. Amelia gently tugged the reins, earning an annoyed snort and foot-stamp. Another tug and the horse relented, swinging her large head downward to crop at some grass instead.

Amelia grinned and gave the lovesick mare's neck an affectionate pat. With a glossy dark brown coat and a black mane, the mare was one of the prettiest horses Amelia had ever seen.

"I think she has a thing for Pepper."

"Too bad for her Pepper's a gelding."

"Oh, dear. Poor Cleo." Then she laughed as the mare moved closer so she could get to the grass right next to where Pepper was eating, practically touching noses with him. He blew through his nostrils but didn't push her away. "Ah, well, I guess it doesn't matter to her. The heart wants what the heart wants."

She shifted back in her saddle, adjusting her seat as Cleo stretched her neck out to steal a clump of grass from Pepper. The western style differed from what she'd used in dressage, and she still wasn't sure how she felt about it. But she *was* sure how she felt about the Circle R ranch.

She loved it.

All around them was a wide swath of grasses and gently rolling hills in about a million shades of green and brown. Off to their left rose a small copse of trees. Beside it was the glimmer of sunlight reflecting off water. If that was the stream Daryl told her they were heading for, that meant they'd nearly reached the westernmost property line.

She took it all in with a happy sigh. "It's absolutely gorgeous out here."

"Yeah, it is." Daryl rested his wrists on the saddle horn as he stared out over the land. "You should see it in the spring when all the grasses and wildflowers are just starting to come alive. It's like being inside a living painting." Then, as though uncomfortable with his own observation, he clicked his tongue at Pepper. "We should keep going. You must be hungry by now."

Falling into place beside the big, speckled horse, she realized that, yes, she *was* hungry. Starving, in fact. Which, considering what she'd eaten for breakfast, was as shocking as it was gratifying.

Who knew chastising nasty old ladies could work up an appetite?

After they reached the stream, they loosened the girths on both horses and tied them so they could graze. Daryl and Amelia settled onto the blanket he spread across the springy grass along the bank. She unpacked the sack of food Kim had given her, keeping one sandwich and apple for herself and passing the other two to Daryl.

Unwrapping the wax paper around the sandwich, she took a small, tentative taste. Absolute deliciousness exploded in her mouth. She took a bigger bite, then proceeded to devour the entire thing with dainty greed.

Her mother's chef might have won all kinds of international acclaim, but she'd never enjoyed a single thing he made as much as she did that simple ham sandwich. She almost wished she hadn't been so quick to give the rest over to Daryl.

Then again, he needed the extra fuel more than she did. He was bigger than her.

A lot bigger.

She watched through her lashes as he took a bite of his apple, white teeth slashing through the fruit's crisp flesh with a loud crunch. His firm jaw flexed as he chewed, tanned throat working as he swallowed. His tongue darted out and licked the juice from his lips before he took another big bite.

Oh. My.

For the second time that day, all the moisture vanished from her mouth.

What the heck was wrong with her? She'd seen the man eat before, for Pete's sake.

So why was she watching him devour that piece of fruit like it was the most enthralling thing on the planet?

Embarrassed by her strange fascination, she looked away, taking a large bite of her own apple, praying he hadn't noticed. She brushed at the juice that trickled down her chin with the back of her hand. Oh, how her mother would be horrified by that 'uncouth' gesture.

Then again, her mother would be horrified by any number of things she'd been doing lately. Amelia gleefully snapped another bite of apple.

And I don't care one little bit.

Okay, that wasn't completely true. Obviously, she still cared a little if she was even thinking about what her mother would think. But she was trying her best not to.

Just like she was trying her best not to think about how angry her parents must be right now.

Or what was going on back in Connecticut with Charles and his parents.

Not to mention the hundreds of guests who, according to Daryl's last conversation with Doyle, were still expecting a wedding at the end of the week.

Stop, stop, stop.

She put the mental brakes on before the spiral could pick up speed.

Not. Thinking. About. It.

They finished their meal, then lounged a bit on the blanket, just soaking up the peace and quiet, each of them lost in their own thoughts. But eventually, the lazy afternoon had to draw to an end.

They rinsed their hands in the stream and let the horses have a long drink before starting back. The fresh air and repetitive thud of the horses' hooves acted like some kind of magic elixir on her. As each mile passed, more of the tension choking her the past few weeks drained away, leaving her feeling calmer. More balanced.

Free.

She let out a happy sigh. "You're so lucky to have been born here." Hopefully, she didn't sound as jealous as she felt.

"I wasn't."

The short answer drew her gaze away from the scenery. "I'm sorry?"

"I wasn't born here."

"Oh. Sorry, I thought you said Hayden was your hometown."

"No."

She waited, then asked, "Where are you from, then?"

"All over."

"Oh." She didn't know what else to say. The clipped responses pretty much shouted to drop the subject. So she did.

Even though she didn't want to.

For some reason, she wanted to know more about him. The rodeo star, the horse whisperer, the fierce defender of little sisters. All the pieces of what was turning out to be an intriguing, complicated man.

Not that it meant anything. She was just curious about him, that was all.

It had nothing to do with the tiny flutters that had struck watching him eat that apple. Or the avid fascination she'd felt when he'd run a dampened bandana over his face and neck back at the stream.

Absolutely not.

She'd just broken her engagement to another man three days ago. She had no business feeling flutters or anything else about anyone, least of all her bodyguard.

Hear that, hormones? Knock it off.

They rode on in silence for a few minutes, but it wasn't nearly as soothing as it had been before. When Daryl finally broke it, his surly tone made it clear every word was grudgingly given.

"Dad was a Marine. I was born while he was stationed at Pendleton in California. We moved a couple of times to different duty stations around the country. We didn't move here until after my mother died."

And just like that, all of that newly released tension came flooding back.

Why had she kept asking questions he so clearly didn't want to answer? They'd been having a lovely afternoon, and she'd gone and ruined it.

Stupid mouth.

"I'm sorry. I didn't mean to bring up such a painful subject."

"It's fine."

She didn't buy that for a second.

As though to prove his point, Daryl offered more.

"Dad was born on the reservation west of town. So, when he had to leave the Corps to take care of me, he went back to the only place he knew. But there wasn't a lot of work to be had there, and being a grunt doesn't exactly translate well to marketable job skills in civilian life. So, he ended up here, doing the only other thing he knew how to do. Wrangle horses."

That was probably the most she'd ever heard him say at one time about himself. And yet it raised more questions than it answered. Which she hesitated to pursue, but since he'd opened the door...

"So, you went from living on military bases to living on a ranch. That must have been quite an adjustment for you."

"I hated it. For the first few months, I hated everything about this place." The admission held a wealth of feeling.

"What changed your mind?"

"I saw my first horse being born. Actually, I *helped* my first horse being born." A small smile of remembered pleasure quirked his full lips.

Her tummy did a little squiggle.

Stop that.

"How old were you?"

"Almost eight."

Her eyes widened. "And they let you help?"

"Being that young was why I could. The mare in labor was having trouble. Her foal was caught up inside and wouldn't come out. The vet was a no-show, and the foal was so big that nobody else could get a hand far enough inside to straighten out the leg that was stuck. But my hands were a lot smaller than any of the adults' were."

Realizing what he meant, Amelia's stomach gave a different kind of squiggle.

"Oh, my goodness. You had to..." She couldn't say it. The picture in her head was bad enough.

"Foal came out slicker than snot after that, as Zeke would say." Daryl laughed at the face she made. "Jasper was the most beautiful thing I'd ever laid eyes on. I never wanted to leave the barn after that. The hands were always chasing me off so they could work, until one day Zeke put a muck rake in my hand and told me if I was going to be underfoot anyway, I might as well make myself useful."

The happiness that radiated from him as he shared those memories changed something about his entire demeanor. He seemed younger, somehow. More vibrant.

It was too good a look on a man already dangerously attractive.

"Zeke, huh?" He'd been resting in the bunkhouse when they

returned from church. The stitches in his leg would keep him off of his feet for a few days, but as he predicted, that and the bruised muscle were the worst of it. "So, he was even working for your father all the way back then."

And just like that, the happiness and vibrancy were gone.

"No. He worked for Kim." He gave Pepper a nudge, sending the horse into a trot.

Cleo, distressed at being left behind, pranced a few steps and gave the reins a mighty tug. Distracted, Amelia let the mare have her head.

Zeke had worked for Kim?

She'd just assumed Hank had purchased the ranch on his return to Hayden. But that didn't seem to be the case. If Kim had owned the Circle R, and Zeke worked for her at the time Hank and Daryl lived there, did that mean Hank had worked for her, too?

Daryl opened the gate between two of the grazing fields, securing it behind them before riding on again, all still in the stony silence that had descended over them.

Amelia's throat ached from holding back the emotions roiling higher with every silent mile they covered. She never seemed to know when to keep her mouth shut lately.

Charles had flung that accusation at her with increasing regularity when she'd tried to get a say in at least some of the final wedding details. It hadn't seemed a lot to ask, seeing as she was the bride. But he'd blamed her for any strife that arose between her and his mother, telling her she needed to learn the art of compromise.

Dipping a hand into the bag slung around her saddle horn, she popped an antacid out of a roll and quickly chewed, the once delicious sandwich starting to feel like a lead weight in her gurgling stomach.

Charles hadn't wanted compromise. He wanted a pretty puppet who would do what he said without question or argument. When she 'overstepped,' he either yelled or went totally silent to punish her.

Not that she thought Daryl was trying to punish her for being too nosy. The end result, however, was the same. Just like a dog beaten one too many times flinches at a raised hand, her body reacted to any perceived disapproval with an overabundance of stomach acid and nerves.

Pepper drew to a halt. Cleo followed suit without Amelia's direction. Looking over at Daryl, it was difficult to tell what he was thinking, his expression shaded under the brim of his hat in the afternoon sun.

"Look." He nodded off to their left.

She let out a small gasp of delight.

About a half-dozen horses grazed in the field, and romping around them were four gangly legged foals. The two larger ones were chasing each other around the group in a fit of the zoomies. The younger two played between the legs of the adults, who were ignoring their antics as they cropped grass with the quiet aplomb of seasoned parents.

After watching the young horses frolic for a few minutes, they turned their mounts toward the final gate and then the barn. Daryl didn't say anything, but it felt like he'd just offered her an olive branch. If so, she'd take it.

Being in discord with him, even for a short time, was making her miserable

When they dismounted in the stable yard, Amelia accepted Ned's offer to remove Cleo's saddle for her because she wasn't certain she could manage it on her own. The last thing she wanted to do was land on her butt in front of everyone.

She did, however, insist on handling Cleo's grooming herself. It was dirty, monotonous work, but it was the price you paid in return to the horse for the service it gave you. That, and a nice flake of hay.

One more thing her mother would have been horrified about. Amelia grooming her mounts after her lessons. Which she would have known about, if she'd ever bothered to show up and watch like most mothers did.

Meredith Westlake didn't do barns.

Daryl had already gone back to the house after grooming Pepper, so she walked there alone when she was done. It wasn't that she expected him to stay glued to her side every minute. But she still had to squelch a small pinch of disappointment he hadn't waited.

After a glass of cold water from the kitchen sink to quench her parched throat, she retreated to her bedroom. She shed her borrowed boots, jeans—now well-secured thanks to a belt from Kim—and top, all of which smelled too much of horse to continue wearing for the rest of the day. She was dirty, sweaty, her muscles ached, and she was pretty sure she smelled just as bad as her clothes did.

She loved it.

And there was still more to do. After her shower, she had to go help Kim with the evening meal. There had already been a few pots simmering on the stove, but she knew there was a sack of potatoes with her name on it waiting.

Hair pinned up to keep it dry, Amelia opened the door to the bathroom. She was reaching for the clasp on her bra when her brain caught up with her senses and she realized there was somebody else in the bathroom, stepping out of the shower.

And he was naked.

She froze.

Time stopped.

The world tilted.

Every reasonable thought she'd ever had went flying out of her head. All she could do was stare at the long expanse of bronzed skin that faced her, still gleaming with water that ran down a strong, muscular back to the taut globes of his—

She must have made a noise because Daryl's head whipped around, his eyes first widening, then narrowing as he saw her standing in the doorway. With slow deliberateness, he reached over and dragged a towel off of the bar on the wall and wrapped it around his waist.

Only then did he turn to face her.

The view was even better from this side, although some heretofore unknown part of her mourned the fact he'd put the towel on first.

His black hair was slicked back from his face, revealing its stark beauty of strong cheekbones and piercing eyes. There was a small smattering of the same dark hair running across a chest that was impressively well proportioned with his shoulders, which looked even broader now that there wasn't a shirt hiding them. That line of hair arrowed down his belly and disappeared under the knot in the towel, leaving her imagination running riot over just what was concealed below it.

A small squeak erupted from her lips.

Stop looking, stop looking, stop looking.

She couldn't stop looking.

How could she? He was in her bathroom. *Naked.* It wasn't her fault her eyes wouldn't listen to her. Or that they were devouring every incredible, delectable inch of him like a hot fudge sundae. Or that the sight of his ass was now forever burned into her memory banks.

She should have been horrified.

God help her, she wasn't.

Reluctantly, she finally managed to wrangle her eyes under control and drag them back up that expansive chest all the way to his face.

"I, ah, was going to take a shower." The words were barely a whisper. "Why are you in my bathroom?" Because, God, he'd been *naked.*

One dark brow raised in what might have been amusement. "It's a Jack-and-Jill."

"I don't know what that means."

"It means it's *our* bathroom." He gestured behind him to the door standing open on the side of the bathroom opposite hers. She'd just assumed it went to the hallway. Evidently, it led to another bedroom. *His* bedroom. Why hadn't she considered that possibility?

Because I'm an idiot.

"Oh." She wracked her brain, but there was no etiquette lesson for her to draw on that covered walking in on a naked man. "I'm, um, so sorry." She stammered over the apology, even as that other naughty-minded part of her was willing the knot in the towel to give way. "I was going to take a shower."

She was repeating herself, but at this point she was lucky there were actual words coming out of her mouth.

His lips twitched at the corners. "I can see that."

She frowned. He could...oh.

Oh!

She was standing there in nothing more than her bra and panties.

Which meant Daryl was getting almost as big an eyeful as she was.

Horrified, she squeaked out, "Oh, my God!" and spun back into her room, slamming the door and leaning against it, hands covering her face in mortification.

That did not just happen. It couldn't have.

But it did.

Not only had she walked in on Daryl and stood there staring at all his glorious nakedness, she'd been practically naked herself.

How was she ever going to face him again?

Chapter 15

Dinner was awkward.

Forking up a mouthful of lumpy mashed potatoes, Daryl did his best to act as though nothing had changed between him and the woman sitting beside him. But Amelia hadn't met his gaze for more than two seconds since he entered the kitchen.

And him?

He hadn't been able to keep his eyes off her.

From the normal tone of the conversation around the table, it didn't seem as though anyone else noticed the strained silence that enveloped the two of them like a bubble waiting to burst. Which was good. Because really, what could he possibly say to explain? *Sorry, but Amelia walked in on me buck-ass naked and she's a little weirded out by it?*

Hell, *he* was a little weirded out by it.

Not so much that she'd seen his ass. Years with the rodeo pretty much cured him of any body-shyness, especially with regard to women. No, the weirdness came from the way her eyes had dilated to a dark, smoky green. That had been the look of a woman in lust.

Amelia freaking Westlake.

Could his life get any more complicated?

Evidently yes, because if he was honest with himself, she wasn't the only one in that bathroom who'd gotten a little turned on.

Sure, he'd always acknowledged she was pretty. But never, not once, had the thought of her being *sexy* ever entered his brain. Dainty. Fragile. Ethereal. But never sexy. But as he'd turned around and her eyes had traveled his body like he was a sculpture she was trying to memorize, he'd been free to look his fill at hers without her realizing it.

And he'd liked what he saw. A lot.

Too much.

She wasn't a buckle bunny, or a bar pick up, or even just an ordinary woman. She was the Westlake princess. Someone so fucking far out of his league he was surprised lightning didn't come down and strike him dead for the lustful thoughts he couldn't keep out of his brain.

Because she'd been pure perfection.

He'd felt her tiny waist all the times he'd helped her in and out of his truck. What he hadn't noticed before were her hips. How they flared in a pleasant curve, giving her a bit of an hourglass shape despite the fact she was so obviously underweight.

And her breasts.

Dear Lord, her breasts.

Even encased in plain white cotton, they'd been delectable-looking little treats. A perfect handful. Impossible to see what color her nipples were, but judging by her almost translucent pale skin, he could imagine them being the most delicate shade of pink. Something like the inside of the seashells he'd used to pick up on the beach as a kid.

Put all together, she was a package that could tempt any man to insanity.

But the fact remained, he wasn't just any man, any more than she was just any woman. He was her bodyguard. True, he wasn't protecting so much as babysitting, but the same basic principles applied. She was a job. End of story.

So why, then, couldn't he seem to stop thinking about her? Or looking at her? Or thinking about looking at her?

Amelia, on the other hand, wouldn't even meet his eyes when she passed him the peas, not skipping a beat in her conversation with Chaz—the bastard—who'd once again claimed the seat on her other side. Passing the dish on to Horace, he stabbed a piece of chicken and forked it into his mouth, chewing hard enough to make his teeth hurt.

Wasn't it just like a woman? *She'd* walked in on *him*, and she was giving him the silent treatment, as though he'd been the one in the wrong.

By the time the apple pie was served, his skin felt about two sizes too small for his body. His temper, the one he'd tamed and caged so many years ago, was jerking its leash, trying to break free.

If Amelia thought he was going to put up with her high-and-mighty act for the rest of their time together, she had another think coming.

For the second night in a row, he escaped the dinner table for the barn.

Too bad there wasn't enough light left for him to take one of the horses out and pound out his foul mood with a good gallop. Maybe grooming the frisky stallion that had put Zeke out of commission that morning would be enough of a challenge to do the job. They'd started to build a rapport in the ring. It would be interesting to see if any of it stuck.

He gathered his supplies and headed for the big box stall in the rear of the barn. Along the way, another horse hung her head over her stall door and gave a plaintive nicker for attention. He detoured over to stroke the palomino's nose, chuckling as she blew a frustrated puff of warm air into his face.

"Feeling out of sorts, Miss Delilah?"

He slipped inside the large birthing stall and ran his hands over the mare's swollen sides. She shuffled restlessly, her tail flicking in irritation. "I know you're uncomfortable, darlin'," he crooned. "But you'll be having this baby soon enough."

Very soon, judging by how low her belly was hanging.

Changing his mind about the stallion, he set to work giving the mare a gentle but thorough brushing. He took the extra time with the curry comb to massage muscles that were likely tight and sore from carrying all the extra weight, and finished by wrapping her tail.

Her hind end was soft and loose, but not enough so that she'd be foaling tonight. Probably. With horses, it was always better safe than sorry. He'd seen mares fool everyone and go into labor without having shown even one of the usual indicators.

By the time he made it back to his room, he not only had his temper back under control, but he was feeling a little foolish for letting himself get so bothered by Amelia's snub. Why the hell should he care if she preferred listening to Chaz than say two words to him?

So what if she'd looked at his naked body with the hot interest of a woman thinking about claiming what she saw? It wasn't as though he *wanted* her to do any claiming. Theirs was a working relationship. Period.

He'd been staring at the ceiling, trying to will himself to sleep for almost an hour, when he heard the faint knock. It took a second to realize it hadn't come from the door to the hallway.

Which meant it could only be one person.

Muttering a curse at the way his heart did a little leap at that knowledge, he pulled on his jeans before stalking to the bathroom door and yanking it open.

Amelia blinked, looking startled by the abrupt opening. "I, ah, hope I didn't wake you."

"No."

"Oh. Good." She fidgeted with the belt on her robe, her gaze darting to his face and away several times. "I, ah, I just wanted to, ah..." She yanked on the belt again as though she didn't know what else to do with her hands before blurting out, "Could you maybe please put on a shirt or something?"

Some perverse part of him that enjoyed her discomfort made him grin.

"Why? It isn't anything you haven't seen before."

Pink stained her cheeks at his sarcastic reminder, making him feel like an ass. With a curse, he retrieved his shirt from the floor and yanked it on, doing up two buttons to hold it closed.

"Better?"

"Yes. Thank you." She cleared her throat and raised her eyes to meet his. "I wanted to apologize. For earlier."

"It's okay. You didn't realize we shared a bathroom."

"No, not for that. Well, yes, for that, too. But I meant for not immediately turning around and leaving the instant I realized you were..."

"Naked?"

"And for being so rude as to stare at you like you were a...a..."

"Naked man?"

"Would you please stop saying that?" Her face was no longer pink but red-hot crimson.

He could probably fry an egg on it.

"Sorry."

The look she gave him said she doubted the sincerity of that apology.

Smart girl.

"Anyway, I have no excuse for my reprehensible behavior. You have my most sincere apologies, and my promise that nothing like that will ever happen again."

He could have been a gentleman and just accepted her apology. But the very pretty words in the very matter-of-fact tone scratched at his temper like spurweed.

"I might think you meant all that, Princess, if you didn't sound exactly like one of your daddy's slick press releases."

The sharp breath she sucked in said he'd hit his mark.

Eyes narrowing, Amelia tilted her chin up, meeting his gaze

dead-on for the first time.

"Okay, fine. If you want simple, tiny words you can understand, then here it is. I'm sorry I walked in on you. I'm sorry I ogled you like you were a magazine centerfold. And I'm sorry you're just so damned good-looking that my tongue gets tied into knots every time I try to talk to you when your shirt is off." She stabbed a finger into his chest. "And don't call me Princess!" She spun and started toward her bedroom.

"Hey!"

She whirled back to face him, her expression belligerent. "What?"

"Just for the record, I looked, too."

Shocked eyes and a pink-lipped mouth hanging open were the last things he saw as he shut the door between them.

He would have laughed if he didn't think she might hear and believe he was laughing at her, when in fact the joke was on him. She got tongue-tied because he was too good-looking?

What the hell was he supposed to do with *that*?

Absolutely nothing. She was still his job, his responsibility. Nothing had changed.

And yet, it felt like everything had.

Groaning into his hands, he sank onto the edge of the bed. Looked like that lightning bolt had come down and struck his sorry ass, after all. All that remained to be seen was if it was going to just singe him a little, or burn him all the way to ash.

⸻◆⸻

I looked too.

Lying in bed, Amelia kept turning the words over and over in her head, trying to figure them out. Were they meant to assuage her guilt by making them even about seeing each other almost naked? Or did he mean he'd *looked*, like, really looked, the way she had?

Her stomach clenched even as her heart raced at the possibility.

She knew she didn't have the kind of body men found arousing. In fact, she was very decidedly *un*sexy. So much so that the only other time a man had seen her stripped to her underwear, he'd left her aching and unfulfilled on the bed while he went to take a phone call.

It couldn't get any plainer than that what she lacked.

That experience had left her with a definite crack in her self-image. Compounded by what happened the night of her engagement party, it was a wonder she hadn't shattered into a million pieces already.

So, sexy? No. The best she could hope for was sophisticated.

And that was with her clothes on.

But the way Daryl said those words...

They'd held an undertone, almost a promise, that had her believing maybe, despite what the mirror told her, he'd liked what he saw.

Even showcased in the no-frills panties and bra from Walmart.

She felt a flash of regret that her practical side had made her put the pretty blue satin bra back on the rack. Which was stupid, of course. She wasn't interested in being sexy for Daryl, or for any other man right now.

But having him express admiration for her body—if that's what it had been—was like a balm helping to hold those fractured pieces of her confidence together.

I looked too.

What did that *mean*? Damn it, he could have been a little clearer, instead of going all cryptic and snarky. At least when *she'd* said—

Oh, shit.

Amelia dragged the pillow over her face to muffle her mortified groan.

Had she really compared him to a centerfold model? And told him that the sight of his bare chest made her too stupid to speak? She groaned again.

That was why she'd rehearsed a very concise apology before getting up the nerve to knock on his door. So she wouldn't trip over her own tongue.

Which she'd gone and done anyway.

She wanted to be angry about him calling her apology one of her father's press releases, but, really, he was right. She'd been so embarrassed earlier she hadn't even been able to look at him all through dinner. The only way she could face him to apologize was to put on her game face and treat the situation like any other social misstep she had to make amends for.

Only, the game face hadn't quite fit her this time. And there was no way to pretend staring at a naked man could be dealt with the same way as spilling one's tea.

Especially *that* naked man.

This time when she moaned, it was for an entirely different reason.

She'd never seen so much male perfection before. Lillian had always drooled over Daryl's broad shoulders and long, powerful legs, and that had been fully clothed. Lil had no idea what she was missing. If she ever got a look at him in all his glory...

A surprising spurt of jealousy burned through her at the mere thought of her gorgeous, confident, vivacious friend getting near Daryl's naked anything.

Then she laughed at herself.

How ridiculous. Lil had admired him through an artist's eye, nothing more. And even if there had been something more personal to her interest, it wouldn't matter. Daryl wasn't hers. She had no right to be jealous.

That didn't stop the tiny bud of possessiveness that took root inside of her.

Or the curiosity about the scars she'd noticed marking his body in several places. Remnants of his rodeo days? She'd love to ask, but doing so would mean admitting, once again, she'd seen him naked.

She wasn't about to open up *that* line of conversation again.

Ever.

No, as far as she was concerned, tomorrow would be a day like any other, the shower incident completely forgotten. Or, at least, ignored.

If only she could believe Daryl would cooperate with that plan. But somehow, she doubted he was going to let her off the hook that easily.

And deep inside, there was a tiny part of her that didn't want him to.

Chapter 16

Eggs were a lot harder to master than pancakes.

Luckily, when cooking for a group as large as the one seated at the Circle R's table, scrambled was the style of choice. Unluckily, Amelia couldn't seem to keep them from getting overdone, which made them about as appetizing to eat as warm rubber. Though that didn't keep the men from shoveling them down like it was the last meal they'd ever get.

She wanted to apologize. But if they were willing to leave the matter alone, she'd go along with their generous silence. Dinner, she vowed, would be perfect.

It wasn't even close.

Though it wasn't really her fault.

The owner of the temperamental black stallion paid an unscheduled visit late in the afternoon. From the tight-lipped expression on Kimama's usually placid face, it wasn't the first time he'd done it, either.

By the time he left several hours later, everything was behind schedule. There were still other horses to be seen to and regular chores to get caught up on before everyone straggled into the house and settled around the table to eat.

What had once been a very choice rump roast had been kept warm so long it was little better than the rubbery eggs.

Amelia was both embarrassed and annoyed.

"Why doesn't Hank tell the man he needs to make an appointment if he wants to come and check on his horse's progress?" she asked Kim as they stacked the dishwasher.

"People like that don't take well to being told what to do by someone they're paying to work for them."

"It's still rude," Amelia muttered, rattling a platter a little harder than necessary to make it fit in the rack. She should know. Her mother was one of those people.

"It is. But the horse world is a small one. We've got an excellent reputation within it, but it wouldn't take much more than a few bad comments from men like him to change that." Kim shrugged. "So, we put up with the rudeness and keep reminding ourselves that while we only have to deal with them for a little while, they have to live with themselves forever."

Amelia laughed. "I guess since Hank was a Marine, he's used to dealing with people he can't tell to their face they're being idiots."

Thea had told her Doyle found himself calling on his own military training more than once since starting up his security business. Not for the actual security part. For the dealing with ridiculous requests from clients part.

Closing the dishwasher, Kim turned and looked at her with surprise. "Daryl talked to you about his father?"

"He mentioned a bit."

"Did he, now?"

Amelia didn't like the keen interest in Kim's stare, intense hazel eyes over a slightly long nose that gave her the appearance of an all-knowing owl. She looked around the kitchen, desperate for something, anything, to do, but everything had been wiped, stacked, or put away.

"Come, let's have some more coffee and talk." She phrased it as an offer, but Kim was already pulling two fresh mugs down from the cabinet.

Torn, Amelia waffled a moment before admitting she wanted to stay. She and Kim had spent a lot of time together in the last two days, but they'd talked about little besides cooking.

And *still* it was the most enjoyable conversation she'd had in the past month.

Well, almost.

Amelia brought the sugar and creamer back to the table. "You wouldn't have any decaf, would you?"

"Are you having trouble sleeping?"

"A little. I think maybe I just haven't adjusted to ranch time yet."

She wasn't about to admit she'd spent the better part of the night tossing and turning because every time she closed her eyes, all she could see was Daryl in all his glorious nakedness. It was like the image had been branded onto her eyelids.

Or that once she'd finally fallen asleep, she'd woken several times with her body all achy and yearning. It wasn't hard to guess what her dreams had been about.

Or who.

She'd never had those kinds of dreams about anyone before. Including Charles. She certainly had no business dreaming about Daryl that way. Even if he was twice the man Charles ever was.

Maybe it was a good thing he'd been avoiding her all day.

Okay, maybe avoiding was too strong a term. He'd been busy with the horses in the morning, and helping Hank with his irritating customer in the afternoon. And he'd made a point to check in with her several times to make sure she was doing okay. But other than that, she'd either been with Kim or on her own.

It was only one day, but the truth was, she'd missed him.

Which can't be good.

"Hmm." Kim reached for the kettle on the stove. "Perhaps tea instead."

"That would be lovely." Come to think of it, she hadn't needed one of Kim's special teas to soothe her stomach since that first time. A minor victory, perhaps, but still a win.

"My son rarely speaks of himself to people, and especially not about his younger years."

Interesting that Kim claimed Daryl as her son, while he'd made it clear she was his stepmother. It said a lot about their relationship. Which meant Amelia *really* wasn't comfortable talking about anything else he'd shared with her the previous day.

"Daryl strikes me as a very private man," she replied with care.

"He's much like his father in that regard."

Amelia smiled. There were many similarities between father and son. Reticence was only one of them. "Did Hank ride in the rodeo when he was younger as well?"

Kim nodded, answering the call of the boiling kettle. "It's where he learned his skill with horses. He was a champion roper before he left to join the Marines at seventeen. The youngest to ever win the title at the time," she said with pride.

"Then that's another thing they have in common." She tried to picture a young Hank Raintree roping calves and came up with an image of Daryl instead. "It's obvious that neither one of them likes to brag about themselves."

"Unlike our Chaska, who doesn't know how to do anything else." Kim said it with a small laugh as she brought two steaming mugs to the table, making the observation affectionate rather than judgmental. She went to the cupboard for a plate and filled it with gingersnaps from the rooster-shaped cookie jar, putting it on the table between them before sitting.

"Yes, Chaz is very much the opposite of Daryl in that regard."

But she sensed there was a reason behind Chaz's braggart ways that had little to do with true arrogance. He might laugh, and joke, and chat her up like a big-time rodeo flirt, but there was a hint of something in his eyes while he did that struck her as almost sad.

They sipped their tea in silence for a few minutes. There were so many questions Amelia wanted to ask. But she didn't have the right to pry, so she stayed silent, nibbling on a cookie as she enjoyed the comfortable sense of peace that always settled over her when she was with Kimama.

"We'll be making ham and eggs for breakfast tomorrow."

Amelia bit into her cookie to hide a grimace. "I'm not so sure the men would appreciate me messing up their eggs a second day in a row."

"They ate them, didn't they?"

"That doesn't mean they enjoyed them."

"They appreciate a good effort. You'll do fine."

Amelia wasn't nearly as confident as Kim. "Sometimes a good effort isn't good enough. Maybe you should just do the eggs and save everyone another round of indigestion."

Kim gave her a look laced with disappointment. "I didn't take you for a quitter."

"I'm not!" The accusation stung. "I just don't want other people to suffer for my ineptness."

But was that it? Were her concerns about the men's stomachs, or her own embarrassment? God, when had she become such a coward?

Oh, right. When her mother made it a mortal sin to show herself being anything less than perfect. In appearance. In actions. In conversation. Her parents' little princess had to exude skill and grace in all things, because it would reflect back on them.

Her throat felt suddenly tight. She was so tired of the pale, gilded-cage life her parents had constructed for her.

No, that wasn't entirely fair. They might have made the cage, but she was complicit in her own imprisonment in it. Not once had she fought for what *she'd* wanted, what *she'd* needed to make herself happy. She'd been too busy worrying about making everyone else happy instead.

Well, screw that shit, as Lillian would say.

Learning to cook fluffy eggs wasn't exactly a lofty goal of self-fulfillment, but she had to start somewhere.

"Okay, if you're sure, then yes, I'd like to give it another try."

Kim smiled. "You'll do just fine."

Amelia wasn't a hundred percent certain she was talking about breakfast.

Eager to get off of the subject of herself, she asked, "I enjoyed riding around some of the ranch yesterday. It was so beautiful I almost didn't want to come back."

"I felt the same way the first time I saw it." Kim's smile turned wistful. "After growing up dirt poor, this looked like heaven to me."

Amelia grew up filthy rich, and she felt the same way.

"Of course, when Buck brought me here, it was called Oak Ridge Ranch, and it wasn't quite as large as it is now. Buck was my first husband," she said in response to Amelia's look of confusion. "He was a good man, my Buck, but not such a good *business*man.

"The place was in pretty bad shape when Hank Raintree showed up, looking for work. Buck was gone about a year by then, and I was having a tough time keeping the ranch afloat, seeing as how I knew even less about the business than Buck had." She shook her head, her expression one of fond indulgence. It was obvious she cared for her first husband, despite his flaws.

"If Hank is even half as brilliant with the horses as Daryl was yesterday with that crazy stallion, I doubt he had any trouble turning things around for you."

"He's amazing with them, no doubt. Not quite in his son's league, but I've yet to meet anyone who is. Daryl has a gift." She looked like she was going to say more on the subject, but took another sip of tea and continued her story instead. "As for turning the place around, well, truth is I almost didn't give him the chance. I didn't think I should hire someone who was already tied down to other responsibilities."

"As a single parent, you mean?"

Kim nodded. "I was sympathetic, of course. The boy had just lost his mother, and his relatives over at Rock Ridge...well, in any case, I felt bad, but I didn't have time to worry about a child being underfoot. I assumed either Hank's work or his parenting would suffer from having to divide his attention, and I told him so when I politely declined his inquiry for work."

Amelia almost asked what happened with Daryl's relatives, but bit back her question at the last second. It wasn't her business.

But oh, how she wanted it to be.

"What happened?"

"Well, Hank being Hank, he refused to take no for an answer. He convinced me to give him two weeks to show he could do the job without either part of his life being undermined."

Kim's lips quirked into a smile. "I was ready to beg him to stay on as foreman after only one. He might not have known much about running a ranch at the start, but he knew horses and he knew how to be in charge and get things done. The rest he figured out as he went. He wasn't about to admit there was anything he couldn't do if he worked hard enough at it."

The smile faded. "He was still grieving his wife then, and I think the hard work gave him something else to focus on. I guess the same way my trying to keep the ranch running kept me going after Buck passed on."

And maybe they'd both helped each other through their grief in other ways as well.

Not that it would have been wrong. Human contact was a vital need. But that might be where some of Daryl's reserve toward Kim stemmed from.

"It took almost a year of hard work, but we finally turned things around. I couldn't have done it without my Hanska. He wasn't always the easiest man to understand, or even get along with sometimes, but at the heart of him, I knew he was everything I ever wanted or needed to be my other half. It took me almost that whole year to convince the hardheaded man of that, but he finally agreed to marry me," she added with a self-satisfied look.

Amelia blinked in surprise.

"*You* asked *him* to marry you?"

"I didn't have much choice. If I waited on him to decide he'd proven himself, I'd probably still be waiting on a proposal. The man had some strange ideas about not bringing anything to the marriage. As if I needed anything but him and Daryl."

She stood and brought her empty mug to the sink, waving Amelia back down into her seat when she moved to do the same. "Finish your tea. The men will be done with evening chores soon, and I want to work more on my project before Hank comes in for the night."

Amelia had learned only that afternoon Kim's "projects" were the gorgeous rugs she'd been admiring all over the house. If she hadn't felt she'd be intruding, she would have asked if she could watch her work for a little while.

Instead, she curled her hands around her mug to anchor herself in place. "Thank you for the tea and conversation. I'll see you in the morning."

Just before she got to the door, Kim stopped and looked back.

"Even if he isn't blood of my blood, Daryl is still the son of my heart and I love him very much. There is nothing his father or I want more for him than to find his way home one day."

Amelia lingered over her lavender-scented tea, thinking about everything Kim had said. And all she hadn't. Clearly, Daryl hadn't left the ranch at his parents' instigation. They wanted him here. And judging by the look on his face while they'd been riding the land, Daryl wanted to be here, too.

So then, why wasn't he?

Chapter 17

"Why are you doing that?"

Amelia didn't look up from the chicken sandwiches she was making. "I thought we could take them with us on our ride."

Maybe it was presumptuous to assume they'd be picnicking again. But she'd been so excited when Daryl asked after breakfast if she'd like to ride out with him, she couldn't help but hope they'd be able to duplicate that almost perfect day.

Except this time, she'd keep her big mouth shut and not ruin it.

When Daryl stayed silent, she glanced up. He was standing in the open kitchen door, Stetson still in hand. His dark hair was in disarray, probably from running his fingers through it the way she'd seen him do whenever he put on or removed the battered hat. He didn't even seem aware he was doing it. It was more like an old habit he'd picked back up along with the hat.

Add in the slight scruff that darkened his face, and it was a very sexy, just-rolled-out-of-bed sort of look.

No, no, no!

She erased the thought in a panic. Not sexy. Not attractive. Not ruggedly handsome. Those were forbidden thoughts. Bad, bad thoughts. No good could come of thinking them.

"I meant, why isn't Kim doing it?" Daryl stuck his hat on a peg and closed the door behind him. The roomy kitchen seemed to shrink to half its size. "It's not your job to cook and clean around here."

She sliced through the last sandwich and wrapped it in wax paper as she answered.

"I'm perfectly capable of both. Granted, I'm still on a bit of a learning curve, but admit it, breakfast was darn good this morning." She knew it had been. Even Horace had complimented her eggs, and Horace never said anything at mealtime.

Until this morning, she hadn't been sure he could do more than grunt.

"Breakfast was great, but that's not the point."

"I'm glad you liked it." Silly to be pleased when she'd all but coerced the compliment out of him, but it still gave her a zing of accomplishment. "And if your point is that I should be sitting around doing nothing, then forget it." She reached into the wire basket hanging near the sink and pulled out two pieces of fruit. "Apple or pear?"

"No, my point is it's not your job to do manual labor."

"I hardly consider cooking or making sandwiches manual labor. And it's not Kim's job to cook and clean for me. Your parents are doing me a huge favor having me here. I'm more than happy to pitch in and earn my keep by helping her out while Ella's away. Now, apple or pear?"

Daryl looked confused. "Who's Ella?"

"Mike's wife. She usually helps with the cooking, but she's away visiting her sister who's having a baby, so Kim has been doing everything for everyone all by herself. I know I'm sometimes more hindrance than help because she has to keep stopping to show me how to do things, but I like to think in the long run I'll make her life a little easier while we're here. And besides, I enjoy spending time with her."

She gestured a little more forcefully with the fruit, temper starting to fray despite her best intentions to not let anything ruin their upcoming ride. "Now, for the last time, apple or pear?"

"I didn't know she had someone helping her."

"She's an amazing woman, Daryl, but she's not Wonder Woman. Cooking for all those men twice a day, every day, takes up most of her time as it is. If she had to do it alone, she'd never leave the kitchen. Fine, you're getting a pear." She put the apple back and placed two pears on the counter next to the sandwiches.

"I don't like pears."

Amelia shut her eyes and counted to five. Then ten.

I am not going to strangle him.

Once the urge lessened, she blew out a cleansing breath and reached for the pears with a forced smile. "Then apples it is."

Just as her hands closed over the fruit, Daryl's large hands closed over hers.

She froze.

Staring at their overlapping hands, her heart started to thud faster. Just like every time he helped her in and out of his truck, the contact did strange, squishy things to her insides. Only now, after what had happened in the bathroom, after those dreams that had haunted her for a second night in a row, the effect was even worse.

I'm in trouble here. Big trouble.

Did he feel it, too? This weird, visceral reaction?

It took a few long seconds before she could bring herself to look up at his face to see. His expression held no heat, no indication touching her instilled the slightest response. It reminded her of his blank work face.

Disappointment pinched her chest.

It seemed *I looked too* hadn't meant more than just that.

"Just...forget about the damn fruit." Daryl drew his hands back, fisting them briefly at his sides before sliding them into his back pockets as he took a step away.

"Okay." Her stupid heart was still galloping. All she could do was pray her face wasn't turning fifty shades of red. "Are we still going for our ride?"

Daryl gave a jerky nod and took another step toward the door.

"Sure. If you want to."

"Yes, please."

"Okay, then."

"Okay. Good." This wasn't awkward at all. "Just, ah, give me a minute to put the food in a bag and clean this up, and I'll be right out."

"Sure. I'll be at the barn."

He was reaching for his Stetson when the phone on the wall rang.

She put the sandwich fixings in the refrigerator while Daryl answered it, but the second she heard him say, "Slow down and tell me what happened," her attention was riveted back on him. It probably didn't have to do with her. Doyle would have called the burner cell.

But her stomach still cramped at the possibility.

It didn't seem like the person on the other end of the line was giving Daryl the chance to say much. Every time he started to ask a question, he was cut off and listened again. Finally, he said, "Okay, we'll be right there," and hung up. "Where's Kim?"

"She went to Gladstone." Ignoring Daryl's muttered curses that Kim had chosen today to go out of town, Amelia followed him as he headed toward the bedrooms. "Who was on the phone? What happened? Is everything okay?"

"It was Winnie. Something happened, but I don't know what. I couldn't understand half of what she was saying through all the crying, just that she needs Kim and she isn't answering her cell." He snatched his keys from the top of his dresser and turned, nearly knocking her over in his haste. He grabbed her shoulders and moved her out of his way.

She followed as he headed back to the living room. "Is it the baby?"

"I don't know." He stopped and looked at her. "I'm going to the school and make sure she's okay. Can you keep trying to get Kim on the phone and tell her what happened?"

"I'll call from the truck. I'm coming with you, don't even try to tell me no."

"Damn it, Amelia—"

"We're wasting time." She walked past Daryl and out the front door. She heard him utter a blistering curse, but a few seconds later he followed, helping her into the truck without another word.

He said nothing during the drive to the school on the Rock Ridge reservation where Winona was a kindergarten teacher. Judging by his expression, that had more to do with his worry about his sister than his aggravation with her coming along.

She hoped, anyway.

By the time they pulled into the parking lot outside the one-story school, Amelia had left two messages on Kim's voice mail from Daryl's burner. She'd also talked to Hank after she realized they'd left without telling him what was going on.

Inside the office, a compact Native American woman with mostly gray black hair worn in a thick braid down her back introduced herself as Mrs. Mantooth, the principal. She greeted them with an air of relief when Daryl identified himself as Winnie's brother.

"I hope you can get her to calm down," she said as she led them to a small staff break room. "She hasn't been able to stop crying."

The loud sobs coming from inside before the door was even opened caused a knot of dread to form in Amelia's stomach. Something was very, very wrong.

Winona sat on a faded gray sofa, her arms crossed tightly over her belly as she slowly rocked herself in time with her sobs. Another woman sat next to her, rubbing her back and talking in a soft, soothing voice.

At their arrival, the woman looked up, an expression of relief equal to Mrs. Mantooth's flitting across her face. She must have said something, because Winona looked up as well. With another sob, she stood and flew into Daryl's arms.

Amelia smiled a thank you to the woman as she left. Mrs. Mantooth stepped out and closed the door to give them privacy.

Uncertain for the first time about her decision to come along, Amelia hovered halfway between the door and the Raintree siblings.

What had she been thinking? She didn't belong here. She was an outsider, intruding on what was clearly a family moment. Why had she even considered she might be needed?

She was just about to go outside to call Kim again when Daryl sent her a helpless look of panic over his sister's head.

Doubt fled in the face of his unspoken plea.

Amelia approached and stroked Winona's shoulder, speaking soft words even though the girl was still sobbing too hard to understand anything other than the comfort being offered. Amelia had been in this very state herself less than a week ago. It wouldn't have mattered to her then if Thea and Lillian had been reciting the Gettysburg Address to her, just so long as they said it with empathy and love.

Daryl looked uncomfortable, but he continued to hold his sister as she sobbed into his shirt rather than try to force her from his embrace into Amelia's. He got major points for that. Slowly, the sobs lessened, turning into hiccups before Winona accepted the tissues Amelia put in her hand and blew her nose.

Taking advantage of the lull in the storm, Amelia took Winona's hands and led her back to the sofa. "Are you okay? Is it the baby?"

Winona shook her head, sniffling into the tissues. "No, the baby's fine. But..." Her eyes welled up again.

"What happened?"

"Kaitlin got...a phone call," Winona said, her voice hitching.

"Kaitlin?" The name rang a bell. "Oh, your roommate?"

Winona nodded. "Her brother...he's down in Texas, working the oil rigs. There was an accident, and h-he..." A sob choked her, then she wailed, "Oh God, he's hurt, and they don't know if...if he..." That was the last coherent thing she got out before she started sobbing into her hands again.

"Oh, sweetie." Amelia looked up at Daryl with a confused frown, rubbing Winona's back some more. "Is Kaitlin here?"

Winona shook her head. "Someone came and...picked her up. And I-I..."

Squatting in front of his sister, Daryl said softly, "Winnie, I know you and Kaitlin are close, but you can't go making yourself sick worrying about her brother like this. It's not good for the baby."

Refusing to meet his eyes, Winona started to rock again. "But he...he..." She darted a glance at Amelia.

As soon as she saw the absolute devastation in the girl's eyes, Amelia put the pieces together. "Oh, Winnie, honey. Kaitlin's brother? He's Kyle?"

A fresh downpour of tears was all the answer she needed.

Biting her lip, Amelia glanced at Daryl when he stood. He studied his sister's bowed head with a look that said he was quickly making the connection between his sister and her best friend's brother as well. Rage darkened his eyes almost to black.

Amelia kicked his foot to get his attention.

"Don't. You. Dare." She mouthed the warning to him as she continued to comfort his sister. The last thing Winona needed was her big brother going ballistic over the news of who the baby's father was.

Like a sign of divine intervention, Daryl's phone rang. He continued to stare at Amelia for a few long seconds, like he wasn't sure how to react to her admonition, before he stalked across the room to answer the call.

Amelia let out a relieved breath. The man was just a little intense when he was angry.

Winona's sobs turned to hitching breaths as she tried to get them under control. Her dark eyes, so like her brother's, were puffy and bloodshot, any makeup she'd been wearing earlier in the day long gone. "What am I...going to...do?"

"You're going to calm down, just like Daryl said you should. I know it's hard, but you have to try and think about the baby. You can't do anything for Kyle right this minute, but you can take care of his child. Do you think you can do that for him?"

"Yes. Yes," she said again with a little more conviction, "I can do that."

"Good." Amelia handed her the box of tissues. "I'll be right back, okay?" After getting a small nod, she went over to where Daryl stood near the door. He was just sliding his phone back into his pocket.

"Kim's on her way."

"Good." She'd managed to give Winona something to focus on for the moment, but it wouldn't be long before grief and worry started tearing at her again and battered down that small bastion of calm.

"So, Kyle is..."

Amelia sighed. "Yes."

"And you—" He bit off his words as the door opened a few inches, allowing Mrs. Mantooth to poke her head in. She glanced over at Winona, still seated on the couch, mopping her face with a wad of tissues, and beckoned the two of them out into the hallway.

"How is she?"

"A little better," Amelia replied, "but she's still very upset. You know about the bad news concerning Kaitlin's brother?"

Mrs. Mantooth nodded.

"Kaitlin was called out of class to take the phone call in the office. She was just devastated. She was too upset to drive herself home, and knowing they're friends, I called Winona down to wait with her until someone could come and pick her up. Only that seems to have backfired, since by the time Kaitlin left, Winona was in just as bad a state as she was." She sounded sympathetic, but confused. "I'd hoped she'd be able to take over her class again after lunch."

It was more of a question than a statement.

Daryl shook his head. "There's no way she's going to be in any shape to stay. Her mother is on her way to take her home."

"Oh, dear. That's going to be a problem."

"And why is that?"

"We've already called in the closest substitute teacher to take over

Miss Blackhawk's, Kaitlin's, class for the rest of the day. The only other one we could get to cover for Winona would take almost an hour to get here, and that's if she's even available."

"Well, can't someone else take over for her in the meantime?" Daryl asked. "What about you?"

"Normally I would, but my assistant is out sick today, and that leaves only me in the office to keep things running. With budget cuts, we're lucky to have enough teachers to fill all the classes we need. We just don't have any extra staff to move around."

"Well, Winnie certainly can't stay. You'll need to figure something out."

An awful, wonderful idea popped into Amelia's head.

"Winona teaches kindergarten, doesn't she?" she asked.

"Yes. Why, do you know someone?" There was a hint of desperate hope in Mrs. Mantooth's voice.

Amelia refused to look at Daryl. If she did, she'd chicken out.

"Yes, I do. Me."

Chapter 18

Daryl stared at Amelia. He must have heard her wrong. "*You?*"

Amelia gave a quick nod. "I'm a teacher."

"You are?" Mrs. Mantooth sounded hopeful.

He sounded as confused as he felt. "You are?"

What the hell?

"Yes. I'm fully qualified at the elementary level. I received my teaching certificate from Brown. And while I'm not accredited in this state, I think my credentials would make it acceptable for me to watch over a kindergarten class for a few hours. Don't you?"

Mrs. Mantooth pursed her lips, clearly caught between need and worry. "Oh, dear. I don't know if I could allow that. It would be most irregular."

"True, but this is something of an irregular situation, wouldn't you say?"

"Well, yes. But still..." The principal looked unconvinced.

Daryl's brain finally came out of its stall. Amelia was a teacher? Since when?

He knew she'd attended some fancy school back East at the same time Thea went west to college in California, but he always assumed she'd just gone to get out from under her parents' thumb for a few years. She'd never struck him as a career-minded kind of person.

Another in a growing line of incorrect assumptions, it would seem.

All he'd ever seen was the princess. He never bothered to look beneath the shiny surface for the woman hiding under all that emotional armor. Most people didn't. Which was why everyone continued to underestimate her.

Including him.

But he was looking now. And damned if he didn't like what he was seeing.

After quizzing Amelia for a few minutes, Mrs. Mantooth agreed she was more than qualified despite her limited classroom experience, and relented.

Not that she really had much choice.

"Given the circumstances, I believe we can make this work until the end of the school day. As long as I stop in frequently to monitor the classroom for myself."

Amelia looked pleased with her decision.

Daryl was less so.

He took Amelia aside. "I'm not sure this is a good idea."

"Do you have a better one?" She smiled when he scowled at her. "Don't worry. I can handle a couple of kindergarteners." Her smile faded. "I really am qualified, you know."

"I know. I didn't understand all of that teacher talk you were doing, but I know you wouldn't lie about something like this."

"Oh." She looked sweetly confused. "Then what's the problem?"

"The problem is...hell." He pulled his hand through his hair in frustration. "I just don't like the idea of you being exposed like this. We got away with no one recognizing you at church the other day, but this is really pushing our luck."

She had the nerve to laugh. "I doubt very many five-year-olds read the society page."

He didn't appreciate her humor. "Don't you think she's going to want your full name and go check out your credentials as soon as she gets back to her office?"

"Oh. I suppose she will." She chewed her lower lip. "But

contacting Brown shouldn't set off any alarms anywhere, should it?"

"Probably not," he admitted. "But it's a chance we shouldn't take."

Amelia placed her hand on his arm. "If I don't do this, then Winona has to stay with her class. Do you really think she's in any condition to do that?"

No, damn it.

That didn't make him like it any better.

"Fine. But I'll be right outside the classroom door."

"Stay with your sister."

"But—"

"At least until your mother gets here."

"Stepmother."

A scowl dragged Amelia's lips downward. "You need to stop doing that."

"Doing what?" he asked, confused.

She sighed. "Never mind. Go sit and wait with your *half*-sister." He found he didn't care for the emphasis she put on the word. "Did Kim say when she'd be getting here?"

"Not long. Half an hour, maybe." Which was about twenty-nine minutes too long for him to be left in sole charge of Winona's emotional well-being.

Especially when he went back into the breakroom and found his sister—funny how he'd never noticed not calling her his half-sister until Amelia said it—had worked herself back up into another round of crying.

He'd almost managed to get the waterworks stopped when Kim arrived and they started all over again. He relinquished his spot next to her with relief and gratitude. After promising to deliver Winnie's car to the ranch, he watched them walk out to Kim's SUV, Winnie leaning into her mother's side, Kim's arm wrapped in a protective shield around her.

A tiny piece of him, usually buried under years of cynical

detachment, felt a pinch of jealousy. He'd never had that kind of close relationship with Kim.

His choice.

One made by an angry, bitter boy who resented having his mother's spot filled by someone else so soon. So, he'd kept his stepmother at arm's length, no matter how hard she tried to get closer. He liked her. He respected her. But he'd never quite been able to forgive her.

Maybe it's time to change that.

Something to chew over later. As he walked down the quiet hallway to Winnie's classroom, he started to worry instead about how things were going for Amelia. She might have a degree, but had she ever even set foot inside of a classroom full of rambunctious kids before?

She was too mild-mannered, her feelings much too tender. They might only be five-year-olds, but those kids were going to eat her alive.

Just one more incorrect assumption on his part, as it turned out.

They freaking *adored* her.

Looking in through the upper glass in the door, Daryl watched in bemusement as the class sat cross-legged in a semicircle, listening with rapt attention as Amelia read from a storybook. The door muffled the actual words, but he could tell from her animated expressions she was using an array of voices to go with the characters. The kids loved it. They giggled, groaned, gasped, until she reached the last page and they begged for another.

And another.

And another.

Finally, Amelia put down the last book. Whatever she said had the class scrambling to their feet and rushing over to the small kid-sized tables with an assortment of crayons, markers, and construction paper. Only one girl stayed behind, staring up at Amelia with the saddest big brown eyes Daryl had ever seen.

After putting away the books, Amelia went back to the girl and knelt in front of her. Following a few minutes of one-sided conversation, Amelia stood again and held out her hand. The girl shook her head and stayed where she was, hugging her knees, face pressed to her legs, curled up on herself like a pill bug trying to hide in plain sight.

Not looking frustrated in the least, Amelia went to the other children. She took the time to stop and talk to each of them, bringing glowing smiles to their faces before they went back to work on their pictures with even more enthusiasm. A few minor squabbles broke out over possession of the choicest crayons, but Amelia handled them with calm efficiency, like she'd been doing it for years instead of hours.

And through it all, Amelia kept circling back to the little girl sitting alone on the floor. She sat next to her, talked to her. But as far as Daryl could tell, the child never responded. She'd just hide her face against her legs and sit as still as a rock until Amelia left her alone again.

What Amelia couldn't see, though, was that every time she walked away to interact with the rest of the class, the girl picked up her head and tracked her every move with a hungry gaze that caused Daryl's chest to tighten in sympathy. The child clearly wanted Amelia's attention, but was either too shy or too afraid to accept it.

As promised, Mrs. Mantooth came by several times to check on Amelia and the class. Daryl stepped away during one of those visits to call Kim. Winnie, it seemed, had insisted on staying at her apartment until they got news about Kyle's condition rather than go to the ranch as planned. Kim was staying with her.

When there was just half an hour left to go until dismissal, Mrs. Mantooth came by again, but didn't bother going into the classroom. She just watched through the glass with him, a satisfied look creasing her face.

"I have to admit, I didn't think this was going to work out quite so well. But it's clear Miss Westlake makes up for her lack of practical experience with natural aptitude."

He winced a little at the use of Amelia's name. But it was true. He'd never seen her so comfortable in her own skin before. Her affection for those kids was crystal clear, as was theirs for her. This was obviously what she was meant to be doing.

So why the hell wasn't she?

Oh, right. She'd been getting married to the dickhead from Connecticut.

Daryl's attention sharpened when the principal let out a small "oh!" of surprise. He looked into the room over her head, expecting to see chaos and destruction. Instead, the children were once more sitting around Amelia on the floor, listening to her read. It wasn't until she turned the page that Daryl saw the small girl sitting in her lap.

Amelia had gentled the pill bug.

"I can't believe it." Mrs. Mantooth shook her head. "How in the world did she get Annelise to trust her so quickly?"

"So, it's not just Amelia she hides from?"

"Oh, my, no. Annelise has to be one of the shyest little things I've ever met. At the beginning of the year, it was a month before she'd even say a word, and longer still before she'd let Miss Raintree—that is, your sister—even give her a hug. She still won't say more than a few words to me or any of the other teachers, and she's known us all year." She looked into the classroom once more and uttered a happy sigh. "Simply amazing."

Watching Amelia cuddle the girl as she read, a strange bubble of warmth welled inside him. "Yeah, she is." When she gave him a knowing look, Daryl added, "With the kids."

"Hmm." She didn't look like she bought it. "Well, I happen to agree with you on that. If Miss Westlake is interested, we have a position open in the next term, and we'd love to have her join our staff. If she's going to be staying in the area?" She gave him a questioning look.

He tried to picture Amelia sticking around tired little Hayden, teaching at the small underfunded, understaffed reservation school. It was like expecting a princess to give up her castle for a studio apartment.

Or a dusty horse ranch.

"No, she's got her own life to get back to." He said it as much for his own sake as to answer Mrs. Mantooth's question.

"Pity." With a sigh, she turned and headed back toward the office. "Dismissal is in ten minutes," she said over her shoulder. "You'll want to get out of the hallway before the bell sounds if you don't want to get trampled."

Daryl thought she was joking.

She wasn't.

A split second after the bell rang, dozens of children of varying sizes swarmed out of the classrooms and the noise level jumped from zero to a hundred. The seething mass flowed down the hallway toward the main entrance, reminding him of a nest of fire ants that had been poked with a stick.

When the door next to him opened, he expected the children to pile out in the same haphazard fashion. Instead, Amelia came out first, followed by her class in a tidy line, like ducklings waddling after their mama. She smiled at Daryl before leading her flock through the chaos, little Annelise clinging to one hand while a boy with a mop of curly brown hair claimed the other.

She's the freaking Pied Piper.

He followed along at the end of the line. When they got outside to where the children were supposed to line up for their buses, the boy holding Amelia's hand tugged on it to get her attention.

"Is he a giant like from the story?" he asked in what Daryl assumed was supposed to be a quiet voice.

She bit her lip and glanced at Daryl, laughter sparkling in her eyes. "No, David, he's not a giant." Louder, she said, "Class, this is Miss

Raintree's brother. Can you say hello?"

"Hello, Mr. Raintree," they chirped obediently. Two of the boys broke formation and crowded around at his legs, looking up with expressions of awe.

Squatting to their level, Daryl raised an inquiring eyebrow.

"Miss Raintree talks about you lots," one of them blurted. Encouraged by a nudge from his friend, he added, "She says you're a horse whisperer."

Not sure if he was more surprised Winnie had praised his talent with horses, or that she'd told her class about him at all, Daryl said, "She did, huh?" He glanced over at Amelia, but she just smiled.

"Yeah." The kid shuffled his feet, and when his friend nudged him again, he elbowed the other boy right back and said, "You ask."

The second boy, a little smaller than the first, squared his tiny shoulders. "Me and Luke were wondering...why do you have to whisper?"

"Why..." Daryl scratched his head, fighting back a laugh.

"Are the horses sleeping?"

"Um..." He shook his head. "No, they're awake."

"Then why do you whisper?" Luke demanded.

"Boys, I don't think that's—" Amelia started to say.

Daryl winked at her before giving the two inquisitive boys his full attention. "Because when you whisper," he said, dropping his voice to one and waiting until the kids had unconsciously leaned in closer, "everybody wants to hear what you're saying."

"Ohhh." The boys looked at each other and nodded, satisfied with his explanation.

"Okay, buses are here." There was amusement in Amelia's voice as she made the announcement. The kids all scrambled back into their line.

"Will you be here tomorrow, Miss Amy?" Annelise asked in a shy voice from where she still clung to Amelia's hand.

"No, honey, I'm afraid not. This was only for today because Miss

Raintree had to go home."

The girl's lip quivered. "Didn't you like us?"

"Oh, sweetie, of course I do!" Amelia dropped to a knee in front of her. "I love all of you. I had the best time this afternoon, truly. I'm not a regular teacher here, that's all. I'm just visiting with Miss Raintree's family."

Annelise thought about that for a second before she threw her arms around Amelia's neck and hugged her. The girl's eyes caught Daryl's for a split second. When she pulled back from the hug, she whispered something in Amelia's ear. Whatever it was made Amelia grin and whisper something in return, earning him another look from the little girl before she darted toward her bus with a final wave.

Mrs. Mantooth was waiting at the doors when they walked back toward the school. "I can't thank you enough for filling in, Miss Westlake."

"It really was my pleasure. The kids were wonderful."

"Judging from what I saw, they think the same about you. You're a natural."

Amelia ducked her head, cheeks turning pink. "Um, I should go and put the classroom back in order." It was an obvious bid to escape the principal's praise.

"No need. I'll take care of it." Mrs. Mantooth looked at Daryl. "Have you heard anything more on the condition of Miss Blackhawk's brother?"

"Nothing yet."

She sighed. "Well, please keep me informed if you can. I'm sure her attention will be focused on her family, as it should be." After pointing out where the teachers' parking lot was located around the side of the building, she thanked them again before going inside.

"'Miss Amy'?" Daryl asked as they headed for the parking lot.

Amelia shrugged. "I know you don't like anyone knowing my last name, and a few had some trouble saying Amelia, so...Amy."

"I like it." Even if it was the nickname Chaz had used for her.

She gave a small smile. "Yeah, so do I."

They made it all the way to Winnie's car before he gave in to his curiosity.

"So, what did Annelise whisper in your ear back there?"

She held out her hand for the keys and opened the Honda's door. The day's accumulated heat escaped in a stifling cloud. "She asked if I was sure you weren't really a giant."

An early bloomer, his height had always made him feel awkward and out of place as a kid, when he already had his mixed Native-Anglo heritage to contend with on that front. It wasn't until he'd become a teen and the rest of him caught up that he started to appreciate his size.

But now, a twinge of that old self-consciousness poked at him.

"And what did you say?"

She slid into the car and started it, cranking the a/c. "I told her you were more like a knight, rescuing princesses and slaying the dragons that kept them prisoner in their towers."

She closed the door and put the car into reverse while he just stood there, staring at her like a dumbstruck fool. After backing up only a few inches, the car stopped and the window rolled down so she could add, "You know, kind of like Shrek."

Daryl watched the car drive away in stunned silence before he threw his head back and laughed. Well, hell. At least a Scottish ogre was a step up from Sloth. And Chaz would be perfect for the role of pain-in-the-ass donkey sidekick. It wasn't until he was in his own truck he remembered even Shrek managed to get the princess despite their differences.

Too bad that wasn't the way this story was going to end.

Chapter 19

There still wasn't any news when they got to Winona's apartment.

Amelia tried to distract her by recounting how things had gone with her class, but she was too far sunk in her misery to pretend to care. Winnie barely gave a flicker of a smile when she heard how the two boys had asked Daryl why he whispered to the horses.

Finally, Amelia gave up and hugged the girl she'd begun to think of as a friend. "You hang in there," she said, squeezing her tight. "Think positive thoughts."

"I'll try." Winnie hugged her back even tighter. "Thank you."

Kim walked them to the door. "I'm going to stay with her until we hear something."

"Of course." Amelia wouldn't have expected anything less.

"That means you'll have to handle getting dinner ready for the boys."

On the outside, Amelia smiled calmly and said, "No problem."

On the inside, she was freaking the hell out.

Handle dinner? On her own? She'd barely mastered eggs, for pity's sake! God only knew what she'd do to the steaks marinating in the refrigerator. Horrid visions of all the ways she could screw up the meal danced through her head, all the while smiling and reassuring Kim not to worry, she'd take care of everything.

Once they were in the truck, Daryl asked, "You don't have the first idea of how to cook steak, do you?"

"Not a clue." The admission came out as a sigh. "But I'll figure it out. Kim needs to focus on Winona right now. She said everything I need is prepped and ready to go. I'm sure I can muddle through it."

I hope.

Daryl's fingers tapped on the steering wheel. "I can handle the grilling if you want."

"Oh, thank God." The last thing she wanted to do was disappoint the hungry men expecting something edible on their plates tonight. If Daryl handled the grilling, she could fake her way through the rest. Probably. "Yes. Thank you."

They drove for a few minutes in silence before Daryl spoke again. "Shrek, huh?"

Shoot me now.

She'd made the Shrek comment after seeing Daryl's reaction when she called him a princess-rescuing knight. He'd looked a little taken aback and more than a little uncomfortable, so she'd used the humorous comparison to lighten the mood.

There was no need for him to know she really had started thinking of him as her own personal knight errant. He made her feel safe. Not only in the physical sense, but he also made her feel safe to be herself. Or, at least, to try to figure out who she wanted to be.

That alone was worth more than all the zeroes in her father's bank balance.

"Well," she said, pretending to give it some thought, "you do have a lot in common. You're both tall. You're both a little intimidating. And you both got stuck rescuing the useless princess from the clutches of the evil dragon." Although the dragon from the movie had been a thousand times more cuddly than her mother.

"As I recall, the princess in the movie wasn't anywhere near useless," Daryl replied, turning the truck down the long dirt road to the ranch. "And neither are you."

"You're right," she said with a burst of surprise. "I'm not." She had been, for most of her life. But now...now she was starting to see she had a lot more to offer than she'd believed.

Than she'd been *allowed* to believe.

She'd been trapped as surely as Princess Fiona before Daryl helped her escape. What she did with that freedom was entirely up to her.

It was a daunting prospect.

"That doesn't mean you're getting out of helping with the steaks," she said when Daryl helped her down from the truck. Having him lift her in and out of the monster truck had become both the highlight and torture of each trip she took in it.

"Don't worry. I don't go back on my word." He stood looking down at her for a long second, his hands still on her waist.

The heat of his touch was like a brand even through her clothes. She stared up at him, holding her breath, caught between wishing he'd take a step back, and wishing he'd take one forward. If he stepped closer, he'd be all but pressed up against her, and suddenly she wanted that to happen.

The breath she was holding came out in a rush when he chose stepping back instead. His hands fell away, leaving her missing the comforting strength of his touch.

"We should, ah…" Daryl gestured with a thumb toward the house.

"Right."

Mortified by the direction her thoughts had wandered, Amelia hurried inside and threw herself into the dinner preparations with a vengeance.

Despite her worry, the meal was a success, even if the edges of the cornbread were a little too brown. Feeling stupidly proud of herself, she made sure to point out Daryl's efforts on the grill, deflecting the men's praise his way.

Which ensured he was treated to a healthy dose of good-natured ribbing he seemed to enjoy more than he would have compliments.

At the end of the meal, Chaz told her the men would take care of the cleanup and shooed her from the kitchen. She understood it was their way of thanking her for helping out Winnie and Kim, but it felt a little too much like being relegated back to useless princess. She would have much rather stayed and been a part of the group effort.

Still, she couldn't turn down the gallant gesture without insulting them. So, she took herself off as requested to the front porch, where she settled into one of the rockers and just...relaxed.

The problem with relaxing was that it gave you far too much time to think.

She tried to stick to things that were safe. The fun she'd had with the children at school. Worry for Winona and her future with Kyle. Wondering what Kim had planned for breakfast and if she'd be up to handling it herself if she had to.

But inevitably, the thoughts she was trying very hard *not* to think wormed their way into her head. What was going on back in Connecticut? Were people getting suspicious about her continued absence? Or, almost worse, had they not even noticed?

She might have been the bride, but she'd never deluded herself into believing she was the star of the show. That would be Charles. Rat bastard that he was, he was probably eating up all the extra attention coming his way because of her supposed illness.

Daryl hadn't told her anything specific, even though he'd been checking in daily with Doyle. She'd almost asked him several times over the past few days for an update. But she refrained.

Sometimes ignorance truly was bliss.

It was the same reason she hadn't talked with Thea, asking Daryl to pass along several messages via Doyle instead. Right now, she existed in a safe little haven of denial and isolation here on the ranch. Talking to Thea would end that. And she wasn't ready for it to end.

Thankfully, Daryl hadn't questioned her on it.

Daryl.

He was the other thing she was trying so hard not to think about.

It was so, so wrong for her to have these little flutters inside her belly every time she was close to him. She'd never felt flutters with Charles, or anyone else. So why the heck was Daryl the one to elicit this crazy, scary, wonderful response?

Wonderful because she'd started to wonder if maybe there was something wrong with her, that she was incapable of feeling this way for anyone, ever.

Scary, because now that she *was* feeling it, she didn't know what to do next.

And crazy, because she was feeling it for a man who'd made no secret of the fact she was nothing more to him than a responsibility. After this was over, he'd go back to his regular life, and she'd...

Well, she had no idea.

But whatever it was, she wouldn't be doing it with Daryl. So she needed to stop thinking about him. Now. This very second.

She was still trying not to think about him when she noticed the dust trail being kicked up by a vehicle coming up the long dirt driveway. Kim was finally home. Did that mean they'd gotten news about Kyle? Was it good or bad? Was Winnie with her? What kind of mental state was she in?

Nerves made her stomach tighten as she raced down the porch steps to meet the car.

It wasn't until the vehicle pulled to a stop in a cloud of dust that she realized it wasn't Kim's dark-green Bronco, but a black SUV. A chill of unease pebbled her skin despite the heat as its doors opened and two dark-suited men emerged.

She didn't know who they were, but she knew *what* they were.

Oh, God, how did they find me?

She hid her sudden panic behind a calm exterior. "This is private property in case you missed the ranch sign out at the road." Speaking first gave her the position of power.

In theory.

Judging by the expressions on the men's faces, she might as well have clucked like a chicken.

"Miss Westlake?" It was the driver who spoke, but it was the other one who had his phone out, looking first at the screen and then at her. With a small nod, he slid the phone into his pocket and they both started walking toward her.

Shit, shit, shit.

Hayden was the back of beyond. What had she done to give herself away?

Precious seconds were wasted with that mental hand-wringing before she realized it didn't matter. Right now, she needed to take control of the situation before it got any worse than it already was.

She crossed her arms and pulled out her best imitation of her mother at her most condescending. "Clearly, you didn't hear me the first time. You're trespassing, gentlemen, so I suggest you state your business and leave."

She must have done a good job, because they stopped.

"Miss Westlake, you have a lot of people worried about you," the driver said.

She considered denying her identity for all of a second. But clearly, they had a picture on their phones, so what was the point?

"Who are you, exactly?" She was pretty sure she knew, but it wouldn't hurt to be sure.

After a second's hesitation, the driver replied, "Lister, ma'am. And McCall." He tipped his head toward the other man, who looked annoyed with his partner for answering her. "We work for your fiancé's family."

"My *former* fiancé, you mean."

Lister didn't acknowledge the distinction one way or the other. "There was some concern when you disappeared five days ago that you might have been acting under duress."

"Duress?" Amelia shook her head in disbelief. "I spoke to Charles before I left Connecticut. He knows exactly why I did."

Well, maybe not *exactly*. But "I'm not going to marry you" was pretty self-explanatory. If he'd been so concerned, he could have spoken up then instead of treating her like some insignificant annoyance he had to work into his schedule.

"Mr. Charles was especially concerned when he wasn't able to reach you by phone."

"*Mr. Charles* should have taken the hint that I don't want to talk to him."

"I'm certain it would put his mind at ease if he could speak to you, ma'am."

"Fine. I'll give him a call."

When hell freezes over.

"It would be better if you came back with us and discussed the matter with him in person, so he can see for himself you're not being unduly influenced in your decisions."

Amelia gave a short bark of laughter. "That's so not going to happen."

The two men exchanged a long look, doing that unspoken message thing she'd seen her own bodyguards do where they seemed to be telepathic. They started toward her again.

"If you won't return with us to Connecticut, we have instructions to see you back into your parents' care instead. You don't have any objection to setting *their* minds at ease over your well-being, do you?"

Lister made her sound like a spoiled child having a tantrum. God, it was infuriating.

But her anger shifted to alarm when it became clear from the determined looks on their faces that her answer and her cooperation were irrelevant. These men intended to complete their assignment with or without it.

Her heart jumped to her throat, blocking her breath as she turned to run for the house, even though she'd never make it before they caught her.

And then she saw him.

Daryl.

He was nothing more than a shape in the growing shadows of the porch, but Amelia knew it was him. Almost instantly, her fear vanished. She wasn't alone. He wouldn't let anything happen to her. She turned back to the two men sent to retrieve her and knew they'd seen him as well because they halted their advance, caution evident on their faces.

Amelia waited, but Daryl didn't come down the steps and take over sending the men on their way. It took a moment for the truth to dawn. He was leaving the situation in her hands. Ignoring the quick somersault her stomach took, she threw her shoulders back.

I can do this.

"I'm not inclined to go anywhere with you, gentlemen." It wasn't her mother that came out of her mouth this time. It was pure pissed-off princess. "I decided, all on my own, to leave Connecticut. My departure might have been abrupt, but it was my choice to make. I don't owe anyone any further explanation. Not the Davenports, not my parents, and certainly not the two of you. You may go back to your employer and tell him you delivered the message and that I declined the *invitation* he so graciously extended."

Damn, that felt good.

Another look passed between the men. "I'm afraid we can't do that, Miss Westlake. Our instructions were explicit. You need to go to either Connecticut or Colorado."

"Unless those instructions include felony kidnapping, I believe the lady already told you she wasn't going anywhere."

Daryl's deep voice sent a shiver of warmth through her. She never heard him move, but suddenly he was behind her, his large hands resting on her shoulders. She didn't bother resisting the urge to lean back into his comforting strength.

McCall's tone was surly. "Kind of hard to swallow she isn't under duress when you're standing right behind her telling her what to say."

"No one's telling me to say anything!"

"Miss Westlake has given you her answer. Twice. I believe it's time for you to leave."

Neither man looked inclined to follow the calmly stated order. They did the little psychic-talk look again and Amelia tensed. Something was going to happen.

She just didn't expect what did.

As both men began to slide their hands under their suit jackets, there was a very loud, very distinctive sound from the far end of the porch that even Amelia recognized as a shotgun being racked. Her eyes widened at the sight of Chaz standing at the edge of the porch, a big, black shotgun held in his hands with an ease that said he knew how to use it.

She got a further shock when she turned toward a noise at the other end of the porch and saw Hank, a sleek rifle held with the same easy confidence and deadly intent as he leaned against the railing with one hip.

Daryl's attention stayed focused on the two men in front of him. The tension radiating off of him was so intense she was surprised her back wasn't scorched by it. Things could go from bad to worse if anyone did or said the wrong thing in the next few seconds. The last thing she wanted was for there to be any bloodshed because of her.

Taking a breath, she tried to take a step away from Daryl's overpowering presence, but his hands held her in place. She gave him a disgruntled look, rolling her eyes when he looked down at her and raised that annoying eyebrow as though daring her to try it again.

With a sigh, she turned her attention to the men, who had been smart enough to bring their hands back into plain sight.

"Listen very carefully, Mr. Lister, because I'm only going to say this one more time. I am not going with you. Not to Connecticut. Not to Boulder. Not anywhere. The wedding is off. Maybe I didn't handle that decision in the best way, but what's done is done. *Nothing* is going to change my mind."

"Under the circumstances, you'll forgive me if I can't accept that you're making these decisions of your own free will, ma'am." Lister shot a speaking glare at the two silent sentries on the porch.

Amelia tilted her head and smiled. "In case you haven't noticed, it isn't me they're pointing their guns at."

Lister looked like he wanted to argue the point, but another glance at the armed men seemed to change his mind.

"You've already been told you're trespassing," Daryl said. "I suggest you leave. Now." There was a dark threat underlying his words.

The Davenport security men evidently heard it as well. After one last angry look at Amelia, they got into their SUV and sped down the driveway, leaving a rooster tail of dust in their wake. It wasn't until they were out of sight Daryl relaxed his stance and his grip, allowing Amelia to turn and face him.

"Thank you." It was only beginning to dawn on her just how bad things could have turned out if Daryl hadn't shown up when he did.

Although, if he'd heard her tell the men they were trespassing, then he had to have been there listening from almost the first moment they arrived. "Why did you wait so long to say something?"

"You were doing just fine on your own."

She snorted. "Right. If that were true, I wouldn't have needed the three of you to come to my rescue." She glanced toward the porch as she said it, but both Chaz and Hank had disappeared. She needed to thank them. And give them an explanation.

Her stomach cramped a little.

"We didn't rescue you. We just backed you up. There's a difference."

The denial was on the tip of her tongue, but she stopped and thought about it.

It was true that when Daryl had first let his presence be known, he hadn't jumped in and taken over the situation as she expected. And even after Hank and Chaz had joined in the united force behind her, neither had said a word. All three had deferred to her, letting her handle the matter as she saw fit, standing ready to step in only if needed.

In the past, when her friends had championed her fights, she always ended up getting pushed aside while they jumped on the mother-sized grenade for her. That same pattern had ruled their entire friendship as far back as she could remember.

God, had she always been such a wimp? Or had she become one because her battles were being fought for her, whether she wanted them to be or not?

Today was different, though.

Daryl hadn't taken over. Hadn't played white knight and pushed her behind him and fought her fight for her. No. He'd stood at *her* back, letting her know she had his support when and if she needed it, and let her handle the situation all on her own.

The most surprising thing was…she had.

And she hadn't felt like throwing up once.

Amazed and thrilled to find she actually did have a spine, she let out a joyous laugh and threw her arms around Daryl in a hard hug. She breathed in the warm, smoky scent he carried from the barbeque, her face pressed tight to his chest, trying to memorize the moment so she could replay it later when she was a little less giddy with adrenaline.

Finally, she pulled back and smiled up at him.

"Thank you for being my Shrek." She went on tiptoe to press a kiss to his cheek. Which ended up being very close to his mouth instead because of their height difference. She wasn't sure which of them was more surprised by the action. She laughed again, a nervous one this time, and backed toward the porch steps.

"I, ah, have to go figure out what to make for breakfast in case Kim doesn't come home tonight." She almost tripped over the bottom step, righted herself, then bit her lip and bolted inside, wondering what had possessed her to do such a stupid thing as kiss him.

And thinking about when she might be able to do it again.

Chapter 20

The woman was driving him insane.

After the confrontation the previous evening with Davenport's security goons, Daryl expected her to be upset. Nervous. Maybe even a little weepy. Instead, she'd spent the morning bouncing around the kitchen making breakfast all on her own like she hadn't just learned to crack an egg a few days ago, looking happier than he'd seen her in...well, probably ever.

It was just wrong.

Didn't she understand what had happened?

The Davenports knew where she was. And it was a safe bet they weren't going to just leave her alone after one failed attempt to retrieve her. Because call it by any other name, that had been a retrieval team. Their attempts to convince Amelia to go with them had been mere formality on the off chance they could do the job quick and quiet. If he hadn't heard the engine, hadn't gone out to investigate, there was no doubt in his mind they would have snatched her.

Some bodyguard he turned out to be.

He couldn't remember a time other than watching Thea almost get shot that he'd felt such rage and terror as seeing those bastards get out of the car. Every instinct he had had screamed for him to get Amelia into the house, out of harm's way.

But then he would have missed the absolute glory of watching her stand on her own two feet and tell those bastards to take a hike. Politely, of course. He wouldn't expect anything less from her. She might have been angry and scared as hell, but she'd done a damn fine imitation of being in complete control.

Which was why he hadn't given in to his instincts. There were too many well-intentioned people always jumping in to save her whenever she began to flounder in deep water.

It was about time she learned she could swim just fine on her own.

What bothered the hell out of him was their safe house being found. He'd been sure it had something to do with the school principal checking on Amelia's teaching credentials.

But no.

According to Doyle, one of his tech wizards was able to locate a single picture on social media of Amelia outside the church Sunday giving the Hayden Harridans a piece of her mind. No name had been attributed to her, but the poster had mentioned she was a friend of the Raintrees.

Between that and the kind of facial recognition software the senator's alphabet agency friends likely had access to, it wouldn't have taken long for them to locate the picture and make the connection to him.

"Big Brother is watching" was no longer a joke.

Doyle had also informed him they were packing up and leaving Connecticut. The Davenports' social secretary had informed them that morning Thea and Lillian's invitations to the remaining pre-wedding events, as well as the wedding itself, had been rescinded. Which was doubly outrageous since Lillian was one of the bridesmaids.

"Interesting timing, don't you think?" Doyle had asked.

"Right when they think they're going to get their wayward bride back? Yeah. They wouldn't want her friends to get anywhere near her once that happened." Which only confirmed Daryl's earlier suspicions that Lister and McCall had been ordered to bring Amelia back, willing or not.

They'd failed in their first attempt. He had little doubt there would be a second.

Staying on the ranch was the safest thing they could do until they came up with a new plan. All the ranch hands had been apprised of the situation and warned to watch for anyone on or near the property.

Judging by their looks at the news, it was clear Amelia had won the men over during her short stay. Every one of them was ready and willing to stand in her defense. The thought of anyone manhandling their "sweet little Amy," as Zeke had now dubbed her, turned them all into a pack of overprotective big brothers.

Everyone except Daryl.

The way he was thinking of Amelia was far from brotherly.

Oh, he could deny it all he wanted, but somewhere along the line he'd started thinking of her as a woman instead of a job. And not just any woman. One who appealed to him in ways he'd never expected she might.

Amelia Westlake was the farthest thing from what he considered his type. And yet, she was the woman who'd been popping up in his dreams for the past three nights, disrupting his sleep and making him irrationally irritable toward her during the day. As though it were her fault he couldn't seem to stop waking up sweaty, aroused, and unfulfilled to the point of pain.

He wasn't sure if he owed Doyle a debt of gratitude for giving him this assignment, or a punch in the mouth.

Breakfast had barely been cleared when the house phone rang. Daryl's stomach clenched when he answered and heard Kim's voice. She sounded calm, but the threat of tears clung to her words as she asked if he would get Hank.

"Is Winnie okay?"

"No, not really. She's not getting any answers about Kyle from the Blackhawks because they don't know anything yet themselves, and she's starting to think the worst. I keep trying to tell her not to think that way, but, well, I'm about at my wit's end. I'm hoping your father might have better luck talking some sense into her."

"Okay. Let me get him." Daryl turned to Amelia, who'd come to stand at his side as soon as he'd uttered Winnie's name. "She's okay," he said in response to the concern etched on her face before handing her the phone. "It's Kim."

When he returned with his father, Amelia was still on the phone, nodding as she listened.

"Uh-huh. No, I understand. Yes, that's not a problem. No, I'm happy to help. I'm sure we can convince her. Them, too." She looked up and said, "Okay, see you soon. Here's Hank." She handed off the phone and motioned for Daryl to join her on the other side of the kitchen.

"Kim was able to convince Winnie to come home to the ranch?" Daryl asked.

"Not exactly. But I'm sure we'll be able to change her mind."

"We?" He got a very bad feeling about that little word.

"Hank and Kim." She hesitated. "And you and me."

"Absolutely not." The reply was instantaneous, no thought needed.

"I know you don't want me to leave the ranch, but—"

"No."

"But this is the only way—"

"No."

"But—"

"No."

"Winona needs to be here, in her home, where she'll have the support of her family. And since she seems to have inherited the same stubborn gene you have, it's going to take all of us to convince her to budge from her place."

"Gang up on her, you mean."

Amelia looked pained by that description, but nodded. "If that's what it takes."

It probably would, based on past experience with his sister once she'd dug her heels in on something. That didn't mean he was willing to put Amelia's safety in jeopardy.

"No."

From the exasperated look she gave him, he almost expected her to stamp her dainty foot.

She didn't. She poked him in the chest.

Hard.

"Look, I know you're just doing your job and trying to protect me, but if you'd stop being a butthead for a second, you'd see that I have to do this. And I'm going to." She emphasized that declaration with a definitive nod.

The princess had spoken.

"It's not just my job," he muttered, rubbing his chest before looking at her in disbelief. "Butthead?" He loved that her cheeks grew pink as he watched, but the determination in her eyes never wavered.

Damn. She wasn't going to back down on this. He almost missed the timid version of her that would have immediately agreed with whatever he told her to do, no matter her own feelings on the matter.

Realizing he was still rubbing the spot she'd poked, Daryl dropped his hand and sighed. "I don't like it."

Amelia seemed to take that as a concession because she smiled. "Everything will be fine. You'll see. We're just driving into town and back again. Nothing will happen. Let me get my purse, and we can go."

Turning to watch her hurry from the room, he caught his father watching him with an amused expression on his face. Evidently, he'd finished his conversation with Kim in time to overhear some of what had passed between him and Amelia.

"I never said yes, damn it." He wasn't sure if he was complaining or asking what the hell had just happened.

His dad shook his head, still grinning, and slapped him on the shoulder as he walked past. "I'll meet you both out front. You drive."

While Amelia and his father chatted about horses, Daryl stayed vigilant for any sign of the black SUV or any other vehicles that didn't belong in the area. One glance in his rearview mirror happened to catch his father in the backseat of the crew cab doing the exact same thing despite his easy banter with Amelia.

He relaxed by a fraction, thankful for the second set of eyes. But he still took a circuitous route to Winnie's place, just to be safe. When he finally parked behind Kim's Bronco, he was confident they'd arrived unobserved.

After a brief consultation with Kim, Amelia sat on the sofa beside Winona. His sister was still in her pajamas, looking like she'd been on a week-long bender, eyes swollen from crying and lips chewed ragged.

Plucking away the pillow Winnie had clutched to her chest, Amelia flung it aside. "Okay, sweetie, this pity party is officially over."

Winnie's bloodshot eyes widened in disbelief. "What?"

"You heard me. Let's go. We need to get you in the shower and into clothes that aren't quite so ripe." She got up, clearly expecting Winnie to do the same.

His sister stared at her like she was crazy.

So did Daryl. What the hell was she doing? Couldn't she see Winnie was upset? What happened to the woman who had all the patience in the world for shy little Annelise? Who'd even been polite to the people trying to freaking kidnap her?

"Why are you being so mean?" Winnie voiced his own unspoken question as her eyes filled again.

"I'm not mean. I'm practical. Sitting here worrying yourself sick over what might or might not be happening with Kyle is a useless waste of time. Not to mention bad for you *and* your baby." She nodded when Winnie's hands went protectively over her belly. "You need to think about that little person first, yourself second, and Kyle last.”

“Last!”

“That’s right. He’s the only one you have no control over at this point.”

“So?” A tear leaked down Winnie’s cheek.

Amelia appeared unfazed by it. “So, you handle the things you *do* have control over, then worry about the rest.”

“I’m scared,” Winnie whispered.

“It’s okay to be scared. It’s not okay to let it cripple you. Trust me, I’m something of an expert on that.” Amelia sounded more than a little self-deprecating before turning all business again. “So, let’s go. Shower, clothes, and something to eat.” She didn’t wait for Winnie to comply, simply took her arm and pulled her to her feet.

“I’m not hungry,” came the petulant reply as Winnie allowed herself to be led toward the bedroom.

“Too bad.”

Daryl would have stepped in and stopped Amelia’s bullying right then if he hadn’t seen the look of relief on Kim’s face. Going against every protective instinct he had, he waited until the door closed behind them before turning to his stepmother.

“Why did you let her talk to Winnie like that?”

“Because she was the only one who could.” Kim took a deep breath and almost managed a smile. “Anyone want an omelet?”

Watching Kim head for the small kitchen, Daryl noticed for the first time she was looking almost as ragged as Winnie did. There were dark circles under her eyes, and while Kim had always worn an ageless beauty, she suddenly looked as though she’d aged a dozen years overnight. It was clear the past twenty-four hours hadn’t only been rough on his sister.

Still, he didn’t see why she thought it was okay for Amelia to bully the poor girl into submission.

He started to get the idea he’d been looking at things all wrong by the time Amelia had finished harassing his sister into eating most of the food Kim put in front of her and drinking a full glass of milk.

Winnie grumbled and complained, but when she was done, he had to admit she looked a thousand percent better than when they'd first arrived. There was still sadness and fear in her eyes, but at least she no longer looked like it was going to swallow her whole.

By the time a small bag was packed and Winnie bundled into Kim's SUV along with both her parents, Daryl had completely reevaluated the situation. He shot a quick glance at Amelia as they navigated the narrow streets out of the neighborhood.

"The two of you planned that."

"It was Kim's idea, but I agreed with her. Winona was making herself sick with crying and worrying. She needed someone to give her a push in the right direction."

"Which is why you were so determined to come, even though you knew it could be dangerous for you to leave the ranch."

"Yes."

He stewed over that for a minute as they sat at the red light Kim's Bronco had made it through. "You should have told me the plan. I could have done the same thing and left you safe at home."

The noise Amelia made could only be called a snort.

"You? Please. The first sign of tears and you would have caved. Hank, too." She lifted her chin in challenge. "Tell me I'm wrong."

The hell of it was, he couldn't. Winnie's tears had always been his kryptonite. As for his dad...yeah, same there. Look at poor Lollipop.

"She wouldn't be so upset if the Blackhawks would just keep her in the loop about their damn son," he muttered. He knew it was an unfair judgment, but hell, this was his baby sister. He got a pass on being irrational when it came to her.

"They were until she started texting them every half hour, even though they'd promised to let her know about any updates they got on his condition. Which isn't good," she added in a softer voice laced with concern. "I'm not sure what will happen if he..."

"Don't borrow trouble." God knew they had enough already.

Thanks to getting hung up at the light, by the time they reached the main road from town leading out to the ranch, the Bronco had outpaced them. It wasn't too far ahead, but it winked out of sight briefly when it disappeared around a curve up ahead.

Daryl's attention stayed firmly on the road ahead and behind. Both were clear of traffic. If anyone tried to get close, he'd see them coming a mile away. Literally. But even that knowledge couldn't stop the itchy feeling his instincts were giving him.

"Do we know why he was in Texas in the first place?" Besides running from his responsibilities.

"Winona said he got the wild idea a few months ago that he could make some fast money working the oil rigs. She didn't want him to go, but he was determined to come back with a pocketful of cash."

"Stupid kid."

Then again, hadn't he gone off and done pretty much the same thing with the rodeo? It hadn't all been about the money, though. Danger had its own kind of high that could be just as addictive as any drug.

"That's why she was so sure he was going to ask her to marry him when he got back," Amelia said.

Maybe. Or maybe the guy had just seen his ticket out of Hayden. Daryl could certainly relate to that. Only, he hadn't left a girlfriend behind to worry about him.

A *pregnant* girlfriend.

It was all moot, anyway. Whatever Kyle might or might not have intended, all that mattered now was making sure no matter what, Winnie and the baby were taken care of.

Something on the road behind them caught his attention in the mirror. It grew larger fast enough to let him know the vehicle was laying on a good amount of speed. That didn't necessarily mean it was trouble, but the closer it got, the more certain he was their not-so-friendly visitors from yesterday had turned up again.

He grabbed his phone and handed it to Amelia.

"What's this for?"

"We may have company."

"What?" She twisted in her seat to look behind them before turning back straight. "Who do I call?"

"If we need help, hit pound nine." He'd set up the signal with his father, just in case.

Amelia looked at the phone in her hand like it was a grenade. "*Do we need help?*"

"Not yet." The vehicle was close enough that he could make it out as a dark SUV. Damn. He really did hate it when he was right.

Daryl punched the accelerator. His truck was built more for off-road endurance than speed, but its engine was powerful enough that he hoped to at least maintain their lead.

Which they did. The SUV got close, but never overtook them. A fact that had him wondering if they were trying to catch them at all. It felt more like they were herding them toward something.

But what?

Instinct flared just before they went around a blind curve. Only intense defensive driving training and the quick reflexes he'd learned on the back of ornery fifteen-hundred-pound bulls kept them from colliding with the vehicle parked at an angle across the road on the other side of the bend.

He jerked the steering wheel to the right, allowing them to slide around the front end of the stationary SUV and off the paved surface into the loose dirt along the side of the road. For a few heart-stopping seconds, the tires spun before they finally caught traction and propelled them back up onto the road, rubber squealing in an angry chirp as they hit the blacktop.

"Oh my God." Amelia twisted in her seat to look behind them, grasping the seatbelt like a lifeline. "Are they insane?"

The pursuing SUV duplicated his end-run maneuver and accelerated toward them again. Easy for them. They'd known about the blocked road and had been pushing them like a cattle dog into the trap.

"More like determined."

"Determined to what? Kill us?"

"Pound nine. Now."

He couldn't take the time to check and make sure that she did it. He put his full attention to staying ahead of the two vehicles that were steadily gaining ground on them, despite the fact he had the accelerator almost pinned to the floor.

If they could just make it to the turnoff for the ranch before either of them caught up, they might have a chance.

That prayer went unanswered when the lead SUV rammed the truck's back bumper. The impact made the vehicle bounce forward and shimmy, almost ripping the steering wheel from his hands. Growling a litany of curses, he tightened his grip and did his best to coax a little more speed from the already straining engine.

But for every inch he gained, the SUV closed the gap, bumping them twice more before easing back and swinging into the oncoming lane to inch up along the truck's left side.

Daryl knew immediately what they were going to do. There was barely time to shout, "Hold on!" as the SUV veered into the truck's left rear fender in a textbook PIT maneuver, pushing the truck sideways.

Training in both performing and evading the Precision Immobilization Technique had him wanting to turn the spin into a J-turn, but the second pursuing vehicle made that defensive tactic too risky. The best he could do was try to control the slide enough so the truck didn't overbalance and flip.

It worked right up until the back tires slipped off the edge of the blacktop and the world went sideways.

Chapter 21

"Are you all right?"

The question was out before the truck came to a full, shuddering stop. A fast glance over showed Amelia white-knuckling the seatbelt strap with one hand and the oh-shit handle with the other. But other than huge green eyes that looked like they belonged on an anime character, she appeared okay. Still, he needed to hear it.

"Yeah."

The word was too breathy to have any substance, but Daryl didn't have time to coddle. Twisting the wheel, he hit the gas, but the tires simply churned up the loose dirt their spin had sunk them into. Cursing, he gave the truck as much gas as he dared without digging them in any deeper. It might be built for off-roading, but even the truck's beefy suspension couldn't help them if that happened.

"They're coming."

The two SUVs had stopped on the blacktop, one ahead and one behind their truck's position, each angled to prevent them from continuing down the road in either direction should he manage to get them back onto it. The drivers stayed with their vehicles, but the passengers were out and approaching the truck.

"Hold on."

Daryl engaged the four-wheel-drive and punched the gas. The truck lurched forward, straining for a second before pulling free of the dirt mire and going up over the lip of the blacktop, sending both men scurrying out of the way. Without slowing, Daryl continued over the road and off the other side.

No one was expecting that, including Amelia, who made a little noise of surprise as they bumped down over the edge.

There was more loose dirt on this side, but he had the proper momentum to power through it this time. As soon as he reached firmer ground, he cut the wheel and made a wide turn back toward the road, where he regained the blacktop twenty yards beyond where the first SUV had stopped to block the road.

A quick look in the mirror told him they weren't giving up yet. Both SUVs were right behind them again, and he doubted they would be quite so gentle if they got close enough to try that trick a second time.

Unfortunately, there was nothing he could do to make the truck go any faster. The SUVs closed the gap with every second that passed.

"Oh God." Amelia pointed in front of them. "Oncoming traffic."

A fierce sense of relief swept through him.

"Not traffic. The cavalry."

Three pickup trucks whooshed past in rapid succession. As soon as the last one cleared him, Daryl dared a look in the mirror.

The trucks had fanned out and stopped abreast in the road, one ahead of the other two in a formation not unlike the tip of an arrow. In the bed of each truck stood one of the ranch hands, rifle propped over the truck cab, focused on the SUVs, which sent up smoke from their tires as they braked to avoid barreling into the blockade.

Daryl held his breath until first one SUV, then the other, did a quick three-point turn and headed back in the other direction. Only then did he lift his foot from the gas, slowing the truck to a more normal speed.

He glanced over at Amelia, who was still twisted around, staring behind them.

"You okay?"

Straightening in her seat, she nodded. "I think so. Yes," she said with more conviction. "That was...intense."

"No, it was dangerous. And damned reckless."

Now that the moment had passed, thoughts of what might have happened crowded his mind. Over and over, visions of pulling Amelia's bloody and battered body from the twisted wreckage of his truck if it had flipped ran in a loop through his mind, ratcheting his fear and fury higher with every replay.

Those bastards. Those stupid fucking bastards!

Pulling up in front of the house, Daryl went around and helped Amelia down, but even after her feet were on the ground, he couldn't let go. All he could think about was how if he'd made one single mistake over the last ten minutes, she might not be standing here in front of him.

Realizing he was staring down at her without saying anything, he willed his shaking hands to let go. And couldn't.

"Damn," he muttered, staring into her wide eyes. "Damn," he said again with more feeling before giving in to the urge to drop his mouth onto hers for a hard kiss. There was no softness, no finesse. Just a hard, fast connection that did little to satisfy the almost overwhelming urge that arose to conquer her mouth and claim it for his own.

Claim *her* for his own.

Even as he thought it, common sense returned.

What the hell am I doing?

He dropped his hands from her like she'd scorched him.

But instead of backing away and giving him a verbal slap, or even a real one, Amelia confused the hell out of him by sliding her arms around him and burying her face against his chest, holding on tight as shaky aftershocks wracked her body. His arms automatically went around her and held on.

He didn't know which of them was shaking more.

Only the arrival of the three ranch trucks made them step apart, and even then, he had to resist the urge to snatch her back again.

What the hell was wrong with him?

Amelia thanked the men, leaving each of them bashful and grinning like idiots. Chaz, of course, was the biggest idiot in the bunch, giving her a theatrical bow like a knight before his princess.

Or a jester.

Only the fact he caught Daryl's eye after Amelia turned away and gave him a slow nod betrayed the act. Chaz knew exactly how serious the situation had become. He might play the fool, but Daryl was glad to have him at his back.

Finally, he and Amelia were alone again. But before he had to worry about how to apologize for his totally inappropriate actions, his father stepped out onto the porch. Amelia glanced between them, then excused herself, thanking his dad on her way inside.

"What happened?"

Daryl gave him a short but detailed accounting of the incident. He did his best not to let his feelings cloud the facts, but his temper rose again as he relived the events through his words. Bad enough the bastards dared to try and take Amelia from him. But they'd put her in danger, and *that* was a line they should never have crossed.

His father was just as incensed.

"What the hell were they thinking, pulling a fucknuts stunt like that?"

"They must be getting desperate."

And desperate people did desperate things.

After two failed attempts, how far would they be willing to go for a third?

<hr />

It took all her years of training for Amelia to hide her rioting emotions from Kim and Winnie when she entered the kitchen.

Winnie had already been dragooned into peeling potatoes for the evening meal even though it was only lunchtime. She wasn't crying anymore, thank goodness. But her gaze kept straying to her phone, which was on the table in easy reach.

Wanting nothing more than to retreat to the quiet privacy of her room, Amelia forced herself to stay and partake in the meal preparation. If she allowed herself to think too much about what had just happened, what had *almost* happened, she might go a bit crazy.

Winona seemed oblivious to any drama having taken place. Kim, on the other hand, kept sending concerned glances her way as though she knew something was up, just not what. Amelia left it to Hank to clue her in about the chase and almost-abduction.

She threw herself into the meal prep and turned her thoughts instead to the *other* shocking thing that had happened.

Daryl had kissed her.

And oh. My. God.

She'd *liked* it. More than liked it. Once she'd gotten past her shock, of course. And by then, the whole thing was already over. But while it had lasted…wow. It had been nothing like the chaste little peck she'd planted on him the other day. Oh no. This had been a kiss that made a statement.

She just didn't know what it was trying to say.

It had to have been a result of the chase. An impulsive act brought on by an excess of adrenaline. He'd been shaking just like her while she hung on him like a baby opossum. That could be the only logical explanation. Because there was no other reason a man like Daryl Raintree would ever kiss a woman like her that way.

But oh, how I wish there was.

The traitorous thought wouldn't shake loose no matter how hard she tried, no matter how many reasons she came up with for it being a terrible idea to have any kind of feelings for Daryl. Yes, it was okay to like him, and she did, she really did.

Clearly too much, since she couldn't keep him out of her dreams, where he appeared nightly wearing nothing but that stupid towel.

And sometimes not even that.

But he was way out of her league. Miles and miles. If she allowed herself to think otherwise, she was just opening herself up to an enormous disappointment.

And, of course, there was the tiny fact that up until a week ago, she'd been planning to marry someone else. It seemed all kinds of wrong to suddenly be having hot flashes over another man.

Telling herself that and getting her body to listen were very different things, however.

She could protest all she wanted, but when she was honest with herself—something she was doing more and more these past few days—despite all the reasons it was a bad idea, she was still attracted to Daryl.

Wildly, ridiculously attracted.

And she wasn't going to do a darn thing about it.

How could she? Her life was still in a state of major upheaval. She'd been so focused on getting through the end of the week and past the wedding date that she hadn't even had time to consider what came next.

But whatever it was, it wouldn't include Daryl.

He deserved someone better than her. He was calm, cool, and in control, and she was just a giant hot mess.

She was still telling herself the same thing hours later as they sat around the crowded dinner table, but the way Daryl's leg kept bumping against hers made it difficult. Every time she got her unruly hormones under control, he'd shift one of those long legs and *wham!* Another jolt of awareness would shock her to her core.

By the time dessert was served, she was so aware of the man she swore she was going to come out of her skin if he touched her one more time.

Clearing the table gave her the excuse to get away from him. She all but jumped from her chair to start collecting dishes, aware he'd stayed at the table while the other men left, drinking his coffee and watching her with the same indecipherable expression he'd been wearing the entire meal.

She hated that face. It made it impossible to divine what he was thinking. Was he sorry he'd kissed her? Did he even remember doing it? Could she find a way to make him do it again?

The dish she was rinsing clattered against the edge of the sink. She pushed that last aberrant thought far, far away. Kissing Daryl again was the very *last* thing she should be thinking about. No. It happened. It was over. It would never be repeated. Period.

Unless...

No.

She refocused her attention on stacking the dishwasher as Winnie wiped down the counters and Kim brought the pots to the sink. Never meant never. It was for the best.

Really, it was.

The sound of Winona's phone was a welcome distraction from lying to herself.

The girl pounced on it before the first chime finished playing. "Katie?"

Amelia wiped her hands off on the towel hung by the sink and walked to where Daryl sat listening to the one-sided conversation, his coffee forgotten. Kim sat beside her daughter. As Winona teared up over what she was hearing, Kim put a comforting hand on her leg and waited for the call to end.

When it did, Winona seemed too stunned to react.

"Is Kyle going to be okay?" Kim asked gently when Winona continued to stare at the phone clutched in her hand.

"He's okay. He's not going to die." It sounded more like she was repeating the words to reassure herself than in answer to Kim's question.

"Thank God," Amelia whispered. Someone squeezed her hand. Only then did she realize she'd placed it on Daryl's shoulder as she stood beside him. Embarrassed by the unconscious intimate action, she tried to pull away, but he didn't release her, his attention focused across the table on his sister.

"What else did Kaitlin say?"

His question made Amelia take another look at Winona. Rather than relieved or even joyful, she looked as though she'd been kicked in the head by one of the horses.

"He's going to lose his leg."

"Oh, sweetheart." Kim slipped her arm around Winona's shoulders.

"It's my fault." Winnie pressed a hand to her mouth and choked back a sob. "He only took that job so he could make enough money to ask me to marry him. It's all my fault." She collapsed against Kim as the torrent began.

"No, it's not. It's nobody's fault." Kim rubbed her back as she sobbed. "It was an accident."

"No. I ruined his life."

The absolute misery in her voice made Amelia's stomach ache in sympathy. Her hand tightened on Daryl's before she realized what she was doing.

"He's alive," Kim said, raising her voice a little to be heard over Winona's sobs. "You have to focus on that."

"But his leg…" Winnie sucked in a shuddery breath before sobbing again.

"Do you love him any less?"

"W-what?" The question was enough to snap through the building hysteria and make Winona look at her mother in shock.

"Do you love him any less," Kim repeated, her voice brisk, "just because he'll be missing a leg?"

"How could you even ask that?" Outrage replaced the tears. "Would you love Daddy any less if something like that happened to him?"

A faint smile lit Kim's face. "Of course not."

"Well, neither would I. I don't care about that. But..."

"But?"

"He will." Winona's lips trembled.

"Then you'll just have to set him straight."

It took little coaxing for Kim to get Winona off to bed. Amelia sank into the chair next to Daryl, wiping away the tears she hadn't dared shed while Winnie was there to see them.

"You're crying for someone you've never even met?" He sounded surprised.

"For him. For Winona." She sniffled and took the napkin he handed her, dabbing at her nose. "Life is going to be so much harder for them now."

Daryl looked like he was going to say something before shaking his head. He got up, holding out his hand. She took it without hesitation. Standing there in the empty kitchen, her hand held loosely in his, staring up at him, Amelia felt a sudden sense of déjà vu and wondered if he was going to kiss her again.

She was doomed to never know.

The outside door opened and Hank came in, breaking the blanket of intimacy that had wrapped around them. Daryl took a step back, letting her hand drop. She wanted to scream at Hank for his lousy timing, then laughed at herself for being so contrary. Hadn't she already decided kissing Daryl again would be a very bad idea?

Clearly, she needed to remind herself a few hundred more times before it stuck.

By the time Daryl finished bringing his father up to speed on the latest development, Kim came back into the kitchen. She went to Hank and wrapped her arms around him. She looked weary to the bone. Hank pulled her close and rested his chin on her head, rocking her gently.

Feeling like she was intruding on an intensely private moment, Amelia slipped out of the room. She didn't make it far before Daryl joined her.

"We still have to talk about what happened this afternoon."

Amelia's heart thumped faster as she continued into the living room. "No, we really don't."

Daryl frowned as he followed. "Yeah, we do."

Heat scalded her cheeks at the mere thought of discussing that toe-curling kiss. "It happened. It's over. Can't we just leave it at that?"

For the love of God, please leave it at that.

"No, we can't. Will you stand still for a minute?" He sounded exasperated. "Look, I can understand you not wanting to rehash it, but it's important we talk about this. Things have changed. This afternoon proves that."

"They have?" She wasn't sure if that was good or bad.

"Of course they have. We can't just keep going on like we were."

"We can't?"

"Amelia, the stunt they pulled today proves that they're willing to go to dangerous extremes to try and get you back in time for the wedding. Surely, you see that?"

"The...oh!"

The car chase.

Not the kiss.

Wishing the floor would split open and give her a convenient hole to disappear into, she did her best to bluff her way through her mortification. "Of course. Yes, you're right. It absolutely proves that." She nodded and started walking again.

"Where are you going now?" There was a definite sigh in his voice.

"I, um, I thought I'd just get some fresh air on the porch before bed." Maybe the breeze would help cool her cheeks before she burst into flames.

"It would be better if you stayed inside."

Right. The danger. She almost smacked herself.

Focus, woman, and stop obsessing about the stupid kiss.

He clearly wasn't.

"You're right, I wasn't thinking." She took a deep breath and tried to calm her jackrabbiting emotions. "What do you propose we do about it?"

He looked at her long enough to make her want to squirm before answering.

"Nothing tonight. It's been a long day. You should get some rest. We can talk about this in the morning and decide what we need to do then."

Sleep sounded like an excellent idea. Until she remembered that with Winona there, she no longer had a bedroom to escape to.

"Where am I sleeping tonight?"

She swore she saw a flash of something wicked in Daryl's dark eyes right before he answered.

"In my bed."

Obviously, he didn't mean with him. Amelia's body didn't care. Just the thought sent a hum of unexpected and inconvenient desire racing through her, making her skin tingle and her belly do a happy little swoop.

Worse, she was pretty sure Daryl recognized her reaction. He kept his distance as they went to his room, where he briskly stripped his bed, put on fresh sheets, and offered her one of his clean t-shirts to sleep in when she said she didn't want to disturb Winona to get her pjs.

After grabbing a pair of sweats for himself, he told her he'd be on the sofa if she needed anything and all but bolted from the room.

Frazzled, off-balance, and feeling a little foolish that she was acting like a teenage girl after her first kiss, Amelia brushed her teeth and changed into the shirt that hung on her like a tent. As she crawled into bed, she was certain it would take hours to get past the embarrassment and fall asleep.

But with the soft cotton tee wrapped around her like a comforting hug, and the faint scent of Daryl coming from the pillow, it was only minutes before sleep dragged her under into its tender embrace.

Chapter 22

"I have to leave."

The calm words froze Daryl as he was reaching for the coffeepot. Sleep had been elusive for the second night in a row, and not just because he'd been stuck on the sofa. No, he'd spent half the night trying to forget the look in Amelia's eyes when he told her she'd be sleeping in his bed.

With little success, if the morning wood he'd woken with was any indication.

He really needed that extra cup of coffee.

After pouring, he turned toward Amelia at the table and lifted the pot. When she shook her head, he took his mug and sat back down. His father and the rest of the men had already left for the barn, and Kim had taken herself and Winona off to her weaving room as soon as the last dish had been cleared away.

"Daryl, did you hear what I said? I have to leave."

"No."

"No?" She stared at him. "That's it? Just no?"

"Yes."

It was probably wrong to get such a kick out of riling her on purpose, but she looked adorable when she got steamed. It was like watching a kitten jack up its fur and try to look all mean and dangerous.

Since he doubted she'd appreciate the comparison, he kept his amusement to himself.

Fingers tapping on the tabletop, she tried staring him down. After several minutes, during which Daryl finished most of his coffee without saying a word, she finally smacked both palms down on the table and stood. "My mind is made up. I'm leaving."

"And going where? Back to Boulder?"

Her little chin came up. "No. Texas. My Aunt Josie will let me stay with her."

"I thought you didn't want to bring this problem to her doorstep? Isn't that why you didn't go to her in the first place? Or to the Fordhams or Beaumonts?"

"Things are different now."

"You're damn right they are." He pushed his chair back and stood. His greater height didn't appear to intimidate her at all.

"They know where I am now. It's not safe for me to stay here any longer."

"And exposing yourself while you travel all the way to Texas is safer?" She wasn't that foolish. There was something more to this sudden desire to leave the ranch. "Weren't you listening to anything that was said during breakfast? Dad has the men watching the house twenty-four seven. No one is getting anywhere near you while you're here."

"That's exactly why I can't stay!" She threw her hands up in the air. "Don't you see? You said it yourself, things have gotten dangerous. We don't know what Charles's people might do next. I don't want anyone getting hurt because of me."

"They might only have ever had to shoot at coyotes and mountain lions, but every one of the men that sat at this table and swore to keep you safe knows how to use a gun."

"Last time I checked, coyotes couldn't shoot back." She took a deep breath before continuing in a calm, rational voice, "I will *not* be the reason one of those men gets hurt."

Ah, now we're getting to the heart of the matter.

"They'd be disappointed by your lack of faith in their abilities."

"Okay, fine. What about Kim and Winona, then? Is it okay for the two of *them* to be in danger because of me?"

"They're not—"

"They are! I should never have agreed to come here."

Daryl walked around the table to her, not liking the agitation she was showing. In the past, he'd been able to count on her doing the smart thing, regardless of her own feelings. She understood the chain of command in a security situation. Now, he wasn't nearly as certain about how she was going to react, and that could be dangerous.

For both of them.

"I always thought that if they found me, the worst that would happen was Charles showing up and causing a big scene, trying to convince me to go through with the wedding. I never in a million years would have believed things could get dangerous. If I had, I would have stayed far away from your family and everyone else."

He had a bad feeling that included him.

"All the more reason not to get your aunt involved."

Although from what he remembered hearing from Doyle, she was one feisty old lady. She could probably take on Charles *and* his father all on her own.

"I already talked to her this morning about it."

Well, fuck me.

That wasn't something he wanted to hear.

"Since they know where we are, I figured it was okay to use my phone again," Amelia said into the silence, her tone both defensive and apologetic. "She told me not to worry. Once I get there, her security will be able to handle everything."

"And until you get there?"

"What do you mean?"

"I mean that as much as I hate to admit it, I can't handle getting you there safely. Not by myself." It galled him, but it was nothing less than the truth. No matter how good he might be, four-to-one odds just did not skew in his favor. And that was if they didn't pull in any more muscle after their second botched attempt to acquire their target.

The thought of those bastards getting their hands on Amelia for even a minute made his gut knot up. They probably wouldn't hurt her—Davenport still needed to marry her, after all—but it was pretty obvious they weren't averse to a little rough handling.

Which was why Amelia wasn't setting foot off the ranch until at least Sunday. *After* Saturday's wedding date had passed.

Amelia worried at her lower lip with her teeth. "I didn't think...oh! Aunt Josie can send some of her people here to escort me."

She sounded so relieved to have found an answer, he almost hated to burst her bubble. But it had to be done.

"Even if they could fly in and out today, which is doubtful, they'd still have to drive several hours in each direction between here and the airport. Unless your aunt sends a small army, the risk of you being out on the open road that long is unacceptable." Then he added the coup de grâce, even if it was playing dirty. "You'd be putting not just yourself, but your aunt's security people in a lot of unnecessary danger."

He could see she wanted to argue. Her expression mirrored her thoughts as she tried to come up with another plan. Finally, her shoulders slumped in defeat. Without another word, she turned and walked out of the kitchen, leaving Daryl uncertain whether or not he should go after her. He'd won the argument. Maybe he should leave well enough alone.

Even as he thought it, he was starting after her.

Only to be nearly run over when his sister barreled into the kitchen, her phone clutched to her chest like it was the Holy Grail. Kim was close behind her.

"Whoa, slow down there, squirt," he said, steadying her with both hands. For a second, he thought she might have gotten more bad news about Kyle, but one look at her face showed she looked more stunned than upset. "What's the hurry?"

"I have to go. I have to pack."

"Pack?" He looked at Kim for more information.

"Kaitlin called a few minutes ago," Kim said. "It seems some charity organization has offered to fly Kyle's family down to Texas to be with him while he's in the hospital. There was also a ticket with Winona's name on it."

Daryl didn't need to hear the confusion in her tone to know what she was thinking. There were certain groups that did good works like this all the time, but how had one gotten involved in this situation so quickly? And why had they included Winnie?

"There's a ticket for Mom, too. But that's not even the best part." Winnie was practically vibrating. "They're also going to pay to have him taken where he can be seen by a specialist. He'll be getting the absolute best care possible."

"Along with the other two men who were injured in the accident," Kim added.

Winnie threw her arms around Daryl in a fast, exuberant hug before scampering out of the kitchen again, saying over her shoulder, "I have to go pack."

"She remembers she doesn't live here anymore, right?"

Kim smiled. "She'll remember in a minute. Right now, she's too giddy about getting to go see Kyle to think straight. When she does, I'll take her to her apartment to pack. Kaitlin's parents offered to pick us both up there on their way to the airport."

Mention of the airport reminded him of Amelia's worries about putting Kim and his sister in danger. "Dad will probably want to drive you into town himself."

And have a few more of the men follow, just in case. There was no reason for Davenport's men to do anything to Kim or Winnie, but he wasn't in the mood to take chances. He knew his dad wouldn't be, either.

"Mom!"

Kim grinned and shook her head at the frustrated wail. "That's my cue." She paused on the way out of the kitchen to add, "Be sure to thank Amy for me."

Daryl didn't need to ask what for. Amelia's pretty little fingerprints were all over this.

Somehow, she'd arranged not only for Kyle to receive the finest treatment possible, but to grant Winnie her greatest wish and gotten her a plane ride straight to his side.

Of course, that still left Winnie needing to explain her presence to everyone in Kyle's family, but Daryl didn't think that even registered for her at the moment. Plus, she'd have Kim there to lean on if things got ugly about the baby.

He smiled. She might not realize it yet, but Amelia's well-intentioned meddling had just handed him the answer to how he was going to keep her on the ranch.

—◆—

After having her carefully constructed plan to go to Texas routed by Daryl and his annoying common sense, Amelia retreated to his bedroom to regroup. There had to be some way she could take the danger away from the Circle R without putting anyone at risk to do it.

The thought of Daryl having to take on the men so determined to get hold of her left her feeling sicker than the stupid duck dinners she'd forced down every Wednesday for the last two months. If anything were to happen to him, she'd never forgive herself.

Sinking onto the edge of the bed, she hugged one of the pillows, resting her chin on it as she thought. Bodyguards had always been a part of her life. Even as a child, she'd known they were the men who protected her and her parents from anything bad that might happen. As an adult, she understood that protection could come at a great cost.

She liked the men who served on her father's security team. But never once had she gotten physically ill thinking about the danger they faced on her behalf. That was their job. Whether she liked it or not, they'd chosen their profession knowing full well the inherent dangers it held.

But Daryl hadn't chosen *this* job.

No. Babysitting her had been thrust upon him by his boss, and then only because Doyle was her best friend's fiancé. How could she, in good conscience, allow him to face the unexpected dangers that had suddenly cropped up?

Groaning into the pillow, she fell back onto the bed, clutching it like a teddy bear. Daryl had changed the sheets the night before, but the pillow still harbored his familiar scent.

Spice and leather.

She'd spent the night letting it soothe her, lull her to sleep. Now, she inhaled it like a drug, seeking that same sense of calm.

Because this sudden attack of conscience had nothing to do with Daryl being railroaded into his current situation. It had everything to do with the fact she was thinking of him not as a bodyguard, but as a man.

A sexy, desirable man.

A man she'd seen mostly naked.

And oh, what a glorious sight that had been.

It would be a sin for anything bad to happen to all that beautiful bronzed maleness.

She groaned again. What was she doing? She was supposed to be coming up with a way to get to Texas without putting Daryl in danger, not mentally reliving the single most exciting thing to ever happened in her entire adult life. And that included meeting the Queen of England.

A knock at the door had her sitting up. "Yes?"

When Daryl came in, she could tell from the look in his eyes he hadn't come to tell her he'd changed his mind. Not that she expected him to. His argument was a valid one.

Stupid common sense.

"Winnie got a call from Kaitlin. It seems some organization is flying the Blackhawks down to be with Kyle, and they included Winnie and Kim in the deal."

It was tough to keep an expression of mild interest instead of letting the relief she felt show. "Really? That's great."

"Hmm." He stepped closer, hooking his thumbs into the front pockets of his jeans. "Strange how this group got involved out of nowhere, and how Winnie ended up involved when she's no relation to him."

He stopped in front of her, forcing her to tilt her head back to maintain eye contact. "You wouldn't happen to know anything about that, now would you?"

"Me? How could I?"

And she didn't, not exactly. All she'd done was mention the very sad situation to her aunt when they spoke that morning and wonder if there was anything that could be done to help. Josie contributed to half a dozen medical foundations and even more charities. There was even a wing of a hospital somewhere named after her.

Amelia had counted on her aunt's connections and philanthropic tendencies to come up with a solution to Winnie's problem. Evidently, she had.

Thank you, Auntie J.

"Hmm." Reaching down, Daryl grabbed the pillow she'd forgotten she was clutching and tossed it aside before taking her hands and drawing her to her feet. "Did you know your nose twitches when you lie?"

Her hand instinctively went to her nose. "It does not." Only when she saw the amusement gleaming in his eyes did she realize he'd played her. "Okay, fine. I might have mentioned the situation to Aunt Josie. Whatever came of that is all her doing, though, not mine."

He bent closer to her. "Thank you."

The kiss he brushed over her cheek was soft and chaste, and still it made her heart zing. She stared up at him, uncertain if he was going to kiss her again.

Praying he would.

Knowing he shouldn't.

She surprised them both when she went up on her toes and pressed her mouth to his instead. At first, he did nothing. Then, just as the doubts wormed their way in and she was about to pull away, he put his hand on the back of her head and took over the kiss.

Oh. My. God.

That was her last coherent thought as Daryl's mouth plundered hers. His lips were soft and firm and definitely knew their way around a kiss. When his tongue delved into her mouth to brush against hers, she moaned. When his arms came around her body and pulled her flush against him, she was pretty sure she whimpered.

He felt *so good*. Better than the pillow she'd hugged all night long, that was for sure. Far from being soft and lumpy, he was hard and strong and giving off enough heat to keep her warm forever.

Not satisfied to play a passive role in the kiss, she slid her arms around his neck and angled her head more, deepening the kiss and drawing a sound of either pleasure or surprise from him. He broke from her mouth and rained a flurry of kisses over her cheek and down her throat while his hands roamed restlessly on her back.

His mouth had just reached the upper curve of her breast when Kim's voice calling from the living room froze them both like a dash of cold water.

"Hanska, if we don't leave now, your daughter is going to walk back to town."

Amelia and Daryl stared at each other, both breathing hard as they heard the faint rumble of Hank's reply, followed by the sound of the front door slamming shut. Slowly, as though he had to convince himself to do it, Daryl released his hold on her and took a step back. Then another.

She was glad he still had enough functioning brain cells to act because hers were all mush at the moment, totally destroyed by that kiss.

Oh, God, that kiss!

Daryl shook his head. "That will not happen again," he rasped. Retreating to the open door, he turned back to add, "And you're not leaving." He shut the door behind him with a definitive snap.

Amelia stared at where he'd been for a long second before collapsing back onto the bed, her legs feeling like they'd turned to pudding. "Wow."

As for Daryl's assertions, well, he was dead wrong about them both. She *was* going to find a way to get to Texas and keep everyone safe doing it.

And that kiss would *definitely* happen again before she left.

Chapter 23

As things turned out, she was the one who was wrong.

It seemed she hadn't thought through all the ramifications of getting Winona and Kim down to see Kyle. With the both of them gone and Mike's wife still off with her sister, whose baby was taking its sweet time making an appearance, it was left to Amelia to make sure the men of the Circle R got fed.

Her disgruntlement at that miscalculation quickly gave way to panic.

Bypassing Daryl, she took her concerns to Hank. Rather than help, he added to her dismay by telling her Kim had only felt comfortable going to Texas for an indefinite period because she knew Amelia would be there to handle meals in her absence.

She wanted to tell Hank his wife's confidence had been grossly misplaced. That she didn't have the first clue what she was doing, or how she'd manage to keep everyone fed without giving them all food poisoning, or at least acute indigestion. She wanted to stomp her feet and argue that she was supposed to be leaving for Texas herself, damn it.

But she didn't do any of those things.

Instead, she retreated and regrouped in the kitchen, where she took stock of everything on hand before placing an emergency phone call to Kim for help. With her calm guidance, Amelia was able to plan out menus for the next few days of simple meals she could handle without too much trouble.

She hoped, anyway.

Zeke became her kitchen helper since he was stuck on crutches for another few days. Of course, the shotgun propped next to him made it clear that drudge work wasn't his only purpose in being there.

She was a nervous wreck by dinnertime, but the men enjoyed the meatloaf Kim had talked her through preparing. And they ate up every last bite of the green bean casserole she'd put together from the recipe she found online to go with it. By dessert, she was feeling pretty pleased with herself.

Of course, that pleasure dimmed slightly when Manuelo and Mike left the table to relieve Chaz and Horace from guard duty so they could come inside and eat. But she never let her smile waver. These men were doing so much for her. Too much, in fact. The last thing she wanted was for them to think she didn't appreciate it. She truly did.

She just wished she'd found a way to make it unnecessary.

After dinner, a sense of restlessness set in. She tried watching television, but clicked through the channels without stopping on any long enough to even see what the program was about. After she'd cycled through the channels for the third time, she gave up and turned it off. No way was she able to concentrate on a show, not when all her thoughts were circling around one man and one thing: Daryl and that kiss.

That made twice now he'd kissed her, and twice she'd kissed him back. But the kiss this morning was different.

More.

More intense. And more problematic.

Because from the way he'd avoided spending time alone with her ever since, it was clear he was fighting what they both felt. And she knew they'd both felt it. For Pete's sake, she'd been pressed up against him like she wanted to wear him, so she was well aware of *exactly* how much Daryl had enjoyed that kiss.

Her tummy did a happy flip at the memory.

Was it really so wrong for her to be drawn to him like this? She might have only known him in a peripheral way over the years, but the past week had put them into such close and almost constant contact it had to count for at least double, didn't it? Maybe even triple, considering the intense circumstances. Add to that the fact they'd seen each other practically naked, and it was like they'd been together for almost ever.

Wow, can I rationalize or what?

Rolling her eyes at herself, she stopped in the kitchen to check on what she was making for breakfast before setting up a pot of coffee for Daryl and Hank to share when they came in from the barn. She'd noticed them spending time each evening talking at the kitchen table before going to bed.

Hopefully, they were working out some of the issues keeping Daryl from feeling he belonged here, where his family so obviously wanted him. Of course, if that happened, and he ended up moving back to South Dakota, she'd probably never see him again.

And she found she very much wanted to keep seeing him.

Not that it would ever happen, of course. Her life was such a mess at the moment she couldn't even think about a relationship of any kind. If he'd even be interested in one. All she knew was that Daryl was as attracted to her as she was to him, and at this moment in time, that was enough.

Which was why she found herself standing in front of the door that led to his bedroom from their shared bath shortly after she heard him retire for the night. She had on one of Thea's satin nightshirts under her robe, and nothing else. The soft material rubbed against her nipples, making them sensitive and erect, and she felt decadent and scared and wanton and nauseated all at the same time.

Could she do this? *Should* she?

She'd never get another chance like this again. And if she didn't take it, if she didn't at least try to be wild and daring this one time, she'd be left with regrets and what-ifs for the rest of her life.

She reached out and knocked before she could change her mind.

One way or another, her life wouldn't be the same come morning. She only hoped the change didn't destroy her.

Daryl put his phone on the nightstand charger with a small scowl. After reporting to Doyle that all had been quiet since the attempt to grab Amelia the previous day, he should have felt relieved. Instead, he was more uneasy than ever.

The wedding, according to Doyle, was still scheduled to take place in a little over thirty-six hours. Rumors had surfaced that the bride was horribly ill and under a doctor's care. That would explain her absence from all the pre-wedding festivities. But when it came time for the main event, they'd either have to produce her or admit the truth: that there wasn't going to be a wedding.

It wasn't hard to figure out which option the Davenports would be aiming for.

Which meant tomorrow was their last chance to rectify the situation or go down in a media fireball. And that meant Daryl wasn't letting Amelia more than two steps away from either himself or one of the other men.

She might not think she was in real physical danger, but a kidnapping could go horribly wrong in the blink of an eye. If the Davenports' goons tried to grab her again, especially now that she was being so well-guarded, things could get very bad, very fast.

Thank God for his father's men.

He hadn't even had to ask for their help. Once they learned the situation after the first encounter in front of the house, to a man they'd appointed themselves Amelia's guardians. Even young Manuelo lost his blush and stammer and demanded to be included.

No one would threaten their sweet Amy if they had anything to say about it.

Daryl wasn't sure how he felt about the somewhat possessive way the men talked about her. Even Zeke, who was old enough to be her father, had become smitten after spending the day snapping green beans with her.

None of them seemed to remember that "sweet Amy" would be heading home to her real life in a few days. A life that included trust funds and mansions and servants. It didn't include dusty ranches in the middle of nowhere. And it especially didn't include dusty ranchers.

Or washed-up rodeo stars turned bodyguard.

It had taken every ounce of strength he had to walk away from the incendiary kiss they'd shared earlier. And more willpower than he'd believed he possessed to stay away from her the rest of the afternoon.

He'd thrown himself into his work with a vengeance just to stay distracted. Not only had he handled Zeke's chores, but most of Chaz's and Horace's as well. Even his father had been giving him curious looks by dinnertime.

Not that all the extra labor had helped. The second he walked into the kitchen and saw Amelia standing at the table, filling the bread basket with biscuits still steaming from the oven, he'd been right back to square one.

No amount of exhaustion could stop the southbound stampede of blood.

It didn't stop the snap of possessive anger, either, when Manuelo jumped up and all but ripped the casserole dish from her hands, insisting it was too heavy for her to carry.

Amy, as everyone seemed to be calling her now, was a lot more capable than they all gave her credit for. But being who she was, she'd smiled and thanked the overanxious-to-please teen and taken the seat Mike held out for her.

After dinner, he'd gone back outside and tried once more to beat his libido into submission with hard physical labor. Sliding into bed after a quick shower, he was almost certain he'd be able to get at least some sleep before the sun rose again.

If he didn't think too hard about the woman sleeping just a few yards away.

When he heard the knock, he thought it was his imagination because of what he'd just been thinking. The second he realized it wasn't, he leaped from the bed like a bobcat scenting a meal. He knew he shouldn't open the door. Nothing good could come of whatever happened if he did, because he was all out of willpower and common sense.

That didn't stop him from walking over and opening it, anyway.

Looking like a startled doe, Amelia blinked those huge, mossy-green eyes of hers and swallowed as she looked up at him. "I, um, didn't wake you, did I?"

He shook his head.

"Oh, good." Her smile looked more like a wince. "I was thinking, that is, I was hoping that maybe..."

It was hard to concentrate on what she said. His eyes kept dipping to the neckline of her robe, trying to determine if she had anything on underneath it. He couldn't tell, and it was driving him crazy.

"Oh, this was a bad idea. Never mind." She started to turn and retreat.

Daryl caught her arm and halted her progress, turning her back to face him.

"Oh, no you don't." He felt her tremble faintly. There was one sure way to cure that. "Well, come on, spit it out, Princess. I haven't got all night."

It was hard not to grin at the spark of fire in her eyes, burning away the unease and uncertainty that had made her tongue-tied.

But instead of telling him, she showed him.

Stepping forward, she took his face in her hands and planted a kiss on him that had him reeling. She'd seemed a bit inexperienced when they kissed earlier, but it appeared she was a fast learner.

When her tongue touched his lips, begging entrance, he not only let her in, he practically devoured her whole. But her hands on his face kept her in control of the kiss, allowing her to pull back just a little and set the level of carnality at a low simmer.

Fast approaching the point of no return, Daryl put his hands over hers and eased himself back from the kiss. Looking down into her flushed face, he struggled to get out words instead of just a primal growl of desire.

"This won't just be a kiss." He stared into her arousal-hazed eyes, willing her to understand what he was telling her. "If we do this, you're going to be mine in every way. Are you sure you want that?"

"I want that." She smiled and slid her hands over his shoulders to twine around his neck. "I want *you*."

It wasn't the words, as important as they were, but the look of absolute sensual commitment on her face that sent him over the edge. By the time they made it to his bed, her robe was gone, as was his t-shirt, although he didn't remember who removed what when.

For the first time since he was Manuelo's age, he had no control, no finesse. Just raw, all-consuming need. But this was a night he wanted to savor and enjoy. He wanted to take the time to look at her. To touch every silken inch of skin that had been driving him crazy ever since he'd seen her in her underwear days ago.

He wanted to remember every single second.

Somehow, he grabbed onto his wildly bucking libido and put a saddle on it. He broke his mouth from hers and sat on the edge of the bed, tugging Amelia to stand between his legs.

Perfect.

Her breasts, lovingly molded by the blue satin of the nightshirt, were right there in front of him, just begging to be touched. Bringing his hands up to cover them, he squeezed, ever so gently. Her nipples, already erect, hardened further against his palms through the cool satin as though trying to break free.

Happy to oblige, Daryl slid his hands down Amelia's sides until he caught the bottom edge of the nightshirt, then reversed direction, sliding it slowly up. Amelia's hands went to his and stilled the action with just a touch.

Okay, she wasn't ready for being naked. He could work around that.

Fuck, he'd be happy to do whatever the hell she wanted, just so long as he got to keep on touching her.

Releasing the nightshirt, he curved his hands underneath it and around her sweet little ass, and nearly came right then and there when he realized she wasn't wearing any panties. His fingers clenched on the silken globes, drawing a small gasp from her as her hands went to his bare shoulders to steady herself.

The feel of her fingers on his skin was like a branding iron.

Their eyes met.

Their bodies stilled.

And Daryl had one moment of clarity to wonder if he was making the biggest mistake of his life before Amelia's hand skimmed up his throat, along his cheek, and brushed back the hair he'd been meaning to get cut. Now he was glad he hadn't, because she seemed to enjoy sifting her fingers through the long strands.

He let her play for a few minutes, touching and exploring his neck, shoulders, and chest. But when she ran a single finger across one of his nipples, he knew he'd almost reached his limit. The zing of that contact was enough to make his cock pulse, the movement clearly visible through his worn cotton pajama pants.

When Amelia's gaze shot down and then up to his face, there was a look of such sweet wonderment there, he would have laughed if he'd been able to.

"Yes, you do that to me." He took her hand and placed it over the tented material. "You've been doing that to me for days. Ah, *Christ!*" He gasped the last words as her hand closed over him and squeezed, thankfully with great care.

She startled and began to release him, but he placed his hand over hers to let her know it was okay. Hell, it was more than okay. She could get him off by hand and he'd die a happy man.

Well, no, that was a lie.

He needed to be inside her at least once before that could happen. Maybe twice. Three times and he'd be dead for sure, and the undertaker would have a hell of a time getting the smile off his face.

It wasn't in his nature to be passive, but he let Amelia explore his erection with those long, nimble fingers all she wanted. Right up until he couldn't stand it any longer and stilled her hand. Kissing her softly, he inched back on the bed, drawing her with him, the kiss both lure and reward.

Their lips never separated as he settled on his left hip and deepened the kiss, letting her know with every stroke of his tongue, every touch of his hand, what he wanted to do to her.

With her.

She might not have been very experienced, but Amelia didn't shy from the increasing carnality. If anything, she responded with such natural sensuality, Daryl thought he just might burst into flames if she got any hotter.

Which she did a few minutes later. Rising up on her knees, she skimmed the nightshirt off over her head, tossing it to the floor, watching him with a subtle air of challenge as she did.

He damn near swallowed his tongue.

Incredible.

Glorious.

His.

"You are...amazing."

It was a thoroughly inadequate word, but it seemed to allay whatever uncertainty lurked behind her eyes. She treated him to what could only be called a wicked smile before glancing meaningfully at his pajamas. It took him all of two seconds to skim them and his briefs off.

Her smile froze as she got her first look at him.

Daryl had a moment's worry she was going to shy at the last fence. He wasn't freakishly huge, but he was a big guy and his equipment was proportional. Some women liked the idea of a well-hung man in theory, only to have second thoughts when faced with the reality rather than the fantasy.

This was why he avoided small-statured women as bed partners. And Amelia, while not petite, was still dainty in build. Fragile, like fine porcelain.

Doubts began to crowd past his arousal.

Maybe this wasn't such a good idea. In fact, he knew it wasn't. What right did a great, hulking beast like him have touching someone like Amelia? She was the fairy princess, and he was...well, he was Shrek.

He didn't know what he might have said if Amelia hadn't taken that exact moment to grasp his erection with one of those dainty hands and bring her mouth down over the tip to lick him like a Popsicle. His hips bucked at the unexpected sensation.

"Fuck!"

Amelia rolled her eyes to meet his as she gave the tip another flick with her tongue. He hissed out another curse as the pleasure caused a close call that would have ended the evening much sooner than planned.

Once he stopped writhing, she smiled up at him sweetly, as though she weren't poised to destroy him with just her mouth. "Mmm. Amazing."

It was the last thing she said as she placed her mouth back over his cock and proceeded to drive him to the brink of insanity. Gritting his teeth, he focused all his concentration on not coming despite the desperate need to caused by her warm, wet licks and gentle suckles.

By the time he begged her to stop, he'd fisted the sheets into a knotted mess.

With one last kiss to the weeping tip of his cock, she smiled with a wicked spark in her eyes. "*Very* amazing."

The kiss nearly did him in.

The smile spurred him to action.

Moving with the speed and agility he'd used to win all those buckles roping calves, he jackknifed up and grabbed her, twisting and placing her flat on her back before she had time to do more than squeak.

"If you want to play, Princess, then I'm happy to oblige. Just remember one thing." He straddled her body, running his hands up her torso, over her breasts, and finally planted them on either side of her head as he leaned down over her.

"I play to win."

Chapter 24

S taring up into Daryl's eyes, which had darkened to almost black, a shiver of sensual thrill ran through her, making her breasts ache and everything below her navel tingle in anticipation. If he'd meant to scare her off with that warning, he failed.

Spectacularly.

So much arousal thrummed through her at that moment he'd have to pitch her into a tub of ice water to even begin to cool her interest.

What had happened to her?

She'd never been sexually aggressive before. Up until ten minutes ago, she would have sworn she didn't know how. But something snapped the moment he kissed her like he wanted to crawl inside and live there for the rest of his life. She'd forgotten who she was, who he was, who they were supposed to be, and how they were supposed to act.

In that moment, there was just a man and a woman, and the woman had wanted the man.

Badly.

So she'd taken him.

All she knew about oral sex had been learned from research in preparation for her wedding night. From Daryl's reaction, though, she'd done a decent job of it, lack of practical experience notwithstanding.

What none of the books had ever mentioned, though, was the overwhelming sense of power that came from performing the act.

She had taken a large, powerful man and reduced him to a writhing mass of moaning, panting need.

Her.

It was a heady experience. She'd been loath to end it so soon, but there had been a thread of desperation in his voice that had hinted if she didn't stop on her own, he'd do the stopping for her.

Which was perfectly okay because she knew she could do it again if she wanted to. And she did want to. Very much. There were so many things she'd read about she wanted to try. But right now, she was on pins and needles, wondering what Daryl might do in retaliation for her sensual assault.

There had been a hint of playfulness in his words, but there was also a dark promise that made her shiver again in anticipation.

She licked her lips. "Stop calling me Princess."

The breathy order only drew a smile from him as he lowered his upper body until his mouth just barely touched hers. "Make me."

His lips skimmed her cheek to the tender flesh just below her ear, which he nipped lightly before working his way down her neck to the upper swells of her breasts. The gasp she let out when his mouth found her left nipple turned to a moan as he alternately laved and suckled the hard peak into an exquisite state of hypersensitivity. Just when she thought she couldn't stand it another second, he switched to the other breast. Again, he worshipped and teased until she was ready to scream. Rolling his eyes up to meet her gaze, he gave one last, long lick in mimicry of what she'd done to him.

She whimpered.

With a grin, he continued kissing a path down her belly, hands smoothing over her ribcage, thumbs dipping towards her navel. She didn't have time to worry about whether he found her ribs too prominent or her hips too bony. All his attention seemed focused on his final destination. When he got there, she didn't have room for any other thought in her brain. There was only the feel of his tongue against her sensitive folds, driving her out of her mind.

"Oh, *God*!"

Her hips bucked as he sealed his lips around the sensitive bud of her clitoris and gently suckled. She gasped in a deep breath, certain she was about to die from the pleasure. Then let the breath out in a shaky moan when he let up on the suction and gently licked his way back down between her thighs.

Never, never had she felt anything like that.

And then suddenly, it felt even better.

As he licked back up to her clitoris, the tip of his finger rubbed along her folds before gently pressing into her. The sensation was pure bliss. Unable to keep from moving, her hips rocked against the intrusion, taking his finger even deeper.

A second digit followed, then a third, until finally the entire universe was focused on the place where he was alternately stroking and suckling and licking and thrusting. Where between one stroke and the next everything exploded in a fiery ball of ecstasy that had her bowing her back and letting out sounds she only later hoped hadn't carried past the bedroom door.

The sensation was indescribable.

Euphoric.

Exquisite enough that she nearly burst into tears. Only knowing Daryl wouldn't understand they were tears of the very best kind kept her from doing it. Instead, she closed her eyes and wallowed in the warm aftershocks that erupted every time he moved his fingers, which were still inside her.

Finally, slowly, she came down from the stratosphere and settled back into her body.

"You've killed me," she murmured, cracking her eyes open to look down her body at him. "I'm dead now."

"Oh, no. We're not even close to being finished." Withdrawing his fingers made her squirm one last time. As he watched her watching him, he licked the taste of her from each digit.

It should have embarrassed her.

Instead, it made her blood burn hotter and her body hum again. He might not be finished with her, but she *definitely* wasn't finished with him yet, either.

As Daryl rose to his knees, her eyes couldn't help but be drawn to where he fisted himself with one hand, spreading some of her wetness along his dark-veined shaft as he stroked it. The primitive fear of "how can that possibly fit?" poked at the sensual fog enveloping her brain, trying to find a way through. But she was still so languorous under the effects of her first non-self-produced orgasm she couldn't find it in her to get all that worried about it.

This was Daryl. He wouldn't hurt her. She trusted him.

She trusted him.

What a heady, terrifying, freeing feeling.

She licked her lips. "I want you."

"I think it's pretty damn obvious the feeling's mutual." Grinning, he lowered himself to her, teasing the tip of his erection along her folds, until he pressed it to the entrance of her vagina, which was still pulsing erratically. Suddenly, he stopped, his entire body going rigid. "Shit."

"What?"

"Fuck, fuck, fuck!" He lowered his head as though he were in pain.

"Daryl, what's wrong?"

"Protection," he growled. "I don't have any with me."

She blinked at him, uncertain she'd heard him right. "You...what?"

"I don't usually plan for sex while I'm working."

Didn't guys always carry one in their wallets? Or was that just something that only happened in books and movies?

"Maybe there's still some left in the bathroom from whenever you were here last?" Because seriously, stopping now was inconceivable.

"This is my parents' house. I never brought women here." He sounded offended at the thought.

"Sorry." Patting his shoulder, she wondered briefly if he realized that he'd just included Kim as one of his parents for the very first time. Probably not. There were other, more urgent issues at hand. "Maybe Winona left some...well, no, never mind," she said when he gave her a look that said "really?"

"I don't believe this." He let out a painful half-laugh. "I'm never...I'm sorry." He leaned down and kissed her. "I am so, so sorry. I should have—"

"I'm on the pill." She blurted it out, cutting off his apology and, she hoped, his withdrawal.

He stilled. "You are." Not a question, but a need to be certain.

Amelia nodded. "Since I—" She bit off the *got engaged* part. Explaining you went on birth control in anticipation of having sex with another man, even if he *was* your fiancé at the time, wasn't exactly the best pillow talk. "Since last year."

Daryl seemed to consider the implications. "I've never not worn a condom," he said finally. Meaning he wasn't at risk from past partners, and, therefore, neither was she.

"And I've never..." Unbelievable after all they'd already done, but she felt her face warming at the thought of confessing her virginity out loud. Thankfully, she didn't need to say the words because he gave a quick nod of understanding.

"Okay."

"Okay." She backed it up by sliding her legs around his muscular thighs and pulling him toward her.

"Are you sure?" he asked, even as the tip of his penis probed at her entrance again. "The pill isn't a hundred percent, you know."

"Neither are condoms."

"But..."

She reached up and curled her hands around his shoulders, letting her nails sink in until she was certain she had his full attention. "You. Inside me. Now."

He took her at her word. The probing became a gentle thrusting, which reignited the sensitive nerve endings and made the sensations all the more intense. He was gentle, but he was big, she was tight, and it took more than a little patience before he finally made the stroke that seated him all the way inside.

It was even better than what he'd done with his mouth and fingers. Everywhere he touched her she throbbed, and with every inward thrust she felt a small, extra burst of sensation as he touched deep inside of her.

She wanted to participate. Honest to God, she did.

But she was so bombarded by the sensations whipping through her all she could do was hang on and offer gasping whimpers of encouragement as his tempo increased. She'd never seen a more beautiful sight than Daryl's stark expression as he held himself above her, his lower body pounding into hers in a dance of muscle and glistening skin while he drove her higher and higher toward another of those amazing orgasms.

"Oh, God," she gasped when the pinnacle approached. Like a mad rollercoaster ride, she fell over the edge and went into freefall, keening her exaltation as she went. Daryl's shout and the last deep thrust he gave told her he'd followed her over.

He collapsed a minute later, angling his body to not crush her. The sigh he breathed against her neck tickled, making her realize her entire body was now highly sensitized and responsive to his touch.

"That was..." She had no words.

"Yeah, that was." He kissed her neck and shifted a little more to the side to give her more room.

She wiggled closer in response. The last thing she wanted right now was distance of any kind between them. Putting a hand on his chest, she felt the rapid drumming of his heart. Good to know she wasn't the only one. Her own heart was beating so fast it felt like a hummingbird trapped beneath her breastbone.

They laid in each other's embrace, catching their breath, until finally Daryl said, "We took a huge risk. We can't do this again without proper protection."

Part of her was elated that he planned for them to do this again, but she felt compelled to say, "I told you, I'm taking birth control."

"I know. I just don't want to have any surprises. My parents only got married because my mom was pregnant with me. My sister's in the same damn boat. And I was only a kid at the time, but I think Winnie was a little big for a preemie." He didn't sound bitter, simply matter-of-fact. "I thought it might be nice for one of us to break the trend of marrying out of responsibility and trying for love instead."

It was both strange and delightful to hear a man talking about love. Usually they shied away from the mere thought, as if to talk about it was like calling Beetlejuice's name too many times and cursing yourself with its presence.

"Well," she said carefully, "from what I've seen, your father and Kim are very much in love. Whether he was or wasn't when they got married, he's certainly crazy about her now, and vice versa."

Daryl merely grunted.

"And I can tell you for a fact Winnie is head-over-heels sick in love with Kyle, and I doubt that has anything to do with the baby."

"But does he love her back, or will he only feel trapped into marrying her once he finds out she's carrying his child?"

A worry Winona seemed to share, since she'd gone to such lengths to keep her pregnancy from Kyle until he popped the question on his own.

"Like how your father felt with your mother?" She felt like she was venturing into dangerous territory, but he'd opened the door.

To his credit, he gave it some thought before answering. "I think he loved her. Or, at least, he grew to love her. I'm not so sure she ever loved him back, though. Not the way he wanted her to." He shrugged. "Not that it really matters."

Obviously, it mattered very much, or he wouldn't be quite so fixated on the issue. But there was nothing to gain from pursuing the matter. Whatever hang-ups Daryl had developed were firmly entrenched in his earliest memories of a dysfunctional marriage, and nothing she said was going to change them.

Besides, who was *she* to talk about love and marriage, anyway?

"Can I ask you something?" Daryl rubbed his thumb in slow circles where it rested against her back.

"Sure."

"Why aren't you teaching? From what I saw the other day, you're a natural."

The unexpected praise warmed her. "I had a job all lined up last year, but then...things happened." *Charles* happened. She'd gotten so swept up in him and his whirlwind courtship, she'd let him talk her into resigning her position before she ever got started. So she could concentrate on the wedding.

What a naïve idiot I was.

Well, not anymore. From now on, she took charge of her own life. Her own future. Her own happiness. And right now, that meant getting away from any discussion that included her jackass ex and back to the one thing that had the ability to make her *very* happy indeed.

Daryl's incredible body.

She traced a finger over the faint scar that ran along his left ribcage. "How did you get this?" The muscles in his abdomen rippled in response to her touch.

Interesting.

"Uh." He glanced down at the scar as though he'd never seen it before. "That one...a horse threw me into a fence during my first rodeo." He gave a self-deprecating smirk. "Not my most shining moment."

She winced in sympathy. "And this one?" She caressed the short, thick patch of scar tissue that broke up the otherwise beautiful symmetry of his left biceps.

"A very pissed off bull who didn't appreciate me trying to ruin his record as unrideable."

"And did you?"

"What do you think?"

"Hmm." Given his tenacious nature, she was pretty sure of the answer. She bit her lip and followed a long, pale line that nearly bisected his right nipple. "And this?"

"Are you going to catalogue every one of my scars?" He grasped her questing finger and brought it to his mouth to nip. "Because if so, we could be here for a while."

She shivered at the reaction that tiny bite of pain caused. "I don't have anywhere else to be, do you?"

Grinning, he pressed a kiss to her palm before rolling her under him again, his rapidly hardening erection pressed tight to her belly. "So let me tell you about this bull..."

Chapter 25

T he woman was insatiable.

Grinning as he stepped under the showerhead, Daryl wondered if all virgins went sex crazy their first time, or if he'd just gotten extremely lucky. He tipped his head back and let the water run over his face and soak his hair.

Lucky? Hell, he'd hit the goddamned jackpot.

Of course, he hadn't realized Amelia was a virgin. Not until it was too late to stop and change their pace, even if she'd been inclined to let him. Which, judging by the sting on his shoulders where her tiny little claws had dug in, she had not.

At the time, he'd taken her "I've never" to mean she'd never taken a man bareback before. Hell, he'd never taken a woman bare before, either, not even in his wild rodeo days of anything-goes-sex. Just the thought of it had pretty well demolished any ability for rational thought.

No, the thought of taking *Amelia* skin-to-skin had demolished him.

Lathering up, he cursed himself for his lack of willpower. After that first time, he should have stuck to his guns and not doubled-down on the risk they were taking of relying solely on her oral contraceptive. But they'd not only doubled, but tripled-down, waking up in the early hours of the morning for a slow, almost tantric bout of sex before drifting back off to sleep again wrapped comfortably in each other's arms.

Not that he didn't believe her when she said she was on the pill. Amelia Westlake might be a lot of things, but a liar wasn't one of them.

No, it was the overwhelming fertility and consistent bad luck of his entire family that concerned him. While condoms weren't foolproof either, they were at least one more barrier between a night of fun and a lifetime of consequence. No kid wanted to know they were a mistake.

That, he knew firsthand.

But for some reason, the fear of perpetuating his family's slipups had faded into the background every time Amelia reached for him last night. The only thing he'd been thinking about was the glorious silk of her skin and the welcoming warmth of her mouth. And other places.

The sex might have been rather tame and vanilla compared to some things he'd done in the past, but it had still been the hottest and most soul-scorching he'd ever experienced. Every touch, every kiss, had been a building block that forged the experience into something he still wasn't entirely certain he understood the ramifications of.

Which was why he'd slipped out of bed just a little while ago, leaving Amelia sleeping, her blonde mass of curls a tangled curtain across his pillow. The same curls that had tickled his thighs and balls as she showed him just how creative she could get with that pretty little mouth of hers. For a virgin, his Amy was a damn tigress in bed.

His Amy.

He had to stop thinking of her like that. She wasn't his, and she wasn't Amy. She was Amelia freaking Westlake. The Princess. The job. But the reminders that had once worked to keep that illusion of unbreachable distance between them fell flat and useless when he tried to invoke them now.

It wasn't the job or the Princess he'd had in his bed last night. It had been the woman. The one he'd come to admire, and desire, much more than he should. Because they were living in a bubble right now. One that isolated them from the rest of the world and created illusions of false possibilities.

Once that bubble popped, once they were back in the real world again, everything they'd had between them would be over. Amy would cease to exist. There would be only Amelia, and Daryl had no place in that woman's life.

He should have been okay with that. Sex with a beautiful woman didn't equal a relationship. He'd spent his entire adult life proving that. He did hook-ups and short-term only, but even those had been fewer and farther between recently.

As much as he hated to admit it, he was getting a little too old to continue enjoying that lifestyle. All he had to do was look at Chaz to know while he'd once admired and emulated the man, Daryl didn't want to *be* him. All alone, with no family and no one or nothing to call his own. Chaz talked a good game, but Daryl had seen the bitter loneliness that lurked just under the cocky smile.

But that didn't mean a future with Amelia was an option.

He'd treasure these last few days they still had together, storing the memories of last night away like a miser hoarding gold. But come next week, he'd let her go back to her life without doing anything to try and change her mind. After the hell of living with parents who could make Machiavelli cry like a little girl, she deserved to be happy.

And much as he might wish different, that didn't mean him.

The shower curtain parted, and Amelia stepped inside, blowing every other thought out of his head as she smiled that naughty smile he was coming to recognize so well.

"Hi."

He made a noise that wasn't quite a word, but damn, who could think when faced with the naked goddess who'd intruded on his shower? Amelia didn't seem to care. In fact, her smile broadened, as though she liked being able to revert him to caveman status.

Biting that succulent lower lip of hers, she glanced down at his cock, which was quickly rising to the occasion despite his decision not to continue taking risks.

The gleam in her eyes when she looked back up at him was enough to make him throw reason to the wind and swoop down to claim her mouth, pushing her against the cool tile wall as he plundered deep with his tongue.

What the hell.

One more time would probably kill them both, but at least they'd both die happy.

When the next attempt on Amelia came, it didn't emerge from the shadows or the dark of night. It came riding down the driveway in a rented silver sedan just before lunchtime.

Alerted to the approaching car by Manuelo, Daryl was waiting out on the front porch, leaning against the post near the stairs, phone to his ear, when it pulled to a stop. Amelia was tucked out of sight inside the house with his father. She hadn't liked the order, but at least she'd been smart enough to accept it without argument.

Almost a minute passed before the driver's door opened. The man who emerged wasn't either of the ones who'd tried to strong-arm Amelia into their car the other day. Daryl stayed where he was, his position on the top step not only strategic high ground, but a statement. The stranger would come to him for anything he wanted, not the other way around.

After lingering at the car for a few seconds, the man seemed to understand the game being played. Resettling the jacket of his dark gray suit, he closed the distance between them with long, easy strides that warned Daryl this man wasn't all he appeared. The expensive suit and neatly clipped brown hair couldn't hide the predator lurking just under the sheep's clothing.

Stopping in front of the bottom step, the man said, "I'm looking for Daryl Raintree."

Not what he'd been expecting.

Expression bland, Daryl slid his phone into his shirt pocket. "And you are?"

The man studied him for a second, as though debating whether he needed to answer. Daryl knew exactly what he looked like. He'd been out working with the horses when Manuelo came to get him. He was dusty and sweaty and dressed like any of the other hands in worn jeans and boots and a threadbare shirt that was one washing away from the rag bin.

"My name is Vaughn. I work for Senator Davenport."

"What do you want, Vaughn?"

"To talk to Miss Westlake."

"Not going to happen."

Cocking his head, Vaughn seemed to reevaluate him. "You're Raintree."

Neither confirming nor denying, Daryl said, "Amelia has already said everything she wants to say to the Davenports. You're wasting your time and mine. There's no way I'm letting you anywhere near her."

Vaughn nodded, although Daryl doubted it was an agreement.

"I was informed of what happened the other day on the road. My apologies. My men were a little too enthusiastic in trying to carry out their assignment, and they might have gotten a bit out of line."

"*Might* have?"

"They've been reprimanded for their ill-advised actions."

"Well, that makes me feel so much better," Daryl drawled.

"I can assure you, harming Miss Westlake was never the intent."

"Yeah, kind of hard for anyone to marry a corpse."

Vaughn's professional smile flickered for a split-second. "As I said, my men have been reprimanded."

Like that was supposed to make it all okay.

"You know, last time I checked, Don Rogers was the head of Senator Davenport's security." Daryl needed to get a bead on just who Vaughn was within the Davenport power structure. He didn't act like hired muscle, but he screamed *dangerous* all the same.

"He still is."

"Then who the hell are you?"

"I handle...a different set of problems for the senator whenever the need arises."

Daryl stiffened. He'd been right. This man was much more dangerous than he appeared. He tapped his right thigh. The prearranged signal brought his father out onto the porch, rifle cradled comfortably in his arm in a way that showed he knew how to use it.

Surprisingly, Vaughn grinned.

"I should probably feel flattered you find me so intimidating you need reinforcements, Raintree, since you already have two guns pointed my way. But I can assure you, I'm simply here to facilitate a conversation, nothing more."

"And I already told you, Amy isn't interested in talking to you," he replied, then cursed his slip of the tongue as Vaughn's smile became more of a smirk.

"Amy, is it? Well, in any case, I wasn't talking about me. Someone else wants to speak with her and get this mess straightened out once and for all."

"She's not going anywhere with you." That was for damn sure. If the bastard made one wrong move toward the house, he was going to find out just how many guns he actually had trained on him at that moment, and it was a hell of a lot more than two.

"She doesn't have to."

For the first time since it pulled up, Daryl took another look at the sedan. The midday sun was creating a glare on the windows, but despite the heavy tint he could just make out the shape of a person in the backseat. So, Amelia's idiot fiancé had finally decided to come after his runaway bride in person.

The thought made his gut tighten. In anger on her behalf, not worry. Or so he tried to tell himself. The man was a raging jackass. There was no way in hell Amelia would give him another chance.

Would she?

Not that it should matter to him if she did. She was a grown woman. She needed to make her own choices. Her own mistakes.

Hell, who was he kidding? If she tried to get in the car and leave with the bastard, Daryl would probably lock her in his bedroom until she came to her senses and his father had disposed of the jackass's body.

"He just wants to talk to her. Right here, in the open. No tricks." Vaughn spread his hands wide, like a magician working his audience. *Nothing up my sleeve, I swear.*

Daryl's knee-jerk reaction was a great big "hell no".

It might be a reasonable request, given the circumstances, but Daryl wasn't feeling reasonable. In fact, he was feeling downright surly. Which only got worse when he glanced at his father and he gave an almost imperceptible nod, indicating he thought they should agree to the meeting.

Well, fuck.

"Right here, out in the open," Daryl repeated, laying the ground rules.

"Absolutely."

He really didn't want to do this. "All right. *If* she wants to talk to him." Because if she didn't, no one was forcing her.

Daryl tipped his head toward his father, who slipped back into the house. A few seconds later, he led Amelia outside, her face a little pale but her expression resolute. A surge of pride welled up in him at her courage.

A week ago, she'd run from this man. Now she chose to face him down. Daryl might have once thought she had no backbone, but this week had proven him wrong.

About a lot of things.

As Amelia came to stand beside Daryl, Vaughn studied her, a small line of puzzlement creasing his forehead as though he wasn't certain she was the right person. Not surprising, since she was dressed in jeans and a t-shirt and not some expensive designer outfit.

"Miss Westlake," he said finally.

"Mr. Vaughn." Snooty princess was firmly in place.

Daryl bit back a grin. Charles didn't stand a chance.

With an arm gesture, Vaughn invited Amelia to accompany him toward the car, but she stopped at Daryl's touch. He held out a hand to Vaughn.

"Keys." He caught them as they were tossed and tucked them in his pocket for safekeeping. "Now the gun."

"Do you really think I'd try anything with all the firepower aimed at me?"

"Do you really think I'll let her anywhere near you while you're armed?"

The fact he didn't continue to argue showed Vaughn had expected nothing less. But rather than turn over his weapon, he walked back to the car. Using exaggerated movements, he withdrew the gun from the holster that was all but invisible under his jacket and put it inside on the driver's seat before closing the door. He held up his hands in a "happy now?" gesture.

"What do you think?" Daryl asked his father quietly.

"I'll keep an eye on him. You keep your attention on Amy."

Daryl nodded. He didn't trust Vaughn an inch, and clearly his father felt the same way. He looked at Amelia. She was staring at the car like it was a snake poised to strike. "Are you sure you want to do this?"

She looked up at him, and he realized it was anger, not fear, shining from her eyes. Squaring her shoulders, she lifted her chin in pure regal fashion.

"Absolutely."

They walked down the steps, three abreast, Amelia between the two men who would protect her, no matter the cost. Vaughn went to the rear passenger side door and pulled it open before stepping back to the front of the car, followed by his father. Daryl ignored them both. He stopped Amelia while they were still several yards from the car, waiting for Charles to get out.

Only it wasn't Charles who emerged.

It was his father, the senator himself, who stepped out onto the dirt driveway and gave the place a disdainful once over before locking his gaze on Amelia. Who, judging by her sudden start, was just as surprised to see him as Daryl.

Clearly, they should have clarified exactly who "he" was.

Amelia rallied and sent out the opening salvo. "Senator, this is a surprise."

"I don't know why it should be, considering the situation you've put us all in disappearing the way you did. Do you know how much trouble I had to go to in order to track you down?"

"I made my position quite clear to Charles before I left Connecticut." Amelia's voice was even and threaded with confidence. "I told him I was calling off the wedding and why. I gave him back his ring. I didn't think I needed to be any clearer than that."

"Yes, yes, I know all about your *reasons*." He said it like it was a ridiculous word.

"Then I don't understand your confusion."

"Charles fully expected you to take a few hours to get over your little fit, not hop on a plane and take off into the middle of nowhere to sulk."

"My little fit?" Amelia gave a half-laugh. A dangerous sound, even if the senator didn't realize it yet. "Is that really how you think of my decisions? What am I saying, of course it is. Well, let me tell you, Senator, that my *little fit* is a permanent state, and I have no intention of changing my mind."

"And I have no intention of standing here baking in the sun

arguing with you about this."

"Well, we can agree on one thing, at least."

Already moving to get back into the car, his tone was brusque and businesslike as though clipping out orders to one of his minions. "Good. Get in. My plane is on standby at the airport. We might just make it back to Connecticut in time for the rehearsal dinner if we're lucky."

Amelia flinched, just a little, but otherwise didn't move an inch.

"I meant I didn't plan on arguing. I have no intention of going with you. Weren't you listening? The wedding is off."

"The wedding is most certainly not off," the senator snapped, turning back toward her.

Daryl bristled at the other man's aggressive posture, but held himself back, letting Amelia handle the man who clearly wasn't reading the danger signals she gave off.

Senator Blowhard was expecting quiet, compliant Amelia.

What he was about to get was a great big helping of confident, pissed-off Amy.

"Do you have any idea the effort that has gone into making this the event of the season?" Davenport asked. "The expense?"

"And every bit of both has been focused solely on making sure Charles got as many interviews and as much column space as possible," Amelia replied. "You were engineering a publicity campaign, not planning a wedding. The entire thing was about his career, not our lives together."

"A fact you knew perfectly well from the start."

Amelia paused before slowly nodding.

"You're right. I did go into the engagement knowing that a lot of the focus would be on Charles. That doesn't mean I expected the wedding to be some elaborate publicity stunt, or the marriage nothing more than a pretty façade to present to the public. It might have taken me a lot longer than it should have to figure that out, and shame on me for being so blind to the truth. But that doesn't mean

I intend to compound my mistake by going through with this sham of a marriage and consigning myself to being miserable for the rest of my life just so Charles doesn't lose traction in his campaign."

"Calling off the wedding at this juncture would mean more than losing traction. It would destroy any chance he has of winning the primary this year."

"Oh, please. I'm sick and tired of everyone harping on how this wedding is the cornerstone of Charles's career. Get over it. If Charles can't win the candidacy without being married to me, then maybe he should consider another career choice."

"Do you seriously think that *you* are in any way a factor in all of this?" Davenport scoffed. "Charles could have married any debutante and gotten the same amount of publicity. What he needs from *you* is—"

"My father," Amelia finished for him. "Or, rather, his connections and influence."

"With William's backing added to mine, Charles will be *the* rising star in the party. He could be sitting in the Oval Office before he's forty. Do you understand what that would mean?"

"Well, I wish you all the best with that, but I'm sorry. I'm not sacrificing myself at the altar of political ambition. Not Charles's, not my father's, and certainly not yours. I don't plan on repeating myself again, so please listen carefully. There isn't going to be any wedding, now or ever. It's over. Now please, just go home and leave me alone."

The senator's face flushed a dangerous red, leaving streaks of white along his cheekbones as he clenched his jaw.

"This is far from over, missy. Do you really think you can just make a decision of this magnitude and not suffer the consequences?"

"Oh, I fully expect to be vilified by you and your PR team in the press." She sounded weary, but resolved. "Do your worst. Nothing you say matters. You can't hurt me."

The senator got an ugly look in his eye, his lips twisting into a

mockery of a smile.
"Maybe not. But I can certainly hurt your friends."

Chapter 26

The senator's words sent a shaft of panic through Amelia's carefully constructed shell of calm. Facing down Charles's father was one of the hardest things she'd ever done. Harder even than giving Charles back his ring. But she'd been doing a fairly good job, despite her quaking insides.

Until now.

The very open threat against the people she loved most was enough to shake her confidence to the core.

"My friends have nothing to do with any of this."

"Oh, I think they had everything to do with it." He shot a glare to where Daryl stood just off to her side. "Especially since it was one of the Fordham's security people who spirited you out of Connecticut, and then again out of Boulder before hiding you away up here in the ass-crack of nowhere so no one could get in contact with you."

"I was leaving Connecticut on my own, anyway. Daryl coming along had nothing to do with my decision to leave. *My* decision," she repeated, trying desperately to head off where she could see this going.

Damn it, this was exactly why she'd refused to stay with her friends' families. She hadn't wanted her decisions to cause them trouble. Coming here was supposed to have kept them safe.

Clearly, she'd miscalculated.

But maybe she could still fix things without having to go to her backup plan. She'd known from the start it might come down to doing the one thing she absolutely didn't want to do, what it disgusted her to even consider doing. But she knew if she had to, if she couldn't convince the senator to leave her friends out of this, she'd have no choice.

They would *not* suffer for her bad decisions.

"In case you've forgotten, my friends' families aren't exactly defenseless. Frank Fordham and Rupert Beaumont didn't have their millions handed to them. They both worked hard to achieve their success." Unlike the Davenports and Westlakes, who had been living off of "family money" for generations. "And they're very well respected by their peers. You can't do anything to them they couldn't brush off and ignore."

Maybe.

She really had no idea what kind of trouble the senator had in mind, but it wouldn't hurt to point out the people he was threatening were pretty powerful themselves. If he struck out, they had the wherewithal to strike back.

The senator's expression said he didn't like that little reminder. But before Amelia could feel a moment's relief, he said, "Not all of your friends." He glanced around with feigned interest. "This looks like a nice ranch. Horses, I believe? Small places like this always run on such a tight margin. Be a shame if anything were to make people shy away from doing business here. They might never recover."

Amelia stared at him in shock as the threat registered, rocking her to her toes. "You would honestly destroy decent, hardworking people just to get what you want?"

"In a heartbeat."

There was no shame in his tone. It sickened her to think this was the kind of man running their government. Worse, he was raising his son to be just like him. Now she knew exactly where Charles had gotten his lack of morals.

"You're a monster."

"No, I'm a pragmatist. I'm willing to do whatever I must to

achieve my goal. The question is, what are *you* willing to do to save your friends?"

Anything. Everything. Even the one thing she didn't want to do.

"Okay." She swallowed hard against the fist-sized lump that was choking her. "You win. I'll go back with you."

"*No.*"

She jumped as Daryl practically shouted the word, and then again when he clamped a hand onto her shoulder.

"Amy, no, you can't—"

"It's okay." She patted his hand, refusing to break eye contact with the senator. "I'll go back with you," she repeated, her voice strengthening, "and my first stop will be to pay a visit to the man whose wife your son is sleeping with."

If she'd had any doubts about whether he was aware of Charles's extracurricular activities, the lack of reaction on the senator's face put them to rest.

"Threatening me with spreading lies isn't going to—"

"Truths, Senator. Although I can understand where you'd have trouble telling the two apart, seeing as how your own moral code is a bit...ambiguous."

"Well, if you're foolish enough to believe everything you hear..." His tone dripped with condescension.

"I didn't hear it. I saw it with my own eyes. Unfortunately," she added with a grimace. The memory of Charles's pale buttocks as he pumped into the moaning woman bent over his desk was forever burned into her brain. "Your son should learn to lock his door when he slips out of a party for a liaison. Especially if it's a party in honor of his own wedding and that liaison is *not* with his fiancée."

The senator's eyes narrowed. "So that's what this is about? You caught Charles with another woman, and now you're being spiteful."

"I think if anyone has a reason to be spiteful, it would be me, since sneaking off to screw your mistress while your future wife is in the house is a pretty slimy move. To be honest, though, I couldn't care less who your son is sleeping with. But I'm pretty sure her husband will."

An expression of pure derision crossed the senator's face. "I told Constance you were too naïve for your own good. If you think a bout of infidelity is going to cause anyone in our circles to even blink an eye—"

"Not even the vice-president?"

It was a toss-up which man's reaction said more about him. While the senator took a step back as though he'd just received a blow to the solar plexus, Daryl stepped closer and aligned his body at her side, giving her his full support.

Although he did lean down and whisper next to her ear, "Be very careful, Princess."

She nodded faintly to show she understood.

The senator seemed to have recovered a little of his equilibrium. "If you think your lies—"

"Truths," she reminded him. "And while you may have no problem with someone playing fast and loose with their marriage vows, didn't the vice-president—and correct me if I'm wrong here—didn't he run on a family values platform? I seem to recall his family played a huge part in all of his campaign appearances. Katrina and the children always at his side, the perfect little family unit."

It had been all too similar to her own father's strategy of using his family as props. She'd actually felt sorry for Katrina and her kids, knowing how hard it was to always have to be "on" and perform for the cameras. Evidently, Katrina had found her own way to cope.

Mottled red suffused the senator's face as his shock turned to rage.

"And didn't I hear that the party is grooming him for the nomination when the president's term is up? What kind of damage do you think would be done to his career if it became known his own wife was having an adulterous affair right under his nose? Or to the careers of anyone even remotely connected to the scandal?"

Because while Senator Davenport might not give two figs about the vice-president's career, he most certainly cared about his own.

"My son wouldn't be that reckless," he replied through clenched teeth.

"He would if she promised to get her husband to back him within the party when primary time rolled around." It hadn't been the most loving pillow talk Amelia ever heard, but then, what Charles and Katrina had been doing had nothing to do with love. Amelia could almost forgive him for his infidelity if it did. But knowing he was whoring himself out for political favors made her want to vomit.

There was no refutation this time from the senator. Evidently, he knew his son better than he was willing to admit. Once again, she wondered how far the apple had landed from the tree.

"Do you know how many people you would destroy by going public with this?"

"More than just the two people who deserve it. Which is why I don't want to do any such thing. Not unless you try to force my hand by threatening the people I care about."

"Who else knows about this?"

Before she could open her mouth to assure him she'd told no one until now, Daryl squeezed her shoulder in gentle warning.

"No one who will say anything without Amelia's express instructions," Daryl said. "But rest assured there are safeguards in place that should anything happen to her, anything at all, the information will immediately be made public in the most damaging way possible."

Her breath caught as she absorbed the implication of his words. That the senator might choose to guarantee no one found out by making sure she suffered some type of "accident" in the not-too distant future.

"Your cooperation for her silence, Senator," Daryl said. "Do we have a deal?"

Looking like he'd rather argue than agree, the senator gave a jerky nod.

"So, the wedding is officially off?" She needed to hear it to believe it.

"We've been telling everyone you've been deathly ill and under a doctor's care all week to excuse your absence. When I get back, I'll announce that we've postponed the wedding because of your ongoing health concerns. After a little time has passed," he continued, cutting off her protest, "and some of the media scrutiny fades, we'll quietly announce that you and Charles have reconsidered your marriage and parted ways amicably."

It wasn't the immediate conclusion to this mess she'd wanted, but Amelia knew how the game had to be played. In order to save face—and votes—the Davenports would need to ease their way out of the situation with as much finesse as possible.

But the longer the faux engagement hung over her head, the more problems she could foresee in her future.

"One month," she said.

"That won't be nearly enough time for—"

"One month. If you don't make the announcement by then, I will." She met the senator's furious stare without flinching.

Seeming to realize she wouldn't be intimidated into reconsidering her edict, he said, "Fine. But if I ever hear so much as a whisper about Charles and Katrina, our little deal is off."

"No, that's not the deal." Amelia's heart started to pound. "I promised *I* wouldn't say anything. I can't control what other people find out about them."

"That's not my problem. If this gets out, all of my plans go up in smoke. Years of planning and maneuvering ruined. So if that happens to me, missy, you better believe that I will destroy every single person you know, starting right here."

Panic like she'd never felt before hit. "No, that's...you can't..." It was suddenly impossible to catch her breath, not even with Daryl rubbing his hand in soothing circles on her back.

"Did you get all of that?" Daryl asked, withdrawing his phone from his shirt pocket with his free hand.

Amelia turned and stared at him in utter confusion.

What in the world?

From the phone's speaker, Doyle's voice replied with a tone that held not one drop of amusement. "Every word, loud and clear."

"What the hell is this?" The senator looked like he was going to explode. "Who is that? A reporter?"

"No, my boss," Daryl replied. "Who now has a very nice recording of you threatening Amelia and her friends. One of whom he's engaged to, by the way, so I'm thinking he's not real happy with you at the moment."

"That's...you..." The senator sputtered before finally getting out, "That recording won't be admissible in court."

"Oh, it doesn't need to be. It just needs to be clear enough for the ten o'clock news."

The senator blanched, then flushed.

"It's simple, Senator. Stick to the deal, and that recording will never see the light of day. Screw with any of us, and it goes public. Now I suggest you leave. I believe you have a plane waiting?"

Amelia was still processing this new twist when the senator gave her a look that, a week ago, would have made her cringe. Now, it only made her chin come up higher.

"You were never worth this much trouble." He straightened his jacket with a jerk and stalked to the car.

Vaughn walked back to close his door, then caught the keys Daryl tossed him and went around to the driver's door. He shot Amelia a short, two-fingered salute, as though to acknowledge who had won the skirmish before getting in.

As they watched the car retreat down the long driveway, Amelia sank against Daryl, her arm going around his waist as much for support as for comfort. "Is it really over?"

He gave her a squeeze. "I think he's scared enough to keep his word. For now, anyway."

"*God*." She buried her face against his chest, breathing in the comforting scent of fresh air and horses that permeated the soft cotton of his shirt. How would she have gotten through this without him?

How would she get through the rest of her *life* without him?

She pushed away the maudlin thought. It was too soon to mourn, not while she still had a few precious days before their strange little idyll was over. If this past week taught her anything, it was to make the most of what you had while you had it.

While Daryl spoke first to Doyle on the phone, then had a lengthier conversation with his father, Amelia sat on the top step of the porch, her gaze never straying far from his strong profile.

Was it really only a little over a week since he'd been forced into the role of her protector? Since she'd been forced to open her eyes and see him as more than Daryl the bodyguard, but as Daryl the man? How was it possible she'd come to know so much about him, to *care* so much about him, in such a short time?

And it wasn't just him. She'd also come to understand so many things about herself in that same short span. She'd always considered herself weak. Spineless. Not good enough for...well, anything. But now she could see she'd thought that about herself because it was what she'd been taught to believe.

Her parents had raised her to see herself as far less than she could actually be. Than she actually was. And that lack of self-confidence had left her malleable and dependent.

The perfect people pleaser.

She'd like to think it was simply neglectful parenting, but part of her new self-awareness meant she needed to stop making excuses for them.

William and Meredith Westlake were terrible parents. Not to mention awful people. She had to accept that and move forward with the knowledge she no longer had to twist herself into painful little knots trying to make them happy.

It was a rather freeing realization.

When Daryl collected her from the porch and led her back into the house, she didn't question when he headed straight for his bedroom. She didn't protest when he locked the door. She didn't put up even a token resistance when he swooped down and attacked her mouth with his, the kiss furious and possessive, making her blood heat and her body leap awake in response.

There was something primal in the way he kissed her, the way he held her close, as though afraid she might somehow disappear.

She held him the same way. If she could find a way, she'd gladly hold on to him forever. But since she'd already decided to be thankful for what she had, not lament what she wanted, she threw herself wholeheartedly into the play of lips and teeth and tongues, enjoying the heart-pounding wildness of it.

Between one breath and the next, they were on the bed. Clothes went flying. Amelia was pretty sure buttons did as well. She didn't care. All that mattered was getting the barrier of their clothing gone.

Now.

This instant.

Finally, they were skin-to-skin, and Daryl stopped. Just...stopped.

For the briefest second, she had a horrible sense of déjà vu, remembering the night she'd tried to seduce Charles after their engagement and he'd lost interest in her before the deed had been done. But one look at Daryl's face burned away any chill that memory raised.

His dark eyes were fierce and tender at the same time as they slowly followed the path his hand took. Starting at her leg, up over her hip, across her belly and through the valley between her breasts, as though inspecting every inch to make sure she was whole. Until finally his long fingers cupped her jaw and he was looking directly into her eyes.

"You scared the hell out of me." The words sounded like they'd been dragged from someplace deep and painful. "If you'd gotten in that car with him…"

"I wouldn't have." Not unless her insurance plan hadn't worked. He probably wouldn't appreciate hearing that, though, so she kept it to herself.

"If you had…*God*." He closed his eyes as though pained by the thought.

Turning her head, she laid a kiss on his palm. "I didn't."

When he opened his eyes again, there was such potent emotion shining from them, Amelia's breath caught in her chest. This wasn't lust. It wasn't fear or affection or anger. It was something she'd never seen directed at her before.

Something that touched a place inside of her that shuddered and slowly stretched as it awakened for the very first time. Ever.

Oh, God. I love him.

Oh, no. No, no, no. This was not supposed to happen. This was supposed to be about the here and now. She was under no illusion about how things stood between them. What the future held. Daryl wasn't her happily-ever-after guy.

No matter what her stupid heart said.

But she could at least be happy right in this moment.

Wetting suddenly dry lips with the tip of her tongue, she asked, "Are we going to keep wasting time talking or are you going to make love to me?"

All of that heat in his gaze instantly morphed to the possessive lust that had left her curling her toes and grabbing the sheets the night before.

With a wicked smile, Daryl moved down along her body until his mouth was poised just above the apex of her thighs, which quivered in anticipation. Keeping eye contact, he dipped his tongue into her folds in one long, hot sweep.

With a moan, her legs fell open, leaving her vulnerable to whatever he wanted to do to her, whatever heights he tried to take her. For now, she'd take everything he was willing to give.

Later, she'd deal with the emotional fallout of everything he wasn't.

Chapter 27

A sharp knock at the door snapped Daryl awake. "What?"

Chaz's muffled voice replied, "Mare's foaling. Hank wants you at the barn."

"I'll be there in a minute." Turning his head on the pillow, he forced the red luminous numbers on the clock into focus. Almost one in the morning. It never failed.

"Amy said she wanted to know when it happened." There was a meaningful pause. "You want me to go knock on her door?"

Daryl looked at the woman blinking sleepily up at him from her pillow beside him.

"No, thanks. I'll take care of it." He ground his teeth at Chaz's knowing chuckle as he retreated down the hallway. The bastard just didn't know when to leave well enough alone.

"What's going on?" Amelia yawned like a little kitten, all warm and cuddly and barely half awake. Not that he could blame her for being tired. He hadn't let her get all that much sleep the past two nights.

"Delilah's finally decided to drop her foal." He slipped from under the covers and reached for his jeans. "It's late. Go back to sleep. You can see them in the morning."

His suggestion earned him a snort of disbelief. Throwing the covers back, she snapped on the lamp and gathered up her clothes. "Are you kidding? There's no way in the world I'm missing this."

As fond as she'd become of the pregnant mare, he didn't bother trying to dissuade her. After yanking on his boots, he tossed her one of his old sweatshirts to wear over her tee, adding a flannel shirt over his own. It might be early June, but the overnight temperatures could still drop into the fifties.

Because it could be a long night, Daryl curbed Amelia's impatience long enough to set up the coffeepot and drag down several large, well-used metal thermoses from the cabinet. All but dancing with anticipation, she grabbed his hand and half-dragged him out the back door as soon as he was done.

"Come *on* already! You're going to make me miss my one and only chance to see a horse being born!"

She'd said it in a laughing manner, but the reminder her stay on the ranch was almost over was a sobering one.

When they got to the barn, Chaz gave a smirking look at their clasped hands. Glaring a warning to keep his comments to himself, Daryl went to where his father leaned against the closed half-door to the mare's birthing stall. Only then did Amelia pull her hand from his to peer inside.

"Oh!" She covered her mouth.

Daryl looked over her shoulder. The mare was lying on the thick bed of straw. Her sides heaved and she let out a strained groan as she struggled to expel the foal. Daryl placed his hands on Amelia's shoulders as she cringed at the sound.

"It's normal. Horses can get very vocal when they're giving birth, just like people."

"She looks so uncomfortable," Amelia whispered. "Is she okay?"

"Delilah's a trooper," Chaz said from her other side. "This is her first foal, so she's taking a little longer than usual, but the last time the vet checked her, he said everything looked fine."

The look he gave Daryl over her head said something else entirely.

Leaving Chaz to distract Amelia with one of his tall stories about a foal he'd helped deliver in the middle of a blizzard, Daryl and his father stepped outside.

"She broke water about fifteen minutes ago," his father said when they were out of earshot. "She's been straining, but it doesn't look like she's making any progress."

That wasn't good news. The foal usually emerged shortly after the water broke. Anything longer than twenty minutes of laboring could mean some type of problem, like a caught hoof or a breech birth.

Or worse.

"The vet?"

"Up in Cactus Flat visiting his grandkids. He's on his way, but it'll take him a while to get here." Maybe too long was left unsaid.

"Damn."

"Nothing we haven't had to handle on our own before."

True. But there were always dangers when a birth required outside intervention.

They went back inside the barn. The vocalizations from the laboring mare were getting louder and shriller. Chaz was still telling his story, but it was clear most of Amelia's attention was focused on Delilah and not him. When he finally gave up and stopped talking, she didn't even seem to notice.

Taking her by the shoulders, Daryl turned her away from the stall and toward the barn door. "That coffee should be ready by now. Would you mind filling the thermoses and bringing them back down here?"

"Okay." She cast a last look over her shoulder, biting her lip as the mare let out another groan before hurrying on her errand.

"That won't keep her away long," Chaz said.

"I know."

"You should tell her to go back to the house and stay there. She doesn't need to see this. It could get bad."

Daryl snorted. "Yeah, why don't you tell her that?"

"Because she's not mine."

Daryl refused to acknowledge the way his heart surged at the implication that she might be his.

Instead, he turned his attention to his father as he stepped into the stall, slowly approaching the mare and crooning soft words. Her ears twitched and turned, listening to him while he placed his hands along her rippling side as another contraction hit. Her entire body seemed to get into the effort to push her foal into the world, but by the time the contraction ended, there still wasn't any sign of it emerging.

Shit.

Amelia returned with the coffee, but nobody drank it.

The long minutes dragged on. And on. And still, no foal.

Finally, Chaz and his father exchanged a look that had Chaz heading into the tack room and coming back with the foaling kit that had likely been prepared weeks ago. Stripping off his jacket and rolling back his sleeves, Chaz grabbed a large bottle of lubricant and let himself into the stall, talking softly to the mare as he approached.

"What's he going to do?" Amelia whispered.

"Give her a little help. Remember when I told you about that foal I had to help deliver when I was a kid?"

"Yeah." Her eyes widened. "*Oh.*"

"You can wait back at the house until this is over, you know."

He grinned at the dirty look she shot him in reply. He'd been pretty sure she'd be that way about it, but he needed to offer her the out. Especially with the way she cringed every time the mare made a sound, her hand squeezing his in time with the contractions.

She did, however, avert her gaze as Chaz pushed his lubed hand into the mare's birth canal.

"Okay, I've got one foot not too far in. And that's the nose." He was quiet for a few seconds before cursing. "I can't find the other foot, and this foal's wedged so damn tight I can't get my hand in any further without the risk of hurting the mare."

"Can you push the foal backward?" his father asked.

"Not enough to make a difference."

"What if we stand her up and walk her, help shift the foal?" Daryl asked.

His father shook his head. "I don't think she's got the strength. She's been pushing too long." He shoved his fists against his hips and stared up at the ceiling, blowing out a frustrated breath. "Damn it to hell."

Daryl understood his father's dilemma. There were very few things they could do at this point that wouldn't be dangerous, but it could be just as dangerous to do nothing. It was a tough decision. If they chose wrong, they could lose the foal, the mare, or both. In the innocence of youth, he hadn't realized what a precarious situation it had been when he'd helped deliver that foal all those years ago.

He stilled.

Slowly, he brought his hand, still twined with Amelia's, up to where he could look at it. He'd been able to help back then because of his small child's hands. They were too big now to do any better than Chaz's. But Amelia's...hers were small, dainty, gentle. They just might be the answer.

"Dad." When his father looked over, Daryl lifted his and Amelia's hands higher. He didn't need to explain.

"It might work."

"What might work?" Amelia asked.

Gripping both of her hands, he said, "When I helped with that foal when I was eight, it was because I had the smallest hands."

She looked at him, uncomprehending for a moment before dropping her gaze to their entwined hands. Understanding quickly gave way to an expression of panic. "I'm not...I can't..." She stammered, her green eyes so wide they looked like they might fall out of her suddenly pale face.

"You can." But he wouldn't tell her she had to. This had to be her decision.

Biting her lip again, she looked toward the stall, where Delilah let out another groan as her body strained. She swallowed. "What do I need to do?"

Daryl kissed her forehead, relief and pride filling him. "That's my girl."

By the time she'd washed up and had lubricant smeared from fingers to elbow, Amelia was looking a little less scared and a lot more determined. As much as Daryl wanted to go into the stall with her, he let Chaz do it. The mare was stressed enough without having to deal with a bunch of people she didn't know well huddled around her.

His father stood by with the pulling straps in case the foal still wouldn't deliver once it was in the proper position. *If* they could get it into the proper position.

Sometimes a malpresentation couldn't be fixed by anything less than a Caesarean section. With their vet still over an hour away, that wouldn't be an option. But since Chaz felt the nose, the odds were good they weren't dealing with one of the more serious—and potentially fatal—situations.

Kneeling behind the horse, Amelia looked at Daryl. He gave her a smile and a nod of encouragement. After a brief hesitation, she smiled and nodded back before turning her entire attention to what Chaz was instructing her to do. She took a deep breath and began.

"Oh, God, this is...so gross." Despite the complaint, she didn't stop. "I'm not sure...okay, that's...that's a foot." She sounded a little awed. "Um...and the nose...yes, that's definitely the nose."

"Okay, good girl," Chaz said. "Now go to the opposite side from where you felt the first foot and try to slide your hand past the head to find the second leg."

Amelia made a small sound of disgust as she complied. Long seconds ticked past.

"Anything, sweetheart?" Chaz prompted.

Daryl fought back his instinctive irritation at the endearment.

"I think..." More silence. "It's not the same. There's no hoof."

"That's okay. That just means the leg is bent at the knee or fetlock.

Ankle," Chaz said, simplifying. "Which is actually what we were hoping for."

"Okay. So, what do I do next?"

"Try to feel your way down until you come to the bend, then ease the leg up into the right position, pointing straight along the foal's body same as the other one. Kinda like he's Michael Phelps getting ready to dive into the pool."

Amelia let out a rough laugh, which Chaz had clearly intended. A look of intense concentration came over her face as she leaned further into the mare's rump, following Chaz's instructions.

Daryl curled his hands over the top board of the stall door, fighting the need to go to her, knowing that even if he did, there was nothing he could do to help her. This was all Amelia.

Suddenly, she let out a gasp. "I think I did it."

"Don't think," Chaz said. "Be sure."

"I'm sure."

"Okay then, pull your arm out, easy like, before she pushes again."

Everything happened fast after that.

Almost as soon as Amelia scooted back, the mare let out a massive groan and pushed. A hoof appeared, followed by a nose, then the elusive second hoof. Then the rest of the foal slid out with no trouble at all.

Chaz whispered soft words of praise to the mare, stroking her neck as she lay breathing hard after all the effort before checking on the foal to make sure the rest of the sac surrounding him had broken properly and he was breathing okay after his prolonged time in the birth canal. He gave a thumbs-up.

His father slapped Daryl on the back with a relieved laugh. "That's one helluva woman you've got there, son. A helluva woman."

Daryl only had eyes for Amelia, who was sitting in the straw with her back against the stall wall, knees drawn up, staring at the newborn foal with a sense of wonder and delight. He wished he'd brought his phone so he could take a picture and capture it forever.

It was a heady experience, helping to bring a life into the world, and not one soon forgotten. The kind that changed a person. It had changed *him*, for certain. He'd known from the moment he'd watched that helpless, beautiful creature being born all those years ago that he'd found his place, his calling.

His home.

Somewhere along the line, he'd forgotten that. He'd lost his way *and* his home, and had been struggling to find both again ever since. Maybe, just maybe, he'd been handed a reminder of what it was he'd been searching for all along.

Amelia turned her head and smiled at him, all the joy of the moment shining from her eyes, and Daryl felt his heart squeeze tight in his chest. His father was right. She was one hell of a woman.

It was just too bad that no matter what his future turned out to be, she wouldn't be a part of it.

⸻◆⸻

She'd helped a horse give birth.

Her.

Mostly useless, perpetually spineless Amelia Ann Westlake.

She'd been asked to do something she never in a million years would have believed herself capable of doing, much less doing *right*. Daryl and Hank and Chaz had put their faith in her, their trust, and she'd come through without disappointing any of them. And in the process had helped bring a fragile new life into the world.

The absolute amazement of that fact still had her smiling almost an hour later. Her cheeks ached from it. Hell, she'd probably be smiling for days before the wonder wore off.

The memory of that little foal sliding out into the world like an Olympic champion—thanks to Chaz she couldn't think of it any other way—had been second only to seeing his mother clean and nuzzle him until he found his wobbly balance and started to nurse, proving that neither mother nor son were any the worse for their ordeal.

Of course, the joy of the event only somewhat mitigated the fact she'd had her arm *inside a horse*. Try as she might to forget that part, there were just too many physical reminders. Not the least of which was the mess that had ended up all over the front of her borrowed sweatshirt.

Once the euphoria of the blessed event had faded, the smell of a combination of things she didn't want to consider too closely became impossible to ignore.

Trying to wipe it off only made it worse. Daryl finally just stripped the sweatshirt off her and replaced it with his own flannel shirt before she had a chance for a single shiver. He hadn't said a word, but he'd kissed her, long and soft, before going back to talking with his father about the ranch's newest resident.

She wasn't sure if it was the shirt or the kiss, but the cold didn't bother her one little bit after that.

Hank and Chaz gave her hugs and words of praise, but neither meant as much to her as Daryl's PDA. He'd kissed her. In front of the other men. In front of his *father*. He wasn't a man who would do something like that unless it meant something. Unless *she* meant something.

Would he?

Caffeine and adrenaline could only carry everyone so far. After fighting off the nods for as long as she could, Amelia must have drifted off, because a gentle shake of her arm awakened her. Yawning into her hand, she staggered to her feet from where she'd curled up on the nest of blankets Chaz had been using while he'd kept watch over the pregnant mare.

"Go to bed." Daryl handed her the empty thermos and nudged her toward the door.

"Are you coming, too?" It took a second for her to realize how that sounded. "I meant, are you *going* to bed, too, not are you coming with me to—*mmpf*." His mouth stopped the embarrassing tumble of words. With a sigh, she twined her arms around his neck and fell into the kiss.

It wasn't wild or carnal. It was simply lips with a hint of tongue to tease the situation from chaste to promise. But when they broke apart and she started walking up toward the house, her head was spinning and her thoughts were on what new and wonderful ways Daryl might have to make love to her when he joined her in his bed.

Which was the only excuse she had for not realizing the man was there before he stepped in front of her. The hazy predawn twilight illuminated his features, sending a thrill of shock and disbelief coursing through her.

"Charles!"

Chapter 28

"You sound surprised to see me."

Amelia didn't trust his calm, almost amused tone. Her gaze darted around, looking for whomever he might have brought with him. Charles rarely went anywhere without an entourage.

"That's because I am. What are you doing here?"

"I might ask you the same thing. What are *you* doing here when you're supposed to be back in Connecticut? *Getting. Married.*" The amusement gave way to anger in the course of those two words.

"Charles, I already explained to you before I left that—"

"Do you think I care about your ridiculous excuses?" He took a threatening step toward her. "Do you have any idea what you've done?"

She took two steps back, but he still seemed closer than before.

"They were reasons, not excuses." She could shout for help, but that might push him into acting on the rage burning in his eyes.

"We had a bargain."

"Silly me, I thought it was an engagement."

"You had one job to do," he said, ignoring her sarcasm. "Just stand at the altar and say *I do*. That should have been easy enough to manage, even for you."

"Even for me?" Her shock at his unexpected appearance started to burn off as her temper kicked in. "What's that supposed to mean?"

"Oh, please." He gave a nasty laugh. "It's no secret my father didn't choose you for your brains."

"No, he chose me for my father's connections." A sore point, but one she'd already come to terms with. Despite any earlier misconceptions on her part, there had been no emotions other than ambition and greed involved in the orchestration of her pairing with Charles.

And it *had* been orchestrated. From their first meeting and the whirlwind courtship, right down to the over-the-top engagement party. Still, it stung that her inclination to appease had been taken as a lack of intelligence.

Of course, she'd thought she was in love with the jerk, so maybe they weren't so wrong.

"And for your bloodlines."

Amelia's lip curled. "Oh, yes, let's not forget that."

Again, the sarcasm seemed to sail right over his head.

"With our good looks and excellent gene pools, our children would have been stunning. Perfect for the camera."

"Sure, a real Norman Rockwell image." The thought of having a child with this cold, calculating man made her ill. She pitied whatever woman he ended up marrying.

"Do you even know what today is?"

It took a few seconds for her to remember what day of the week it was. She'd had next to no sleep the night before, making the days seem to bleed together into one. But the senator had come on Friday, and although it felt like longer, that was only yesterday. So that meant today had to be...

"Saturday." Even as she said it, what he was really asking hit her. Today was supposed to be their wedding day.

Panic sent her stomach nosediving to her toes.

"I'm not going back with you." She took a step back, ready to run. She might not get away, but if she screamed, she had no doubt someone would come to her aid before Charles could drag her off anywhere. "I spoke to your father. We reached an agreement. The wedding is off. He must have told you."

"Oh, yes," Charles said silkily, "my father told me all about your *agreement*. Right *after* he sent out a press release postponing the ceremony, and *after* he'd already informed all the guests. Oh, but they were still invited to the reception, with the bride and groom's deepest apologies. Like feeding them cake and champagne will make them all forget that I couldn't get my own *fucking* bride to the *fucking* altar."

Another step back. "It was the best solution."

"The best solution?" He sounded incredulous. "For who? Certainly not me. You told my father I was screwing the vice-president's wife!"

"Which was the truth."

"It was politics," he replied, hands fisting. "Katrina was my best shot at getting her husband's support in the primary. With his backing, it would have been a sure thing. And you *ruined* it."

"Me? How? I promised to keep your secret."

"My father ordered me to break things off with her. *Ordered me*, like I was some kind of child or something. And it's *all your fault*."

Pointing out he was *acting* like a child, and a spoiled one at that, wouldn't be helpful.

"Your father seemed to think the risk of what would happen if the vice-president found out about your affair outweighed any potential gain."

"He wouldn't have found out."

It was amazing how very unconcerned he seemed about the possibility, which prompted her ill-advised, flippant reply. "Well, *I* did, so I wouldn't be so cocky if I were you."

His eyes narrowed. "Yes, how did you find out? Father wouldn't say, but he seemed certain whatever you told him was the truth."

Cursing her untamed tongue, she shrugged. "It doesn't matter."

"Oh, I think it does." He stepped closer. "How did you find out, Amelia Ann?"

"I saw you. During the party last week." Had it really only been that long? "I went to your suite looking for you, and I walked in on the two of you doing...well, each other."

Charles looked surprised before he laughed. "You walked in on us screwing? Damn, you must have gotten quite an eyeful." The laughter turned cruel. "Is that why you ran away, Princess? You couldn't deal with seeing what a real woman could do for her man? Did it shock your puritanical sensibilities?"

"Puritanical sensibilities?" She crossed her arms, more annoyed by his use of the nickname she'd come to consider an endearment from Daryl than by his weak barb at her self-esteem. "You do remember that *I* tried to seduce *you* into bed once upon a time, right?"

"And we both know how well that turned out."

Twin fingers of insecurity and inadequacy poked at her confidence.

At the time, she'd thought he'd been as in the moment as her. He'd dashed that belief like delicate crystal on a marble floor when he'd left her, trembling with unsatisfied desire and mortification, to take a phone call.

But then a different memory superimposed itself on that one.

Of a wildly aroused Daryl pressing her to his bed and worshipping her naked body until she thought she'd die from the pleasure of it, before she turned the tables and did the same to him. Wild mustangs wouldn't have been able to pull Daryl away from their bed, much less a stupid phone call.

"What the hell are you smiling at?" Charles snapped, shattering the memory.

"Am I?" Amelia realized she was. "I guess I was just thinking about what a close call I had that night."

He scowled. "What's that supposed to mean?"

That she was glad her first time had been with a man who cared about her and her enjoyment, not with a selfish butthead like him who would have probably ruined sex for her completely.

This time, though, she kept her wayward tongue under control.

"Why are you here, Charles?" She hadn't meant to sound impatient, but she was exhausted and running on the last fumes of adrenaline his sudden appearance had produced. "Your secret is safe as long as your father keeps his word, so you can continue on with your life just as it was before we ever had the misfortune of meeting. We never have to see one another again."

Preferably ever.

"Now, that's where you're wrong. I can't just go back to my life, and do you want to know why? Because of *you* and your goddamned big mouth, that's why."

"I don't—"

"My father doesn't feel it would be in my best interest to continue trying to get onto the ticket for the next election cycle after all. He feels that I've displayed an unfortunate tendency to act *precipitously* and without giving enough thought to the full ramifications of my choices. So he's shut my campaign down. *He shut it down*"—he repeated, his voice taking on the shriller pitch of someone working themselves into a full-blown fit—"and said maybe, *maybe* he'd revisit that decision after enough time has passed to be sure none of my actions will have any far-reaching consequences."

Meaning the senator wanted to see if the vice-president ended up in the Oval Office before he risked letting his son back into the party's spotlight. Just in case any fallout from Charles's ill-advised choice of bed partners blew back onto him.

Sucks that daddy's willing to cut you loose to save his own neck, doesn't it?

"I'm sure that once everything has settled down, you'll be able to—"

"—pick right up where I left off?" Charles made a derisive noise. "No. Even if I could make a second successful start, which is doubtful, there would always be questions about what happened. And where there are questions, there are people digging up things best left buried. So no, I can't just pick up and go on as before. Thanks to *you*. I had it all. But now it's slipping through my fingers, because you couldn't keep your damn mouth shut and do what you were told. You've ruined my life, Princess, and now I'm going to return the favor."

He lunged.

As he grabbed her left arm, he got mostly the material of Daryl's oversized flannel shirt. She let out a scream of fear, outrage, and absolutely furious woman as she swung her free arm to fend him off. True to form, her fist missed him entirely. But the heavy metal thermos she'd forgotten she was still holding by the strap connected solidly with the side of his head with a dull thud.

There was a split-second when the two of them stared at each other in shocked surprise before Charles's eyes rolled back into his head and he went down like a sack of dirt.

While she stood over him trying to process what had happened, raised voices came from both the barn and the bunkhouse. Within seconds, she was surrounded by men, most of them armed, some only half-dressed, all of them talking at once.

It was all an indistinct drone of noise.

Her attention was all for the silent man who stood beside her, staring down at the now groaning man at their feet. Daryl looked like he was about to rip Charles into tiny little pieces. The longer he stayed silent, the more nervous she got.

Finally, she laid a hand on his arm and felt a small shudder as he seemed to wrestle his emotions under control. He took the thermos from her lax grasp and held it up, exposing the dent that now warped the metal casing.

Trying to play it off as nonchalantly as possible to keep him from losing his cool, Amelia shrugged. "He called me Princess."

Daryl's expression remained stony for a moment before that wicked twinkle she loved so much sparked in his eyes. He wrapped his arm around her shoulder, pulling her close as Hank and Chaz yanked a groggy Charles to his feet. Daryl shook his head at Charles, a ghost of a grin on his lips.

"Big mistake, asshole. Don't *ever* call her Princess."

❖

Daryl studied the familiar curves and angles of Amelia's face on the pillow beside him. Soft with sleep, her mouth was a tempting little rosebud, ripe for kissing. He resisted the urge. She needed her sleep more than he needed to make love to her again.

After playing midwife to a horse the night before, followed by the unexpected arrival of her ex and all the excitement surrounding that charming little scene, the few hours of catnaps she'd managed over the course of the day would be nowhere near enough.

His caveman-like need to reassure himself she was all right by having sex with her every time they were near a horizontal surface hadn't helped, either. Not that they'd needed it to be horizontal.

The wall had done just fine. And the shower.

So, as much as he might want to kiss those rosy lips until she woke, then bury himself inside her until the hint of panic burning low in his gut subsided again, he resisted. Even if she hadn't been exhausted, there were other things to take into consideration.

She probably wouldn't admit it, but he had to assume someone who'd been a virgin until only three days ago would have to be a bit tender by now.

He almost groaned out loud. That night was seared into his memory like a supernova. He'd treasure her gift forever. He didn't deserve it, but damned if he could find it in him to regret it for even one second.

Giving in to the need to touch her, he brushed a finger along her soft cheek.

A puff of breath escaped through her parted lips as her eyelids fluttered and opened, taking a second to focus before she smiled sleepily at him. "Hi."

"I didn't mean to wake you." Or had he? "Go back to sleep."

"Is it morning already?"

Almost. "Not yet."

"Good. I don't want it to be tomorrow yet." She snuggled closer and pressed a kiss to his chin. "I don't ever want it to be tomorrow."

Because tomorrow meant their time together was over.

The threat of the wedding was past.

The senator had sent his man Vaughn to collect Charles. Escorting him from the bunkhouse where he'd been confined, Vaughn had whispered something in his ear that had stopped his ranting threats of pressing assault charges and made him look ill before he meekly got into the car. It was a safe bet he wouldn't be back.

Even Mike's wife was finally back from her visit with her sister. She'd be taking over the kitchen duties in time for tonight's dinner.

All of which meant there was no reason left for Amelia to stay at the ranch.

She kissed him again, this time on his lips, her hot little hand snaking its way under the covers to press against his chest.

"You need sleep," he said, even as his heart picked up its pace.

"I don't want sleep." She nipped at his chin. "I want you."

He didn't resist as she rained kisses along his neck and down his chest. How could he when he wanted her, too? When she took the hard length of him into her mouth, he pressed his head into the pillow on a low groan and swore he saw stars.

She licked and sucked like he was a treat from the sweet shop. He climbed steadily closer to the edge of his endurance, but he hung on the way he had to the back of that demon bull who'd tried to do him in.

This was a much more enjoyable ride.

Eventually, though, his fortitude reached its limit. He flipped them around so he was above her on knees and elbows, muscles quivering like a bronco waiting in the chute.

"I want you." This time when she said it, there was no teasing, no laughter. Her eyes were solemn as they bore into his with steady intensity.

He responded the only way he knew how, pressing into her as they stared at each other in the early morning twilight. Using the slow give-and-take of the act to stoke the anticipation kindling between them from a warm glow to a white-hot simmer.

I want you.

He angled himself so he went even deeper.

I need you.

She gasped when he hit the spot that gave her the most pleasure, and he concentrated on running himself over and over it until she was thrashing her head against the pillow.

Don't leave me.

Reaching down with one hand, he found her clit. The added touch tossed her over the edge of her climax with such force he had to clamp his mouth over hers to contain her scream. As her inner walls pulsed, it pulled him into a freefall of his own.

He pumped his release into her, his body shuddering and shaking, until he finally held himself still, deep inside of her as he stared down into her pleasure-hazed eyes. It was as though he'd torn a piece of himself free and sent it into her, never to return.

Stay.

But she didn't answer him.

Because none of his heartfelt words, none of his desperate pleas, had been spoken aloud. He tried, damn it. He really did. But he just couldn't push the words past his lips.

Slowly, as he watched, the pleasure melted from her eyes to something that looked more like weary acceptance. It made his chest ache, but as much as he might want to say all those things to her and more, it would only be selfish and cause her more pain in the end than if he just remained silent now.

She kissed his chin and snuggled close with a soft sigh.

Even though she was right there in his arms, he could feel the distance that had already settled between them. The fairytale was over, and later today—or tomorrow at the latest—he'd be returning the princess to her proper place in the world, while he...

Had no idea anymore where that might be for him.

The only thing he did know was that it wasn't with her.

Chapter 29

"How are you doing, sweetie?"

Sucking hard on her straw, Amelia did a mental count to five before answering Thea's anxious question.

"I'm fine." Or as fine as anyone could be who'd spent the last twenty-four hours being smothered to death by love and concern.

"Are you sure?"

Forcing a smile, she replied, "Very sure. Thanks."

It had been like this since the moment Daryl brought her back to Boulder and left her in the tender care of Thea and Mrs. Fordham. She'd been cosseted, worried over, and assured at least a hundred times already that she was more than welcome to stay with them for as long as she liked.

If she lasted a week before she lost it and ran screaming into the streets, it would be a miracle.

Not that she didn't appreciate everything her friends were doing. They were the lifeline that had held the fragile threads of her existence together for the past ten years. But one thing she'd come to understand during her time on the Raintree ranch was she didn't have to be that pathetic, needy person anymore.

She *wasn't* that person anymore.

But her friends were still treating her like she was made of spun sugar, ready to dissolve into a gooey mess at any second.

It had to stop.

"Mellie..."

Thankfully, Thea's latest outpouring of concern was cut off by Lillian's return.

Sauntering up to the round glass table by the pool they'd been lounging around all afternoon, she placed a large platter of cookies in the center with a triumphant "ta-da!" before dropping into her chair.

"Rosa's version of snickerdoodles." Lillian bit into one of the cookies that was almost as big as her hand and groaned. "Sooo good."

Amelia took a bite and wanted to groan herself. The cinnamon-sugary taste danced on her tongue, awakening her taste buds with a vengeance. Finishing off the cookie with what was no doubt unladylike greed, she grabbed a second and was about to bite into it when she noticed her friends watching her with something akin to fascinated confusion.

"What?"

"You ate the whole cookie." Thea sounded shocked.

"And took another one," Lillian added.

She shrugged. "I'm hungry."

In the past, if someone had commented on how much she was eating, she would have felt compelled to stop. Or at least lost her joy in the food as she forced it down. Now she took a big bite of the cookie, relishing every sweet crumb as she chewed.

She looked out at the pool's soothing waterfall feature and did her best to ignore the way she was being studied by her friends. Like she was some strange new life form they couldn't quite figure out.

Which she guessed she kind of was.

She wasn't the Amelia who'd blindly allowed her life to be directed by others while her health and mental well-being paid the price. She wasn't even the Amelia who'd walked out of their hotel room in Connecticut after taking the first hesitant grasp of control over her own future.

She was *this* Amelia. The one who'd stood up to Senator

Davenport's threats. And helped deliver a foal. And nearly knocked her idiot ex-fiancé's head right off his stupid neck, even if that last one was sort of a happy accident. She was…Amelia two-point-oh. New, improved, and ready to get on with the next stage of her life.

Right after she cleared up a few things to close out the old one. Starting now.

After finishing the last of the cookie, she brushed her hands and turned back to look at the women who were as close to her as any blood sisters could ever be. Maybe closer.

"You know I love you guys, right?"

"Yeah, that doesn't sound ominous at all," Lillian muttered.

Thea shot her a look. "Of course, sweetie. And we love you too. You know we'd do just about anything in the world for you. Just name it."

"You can stop."

Thea blinked at her in confusion. "I'm sorry?"

"Stop," Amelia repeated. "I appreciate everything you guys have ever done for me, everything you're doing for me now. But seriously, you have to stop treating me like I'm the walking wounded or something. Like I can't handle hearing anyone talk about anything even remotely connected to the wedding or what happened after I bolted. I'm fine. More than fine, actually. I'd say I'm pretty damn great." She picked up another cookie and snapped off a bite as if to prove it.

"Oh." Looking a little bewildered, Thea sat back in her chair, her own cookie forgotten in her hand as she absorbed Amelia's words.

Lillian seemed to take the declaration a little better. "I don't know what was in the water up there in Hayseed, but it looks like it agreed with you."

"Hayden," Amelia said, feeling protective of the little town and the people she'd come to like very much while she was there. Well, most of them, anyway. The Harridans she could definitely live without. "And yes, I think being up there, where no one knew me, far away from my parents and from everyone's expectations...it was definitely good for me."

"Being away from *us* was good for you, you mean," Thea said in a quiet voice.

Hating the wounded look in her friend's eyes, Amelia quickly said, "No! Not at all." But that was the old Amelia talking, trying to soothe other people's feelings by downplaying her own.

"Okay, not exactly," she forced herself to say. "Being on my own made me face the changes I needed to make in my life without having you two to lean on. I love that you've fought my battles for me when I couldn't, but, well, now I can, and I have to start as I mean to go on." She took a deep breath. "Which is why I'm going to go spend some time with my Aunt Josie while I figure out what comes next for me."

Right after she dealt with her parents, even though she'd much rather not.

"Oh, but Mellie, I love having you here," Thea said.

"And I love being here, but..."

"But we're making you crazy, aren't we?" Lillian asked.

Amelia gave a rueful grin. "Maybe just a little."

"But—" Thea's mouth closed with a snap over her protest. She sighed. "Okay, yeah, I guess maybe we've been...overcompensating a little. But we can stop. Really. You don't have to leave again."

Yes, she did. There were reasons other than the incessant coddling that had her stay with the Fordhams scratching at her nerves.

Namely one large, silent man who hadn't even bothered to stop in at the house once to see her since he'd deposited her on the front steps the day before like a piece of luggage. Every time she turned around, she kept expecting him to be there. Only he never was.

It was making her demented.

"It's just for a visit. I'll be back."

Amelia reached for another cookie, pretending she didn't see the look her friends exchanged. She hadn't lied. She *was* hungry. All the time, it seemed. Without the things going on that had always sent her into painful bouts of dyspepsia, she was enjoying food like never before. She certainly didn't need a belt to help hold up her pants any longer.

Not that Daryl minded her curves filling out a little. The reverence in his eyes as he'd worshipped at her naked body their last night together told her he liked her however she looked.

"So, how was it spending a week alone with the very hunkalicious Daryl?" Lillian asked, finally breaking the silence.

Amelia inhaled hard and choked on a cookie crumb. As always, Lillian seemed able to read her mind.

Or maybe it was just her expression, because before Amelia could reply, Lillian's glass thumped down on the table as she sat forward in her chair. "Oh my God, you totally did him!"

"What? No." Thea's head swiveled between the two of them before she stared at Amelia, her mouth hanging open. "You and Daryl?"

Still coughing, Amelia reached for her iced tea.

"I knew it," Lillian crowed.

Thea still looked stunned. "Holy shit. How did I miss that?"

"I want details."

"You and Daryl?" Thea repeated.

Amelia gave Lillian a repressive scowl before answering Thea.

"Yes, Daryl and I got...close during our time at the ranch." Unfortunately, it seemed she'd gotten a little closer than he had. "And no," she added when Lillian opened her mouth again, "I will not share details."

"Oh, come on," Lillian all but whined. "The man is so fine, and you *know* how much I always wanted to draw his—"

"Lil," Thea broke in.

"What?" Glancing at Amelia, Lillian's expression changed from joking to understanding. "Oh. Sorry."

"Sweetie," Thea said, "you got more than just a little close, didn't you?"

Amelia swallowed the lump that wanted to form in her throat. She'd known going into the affair it would end once they returned to their real lives. She just hadn't expected it to be so damn hard to accept. Even though her dreams had been filled with Daryl, last night had been one of the loneliest she'd ever spent in her life.

"I want to go down to the security bungalow and talk to him, but I'm too chicken."

Because if there had been any words to be spoken between them, they would have been said during the drive back to Colorado the day before. Instead, the stilted silence had stretched her nerves almost to the breaking point.

"Oh." Looking like she wasn't sure she should, Thea said, "You can't. I mean, he, um, he asked for some vacation time yesterday. He left as soon as Doyle okayed it."

"Oh." What else could she say?

"You could go see him at his apartment," Lillian said.

"No, actually, you can't." Thea sighed. "Doyle said he mentioned spending some more time with his family back in South Dakota." She offered Amelia a sympathetic look. "I'm sorry, sweetie."

"No, it's okay."

And in a way, it was. The fact Daryl was with his family after avoiding them for so long meant maybe they'd mended some fences. If so, then at least *something* good had come out of the mess of the last two weeks.

"You could call him at the ranch," Thea said.

"True." But not going to happen.

"You know," Lillian said slowly, "this might actually be a positive sign."

"Really, Lil?" Thea gave her an exasperated look. "Running away is positive?"

"Not running. Retreating. Think about it," she said when they stared at her. "What did Doyle do when you were starting to get to him last year? I mean, really get under his skin, where he couldn't stop being tempted by you no matter how much he thought he was wrong for you? He ran as fast as he could in the other direction."

"Well, figuratively, yes. But he didn't actually *run* anywhere." Thea shot Amelia an apologetic look.

"Only because he couldn't," Lillian said with a flick of her hand. "He was too busy protecting you from your stalker. If not for that, I guarantee he would have been on a plane back east to visit his family like that." She snapped her fingers.

"Maybe."

"I don't know." Amelia had to fight the small burst of hope Lillian's words sparked. "We never really discussed what we were feeling or what we were going to do about it. It all just sort of...happened. I don't know that he wanted anything more than what we had."

Surely, he would have given her some kind of hint when he was saying goodbye yesterday? Even a "see you around sometime" would have been enough to leave the door open a crack. Skipping town seemed more like he was slamming it shut.

Then again, hadn't he told her a strategic retreat could sometimes be the smartest move?

I'm so confused.

In the end, she broke down and told them everything, from the time she'd left their hotel in Connecticut to her final tearful goodbyes to the men on the Circle R. Thea looked a little queasy when Amelia described how she helped deliver the foal, which was kind of funny because that was usually Amelia's reaction to anything disgusting. But queasy or not, Thea and Lillian seemed impressed with everything that happened, most of all the fact she'd been the one to lay Charles out flat with her trusty thermos.

She had to admit, that was her favorite part, too.

There was, however, some serious redacting done when it came to certain *intimate* details. Some things were too personal to share, even with her best friends. Amelia's face heated when she admitted she'd been the one to go to Daryl the first time, not the other way around, but she felt a little proud at the same time. Especially when Lillian gave her an enthusiastic thumbs-up.

For Amelia, that night had been the turning point. She hadn't been afraid to go after what she wanted.

So why was she so afraid to do it now?

In her past, failure had never been an option. If she couldn't do something to perfection, then she wasn't to try. A lesson drummed into her since childhood. It would seem there were still some old habits she needed to break.

But first, she needed to decide if Daryl was worth what it would cost her to try.

Chapter 30

Driving up to the massive marble steps at the front of her parents' house, Amelia experienced a vivid sense of déjà vu. Exactly two weeks ago, she'd made this same trip. Same car. Same driver. Only this time, she didn't have the comforting presence of Daryl Raintree to keep her feeling protected as she prepared to enter the dragon's lair.

It was amazing how fast she'd come to think of him as her safe harbor.

Not that she'd come alone today. Even if she wanted to, Doyle would have pulled what Thea called his "bossy routine" and insisted someone else accompany her. The fact he'd chosen to come himself meant Thea had done some behind-the-scenes bossing of her own.

So, between Brennan Doyle and Sam Britten, plus the additional men there to help move the few things she'd come to retrieve—and judging by the size of them, they weren't your everyday ordinary movers—she was more than adequately protected. Not that she really needed it. Without the wedding hanging over her head, there wasn't anything her parents could do to her now.

Nothing mere bodyguards could protect her from, anyway.

The head of her father's security team, Paul Kent, met them at the front door.

Leon hadn't waited to see if he was going to be fired. He and several other members of the security staff had quit and were now working for Doyle at Praetorian Security. Which probably accounted for the terse nod of greeting the two exchanged.

After taking in the small show of power standing behind her, Paul offered Amelia a knowing smile.

"It's good to see you're well, Miss Amelia. I'd say welcome home, but..."

"But it's not my home any longer." She patted his arm when he winced. "It's fine. I understand this situation is awkward for everyone, so let's try to get through it as quickly and painlessly as possible, shall we?" She hesitated. "Will my parents be joining us to make sure I don't make off with the silver?"

Looking uncomfortable, Paul replied, "No. They, ah, left that to me."

"Of course they did."

Amelia absorbed the sting of the very calculated action meant to let her know just how unimportant she was to them. Fine. She'd dreaded a confrontation with them, anyway. Perhaps this was better. No yelling, no drama, just the quiet dissolution of their familial ties.

Sort of like a Reno divorce.

There wasn't any of the sadness or sense of loss she'd expected as she walked through what had always been her home and now, by the whim of her parents, wasn't. Instead, all she felt was an odd sense of relief. How had she never noticed before how sterile the mansion was? How completely devoid of any warmth or personality? Of soul?

How had she managed to live here without becoming just like them?

Shaking off the feeling of a lucky escape, she opened the door to her bedroom and walked in, only to stop and stare. The last time she'd been in here, it had been to box up her possessions for shipping to what was supposed to be her new home in Connecticut.

Now, those boxes were strewn haphazardly about the room. Every one of them was open, and most of them looked a lot emptier than they used to be.

She started as Paul cleared his throat.

"We were instructed to inventory the contents of your room, including the boxes." Apology lay heavy on every word.

Son of a bitch.

It shouldn't have surprised her. After all, it had taken two days and the flexing of a little legal muscle by Mr. Fordham's high-powered lawyers to get her parents to agree to let her retrieve her personal belongings.

This was their retaliation.

"I take it there were some things my parents decided weren't mine to take?" The question came out more terse than intended as she fought down her temper. Paul was only doing his job, one he clearly took no pleasure in. There was nothing to be gained by getting angry at him.

"There were." He removed a sheaf of papers from the clipboard he was carrying and handed them to her. "This is the full inventory. The items marked in red were the ones deemed as having value and belonging to the estate. The rest were determined to be your personal possessions, and the ones you'll be allowed to remove from the premises."

Taking the list with numb fingers, Amelia barely glanced at it. She'd known her parents would strike out at her in whatever petty way they could, because that was the kind of people they were. If you didn't conform, you were punished.

Having people pick through her belongings rankled more than the things her parents had taken away from her ever could. Her mother would have known that.

Doyle touched her shoulder. "Amelia?"

Finding her legendary calm façade was getting harder by the second.

She offered Doyle a small, tight smile. "I'm fine. It's fine." The pages in her hand crinkled. She took a deep breath and fought to relax her grip. "I guess I need to go over this and see if we agree about what is and isn't mine."

It took longer than she expected.

Not because there was so much left in the boxes to inventory, but because there wasn't. Almost all of her clothes had been removed, along with the shoes and accessories that went with them. Only the non-designer items, the "cheap" things her mother hated her wearing, had been left behind.

That and her underwear, which had been listed right down to the last satin demi-bra. Her face burned as she boxed those back up. She soldiered on, though, determined to get this finished before she burst into actual flames from the mortification.

Gone, too, were all of her electronics. She passed over those redlined items with little more than a twinge. Her pictures were backed up on the cloud. She didn't care about the rest.

The same for her jewelry. She'd abandoned most of it back at the Davenport estate, but the few pieces she'd left at home were gone. She could argue that much of it had been gifts—birthdays, Christmases, and such—and legally were hers, but it wasn't worth the effort.

Except for one thing. The bracelet Thea gave her for high school graduation.

It was probably the least expensive piece she had, but it meant the most. A delicate triple braid of white, yellow, and rose gold, it was the perfect representation of Thea, Lillian, and herself. Three very different people who, when put all together, blended into a beautiful friendship.

Since Thea had one custom made for each of them, there was no way her mother could claim it didn't belong to Amelia. But she was going to make her beg for it back anyway.

Surprise, Mom. My begging days are over.

She had Doyle put the bracelet on the list of things she was disputing ownership of. Let the lawyers fight it out. She was done being bullied.

It went on like that for hours. Item by item, box by box.

When they got to the last box, Amelia was more than ready to be done with it all. Having her entire life reduced to items on a checklist was every bit as demoralizing as her parents had intended it to be.

The only thing left now was the furniture, and there was only one piece that was hers to take: the antique mahogany dressing table and mirror her Aunt Josie had given her for her sixteenth birthday. She'd have to tell the movers waiting outside to be extra careful in packing it up, since it was very old and very special.

Amelia turned to point it out to Doyle, only to keep turning when she didn't see the table where it normally stood. Thinking it might have been moved out of the way when the boxes had first been inventoried, she did another full turn. Panic bloomed in her chest like an air bubble in a diver rising too fast to the surface.

No table.

Frantic, she turned to Doyle, who had taken over possession of the inventory list while she went through each box. "The table."

"Which table?" He flipped to the page that held the list of bedroom furniture. All of it was marked red.

"An antique dressing table. It should be right *there*"—she pointed emphatically—"and it's not."

Doyle ran a finger down the list, shaking his head. "I don't see anything like that. Maybe they listed it as something else?" He offered her the sheaf of papers.

Amelia scoured the list, looking for anything that might even remotely match the description of her table, but there was nothing. "Where is it?" she asked, not sure who she was asking as she went through the pages a second time.

Still finding nothing, she looked at Paul, who had tried to remain as unobtrusive as possible through the process. She shook the list now crumpled in her fist at him. "Why isn't my table listed here? What happened to it?"

"I'm...I don't know." Paul looked both confused and uncomfortable. "That's everything that was in this room as of yesterday when I got the order for the inventory. If this table you're looking for isn't on it, then it wasn't in the room when that happened."

Amelia stilled at his words.

"The table's important?" Doyle asked.

"To me, very. Which is exactly why my mother had it removed." Possibly destroyed.

One last spiteful act of punishment for her disobedient daughter.

"We can add it to the list we'll be giving to the attorneys—"

"There's no need." With the grim sense that the entire day had been heading toward this moment with all the inevitability of the Titanic and its iceberg, Amelia turned to Paul again.

"Where exactly might I find my mother?"

❖

The formal dining room in the Westlake mansion was a cavernous space filled with polished mahogany furniture and Swarovski crystal chandeliers. The ceiling was covered in a Renaissance-inspired fresco that would have looked more at home in the Sistine Chapel than a private home.

It was a room meant to impress and intimidate in equal measure.

For Amelia, it was the site of far too many uncomfortable meals with her parents, and almost as many unhappy disagreements with her stomach. In a room able to accommodate thirty, the three of them eating there alone had felt oppressive, not to mention ridiculous.

In retrospect, maybe even a little sad.

There was a smaller dining room much more appropriate for when they were eating *en famille*, but she couldn't remember anyone ever using it but her.

As usual, her mother was ensconced at one head of the long table.

Someone else might have thought the elaborate place setting of china and crystal had been laid for Amelia's benefit, but the truth was her mother always dined in similar splendor.

Limoges and Waterford at every meal, even when it was lunch for one.

That her mother had sat down to a meal while her only daughter was picking through the miscellany of her life just a floor away was supposed to be another slap in the face. But Amelia was too bloody furious to care.

Her mother had done a lot of awful things over the years, but this time Amelia had no intention of backing down for the sake of preserving the peace. For the first time in her life, she was looking forward to blowing that peace right out of the water.

Stalking to the end of the table, she curled her fingers around the back of the chair at her mother's left and demanded in a low, firm voice, "What did you do with my table?"

At first it appeared her mother would ignore her, as she finished chewing her bite of food and then took a measured sip of wine. But Amelia recognized the tactic for exactly what it was and decided it was past time to fight fire with fire.

Because it would drive her mother insane, she pulled the chair back with a loud screech against the polished wood floor and dropped into it with a sigh.

"Must you?" Her mother used her most put-upon tone, touching her temple with one manicured hand to emphasize how distressing she found the sound.

"Must I what, Mother?" She leaned back and crossed her legs, not her ankles, letting her foot swing in defiance of every etiquette lesson ever drummed into her.

She thought she saw her mother's eye twitch.

"Must you prove yet again what a complete and utter failure you've turned out to be at becoming the daughter I'd hoped for?"

Amelia's foot swung a little faster. "Hmm," she said, as though considering the matter. Then she smiled. "Yes. Yes, I must. Although if you were the one trying to mold me into your perfect image of what a daughter should be, doesn't that mean that *you've* failed as well?"

The tightening of her mother's lips showed a direct hit.

That felt good.

"Why are you even in here?" Her mother sliced viciously into her salmon, which was drowning in thick cream sauce and truffles, one of the heavy meals turned out by her mother's snooty chef Amelia had truly despised.

Even now, the smell made her want to gag.

"Mr. Kent had explicit instructions that you were to be allowed into the upstairs bedroom only, and then only under his direct supervision. You have no business coming into any other part of the house."

The bedroom, not *your* bedroom.

A deliberate choice of words meant to cut as deeply as the knife slicing through the fish on her plate.

"Oh, please, Mother, let's just cut the crap, shall we?" She felt a spiteful burst of satisfaction when her mother flinched at the casual vulgarity. "You not only knew I'd come and find you, you made sure it would happen. Because that's what you do. You manipulate people into reacting exactly the way you want them to."

"Do I?" Her mother took another sip of wine. "How positively Machiavellian of me."

"Oh, I'd say you put good old Niccolo to shame. But we've strayed from my original question. What have you done with my dressing table?"

"Yours? You're quite mistaken. There isn't a single thing in this house that is yours. That I'm allowing you to remove anything at all is only done out of the goodness of my heart."

At that, Amelia couldn't help but laugh.

"Heart? You don't have a heart. You have a balance sheet. Every single thing you do is weighed against what it will cost you and what it will gain you. Sentiment plays no role in your life choices. It never has. Especially when it comes to me."

"Please." After tapping the corners of her mouth with the pristine white linen napkin, her mother placed it on the table. "If this is leading up to a 'poor me' party, spare me."

"It's pity party, and no, I wouldn't waste my time. Because in order to elicit pity, one must first have some sort of empathy. And you, Mother, don't have an ounce of that in your body."

"Why, because I didn't spend my days coddling you as a child?"

"Coddling? I can barely remember a time that you even *touched* me as a child unless it was to correct my posture or to pose for the cameras. I had a closer relationship with my nannies than I ever did with you."

"You never understood. You never appreciated how much effort went into supporting your father's career. How important that was."

"Oh, I knew. I just thought that maybe someday the two of you might decide to put at least a tenth of that effort into your parenting." She laughed softly at her stupid, naïve younger self. "More fool, me."

"We gave you every advantage, everything you could have possibly wanted or needed to succeed. The right schools, the right clothes, the right social circle. And yet, you persisted in fraternizing with the wrong people and acting so...so common. *Your* failures are not *our* fault. We tried our best."

Recognizing the martyred tone, Amelia shook her head in disgust.

"You tried your best to make sure I was exactly what you wanted me to be. Malleable and manageable. Whenever I started to think on my own, tried to rise up and become who I should have been, who I wanted to be, you were right there to knock me back down again with your cutting remarks and biting criticisms. *That's* why you hate Thea and Lillian so much. They were the ones who gave me the courage to try and stand up for myself, not just let you railroad me into being your little wind-up doll, doing what you wanted, saying what you wanted, marrying who you wanted—"

"I knew they were behind this entire debacle!" Her mother's nostrils flared in anger. If she'd been the dragon her friends jokingly called her, she'd be breathing fire right about now.

"They weren't behind anything."

"Everything was going along exactly as planned until *they* showed up at the party."

"You mean *I* was going along exactly as planned." Uncrossing her legs, she sat forward, hands gripping the edge of the table to keep them from turning into fists. She looked her mother directly in the eye, something she couldn't remember ever having done before during an argument.

"Listen to me carefully, Mother. *I* called off the wedding. *I* decided that I didn't want to...no, that I *couldn't* spend the rest of my life with Charles." Just saying his name left a nasty taste on her tongue.

"My friends, unlike you, trusted me to make my own decisions and, *very much* unlike you, supported me in them. That is the beginning, middle, and end of their involvement. I take full responsibility for handling the situation badly, but I won't apologize for it, either. I did what I felt I had to do."

"Well, then I suppose I have no choice but to do the same." Pushing back her chair—noiselessly, proving her better manners—she stood. "It pains me greatly, Amelia Ann, but I find you leave me no choice. After what you've done, your father and I have no alternative but to distance ourselves from you in order to avoid the taint your precipitous and thoughtless actions have caused. Throwing away the advantageous opportunities that we secured for you was—"

"Can we just cut to the chase, please?" Amelia asked tiredly.

Bristling at the rudeness of the interruption, or perhaps it was simply having her prepared speech cut short, her mother sniffed. "I can see that just a few weeks with your *friends* has undermined all the years I spent instilling you with a sense of proper behavior."

She refused to rise to the bait. "The chase, Mother."

Throwing her head back and squaring her shoulders, all the better to look down her thin nose at Amelia, her mother said, "We're disowning you." When Amelia said nothing, she continued, "I know that might seem harsh, but you of all people should understand your father has to protect his reputation within the party."

Which, of course, was so much more important than protecting his daughter.

"Harsh? No." Amelia stood as well. "That's actually nothing less than I'd expect from the both of you."

She replaced her chair with silent care. Emotions swirled inside of her, but they weren't the ones she'd expected to be feeling. Every confrontation she'd ever had with her mother had been an agony of tension and sickening nausea, twisting her insides until she would agree to just about anything to make it stop.

But this time...this time she felt none of it. Not a pain, not a twinge, not even a Pavlovian urge to reach for an antacid. Which, she realized with some surprise, she hadn't used since shortly after her arrival at the ranch.

Instead, she felt a sense of relief that she never had to entrust her well-being to these unloving people ever again. By cutting ties to protect themselves, they'd actually done her a huge favor without meaning to.

She was free.

"What on earth are you smiling about?"

Amelia's fingers rose to her lips, which were indeed curved upward. "I guess I'm just glad to finally have things settled so I can get on with my life."

"Get on with your life?" Her mother made a scoffing sound. "Doing what?"

"Whatever makes me happy." It might take some time to figure out what, exactly, that might be. But it definitely wasn't anything she would find here.

Suddenly weary of the entire episode, she said, "Since you feel the need to keep playing games, I'll just add my dressing table to the list of items we'll be submitting through the lawyers to contest ownership of. I'm done here."

In more ways than one.

Eager to escape into the fresh air and sunshine so she could breathe again, Amelia turned and walked away without offering her mother any kind of farewell. Not because she wanted to thumb her nose at the manners her mother held so dear, but because she honestly had nothing left to say.

"You were always a great disappointment to us, Amelia Ann," her mother called, looking to draw that last drop of blood.

Amelia hesitated for only a second as she reached the doorway.

"Funny," she said over her shoulder, "I was going to say the same thing about you."

Chapter 31

"**I** never took you for a fool."

Ignoring the barb and the man delivering it, Daryl continued to groom the stallion cross-tied in the barn. He'd gotten onto his back and rode for almost a full five minutes today. For that, he was treating the horse to an extra rubdown to celebrate their uneasy truce.

He and Chaz, however, were another matter.

The man had poked at him nonstop since he returned to the ranch. After a week of it, he was close to losing his patience.

Which seemed to be Chaz's goal. Every chance he got, he brought up Amelia. "Do you remember when Amy cooked those godawful rubber eggs?" "Amy would love to see how big the foal is getting." "If Amy were here, I bet she'd cook us up a big batch of those cookies that tasted like chocolate chip heaven."

It was fucking annoying.

Not to mention painful.

"Course, I never took you for much of a coward, either, but I guess I was wrong on both counts."

Not wanting to spook the stallion and ruin all the progress he'd made, Daryl kept his tone calm despite the temper those words ignited. "Only the fact my dad's already short a man until Zeke's leg is a hundred percent is keeping you from spitting a few teeth right now."

"Are you denying you let her go 'cause you were too afraid to ask her to stay with you?"

"I let her go because she didn't belong here. It was the right thing to do." He shot Chaz a glare when he made a derisive noise. "It was."

"Bullshit. You let her go because it was the *easy* thing to do."

Easy? Hell, no.

Bringing Amelia back to Boulder had been the hardest thing he'd ever done.

But coming back to the Circle R without her had been a close second. Every piece of the ranch seemed to have absorbed her essence, reminding him of her. No matter where he turned, how hard he worked himself, how many times he tried to convince himself he'd done the best thing, the *right* thing, he couldn't escape thoughts of her.

She was a part of the place now, a part of him, and he missed her like hell.

Not that he'd say any of that to Chaz, who was still scowling at him. He scowled back.

"What the hell business is it of yours, anyway?" Daryl laid a calming hand on the stallion's flank when it shifted unhappily at his tone.

"That girl wanted you to ask her to stay. She loved this ranch."

"Then maybe you should call and ask her if she wants to come visit if you think she wants to be here so badly."

"She wanted to stay here with *you*, you ass." Chaz shook his head. "Makes me sick to see you throwing away a chance that I'd..." He shook his head again.

"That you'd what?" Daryl put away any pretense of grooming and walked toward him. He'd tolerated Chaz's teasing and flirting, but if he thought Daryl would just stand aside while he went after Amelia in earnest, then he was chewing locoweed instead of hay.

Chaz plucked the ever-present stalk from his mouth and tossed it aside with an angry snap. "That I'd kill to have. The chance to make things right before it's too late. And believe you me, those don't come around all that often. If you don't grab it while you can, you'll regret it the rest of your miserable, lonely life."

There was such a wealth of pain and self-loathing in his voice Daryl had no choice but to take Chaz's warning to heart. Not that it changed anything. He was still who he was, and Amelia was who she was. Different people. Different worlds.

"What could I possibly have to offer her?"

Chaz held his arms out wide, indicating everything around them. He didn't actually say "duh" out loud, but his expression said it for him.

"The ranch isn't mine."

"I wasn't just talking about the ranch, dumbass." Shaking his head, Chaz brushed past him and started untying the stallion's leads. "I'll finish up. The black needs to get used to the people who actually work here."

A pointed reminder Daryl's stay at the Circle R was a temporary one.

After delivering Amelia into the arms of Thea and Evie Fordham, he'd filed his reports with Doyle and claimed two weeks of vacation time. Doyle had approved it on the spot. Without giving it any thought, he'd found himself right back on the road, heading for South Dakota again.

Now, half that time was gone, and he still didn't know why he'd come back to the place he'd spent so many years avoiding.

He found his father sitting at the kitchen table, a steaming mug of coffee at his elbow, as he looked over some papers. Training contracts, judging by the look of them.

After pouring a cup of coffee, Daryl joined him. "I made some progress with the black today."

"So I heard. That one's taking longer than I expected to come around. Too stubborn for his own good," he added, taking a sip of his coffee.

Subtle his father wasn't.

Daryl gave a silent sigh and waited for another round of "you don't come home to see your family often enough." At least Kim wasn't there to add her special brand of guilt to the mix.

"It's been good having you here," his father said, staring into his cup rather than meet Daryl's eyes, which was very unlike him.

"I've enjoyed being here." Oddly enough, it was true.

Helping with the ranch chores and working the horses had helped fill the gaping pit that opened up inside him as soon as he'd driven through the gates of the Fordham estate, bringing Amelia back into her world.

Seeing her dressed in her borrowed jeans and t-shirt in that setting had driven home how far down she'd brought herself to fit into his world. He'd done the right thing, leaving her where she belonged.

Even if it did eat at him every night when he lay alone in his bed, imagining he still smelled the scent of her shampoo on the pillowcase.

"But you don't plan on staying." His father set his cup down with a heavy thud and finally met his gaze with eyes the same dark shade of brown as his own.

Nope. Definitely not subtle.

"I haven't decided yet." Daryl hedged. "I've still got a little time left to think."

"I wasn't talking about just the rest of your vacation."

"Neither was I."

Both men stilled. It was a toss-up who was more surprised by the admission.

Daryl had barely begun to consider the possibility of staying, even in the abstract. But it was out there now, and his father wouldn't let him pretend otherwise.

He cleared his throat. "I've been giving it some thought, and, well, I guess I realized staying away hasn't really solved anything."

"See now, that's what I don't understand. What was there to solve?

I thought you'd come to love the ranch after we settled in here. Next thing I know, you're off running the rodeo circuit and coming home less and less. Then you move down to Colorado, and you finally stopped coming home altogether. What the hell *happened*?"

So many things that to a child who'd just lost his mother, his home, his entire world, had seemed overwhelming and unfixable. But how did he explain the messy emotions of a wounded, lonely boy who'd grown into an angry young man?

"You married Kim." Judging by the look that crossed his father's face, that hadn't been the right place to start.

"What the hell...are you saying it's Kim's fault you left?"

"No. Yes. Fuck!" Daryl ran a hand through his hair and drew a breath, trying to find the right words.

"That woman has always loved you like you were her own." There was a sharp edge of temper to his father's words.

"I know, I know. She always acted like a mother toward me. Maybe a little too much, sometimes," he added half under his breath before finishing his coffee and staring down into his empty cup.

"Was it because I married her so soon after we lost your mother?"

"Partly, I suppose." It had been over a year. But to a child who was grieving, a year was like no time at all.

There was a long, uncomfortable silence. "Son, I...there was—"

"I know, Dad." He glanced at his father, taking in his tight jawline and the squint that always betrayed his discomfort. "I can count," he added, trying to lighten the mood. "And Winnie was a little porky for a preemie."

As he'd hoped, his father chuckled.

"Don't ever let your sister hear you call her that." The look he gave Daryl was sharp. "Is that it, then? Did you feel left out somehow after Winona was born?"

"A little, I guess." A lot, actually. Not that he ever blamed Winnie. His sense of not fully belonging to their new little family while she did was entirely his issue.

"Just so you know, I would've married Kim anyway. I loved her. I love her even more now. And it's always hurt her you never seemed to think of the ranch as your home."

"But it's not my home." How to explain what he barely understood himself? "When we were living out in the foreman's cabin, just the two of us, I thought it would be the best thing in the world if we could live here forever."

Especially after the month they'd spent staying with his father's parents when they first returned to South Dakota. The wide-open spaces seemed like heaven after that cramped little house brimming with spite and resentment.

"After you married Kim, for a little while it seemed like I'd gotten my wish. But then…"

"Then?"

"I was reminded that even though I'd moved up to 'the big house' I was still just some stray living here on Kim's charity. We both were. The ranch was hers, and you married into it."

"Reminded? By who? No, never mind, I can guess." His father growled, calloused fingers drumming on the tabletop. "Those nasty bitches who just love to stick their nose into everyone's business and make it their own. What did you call them? The Hayden horse faces or something?"

Daryl grinned. "Harridans. Although after seeing them in town a few weeks ago, I think horse faces works, too. They haven't aged well, have they?"

"And they haven't changed, either, not a one of them." He muttered one of the words Kim would lose her mind over if she heard it uttered in her house.

And that was the problem in a nutshell. His father might run the place, might have even brought it back from the brink of foreclosure, but at the end of the day, it was still Kim's house. *Her* ranch, *her* home. Not his. Not really.

"They might be bitches, but they were right," Daryl said quietly.

How he wished they weren't. "Kim marrying the hired help doesn't make any of this really ours. We just showed up at the right time and benefited from her being alone and desperate."

All these years later, those words still rang clear and true in his head.

His father drew a deep breath. But instead of uttering what Daryl guessed would be another colorfully descriptive phrase, he pushed the chair back with a hard shove that nearly tipped it backwards and stalked from the room.

His whole body one tense knot, Daryl watched him go, then leaned both forearms on the table and hung his head with a soft curse of his own.

"Well, you certainly managed to fuck that to hell and beyond, dickhead."

He was debating whether he should go after his father and try to smooth things over when the ring of boot heels came stomping back toward the kitchen.

Here we go.

But instead of hurling angry words, his father threw a folded piece of paper onto the table in front of him. "Read it."

Warily, Daryl opened an old photocopy of a document. The word "deed" jumped off the page first, followed by the name of the ranch. He skimmed over the large block of legalese down to the name Hanska Raintree. "So, she legally signed the ranch over to you when you got married." That didn't change anything.

In fact, it made it worse.

The Harridans had used worse words than hired help and strays. Terms like gold diggers, opportunists, and even grifters had also come up during the many conversations that *just happened* to take place where he—and others—would overhear them. Most right under that same dogwood tree outside the church, where they'd launched a similar whisper campaign against Winnie.

His father dropped into his chair with a scowl.

"No, she signed it over to me when I bought it from her. *Before* I married her."

"You...what?" Daryl stared at his father in surprise. "When you *bought* it? Where would you have gotten the money to do that?" Because if there was one thing he remembered clearly about his mother, it was her complaining there was never enough money to afford the little luxuries she wanted.

And a ranch sure as hell cost more than a bottle of fancy perfume.

"From your mother's life insurance." For the first time, his father sounded uncertain and more than a little uncomfortable.

"There was a small policy through the Corps we took out when you were born. I'd planned on leaving it in the bank for you to use for college or whatever else you wanted to do with it when you were old enough. But then I decided using it to make sure you had a home that was always there for you, and where you would always feel welcome, was more important than worrying about student loans."

A home where you would always feel welcome.

Unlike his father, whose own parents had treated them both like lepers. They'd only taken them in, grudgingly at that, because it would have looked bad to turn them away while they were in mourning.

"A small policy wouldn't pay enough to buy a ranch this size."

Daryl was still trying to wrap his head around this new information, and the change it made to the worldview he'd had since he was nine years old.

"Not now, but don't forget, when we first came here, the place was smaller, and on the verge of going bankrupt. Even after things started to turn around, there wasn't a whole lot of value past the liens and outstanding debt for feed and supplies and such. Kim insisted I only pay her what it was worth at the time."

A small smile softened his face. "That was an argument for the ages. Do you know she refused to marry me until I agreed to her price and we had everything all legally signed, sealed, and notarized? And with her...well, under the circumstances, that was a pretty bold thing for her to do."

Being pregnant and unwed twenty-some years ago in Hayden, it had been *very* bold. But Daryl had never found Kim to be anything less than fearless. Even when dealing with a sullen, resentful stepson who never showed her a tenth of the affection she showered on him.

I have some serious apologizing to do.

"Why didn't you ever tell me about this?"

His father shrugged. "It never dawned on me I needed to. This was our home, and we were a family. All four of us. As far as I was concerned, that was that. It didn't matter whose name was on what piece of paper or who owned what when. I never knew you felt different."

"I didn't, until..."

"Yeah, until you got an earful of spite from the horse's asses." His dad drummed his fingers on the table again. "You know that even if I hadn't officially bought the ranch from Kim, this would still be your home, don't you? Yours and Winona's equally."

"More Winnie's than mine."

"Equally," his father repeated. "Why do you think I picked the name Circle R for the place?"

"Well, the R is for Raintree, obviously." He'd never much thought about the rest.

"And the Circle is for the Medicine Wheel. The circle of life and death, the continuation of all things. This family is a part of that circle. No matter what comes, we're all tied here, to this place. It's special to us because it's home. Even if we move a thousand miles away."

When Daryl didn't say anything, his father heaved a frustrated sigh. "Son, how do you think Kim came to own this ranch in the first place?"

"It belonged to her and her husband."

"Yes, but she was Buck's *second* wife. He already owned the place when she met and married him. And she only lived here a few years before he died. He didn't have any children from either marriage, so she inherited everything."

"Huh." He'd always assumed Kim and her husband bought the ranch together. Yet another new wrinkle in his worldview.

"She didn't tell me until years later, but those women who put a bug in your ear about me taking advantage of the poor, grieving widow for my own profit? They said pretty much the same thing about Kim when she'd married Buck a few years earlier. She was the younger second wife. His first missus hadn't been gone all that long, and some folks didn't take too kindly to his choice of marrying an outsider. Or the fact she was suddenly a young widow who just happened to become one of the major landholders in the area. More than a few were rooting for her to fail and lose the ranch."

"And then you came along and turned things around, spoiling their petty vengeance." And gave them a whole different set of targets to vent their spiteful frustration on instead.

So many years trying to prove he wasn't a greedy, grasping boy out to take what wasn't his to claim, trying to prove his worth, and to whom? A gaggle of prune-faced old biddies whose only pleasure came from inflicting their own narrow-minded views and biases on those around them?

Why had he ever cared that much about what they thought of him?

Because he'd been an impressionable child, desperate to be accepted, and they'd known just the right poison to drip into his ear. The harder he tried to prove himself, the more he seemed to fail, at least in his own eyes.

And the more he failed, the harder it became to come back to the ranch and face the people he felt he was disappointing the most, until finally it had just become easier to stay away. When all along it was by staying away that he was failing them.

Chaz was right. He was a fool *and* a coward.

He'd let the past rule his life. No, worse, he'd let the insecurities of a nine-year-old boy rule his life. And because of that, because of the distorted picture of who he saw himself as, he'd lost so many years with his family that he could never reclaim. Moments that should have been precious that he'd thrown away without a second's thought.

Fool, he was. But he would have to be a *damned* fool if he didn't start fixing the mistakes of the past. Starting with the biggest one of all.

Chapter 32

It wasn't even ten a.m., but the Texas heat was already inching up into the uncomfortable range. Which was why Amelia had learned to take advantage of the morning and evening hours to enjoy the peace and beauty of her aunt's gardens. Going outside in the middle of the afternoon felt like stepping onto the surface of the sun. Not that she hated the heat, but her body was still attuned to the milder temperatures of Colorado.

And South Dakota.

Nope, not going there.

She'd already done her thinking about what happened back in Hayden, and made her decision what to do about it. Now she just needed the courage to stick to it.

Setting the wooden glider into motion with her foot, she leaned her head back and stared through the leaves of the towering sassafras tree. The glider hadn't been here when she first arrived almost two weeks ago. It just appeared one day after she'd taken to spending so much time in the garden, thinking and, yes, licking her wounds.

The events following her wedding-that-wasn't had definitely taken their toll.

She still felt a little guilty about the way she'd abruptly left Thea's home after only a few days. As much as she loved her friends, they were having a hard time figuring out an Amelia who didn't need them in quite the same way as before.

Which was only fair, since she was having the same problem.

New, independent Amelia was still standing on the shaky legs of a newborn foal. Wobbly, a little unsure, but getting stronger every day.

That didn't mean she wasn't forever grateful to Thea and Lil for all the battles they'd fought for her in the past. She owed them so much. Just like she owed Daryl for showing her she could fight those battles herself going forward.

A small slice of pain and frustration wedged into her chest at the thought of him. But like the errant thoughts of Hayden and the ranch, she pushed it away.

She'd done more than her share of thinking about *him* over the past few weeks. Impossible not to when he filled her dreams every night. No matter the control she had to keep things in their proper boxes during the day, once she fell asleep, her brain did whatever it wanted.

And it liked to think about him.

A lot.

I really hope I made the right choice.

It didn't matter. Right or wrong, it was made. And she was through with worrying so hard about doing the right thing that she ended up being frozen into doing nothing.

Or, worse, doing what she was told to do.

From now on, she was following her heart. If she made a mistake, if she crashed and burned, well, she'd pick herself up and try again. Not focusing on pleasing everyone else meant she could finally concentrate on trying to please herself.

Seeking her Zen place, she closed her eyes and breathed in the aromatic scent the sassafras tree permeated the air with. The dappled sunlight played along her face, probably causing more of the freckles her mother so abhorred. There were no cameras to worry about anymore, so it didn't matter.

In fact, other than a quick swipe of mascara and some moisturizer, she didn't even bother with makeup most days. She'd gotten out of the habit back at the ranch, and found it too much like layering on a mask to go back to a face full of cosmetics now. She was who she was, and she was okay with that person, spots and all.

If anyone thought differently...well, that was their problem, not hers.

It was hard not to feel like she'd been reborn.

Thinking back to what her life had been before, she could hardly believe she'd ever been that silly, weak person. It saddened her to think of all the time she'd wasted, the opportunities she'd never have again. All because she'd been so thoroughly indoctrinated into the belief that her wants and needs came after everyone else's.

She wasn't foolish enough to think she'd passed all the hurdles that came with taking charge of her own life, but at least now she *was* taking charge of it. So far, she thought she'd been doing a pretty decent job.

There was a lot more to do, of course. Her next hurdle would be the most difficult yet, but she was fully prepared to do whatever she needed to achieve her goal.

"You've come a long way, baby," she murmured with a smile.

"It's good to see you can still do that. I was starting to wonder if the bastards had stolen your smile as well as your inheritance."

Amelia's smile turned wry at the acerbic comment. She opened her eyes and stopped the motion of the glider so her aunt could sit down beside her.

Somewhere in her eighties—though she'd never admit to exactly where—Josephine Pierce still had the vibrant energy and biting wit that had been her lifelong trademark. She did yoga every morning, swam every afternoon, and though she carried a cane when walking any distance, it seemed to Amelia she used it more as a weapon to swat uncooperative people out of her way than she did to steady her gait.

There were a lot of reasons Amelia loved her great-aunt. The fact she took no crap from anybody was one of them.

"Yes, I can still smile." She ignored the comment about her

inheritance, but Josie wasn't deterred so easily.

"I always knew Meredith was a slave to her image, but to kick her daughter out of her own home..." She shook her head and made a *tsking* sound. "Bad form, even for her."

At least her mother's obsession with image had worked to Amelia's benefit for once. Mr. Fordham's lawyers had put the fear of bad press into her and retrieved most of the items on the contested possessions list, including the bracelet and dressing table.

As far as Amelia was concerned, she'd gotten a win.

"Really, it's fine," she said, hoping to head off another anti-Meredith rant. "I wouldn't have stayed with them for long, anyway. They did me a favor. Now I can move forward without looking back."

"Some favor." Josie sniffed, but this time was successfully diverted. "So, you're still set on this plan of yours, then?"

"Yes."

"There's nothing I can do to talk you out of it?"

"I'm afraid not."

Her aunt pursed her lips. "I'm not as young as I used to be, you know. It would be nice to have you stay here with me. This is all going to be yours when I'm gone. Why not start enjoying it now?"

Amelia's heart pinched. Her aunt might just be testing her resolve, but there was still truth to her words. Despite her good health and the pure contrariness that would probably have her outliving her own doctors, Josie was still getting up there in years. One day, she wasn't going to be with them anymore.

As much as she hated to think about that, she couldn't live her life around anyone else's expectations. Not again. Not even for Josie.

"I told you I didn't want you making me your primary heir." It was a waste of breath, of course. Once her aunt made up her mind about something, not even a team of wild horses could get her to budge.

"Who else am I going to leave my money to?"

"You do have other relatives besides me."

"And if any of them gave two figs about me and not the money, I might consider letting them have some." Josie thumped her cane hard into the ground to emphasize her displeasure. "Money and power do strange things to people, my dear girl."

An image of Charles lunging at her with crazed, hate-filled eyes flashed through her mind, sending a ghost of a shiver through her body.

"Don't I know it."

"Yes, you do. Which is why I know you'll do something good with your inheritance. Not just turn into another billionaire bimbo jetting around the world flashing your coochie to the paparazzi and providing headline fodder for the rags."

Even though she laughed, Amelia felt a flicker of interest stir at her aunt's words.

She *could* do something good with the money. A lot of somethings. There were so many worthy causes...

She tucked that thought away. Hopefully, it would be many years yet before she ever had to think about it.

"As much as I'd love to stay here with you, Auntie, and as much as I appreciate you letting me stay here these past few weeks, I have to be true to my heart. If I'm not, then I haven't learned anything at all from this mess I made."

"The mess wasn't all yours. You just got stuck cleaning it up."

Amelia cut her off before she could get ramped up again. "Still, I can't stay. That doesn't mean I won't call all the time and visit whenever I can."

"It's that young man of yours, isn't it?" Josie asked with a knowing gleam in her eyes. "The cowboy?"

"He's not a cowboy, he's a bodyguard," Amelia said before she saw the trap. She rolled her eyes as her aunt cackled and thumped her cane again. "Okay, yes, fine. Part of this is about Daryl. Well, about Daryl and me. About us. Not that there's an us right now, but...well, there was once, or at least I think there was, but I'm just not sure that..." She trailed off as her aunt placed a hand on hers, patting it affectionately.

"You love him."

Amelia stared at her helplessly. "I really do."

"Well, then, that's good, seeing as he's sitting in the library waiting for you."

"He...what?"

"It would be a shame for him to come all this way just to find out you didn't care one way or the other, now, wouldn't it?"

"Wait, wait, wait." Amelia shook her head. She must have heard that wrong. "He's here? Daryl is *here*, right now, inside the house?"

"And probably starting to sweat a little about how long it's taking you to get in there to see him." Josie cackled again, enjoying herself. "Do him some good, too. Handsome ones like that are always too cocksure of themselves. A little uncertainty keeps them humble."

"He...oh, God." She jumped to her feet, took several steps toward the house, then turned and paced back to the glider, wringing her suddenly damp hands. "He wasn't supposed...I was going to...what do I *do*?"

Her aunt stopped her frantic pacing by swinging her cane out into her path. When Amelia looked at her, Josie said, "Go talk to him."

"Right, right." Her head bobbed so much she must have looked like a nervous quail. "I'll go see what he wants." She set off toward the house at an unladylike pace, ignoring her aunt's cackled laughter as it drifted behind her. All of her attention was focused forward.

He's here. He's here. He's here.

The words spun through her head as she hurried across the flagstone patio. Why was he here? Why now? She hadn't heard a single word from him in over three weeks. Not since he'd brought her to the Fordham estate.

He hadn't even bothered to say goodbye before he left.

Not that she'd expected a sudden declaration of love or anything. But after their last night together, she'd thought...a lot of things.

She'd come so close to begging him to let her stay. To keep on holding her forever, and never letting go.

Only self-preservation had held her back. That, and knowing there were more than a few roadblocks in their way that needed to be torn down and overcome before either of them could move forward, with or without each other.

She'd managed to knock over some of her obstacles during her time with Daryl, but she'd needed to work through a few more before she was comfortable taking the next step. She'd made it through a few, but she wasn't quite finished yet.

And now he was here, throwing all of her plans into utter disarray, and she didn't know what to think about it.

Stopping on the patio outside the French doors to the library, she drew in a deep breath and shook out her damp hands, then rubbed them on her shorts with a grimace.

Get it together, woman.

She was just going to see him. Talk to him. There was no reason to be this freaked out. She'd seen the man naked, after all.

Which was *so* not the thought to have on her mind as she stepped inside. Her entire body prickled with goosebumps at the sight of him as he studied a painting of a longhorn steer on the far wall. She could have lied to herself and said it was the air conditioning, but it wasn't.

It was all him.

He turned, and they stared at each other across the room in silence. He was back to looking the way she was used to seeing him, dressed in a dark suit that hugged his form to tailored perfection. Like an extra-tall, super-sexy James Bond, only with longer hair. And broader shoulders. And a really great butt.

She cleared her throat and tried to tamp down the way her body was perking up. "You're here."

"You sound surprised."

The deep rumble of his voice sent familiar warmth rushing through her, undermining her efforts to keep her rowdy hormones in check.

"Well, you didn't call, or text, or..." *Acknowledge my existence in any way for the last three weeks.* "Or anything."

"I'm sorry." He looked uncomfortable, but sincere. "I needed some time to work out a few things without any distractions."

"Oh." It was good he thought of her as a distraction, right? "And did you? Work them out, I mean?"

"I think so. I thought so, anyway." He didn't sound very sure. In fact, he sounded pretty *un*sure. Maybe even a little nervous. That worried her. But the fact he'd traveled all the way here to see her offset her concern with a good dollop of hope.

"Do you want to sit down?" She indicated the cluster of leather chairs and love seats in front of the bay window.

"No, thank you."

"Oh. Something to drink?"

"No."

Out of polite hostess options, Amelia chucked the usual pleasantries.

"Why are you here, Daryl?"

"I've been wondering that myself," he muttered, running a hand through his hair and sending it into familiar disarray. "I thought I had it all figured out. The time we spent together, I thought I'd gotten to know you, to understand you, but I spent that week with Amy. Amy cooked for the hands and washed dishes and made love like a starving sex kitten."

He gestured around the large room, or possibly the larger mansion surrounding it. "But Amelia...she belongs in this world, and I can't compete with that. Seeing you here, knowing you deserve every luxury this kind of life can offer, everything that I *can't*, I think I—"

"One month," she blurted.

He looked at her like she'd lost her mind. "What?"

"I was waiting one month. And then I was coming after you."

"Amelia, you don't have to—"

She held up her hand. "You weren't the only one who needed to work out a few things. I wanted to make sure two of the biggest ones that might trip us up were taken care of before we saw each other again. One, that the senator made the announcement he promised, about the end of my engagement to his son."

After Charles's little stunt at the ranch, the senator had become extremely cooperative. Likely in the hope there wouldn't be charges brought against his troublesome offspring.

"And two?"

She took a quick breath. "To make sure I wasn't pregnant."

If a man could be said to turn to stone, then that was what happened to Daryl. Amelia wasn't even certain he was breathing.

"Are you?"

"No." There had been mixed feelings over the arrival of her period. The same confused emotions flitted along Daryl's expression now.

"Just for the record, I would have been very okay with it if I was," she said quietly. "I just wanted you to know for sure that I was coming to you because I wanted to, not because I had to. And so I'd know that if you wanted me, it was for me, not because of some misplaced sense of obligation."

"*If* I wanted you?" Daryl finally moved, crossing to her in swift, distance-cutting strides reminiscent of how he'd walked across the corral after calming that demented stallion. He grasped her shoulders and stared down at her with dark, serious eyes. "Woman, I've done nothing *but* want you since the minute you walked away from me three weeks ago."

"I believe you walked away from me." She used a hint of teasing to hide her dawning hope. "If you want to be entirely accurate."

"What I *want* is to not make the same mistakes I've been making all my life, turning my back on the things that matter most because I felt I didn't deserve them."

Had he just intimated that she mattered to him? Or that she was a mistake?

"I don't understand."

Sliding his hand down her arm, he took her by the hand and led her over to sit on the love seat. "I won't get into the whole drama, but when I was a kid, I got an earful about how my dad only married Kim to get the ranch, and that I'd gotten both a home and a mother that weren't really mine, like I somehow didn't deserve either. After a while, I started to believe it."

Because after you heard something enough times, you couldn't help but think it's true.

She was a perfect example.

"That's why you've always called her your stepmother. To prove you're not claiming what you thought you shouldn't." Her heart ached for that confused, insecure little boy. "Is that why you got so involved in the rodeo? To get you away from those people? From the ranch?"

"Yeah. But even that wasn't mine." He rubbed his thumb over her knuckles like they were a worry stone. It was clear this wasn't easy for him to talk about.

"I felt like I was just following in my father's shadow, riding the coattails of his reputation there. It's why I rode the toughest bulls, took more chances than I should. To prove I was good in my own right."

She thought of all those championship buckles he'd won.

"But it was never enough, was it?"

He shook his head.

"It wasn't until I got the job working security for the Fordhams that I felt like I was finally finding my own way, my own life. It had nothing to do with my past, so no one could say I didn't earn what I had for myself."

That didn't sound promising for what she had planned, but she held her tongue.

"But every time I went home to visit, I came back to Boulder feeling dissatisfied with the life I was building there. So, I started going home less and less."

"Until you finally stopped going all together." She gave him a wry grin. "I'm something of an expert on avoidance techniques, remember? You weren't ready to face the issue, so you ignored it instead."

"Yeah, I did." He sighed, tugging her a little closer. "Until I had no choice but to go back and face them down, ready or not."

"Sorry."

"Don't be." He slid his arm around her shoulders, anchoring her to his side.

She could feel the rigidity in him, as though he worried she might push him away. Instead, she sank into the embrace, catching the familiar scent of him and only just resisting the urge to tuck her nose into the curve of his neck and shoulder and inhale as deeply as she could to fill herself with it.

God, I missed him.

"So, what now?" she asked.

"Now, I think I finally know what I really want."

"And what's that?"

"You."

As thrilling as that one little word was, it wasn't enough.

"Well, that might be a problem if you're staying in Boulder, because I'm moving to South Dakota." She felt him go still and offered a quick, silent prayer she wasn't about to screw everything up.

"Why would you do that?" he asked cautiously.

"I've been talking with Mrs. Mantooth. You remember, the principal at Winona's school? It seems if I can get my teaching credentials transferred in time, there's a position at the school for the fall term that's mine if I want it."

"And do you?"

"Yes, I really do. More than almost anything." Thoughts of getting to spend her days with the children had been the balm that kept her ragged nerves from getting the better of her as she waited out her self-imposed timeframe.

But she'd made those plans based on the way Daryl had been while they were on the ranch, and the fact he'd gone back to spend even more time there after bringing her home. She'd thought she knew where his heart lay.

Now, though, after hearing about all the reasons he'd had for staying away, she might have made a serious miscalculation.

"But not as much as I want you." She needed to make that very clear. "If you don't plan to move back to Hayden, I'm sure there are plenty of schools in Boulder I can—"

"Two weeks."

She stared at him in confusion. "I'm sorry?"

"Two weeks." He pulled himself away from her so they could see each other clearly. "That's how long ago I gave my notice to Doyle."

"You..." The doubts started to give way to hope. "You're moving back to the ranch?"

"I'm buying into it, actually, once I can work out all the details with my father." Daryl pulled a face. "He's resisting the idea, but I think we can come to an agreement. Once we do, I plan to build a second house a little ways from theirs, so we'll have some privacy. I've got a few ideas about it, but, well, I wanted to wait and see what you thought."

Her breath caught. "About the house?"

"About the house. About the ranch. About us." He seemed to steel himself, waiting for her reply, his expression an endearing mixture of hope and fear that mirrored her own.

"I won't marry you right away. I've only just gotten rid of one fiancé. I don't want anyone to ever say to you that you got someone else's bride. No one," she said fiercely, "is ever going to say you didn't have to work damn hard to earn your I do."

Daryl laughed. "I get the feeling you're going to enjoy every second of putting me through my paces."

"Every single one." She kissed him, then gave a contented sigh and ran her fingers over his strong face, cupping his cheek in her palm. "One day," she whispered.

"One day?"

"That's how long it took me to fall in love with you." Saying the words out loud sent her stomach into freefall, but she wasn't sorry. Never again would she hold back her true feelings and wonder what might have been. She would take life by the horns and live it, even if it ended up kicking her in the teeth once in a while.

"Oh, Princess, I've got you beat. It only took me one night."

"The night I came to your bedroom?"

Daryl shook his head slowly. "The night of the party back in Connecticut. When you walked down those stairs like a queen in that purple dress, thumbing your nose at everyone and not giving a damn what any of them thought, especially your mother. Not that I was willing to admit it to myself at the time," he added with a chuckle, using his finger to close her mouth, which had fallen open in surprise, "but that was the beginning of the end for me."

And it had been the beginning of the future for her.

She twined her arms around Daryl's neck as he pulled her into his lap. "Are you ever going to stop calling me Princess?"

"Probably not."

Smiling as she settled into his firm embrace, Amelia sighed. "Forever. That's how long I've waited for someone like you to come into my life." And how long she'd keep him there now that she had him. They were a team now, and they'd face everything that came their way together.

Forever.

Author's Note

Thank you so much for coming along on Amelia and Daryl's rocky road to love and self-discovery. Authors aren't supposed to have favorites, but I have to admit that this couple is one of mine. I hope you enjoyed reading their story as much as I did writing it.

If you're wondering whether Lillian is ever going to get her own happily-ever-after hero, you can find out right now in ***Can't Help Loving You***. And if you missed Thea and Doyle's story, you can catch up by reading ***What the Lady Wants***. Just scan the QR code below to visit my website's book page and pick your retailer of choice to get started. While there you can also sign up for my newsletter to be sure you hear about all upcoming book news, contests, and freebies.

Lastly, if you've enjoyed reading any of my books, please consider leaving a rating and/or review. Those are the fuel that keep authors going. Thank you!

Acknowledgements

Writing is such a journey of experiences, and so many thanks are due to the people who've helped me along the way. My #GooPooGirls, Lauren Rico, Patty Blount, and Jennifer Gracen, for being my sounding boards, head cheerleaders, and overall best friends a person could wish for. My family, for not making (too much) fun of me for writing "those kissing books." And especially my husband, Danny, for encouraging me to follow my dreams and being understanding about all the hours I spend locked in my office pounding away at the keyboard. Love you, babe!

Also By Nika Rhone

<u>Boulder Bodyguards series</u>
What the Lady Wants
Finding Forever
Can't Help Loving You

<u>Boulder Beaumonts series</u>
Worth Any Price *(coming soon)*

About the Author

Nika Rhone spent her childhood wearing out library cards as she read her way through the extraordinary worlds far beyond her small hometown on Long Island, NY. By her teens, her imagination was taking her places all on its own, forcing her to learn how to type (badly) so she could get all the stories down on paper. After a long love affair with science fiction and fantasy, she finally discovered romance, fell head-over-heels, and now spends her days crafting happily-ever-afters for the characters who still tell their stories faster (and better) than she can type them.

You can keep up with all the latest book news, events, and giveaways by visiting her website www.nikarhone.com and joining her newsletter.